Song of the Goddess

by

Jason Argos

Vabella Publishing
P.O. Box 1052
Carrollton, Georgia 30112
www.vabella.com

Cover design by T.L. Gray

Image Copyright Unholy Vault Designs 2013
Used under license from Shutterstock.com

13-digit ISBN 978-1-938230-39-4

Library of Congress Control Number 2013906264

10 9 8 7 6 5 4 3 2 1

This book is deicated to my mother.
Thanks for all of your support.

Acknowledgements

Thank you to T.L. Gray for her invaluable advice, unwavering support, and believing in me as I stumbled my way through the publishing process. Thanks also to my editor, John Bell, for giving me this opportunity, and to everyone on Scribophile for their enthusiasm and support.

Chapter One

A raven soared passed a crescent moon hanging over one of many lush forests in the region of Austuria. Winged predators screeched, soaring through the shadowy green and brown treetops searching for a meal scurrying along the forest floor; stalking their prey and striking from darkness.

Ikari Sanada stood atop a thick branch and smiled, enjoying the warm breeze blowing over his youthful features and brown hair. He wore the traditional garb of the Sanyoshu: black clothing with red trim, light but sturdy arm and shin guards, and the crimson sigil of House Sanada on the back of his tunic. The only difference between himself and the rest of his cohorts was the short sword he carried on the back of his hip, rather than the long blade the others wielded.

The sound of horses trotting over dried leaves drew his attention to the road below. Two men sat on top of a dark-colored wagon, each armed with crossbows and peering around with a nervous look, while a third worked the reins. Ikari glanced over to the tree across from him and nodded at the young man kneeling on a thick branch. Saskai Tri'on returned his nod before making a chopping motion with his left hand.

Responding instantly, four hooded Sanyoshu, each with their sword in hand, leapt from their perch atop the trees and dropped down onto the wagon. Moving in sync, six more sprang from the brush and yanked the two armed men off of the wagon before they could react. Saskai followed them down, kicking the driver as he landed on the wagon.

The Sanyoshu lined up the driver and his compatriots behind the wagon while Saskai moved to inspect its cargo. Smiling again, Ikari let himself fall forward, flipping head over heels, to land softly on the leaf covered ground.

"Who're you?" one of the men asked.

Ikari walked slow and purposefully, eyeing each of the men as he circled around them. "Tell me who you work for and I'll let you live."

"May Yun'Harrar feast on your soul for a thousand years."

"You will be respectful or die." Saskai picked up one of the fallen bows and struck the man on the back of his head.

"Who sent you?" Ikari repeated, adding a hint of menace to his voice. "Speak now, or even the gods won't be able to save you."

"I know only that we were given orders to deliver our cargo to House Borga," the driver replied.

"What's the cargo?"

"Weapons," Saskai answered. "Enough to furnish a small army and some ancient looking scrolls."

Ikari grinned, then glanced back at the driver. "You're going to deliver a message for me."

"You expect us to accept orders from you?" one of the men spat.

"No." Ikari shrugged, gesturing toward the third man. "I expect *him* to." Before either of the men replied, Saskai shot them both in the neck. "You will tell your master that the Sanyoshu will kill all who trespass in our territory. You will also tell him that it'll be House Sanada, not Borga, that will reign over this realm." He stepped to the side and motioned for the driver to leave.

"Lord Ikari, do you really believe Danothir will make a grab for power?" Saskai followed Ikari over to the wagon as the man ran off.

Ikari nodded. "He's been gathering weapons and soldiers for months now, but I can't figure out why he's been looking for ancient texts." He climbed into the wagon, glancing at the crates for a long moment. "Whatever his intent is, if it doesn't benefit the Sanada, I'll crush it and him."

* * *

An old Jeep Cherokee bounced its way up a winding dirt trail. Amy Price sat next to her sister Lucy in the back, staring at the dense jungle and mentally thanked the person who had invented air conditioning. True to form, Lucy had spent most of her time complaining about the humidity, the bugs, and anything else she could after they'd gotten off the plane from London. They had flown down to Belize to join their father on a dig where he found something he had described as *frightfully smashing*.

"So Diego, how long till we reach the camp site?" Lucy leaned closer to the driver, a tanned man in his late twenties.

"Not much longer."

"What exactly has my father found?" Amy asked, remembering how excited he sounded during their last conversation when he convinced her to fly down to see for herself. She usually only joined him for brief trips in-between semesters, and only when he needed extra help with translating or was trying to convince her to follow in his footsteps.

"I saw for myself what he found, but it held no meaning for me."

"But what was it?"

"I would tell you, but Dr. Price has sworn me to secrecy."

Giving up on coaxing the information out of him, Amy sat in silence and pulled her auburn hair back into a black elastic band while Lucy asked about Diego's interests.

Reaching the camp, Amy stepped out of the jeep and stretched, wearing a comfortable pair of brown hiking boots with light brown pants and a tan blouse. A few tents were set up in a loose circle around a fire pit and various pieces of digging equipment lay scattered about as people moved around carrying steaming bowls.

"Lucy!" Recognizing the voice, Amy turned just as their dad came rushing toward them with open arms. "I didn't know you were coming too."

"I wanted to surprise you." Lucy returned their father's embrace.

"I'm glad you came." Dressed in a dusty tan shirt and slacks, Dr. Price stepped over to Amy and put his arm around her shoulder. "How are things back home?"

"Good," Amy replied. "I'll be graduating a semester early."

"My little girl is getting her first degree. Don't suppose you've given any thought to joining me out on the field? Might as well put that college degree to use."

"I haven't decided what I'll do yet." Amy smiled, unsurprised by his latest attempt to recruit her. "So Dad, I'm dying to know what's got you so excited."

"First we eat and catch up, then I'll show you." His smile spread from cheek to cheek as he looked over to Amy. "You'll love this."

* * *

An hour later, they had finished dinner—which fortunately had tasted better than it looked—and headed into the jungle while listening to their father recount the last month of research.

"My team and I started finding some pottery and a few spear heads early on. A week later, Diego and I stumbled onto a sealed chamber and found half a dozen ivory caskets."

"Whoa…" Stepping into a large clearing behind her dad, Amy looked past him to stare at the stone temple in front of them. Standing about one hundred feet tall, the structure was almost completely covered by vegetation.

Making their way inside, her dad led them to a metal ladder and climbed down into the casket chamber. "Besides the bodies, we found quite a bit of jewelry and some rather fancy looking spears."

3

Lucy walked into the center of the artificially lit room and looked around, adjusting the camera hanging around her neck. "I know I'm no expert on long dead things, but this looks a bit normal."

"She's right," Amy confirmed, glancing over one of the caskets in the circular room. "The caskets are a bit unique, but it looks like a typical Mayan burial chamber."

"The team and I thought the same thing, but when I started to examine that wall—" He pointed behind the sisters, directing Amy's attention toward a section of the wall that had been broken through. "—I found the wall was hiding those stairs."

"Where do they go?" Amy followed Lucy over to the hole and peered through, growing more intrigued by the second.

"Down aways."

"You're being annoyingly vague on purpose, aren't you?" Amy turned to glare at her father.

"Playful teasing sweetheart, and I figured you could help a bit since you beat the team I have flying down from the Smithsonian." Dr. Price led them down the narrow stairs. The walls were covered with a thick layer of cobwebs while cables ran along the ground providing power to the small lamps that lit their way down the long, zigzagging stairs.

They emerged in a large chamber where the air was warm and stale. Ancient writings covered the stone walls. Six columns, each evenly spaced on either side of the room with carvings of their own, held the cathedral ceiling above them. Five large archways were fixed into the wall ahead of them, with more writing covering the space between each.

Amy walked over to one of the walls and felt her eyes widen in surprise before rushing to another. Running her hand over the writing, she turned back toward her father only to find a wide grin staring back. "This is amazing, and impossible."

"I knew you'd want to see this." Dr. Price's smile widened. "Linguistics was always your strong suit."

"I don't see what's so special about some Mayan writing." Lucy stared at one of the columns.

"It's not all Mayan." Amy turned and looked at her sister, eyes wide with excitement as she pointed to the wall next to her. "This is ancient Greek." She walked over to another section of writing. "And this is Babylonian. Over there I saw Egyptian and Gaelic."

"So?"

"So?" Amy laughed, trying to decide which wall to look over next. "These are cultures separated by thousands of miles and hundreds of years."

"What's it say?"

Amy walked along the wall, unable to believe what she was seeing. "Most of it seems to focus on mythology. There are references to Zeus, Cali, Loki, Ra, and others."

"Can you translate this wall?" Her dad motioned toward the front wall.

Glancing at the archways on the wall while stepping over to a stone podium a few feet away, Amy tried to slow the questions racing through her mind. "I can try, but I've never seen writing like this before."

Dr. Price shook his head. "No one else has either, that's why I called in a team from Washington. Still, you've always had a talent for picking up languages. I was hoping you might be able help, and you'll get the chance to work with some of the best archeologists in the field."

Amy forced a smile, wishing her father would give up trying to get her to follow his career path. Turning back to the wall with the strange writing while Lucy and their dad began taking pictures, she started to ponder the significance of the archways.

"You know you don't have to solve this tonight," Dr. Price stated.

"I know." Amy nodded, focusing on the podium. "There's something about the writing though, it's... almost like the translation is right on the tip of my tongue."

Kneeling to get a closer view of the podium, she felt a soft breeze and began to notice a low voice. "What?"

"I didn't say anything," Dr. Price replied.

As Amy glanced back at the writing, her vision blurred. Rubbing her eyes with a pained groan, she looked again and gasped, taken aback by what she saw.

"What's wrong?" Lucy lowered her camera.

"I, I can read this," Amy stammered, feeling light headed as she stood. "I was looking down and then, then I could read it."

"What do you mean?" Her dad turned toward her.

"It says that these are passageways to other realms." Amy read, unable to focus her thoughts. A stronger breeze swirled around her as the sound of a woman singing filled the chamber. "Who's singing?"

"There's no one singing." Concern edged her father's voice. "Are you alright, sweetheart?"

5

"You can't hear it?" Amy asked as the singing grew louder. "…And that breeze."

"Honey, there's no breeze. Look, it's late and you had a long flight, you should get some rest." Dr. Price put a hand on her shoulder.

Before Amy could protest, the stone within the forth archway ripped away, pulled into a howling indigo vortex of shimmering light.

"What is that?" Lucy jumped to her feet, mirroring the shock Amy felt.

The gusting winds continued to pick up, matching the increasing volume of the singing voice. Amy stared at the whirlpool—her mind numb and devoid of the fear that should have been racing through her—and started toward the swirling vortex.

"What are you doing?" Lucy shouted.

"It's calling me." Amy heard her own voice as if in a dream.

"No, it's not." Her father reached for her arm, but a blast of wind slammed into his chest, knocking him back.

A shimmering fog poured out of the light and wrapped around Amy, pulling her into the vortex. Feeling as if she was underwater, she heard her father and sister screaming her name as she stepped through the whirlpool. Then she heard nothing.

* * *

When Amy stepped through the vortex, she felt like she was in a trance. Whatever had compelled her to pass through the opening had her feeling calm and serene. Now, she was terrified.

Bright lights swirled around her as she sailed through a vast cobalt void. The Sound of swords clashing rang in her ears. She caught the scent of ocean water and looked down to find herself falling toward an immense green sea. Splashing into the water, she frantically tried to swim to the surface, but the more she struggled, the more she felt like she was being pulled down. She fought to hold her breath while the water began to swirl and bubble around her until it exploded in a bright flash.

Gasping for breath, Amy found herself standing on a floating slab of rock. All around her, she saw flashes of people dressed in old fashioned tunics or robes. Images of a man and woman dressed in black and red flashed in and out of view. Other images of a lean woman in a purple gown floated passed one of a man dressed like a knight. Voices shouting happily or angrily became drowned out by the woman's harmonious singing.

The cobalt void melted away to reveal a turquoise sky hanging over a grassy field covered in blood. People in strange, blood red armor slaughtered the men and women on the field while a black shadow poured over everything in sight, leaving her in darkness. Turning away from the dark, she found herself looking down at a small island with a round palace in its center. The palace erupted in flames, and a malicious laugh replaced the singing.

Amy screamed as the stone slab crumbled beneath her feet and sent her plummeting into the dancing flames. She closed her eyes, throwing her arms up to protect her head just as she was about to hit the charred ground, but after a long moment, she discovered that she was standing in a narrow, wooden box. Her heart about ready to burst from her chest, she pushed and scratched at the top of the box trying to free herself, pleading to be let out.

A moment later she heard a man's deep voice. "Open it."

Chapter Two

The sun shined high above the large market as villagers hurried about their business. Some carried baskets filled with exotic fruits while others held bags of rice or grain. Venders in wooden carts lined the sides of the road, selling cloth or inexpensive jewelry to young women who passed by. Others tried to sell blatantly fabricated scrolls that promised good fortune and health.

Unfazed by the venders competing to be heard, Hayate Thane made his way through the bustling crowd, heading toward the warehouses at the edge of the village. He glanced to his side and noticed a group of women staring at him. Nodding with a quick smile, he continued on his way, eager to complete his task. He had traveled to Nel'Oskow to speak with the head of House Borga—a man not known for his hospitality—but just as he arrived, he had learned that Lord Borga was *coincidentally* away. Hayate was told that he could find Borga's second in the warehouse district. He knew little about General D'Gust Svipdag except for tales of his ruthlessness and lack of compassion.

A man from behind a booth filled with weapons stepped out in front of Hayate. "Good sir knight, might I interest you in a shield?"

"Thank you but no."

"But you don' understand sir knight. This is the shield used by the legendary Primus himself."

"I doubt that." Hayate tried to step by, but the man blocked him.

"Perhaps I can sharpen your sword then?" The man gestured to Hayate's weapon hanging off his hip.

"Next time." Hayate pushed past the man and continued down the road. After a few minutes, he reached the warehouses and spotted Svipdag overseeing the unloading of large crates. He was a scruffy looking man with dark unkempt hair and a graying beard. His deep, raspy voice had the workers running frantically about. "Pardon the interruption, but…"

"Who in Ako'Reah's name are you?" Svipdag demanded, pulling out a knife before storming toward Hayate.

"I'm Hayate Thane of Ithor."

Svipdag crooked his head. "A bit far from Ithor aren't you, knight?"

"I'm here to discuss the recent thefts of Ithorian shipments in this region." Hayate glanced around, noticing two soldiers approaching with crossbows. "I see that some of those crates have Ithorian markings."

"We get shipments from lots of places, so what?"

"A week ago an Ithorian freighter was attacked. The crew was found dead and the shipment is missing."

"That's too bad, but I could care less," Svipdag sneered. "Look kid, these crates—and whatever they hold in them—belong to Lord Borga."

A soldier in gray armor walked over to Svipdag and placed his left hand on his right shoulder in salute. "Sir, we've located the item."

"Show me." Svipdag turned and followed the soldier into the warehouse. "And get rid of the knight."

Hayate darted around the soldier, matching Svipdag's pace. "These crates belong to Ithor."

"Tell it to someone who cares."

Passing a large stack of boxes, Hayate followed the older man into a well-lit loading area and noticed a mahogany casket with the golden crest of Araia, the warrior goddess, affixed near the top.

Svipdag let out grunt, gesturing with his knife still in hand, toward the casket leaning against a smooth wall. "Open it."

"If this is…" Hayate started as the soldier pried the casket open, but let his voice trail off as a young woman with auburn hair burst from inside.

The woman—around the same age as Hayate—looked up, her face pale and eyes wide as they darted back and forth, and started stammering in a strange language, but in mid-sentence, she began to speak Terran. "…are you people? Where am I?"

"What is this?" Svipdag demanded, turning toward Hayate. "You! You knew. You knew about her so you came to get her."

Hayate shook his head, surprise still flooding his thoughts. "I don't know what's going on here but I'm putting a stop to it."

Hayate drew his sword and knocked the bow from the hand of the soldier to his left. He turned and ducked, avoiding an arrow from the right before rolling behind a stack of crates to avoid a second arrow. Another soldier came from around the other side and attacked with a large broadsword. Blocking the first strike, Hayate kicked the soldier in the chest then slashed him below his chest plate.

Climbing over the crates, Hayate leapt to the other side. Svipdag flung a knife at him as he landed, which he managed to deflect with his sword. Hayate lunged toward the General, but Svipdag drew his own sword and parried his attack. Raising his sword above his head, Svipdag swung it down, causing sparks to erupt as Hayate blocked and tried to push him back.

"Brave kid, but stupid." Svipdag flashed a lopsided grinned an instant before Hayate felt the butt of a bow crash into the back of his head. Hayate cried out as a jolt of pain flashed through him and struggled to remain standing until Svipdag struck him with the hilt of his sword, sending the woman, and everything else, fading into darkness.

* * *

The crossbows manufactured in the more affluent regions of Terra were usually made from the trunks of the amber caius tree's, a sturdy and elegant looking wood that was growing more popular than oak bows. Startling back to consciousness, Hayate found himself lying on the floor of a well-furnished bedroom, grateful that the soldiers of Nel'Oskow were outfitted with the cheaper and softer oak version.

Staring up at a brilliant crystal chandler, he rose to his feet and looked toward the wide balcony window to his left, finding the strange woman staring out. Stepping toward her, he reached out and lightly touched her shoulder. "Are you unharmed?"

Startled, she pulled away and looked him over while ringing her hands. "I'm fine."

Looking over the railing, Hayate realized that they had been taken the Borga estate. He silently cursed himself for being reckless and forgetting about the other soldier. "We have to get out of here," he stated as he went to the double doors and tried to open them. *Locked.* He moved back to the balcony and considered jumping but decided that it was too far of a drop.

"Who are you?"

"My name is Hayate Thane."

"Amy, Amy Price." She extended her arm.

Taking her hand with a reassuring smile, he brought it to his lips and kissed her fingers. "My honor to meet you. Tell me, why were you in the casket? Were you stowing away?"

"I, I don't know how I got there."

After listening to the improbable tale of how she ended up in the casket, Hayate found himself unable to hide his astonishment. Travel from one realm to another was common enough, but if you traveled through a Gateway from one realm, you would exit through another, and the Gateways to and from this realm were on Hapes Island.

"Travel between realms is impossible without passing through the Gateway of the God's."

Amy shook her head. "I can't explain what happened. I don't even know where I am, and I certainly don't know anything about different realms."

"This is the realm of Terra." Hayate smiled at her reassuringly. "Don't worry, I'll get us out of here, somehow, and I'll help you find a way home."

Still looking uneasy, Amy returned his smile. A moment later the doors burst opened and two soldiers marched in followed by Svipdag.

"Lord Borga wishes for you to join him."

* * *

Following behind Hayate and the men escorting them through a series of well decorated corridors, Amy kept her arms tight to her chest as they passed paintings of some unknown countryside. A few large vases sat on polished mahogany tables placed between paintings while thin lace curtains were pulled open in front of the tinted windows.

Pausing as they reached a large door, Svipdag pushed it open and stepped into the spacious chamber before motioning for them to follow. "Your guests, my Lord."

Amy stayed close to Hayate, desperate for some sense of where she was and what was going on as she stepped into the warm room. A plush rose-colored rug with gold trim lay on the hardwood floor while a wide mahogany desk with a pair of lanterns sat in front of a large window.

A middle aged man in a crisp, burgundy shirt turned away from the window. Light pouring from the lanterns reflected off of his graying hair and beard giving him an air of malice that sent chills throughout Amy's stomach.

"Thank you, General. That'll be all." Waiting until Svipdag and the soldiers left, Lord Borga stepped around his desk, picking up Hayate's sword and glancing over it. "So, Knight of Ithor, why have you come to my land?" His deep voice echoed off the walls as he glared at Hayate, adding to Amy's apprehension.

"I am here with the full authority of the Consortium to…"

"Spare me. I know of your meeting with those fools and what you claimed you would come here for." Danothir held the sword at eye level, anger shimmering in his eyes. "This is a beautiful sword, but do not think I would hesitate to use it to cleave your head from your shoulders."

11

Hayate held his gaze on the older man, unfazed by the threat. "I demand that you release us from this unjust imprisonment."

"You are hardly in any position to demand anything, Knight." Borga set the sword down and sat behind his desk. "Why are you here?"

"I'm here to investigate recent thefts of Ithorian goods."

"Lies. You are here to rescue that woman. You have come to take her to Ithor and save your dying kingdom."

"She has nothing to do with Ithor, she's just a stowaway."

Borga laughed incredulously. "Come now, you know as well as I that her appearance in that casket means more than that." He looked over to Amy. "Tell me, what is your name?"

"Amy."

"Well Amy, tell me, why do you cower behind him?" Borga paused for a moment and smirked. "Is it because you are afraid? How can one such as you be afraid of a mere mortal? For you to fear me means that you have yet to discover your power."

"I don't know what you're talking about." Amy tried to keep the fear out of her voice. "I got sucked through some purple light and ended up here. I don't know who any of you are, and I don't care. I just want to get back home."

"Allow me to introduce myself. I am Lord Danothir Borga, head of House Borga, and you needn't fear me. You are the Protectorate Goddess. Cooperate and I shall not harm you."

Amy stared at the gray haired man for a long moment. "Cooperate with what?"

"I have been searching for you, my dear, for a very long time now." Borga leaned forward on his elbows with an unsettling smile. "You will lend me your power—all the power of the heavens—and with that power, I will destroy the ineffective and obsolete Consortium and usher in an era of amity in this chaotic realm."

"That's insane," Hayate spat. "The Consortium has existed for nearly three hundred years. Even if you could defeat the Consortium, the other Houses would never allow it."

"There is some truth in what you say. That is why Amy here is going be of use. With her power, even the other Houses would bow before me. Think about it. One House ruling over the realm, there'd be no more squabbling, no more bickering over land or fighting over every petty thing. Under my unchallenged rule, this realm would prosper."

"You are talking about subjugating an entire realm."

"Isn't a golden age under my rule preferable to the chaos that has been strangling our realm for centuries? If the realm is to grow, the old ways must be undone." Danothir stood, picked up the sword, and called for his soldiers. Handing one of the three soldiers that entered Hayate's sword, he motioned for them to leave. "Take the knight and the girl upstairs and lock them in separate rooms."

Pushed out the door along with Hayate, Amy silently wished that she was home with her father and sister, sitting in front of a warm fire telling each other about their days. Looking out one of the windows they passed, she noticed that the sun was beginning to set in the orange horizon and began to wonder if she would ever see another sunset when Hayate grabbed a vase and smashed it against the head of the soldier in front of them.

Amy jumped back, startled, while Hayate rushed the second soldier, pinning him against the wall and punched him. The remaining soldier quickly yanked him off the second and started to aim his crossbow, but Hayate tackled the soldier, trying to wrestle the weapon free. The second man shook his head, regaining his composure, and kicked Hayate in the ribs, knocking him off his compatriot. Slipping behind the man as he readied his weapon to strike, Amy grabbed a vase and smashed it over his head, knocking him unconscious.

The last soldier punched Hayate on the jaw before reaching for his sword, but Amy grabbed him by the collar and pulled him back. Snarling, he lashed out with the back of his fist, knocking her to the floor and sending a bolt of pain shooting through her cheek. Towering over her, he reached out to grab her when he let out a pain grunt before toppling over with an arrow sticking out of his back.

Looking up, she found Hayate holding a repeating crossbow as he hurried over and helped her to her feet. "Are you okay?"

"Yes." Amy swallowed, all too aware of the pounding in her chest and the tremble of her hands, while he retrieved his sword from the downed soldier and put it in its sheath.

"We need to go before someone comes to investigate the noise." Holding the bow close, Hayate took her hand and led her downstairs.

Hurrying down another well decorated hall while trying to stay ahead of their pursuers, Hayate pulled Amy into and a dark room and closed the door moments before a group of soldiers rounded the corner and rushed passed.

"If we can get to the forest, we might stand a chance of getting out of here." He went over to the window, kneeled, and peered out. "We'll wait here until the sun sets then make a brake for it."

"Is that a good idea?"

Hayate shrugged. "Better than making a run for it over open terrain while there's still a bit light left. We'll just have to hope this place is big enough that it takes them a while to search."

Amy nodded and crouched next to him, trying to stifle her terror and slow her racing thoughts. They waited in silence for almost twenty minutes before cautiously opening the window and climbing out.

Ducking behind a large hedge to see if it was clear to continue, they crept along the shadows, avoiding any soldiers and the occasional grounds keeper in the direction of the forest. Half way across the lawn, they spotted a pair of soldiers talking on horseback.

"Wait here," Hayate instructed. He slowly advanced on the soldiers then fired two arrows, killing them both.

"Hey, over there," someone yelled from the distance.

"Come on." Hayate mounted one of the horses in a fluid motion and gestured toward the second. "Take the other one."

"I'm not very good on a horse." Amy ran over to him.

"Get on." Hayate extended his hand and helped Amy climb up behind him. An instant later, the horse bolted toward the tree line. Fear rushing through her like the wind in her hair, she wrapped her arms around his waist, praying not to fall, as Hayate navigated through the sea of large trees.

Glancing over her shoulder, Amy managed to spot the outline of their pursuers in the darkness. Turning sharply, the horse galloped along a narrow path, sending a fresh gust of cool air washing over her face. Tightening her grip on Hayate, she shifted to her right to avoid a low branch, wishing she had taken riding lessons with her sister when she had the chance.

"Hold on," Hayate shouted over his shoulder.

She opened her mouth to say that she didn't need to be told that when three arrows whizzed past her head. A second later, the horse veered left and plunged into a denser portion of the forest. Amy looked back over her shoulder and noticed that they had gained some distance on the soldiers. Swerving to the right, they rode for another hundred yards before making an abrupt stop.

"Let's go." Hayate jumped off then helped Amy down.

"We're not taking the horse?"

"They'll track the horse." Hayate slapped the steed and sent it running deeper into the forest. He threw the bow to the side then grabbed her hand, pulling her behind one of the larger trees. "It'll be easier to avoid them on foot."

"But what about the crossbow?" Amy pointed to the discarded weapon. "Aren't you going to, you know, shoot them."

"It won't do much good now, unless you happen to have extra arrows on you."

Amy nodded in understanding just as the sound of hooves began to race toward them. Ducking low, they watched as two soldiers darted passed a few seconds ahead of four others. Waiting until it was clear; they emerged from behind the tree and took off on foot.

They ran for almost an hour before stopping in a small clearing. Collapsing beneath a large tree while trying to suck air back into her lungs, Amy glanced up and noticed for the first time the two pale moons that hung overhead as the stars shined brightly against the black backdrop of the night sky.

"Wow, two moon's," Amy gasped between breaths, amazed by the beauty of the shining orbs.

"There's a third," Hayate replied. "We call it the mystic moon because of its reddish color and that it can only be seen a few nights of the year."

Amy looked back at the stars—admiring their beauty—and exhaled slowly, realizing just how far from home she really was. Her fear creeping back up, she began to question if she would ever find her way back or if it was even possible. Intellectually, she knew that if there was a way for her to get here, then logically, there must be one back.

Looking back over toward Hayate, she noticed a bruise on his handsome face. "Thanks, for taking me with you."

"I, I won't let him use you," Hayate stammered. He stood in front of Amy and locked his gaze into her eyes.

She looked back into his pale gray eyes, unsure of what he meant. "Why does he want me?"

"There's a legend," Hayate peered up at the moons. "A girl not of this realm will traverse the stars and emerge from the casket of the warrior goddess. She will become the Protectorate Goddess, the guardian and protector of Terra and its people." He looked down at her again. "You told me that you came from a place called London, and you were in Araia's casket."

"And you think I'm part of some legend?" Amy stared at him in disbelieve. "I'm not a bloody god. I'm just me, a plain human being from London."

"You came here without passing through the Gateway of the Gods. It's said that only the gods can do that."

"I don't care about gods, or Gateways, or whatever..." Amy pulled her legs to her chest and leaned back against the tree. "I just want to go home."

"Whatever your destiny is I'll help you." Hayate knelt down in front of her. "I swear, I will protect and aid you. Whether you ascend to the heavens or return to your home, I will stay by your side." He smiled warmly at her. Amy returned his smile, but turned away when she felt her face redden. He rose to his feet and offered his hand to help her up. "We should get moving. If we head north, we should come across one of the half dozen towns that are just outside the forest."

"Okay." Amy took his hand. She smiled at the warmth of his touch then rose to her feet. She couldn't explain why, but she felt herself relax a little. However, she couldn't shake the slight feeling of dread that crept up as she thought about what Borga had said. There was something disturbing about how he had laughed. Something familiar.

Chapter Three

Emerging from the forest, Amy and Hayate reached a large town just after dawn. As early as it was, people were already beginning to fill the streets, opening shops or setting up trade stands. Most of the structures were made from a pale, unfamiliar stone with wooden or straw covered roofs. A cool breeze carried the scent of baked goods as they passed by a small shop and entered a large structure made from tan colored stone with a worn narrow door.

The inside of the building had a glass skylight that let the morning sun illuminate the plain looking room. Two women stood behind an old looking bar made from a white timber while a few men sat around a small wooden table, talking softly as a woman in a gray apron set plates with steaming food in front of them.

Amy's boots thudded against the wooden floor as she and Hayate headed toward a small table near a round window. She smiled at Hayate as he pulled her chair out then lightly pushed her to the table when she sat. Sitting in the seat across from her, Hayate waved a waitress over and a short chubby woman with curly blonde hair walked over and greeted them.

"Morning folks, what'll ya be having on this fine day?"

"What do you have?" Hayate asked.

"I personally recommend the pheasant soup with dried mutton."

"I'll take that then, and some ergon tea."

"And you miss?"

"The same," Amy responded, unsure of what else to order. The waitress hurried off into the kitchen and began talking with the chief. Peering out the window, Amy saw that the streets were beginning to swarm with more people. A few minutes later, the waitress brought two mugs filled with a hazy brown liquid and set them down.

Amy picked up her cream colored mug, examining its content with a cautious eye. "What is this stuff?"

"It's made from ground cinaroot and honey. It's really good." Hayate drank from his mug.

Slowly raising the mug to her lips, she let the strange tea roll over her tongue then swallowed, surprised by its sweet cinnamon flavor. "Okay, it is pretty good."

"Once we finish breakfast, we need to find a way to get to Ithor."

"How?"

Hayate robbed his eyes, stifling a yawn. "I'm hoping that we can buy our way into a caravan headed east or maybe gain passage on a trading ship. Towns like these always have people coming and going, so we just need to find one that's going our way."

"Will going to Ithor really help?"

The waitress brought their food over and set it in front of them. Hayate waited until she had left before answering. "I'm sure that King Ryoma would help you, if we can get to him."

Realizing that she hadn't eaten since she first arrived at the temple ruins, Amy picked up the spoon that sat in her soup and tasted it. Finding it to her liking, she shoveled the brownish brew into her mouth. She then picked up a strip of spiced meat and bit a small piece off before finishing her tea. Amy glanced up from her now empty plate and found Hayate staring at her. "What?"

"It's nothing." Hayate shrugged, returning his attention to his own plate.

The room began to fill with customers, causing the noise level to rise from various conversations talking over each other. Some talked about how their crops were growing; others spoke of trips to neighboring regions. Glancing from table to table, it seemed as if Amy could hear what any particular person was saying without them being drowned out too much by everyone else.

Hayate finished the last of his meal and set three silver coins on the table. "We should get going. Hopefully we can be on our way by noon." He stood then offered his hand. Amy nodded, following him back out into the now busy street.

* * *

Hayate let out a long, exasperated groan as he sat on a worn weathered bench beneath the afternoon sun. He spent most of the morning talking to traders, hoping to buy their way onto their ships with no success. He had come across a group of traveling performers but they were headed south toward Osaka Major.

Amy sat on the bench next to him, watching a small child playing a viola on a stone slab. Glancing at Amy, he couldn't help but think how out of place she looked, but considering she was from another realm, it was to be expected. *If she really is from another realm.* Hayate looked away from Amy, dismissing the thought. She had to be the woman in the legend. Why else would Danothir hold her and risk war with Ithor by killing one of its knights on official business sanctioned by the Consortium. *She must be the one. She is the one who can save the people of Terra.*

People began to crowd around the performing boy as he continued his energetic song. It was an older melody with an upbeat tempo that was typically played at banquets or large gatherings. As the crowd grew larger, two girls, clad in colorful garments, climbed on the stage and started dancing around the boy.

"I'm going to get a closer look." Amy stood, moving toward the crowd.

"Okay." Hayate watched her as she began clapping along with the audience.

An old man in a maroon tunic walked over and stood next Hayate. "I hear you're looking for a way east?"

"I am, but who are you?" Hayate eyed the bald man suspiciously.

"Forgive me. That was rude of me. My name is Bernard Legan, but most people simply call me Gramps."

"I'm looking for passage to Ithor for myself and one other, why?"

"Those are my grandkids playing on stage." Bernard pointed a frail finger toward the stage, radiating a hint of pride. "My grandson really has a knack for playing. I travel around with my family looking for work. We take what jobs we can find then move on. The kids put on little performances like this to earn money for food and such."

It was a common story, Hayate had heard about families losing their homes in wars waged by rival Houses and being forced to roam from town to town. Many of those families had remained nomadic over the years, finding the relative freedom to their liking.

"We are heading to Ord Vista, but there's been talk about bandits and other malcontents roaming the countryside lately. I hopped to hire some men to escort us, but we are simple folk with little money to spare." Bernard looked over toward the children. "I would hate for anything bad to happen while we traveled."

"I don't see why you'd tell me about this?"

"You are a strapping young knight aren't you? We can't afford to pay you to protect us, but, I'd gladly take you and your friend with us if you agreed act as our guard."

Hayate nodded, a sense of hope pushing back his exhaustion. Ord Vista was a half a day's ride from Ithor, and he needed to get Amy as far away from Danothir Borga as fast as the gods would allow. "Alright, when do we leave?"

Bernard beamed. "If it's all the same to you, I'd like to leave within the hour."

Hayate nodded before Bernard hurried down the street and began talking to a large group he assumed was Bernard's family. A woman called for the children—who quickly scooped up the coins the crowd had dropped for them—and ran over to the woman. As the crowd dispersed, Amy walked back over to him and smiled. He returned her smile and held her gaze for a moment as the sun reflected off her auburn hair. "I found us a way to Ithor. The boy's family is headed that way and they offered to take us along."

"That's great." Amy's smile faded as she sat.

Hayate sat down on the bench next to her and looked up at the clear sky. Taking a long, slow breath in an attempt to relax, he knew that as long as they were still in Nel'Oskow, Amy would still be in danger.

* * *

Danothir stood in front of an amber colored shelf that displayed several antique daggers inside his personal office. He could feel his hand beginning to tremble with rage while a man he had paid to deliver a shipment of weapons and ancient text, explained why he now arrived empty handed. Already furious with the fools who had let the girl escape, his vision began to tunnel as he listened to the frightened man.

"He, he said they would kill anyone who entered their territory."

"Who? Who has the gall to interfere in my affairs?" Danothir reached toward the case and withdrew a long silver dagger, enjoying the weight of it.

"It was the Sanyoshu, led by a member of the Sanada family." Sweat poured down the pale man's face. "He, he said the Sanada would rule, not Borga."

In a flash of pure rage, Danothir lunged at the terrified man. Snarling, he plunged the dagger deep into the man's chest and watched as the man fell to the floor, gasping, while blood poured from the wound. "Incompetent fool! You should have killed the Sanada instead of fleeing in cowardice."

Svipdag let out a slight chuckle from the back of the room. "I did warn you about shipments passing through their territory."

"I will see them battered and broken, groveling at my feet." Danothir clenched his fist.

"Lord Borga, with respect, I'm confident that once we retrieve the girl, your forces can crush any opposition. But the Sanada are a dangerous threat, one that can spoil your plans before they've started."

"And what do you propose?" Danothir pulled the bloody dagger free from the man's torso and sat down behind his desk. "The scrolls may give the location to what I need in order to obtain the army of the gods."

"I'm aware of that my Lord, but it's possible that the Sanada don't know what they took. They probably only bothered with the shipment because it crossed into their territory." Svipdag stepped over the man's body and walked over to the desk. "Let me deal with the Sanada."

Danothir glared the General, gesturing with the bloody knife. "Oh you'll deal with them; you will retrieve my box and ensure that they do not intrude upon my affairs again."

"What about the girl?"

"I will deal with fixing your blunder. Now go, and send someone to clean this mess." Danothir waved Svipdag away. He waited until Svipdag reached the door before letting his face grow cold and added, "And do not fail me General."

"As ordered my Lord," Svipdag replied with a hint of fear in his voice.

Chapter Four

Bernard's family traveled along a well-used dirt road that headed toward a lush forest. A broad, bluish green field encompassed the caravan as the sun's last rays of light faded into the horizon. The family had a few wagons that carried what little belongings they owned as well as some tools and food.

Some of the older family members rode in wagons, laughing at stories being shared or entertaining some of the younger kids. Amy sat on top one of the wagons and watched the children running besides her, playing a game that reminded her of tag. A young girl named Lana sat cross-legged in the back of a cart ahead of her, occupied with a music box.

Amy looked ahead and found Hayate conversing with Bernard at the front of group. Over the last two days, he had gone out of his way to make sure she didn't go wanting for too long, offering water or fresh fruit before she would ask for anything. She caught him peering over his shoulder a few times; *to make sure she was alright*, as he would often put it. She wondered if he had even noticed that most of the younger women, and a few of the older ones, would gaze at him or talk in a flirtatious manner whenever he was around. Admittedly, she too thought he was attractive, in a chivalrous, sweet kind of way; and his brown locks and gray eyes gave him a boyish charm.

"So how long have you two been together?" A woman named Mezza asked in the seat next to her. She was a few years older than Amy, but her age was well hidden behind her elegant features. "You and the knight?"

"We're not together," Amy replied, looking away from Hayate. The group turned along the path, putting the forest to their left. "I mean we are, but not together, together."

Mezza arched an eyebrow. "Really? Half the women here fling themselves at him and he ignored them, focusing only on you."

"I guess he's just distracted."

"Maybe, but he keeps sneaking a peek at you." Mezza smiled, nodding toward Hayate, who quickly looked away. "Any minute now, I bet he'll come over asking if you're cold."

"He's a nice guy, that's all." Amy felt her face redden, and looked away.

"Well I think it's sweet. I make a living reading people, and he is drawn to you. That's as clear as rain is wet." Mezza smiled. Amy again glanced at Hayate and remembered what he had told her about the legend of the Protectorate Goddess, hoping that he would accept that she was just an ordinary woman.

A shadow darted along the edge of the trees, drawing Amy's attention. Returning her vision forward after a moment, she noticed that Hayate and the others in front had stopped a few yards short of a wooden bridge. Two large men blocked their path, each armed with spears.

"Sorry folks but roads closed," one man stated. They each wore dark clothing with lavender armor and a black pentagram inside an inverted triangle was engraved on their breastplates.

"Let us pass. We're not looking for any trouble." Hayate glanced around, raising a slow hand to his belt.

"Then head back to where you came from." The man gestured down the road.

"We can't do that."

"Then you got a problem kid," the second man spat.

Another man in lavender armor burst out of the forest and jumped onto the wagon with Lana. He sneered and grabbed the girl by the arm, yanking her to her feet. "Gotcha."

"Lana!" Mezza leapt at the man but he shoved her away as another pair of men appeared out of the trees, swords in hand.

"Let her go." Hayate started to run toward them when three more men stepped into his path. Drawing his sword, he attacked, trying to push passed them. The two men at the bridge charged forward, but one was tackled by Mezza's husband while the other was tripped by Bernard.

"I got the girl Danothir wanted." The man that had Lana jumped out of the wagon and ran off into the forest with the young girl struggling in his arms.

Without thinking, Amy leaped off the wagon and sprinted after the crying girl. Faintly aware of Hayate yelling her name, she chased after the man. She had to help Lana. If they had grabbed Lana mistaking her for Amy, then it was her fault. Even as she ducked under a low branch, she realized that she didn't have a weapon—not that she could have used one if she did—but she refused to sit and watch a girl get kidnapped.

Weaving to avoid trees, Amy ran, following the cries for help through the darkness. Noticing a set of dark figures joining the one she was chasing, she felt her legs burning and tried to make up the distance they had gained as they began to disappear into the night. Seeing them come to halt ahead of her, Amy slowed and began to circle around to the left of them.

Picking up a thick branch that lay on the ground, she inched her way toward the men while trying to keep her breathing under control. She was surprised that they hadn't noticed her following, but once she got a little closer, she saw what had caused them stop.

Standing on the other side of the clearing was a young woman dressed in tight fitting black and red clothing with gold trim. A short sword in a black sheath hung on the back of her hip. Her brown eyes, catching light from the moons, narrowed as she glared at the four men, who had now drawn their swords.

"Get out of the way woman." One of the men inched forward.

The woman tilted her head with a smile and moved a lock of her long brown hair from her eyes. "Give me the girl or die." Her voice carried an eerie, sultry, calm tone.

The man snarled and rushed forward, bringing his sword over head to strike. He heaved his blade downwards, but just before his blade reached her head, she spun behind him and struck him hard on his exposed neck.

Blinking in disbelief, Amy wondered how anyone could move that fast and noticed a red serpent coiled around a spear on the woman's back.

"Come on." The man holding Lana threw her down. "We'll take her at once. Even if she is Sanyoshu, she can't fight all of us."

Peering over her shoulder, the woman smirked at the three remaining men. "If you say so."

The eerie woman spun on her heel as the three men shot forward, catching each of them with a heel kick in one wide arc. Punching one of them in the throat—crushing his windpipe—she extended two fingers on her left hand and elbowed a second on the side of his neck before spinning behind him and chopped his neck with the two fingers.

Amy winced at the sound of snapping bones as the warrior woman's blow broke the man's neck and sent him tumbling next to his fallen comrade. The last man tried to stab the woman's head but she easily ducked under the blade, grabbed his sword by the hilt, broke his elbow, and impaled him with his own sword.

"Don't move." The woman glanced at Lana then stepped over to the first man she had struck. He started to stir as he picked his head up off the ground. "Your friends are dead. Tell me why you're here."

"I'll be killed…" the man groaned.

"Talk or I'll kill you slow." The woman picked up his sword, waving it around playfully. She waited for a moment for an answer but all she got were muffled cries. Letting out an annoyed sigh, the woman drove the sword into his right thigh and let it stand on its own. "Why are you here?"

Amy watched, unable to steady her shaking legs as the woman continued to torture the man. Swallowing, she dropped the branch and started to move toward Lana, mindful of each step she took. Ignoring the man's screams, Amy put a hand on the young girl's shoulder, motioning for her to keep quiet. She picked up Lana and started to turn to leave when the bloody sword flew toward her and landed an inch in front of her foot.

"Don't try it," the woman said coldly then looked back at the man for a long moment. She raised her foot with a sigh an instant before she drove it down onto his neck, killing him. "Worthless."

"Stay away from us." Amy stepped back as the woman stalked toward them. Putting Lana down behind her, Amy pulled the bloody sword out of the ground, trying to keep her arms from shaking and her legs firm.

"Don't be stupid." The woman continued to advance with a predatory gleam in her eyes. "I'd hate to kill another woman. So why don't you tell me what's going on here?"

* * *

Blocking a downward strike from one of his attackers, Hayate countered with a kick to the ribs followed by an uppercut and looked toward the forest, hopping to spot Amy near the trees. He needed to go find her, but first he had to deal with these attackers. Evading another attack, he recognized the crest on their breastplates and began to wonder why members of House Inara would attack a group of nomads. Toward the back of the caravan, he glimpsed a man digging through a wagon and emerging with a small wooden box.

Another attacker swung his blade, aiming for Hayate's chest, forcing him back and keeping him on the defensive. Spotting an opening in the man's assault, he countered, swinging his sword to the left and catching the man across his throat.

He caught the sound of a third man rushing toward him from the right and once again pushed aside his desire to find Amy. Turning, he blocked the man's strike while pushing him back. Hayate swayed to his right, trying to avoid the enemy's blade but wasn't fast enough and felt the cold steel lacerate his arm.

The man lunged at Hayate, intent on finishing the young knight off. Parrying the man's sword to the left, Hayate swung his blade back, across the man's face, then just under his breastplate. Letting the man fall lifelessly to the ground, he scanned the road and found that the remaining men were beginning to withdraw back into the forest.

Hayate spotted Bernard next to Mezza's husband, pressing a piece of cloth to his wound, and crouched beside him. "How bad is it?"

"My shoulder," Mezza's husband replied through clenched teeth.

"I'm going after Amy and Lana." Hayate stood, sucking in air as he surveyed the caravan. Seeing that no one else appeared to be hurt, he ran after the men. He sprinted, zigzagging through the trees, in the direction he had seen Amy take, praying that he could catch up. Pushing back his growing alarm, he continued running through the moonlit forest until he heard the sound of swords clashing and a man's scream.

Slowing his pace, Hayate walked with his sword at the ready, into a small clearing and found the bodies of the men he was chasing lying mangled in a growing pool of blood. Two hooded Sanyoshu stood in the center of the slaughter, one of which placed the stolen box into a black satchel. Before he had time to question why the Sanyoshu were so far from Austuria; the one with the pouch motioned toward Hayate, sending the second charging forward.

Hayate parried the speedy attack only to catch a painful kick to the chin. The hooded figure continued his attack with a flurry of swings aimed at his limbs and head. Hayate staggered back, trying to keep his feet under him while avoiding getting slashed. The man in the hood swung high before switching the angle of his sword to a downward motion in anticipation of Hayate ducking. Eyes wide, Hayate jumped back, swinging his sword at the man's ankles. He felt his blade find its target—an instant before the man cried out in pain—and then slashed him across the ribs as he fell.

"Bastard," the second hooded figure cursed. Setting the satchel aside, the man drew his sword and dashed forward. His attack seemed to parallel the first Sanyoshu, but instead of swinging down, he caught Hayate with a harsh kick and moved with greater fluidity.

Hayate tried blocking the continuing attacks, but a few managed to slip passed his defenses, sending painful surges through his arms and chest. Hopping to use their surroundings to his advantage, Hayate darted around a tree, but his foe matched his maneuver. Growing tired, he reached for his opponents mask, grabbed it, and landed a solid punch.

He tried to punch again but the man twisted away while placing a harsh foot into his gut.

With the hood still in hand, Hayate looked up, surprised to see long, raven colored hair fall over the young fighter's shoulders. "A woman?"

"That a problem?" the woman asked, renewing her attack. She came at him with a flurry of kicks and slashes until a kick caught him on the ribs, knocking him down. "I don't have time for this." She kicked him in the face then turned and ran, scooping up the satchel as she went.

Hayate forced himself to his feet, willing himself to keep moving despite the pain racking his body. Amy still needed his help. Dizzy and out of breath, he took off after her, but not nearly as fast as he wanted to.

* * *

"Well, start talking," the woman in black demanded.

Amy lunged forward to strike but the woman easily evaded, punched her in the stomach, and shoved her back. Gasping for air, she climbed to her feet and positioned herself between the woman and Lana. A moment later, a raven-haired woman emerged from the trees dressed the same as the first woman.

"Lady Yuki, I have what they wanted." The tattered woman handed the other one a black bag.

"What happened E'Lan? Where's Kurt?" Yuki asked.

"He's dead."

"How?" Before Yuki could get her answer, Hayate emerged from the woods covered in blood.

"Hayate." Amy and Lana ran over to him but he pushed them behind him and stood in a defensive stance.

E'Lan turned to glare at Hayate, anger burning behind her eyes. "He killed him."

"And you are?" Yuki shifted her gaze toward Hayate.

"I am Hayate Thane of Ithor."

"And what are you doing here?"

"I would ask you the same question. Are the Sanada working with House Borga?"

"What does Danothir have to do with any of this?" Yuki glared at Hayate. "You killed one of my men, so I should kill you on the spot. On the other hand, you're already too hurt to fight, so killing you now won't mean much. Tell me what's going on and I'll let you and your friends go, for now."

"I don't know what's happening. We fled Borga's forces then got ambushed by those men from House Inara."

Yuki crossed her arms. "Why did they take the girl?"

"I don't know?"

Yuki laughed to herself. "Then what good are you? Alright knight, since you're of no use anyway, you can live."

"What about the box?" Hayate asked.

"It's mine." Yuki turned and started to walk into the forest before glancing over her shoulder. "Unless you want to *take* it?"

E'Lan glared at Hayate, fury twisting her lips into a snarl. "Hayate Thane, remember this name, 'cause it'll be the one that kill's you. I'm E'Lan Barda, and I will avenge my comrade's death." She turned and followed Yuki into the forest, disappearing in the darkness.

Hayate fell onto his knees in front of Amy. She knelt beside him, putting his arm around her shoulder to help him stand as a fresh wave of fear flooded over her. "You're hurt."

"I, I'm fine," Hayate replied.

"No you're not. We need to get back to the caravan." Amy helped him to his feet and started through the forest with Lana sniffling in front of them.

Realizing that he must have gotten hurt trying to find her, she silently chastised herself for running off without thinking. A sense of urgency crept through her as they walked and questions about why that Yuki woman, and everyone else, seemed so interested in her filled her mind.

Chapter Five

The sun shined brilliantly over the blue green fields that surrounded the kingdom of Ithor. Farmers worked the fields, picking vegetables out of the soil while others loaded baskets into small carts or passed around water. A gentle breeze swept passed, carrying the scent of fresh soil and grass. Amy smiled at the farmers, who cheerfully greeted her and Hayate as they trotted passed on horseback.

A large town encircled the impressive stone castle. Entering the town, Amy saw many people laughing and smiling as they went about their business. Children played outside of shops, kicking a lopsided ball back and forth. They passed buildings made from various woods or stone as they headed down the main road toward the white castle.

Amy rode behind Hayate holding on to his hips, careful not to put too much pressure on his wounds. They had reached Ord Vista two days before and stayed with Bernard's family while Hayate recuperated from his injuries.

Passing under a stone archway, Amy marveled at the low shrubs that lined the roadway, each bearing colorful flowers. They reached the main entrance and dismounted, giving Amy the sense of living in some Arthurian legend. A young squire greeted them with a cheerful wave, taking the reins of the horse from Hayate.

Amy followed Hayate into a small chamber with a smooth stone floor and a low ceiling. A few modest decorations adorned the walls and a small wooden table sat in the center of the room, holding a colorful potted plant.

Walking over toward them from an archway on the opposite side of the chamber, a man in a sky blue suit with tails gave a short bow. "Sir Hayate, it is good to see you returned."

"I need to speak with the King," Hayate nodded. "It's important."

"I will tell his majesty at once." The man bowed again before turning to hurry off.

"Since it'll take few minutes for the King to see us, I'd better change." Hayate glanced at the brown shirt he wore since leaving Bernard's family. He led Amy through the archway to the left and up a flight of stairs before continuing through the many passages.

"This is where you live?" Amy let out a breath, trying to take in everything.

Tapestries bearing unfamiliar symbols or images hung on some of the walls. Mirrors placed throughout the castle reflected sunlight, illuminating areas with few windows. Small plants placed in silver pots sat in front of cherry colored windows. Pausing to push open a large hand carved door, Hayate motioned for Amy step through.

"Make yourself comfortable. I'll just be a few minutes." Hayate stepped into a small room to the side and slid the door closed behind him.

Amy looked around the large room and smiled to herself. *So this is a knight's room.* Light flittered in through a wide window that led to a small balcony. A pair of bookcases lined the far wall, and a wide bed sat on the opposite end of the room. She spotted a stack of papers and a few worn books sitting on a small desk and stepped over to it. Flipping through the pages, she saw various references to a warrior goddess. Another passage told about the Protectorate Goddess and how she would save the realm from darkness.

Letting out an annoyed groan, Amy closed the book and began to wonder why Hayate believed she was the one mentioned in the book. She hadn't done anything miraculous or extraordinary, or anything to suggest that she was a goddess sent to save a world she knew nothing about. How could she save a place she didn't care for and never wanted to be in? The last thing she was responsible for was her sister's cat; and it died because she forgot to leave food for it when she left on a trip to Cairo.

She pushed the book aside, deciding not to think about something so absolutely ludicrous. She followed Hayate here to find a way home, and that's all that mattered.

"Something wrong?" Hayate stepped out of the side room wearing black pants and a brown jerkin over a white shirt. A brown belt held his sword and sheath against his hip, reminding Amy of the stories she used to read as a kid.

"Look Hayate, I know who you think I am, but..." Amy trailed off. "I'm not your goddess."

"I think you are. How else could you have gotten here? You're the one who will make this realm a better place." Hayate looked away, his face reddening. "But even if you're not, there are others who think you are. Until you can return to your rightful place, you'll be in danger. I promised I'd help you, and that's what I'm going to do."

"How can you believe in me so much?"

"Because I think you ended up in that casket for a reason; and I believe that we are meant for something more than fighting and death."

Hayate stepped over to the window. She couldn't help but smile at how confident he seemed one minute and nervous the next. "We should get going. The King is probably waiting."

Amy nodded, following Hayate back into the halls. They made their way until they reached a large iron door bearing the image of a lion roaring on a hill. Hayate started toward the extravagant door, and the attendant who stood beside it, when a man walking through the opposite hall caught his attention.

"Too busy to find a friend and tell him you're back from your travels?" The man, dressed tan pants and a dark gray tunic, smiled broadly and embraced Hayate. "I have to hear of your return from a stable boy?"

"I just returned." Hayate returned his smile. "I'm surprised you didn't hear about it from one of the chamber maids."

"Words can hurt. And who is this lovely thing?" Hayate's friend flashed Amy a practiced smile as he stepped past him. A few inches taller than Hayate, and a few years older, he had short black hair which he wore slicked back. "You *were* planning to introduce us?"

"Of course, so long as you behave." Hayate turned to face Amy. "Amy, this is…"

"Gaius Dualla, knight of Ithor, and at your service." Gaius reached down and brought Amy's hand to his lips as he bowed. "A woman like you truly belongs with us, roaming the gardens of paradise."

"Thank you." Amy pulled her hand free and glanced at Hayate, who rolled his eyes. "So you two are friends?"

"Yes. I've pulled his backside from perditions gate and traveled across the realm with Hayate. He's the best damn knight in the kingdom. Well, second best." Gaius smiled again. "I never could get him to loosen up though."

"We trained together when I first decided to become a knight." Hayate looked toward Gaius. "Although, I could never get him to take his duties seriously."

Gaius let out an amused laugh. "Life is only worth living if you're having fun."

"You'd like my sister. She's always been a… free spirit." Amy smirked, remembering some of the cheesy dates her sister had brought home.

"Alas, I've already set my eyes on a more heavenly beauty," Gaius replied.

Hayate held up a hand. "Amy is a guest. Try to keep that in mind as you troll the halls."

"You wound me." Gaius clutched his chest as if he'd been stabbed.

"Well, you'll have to forgive me later. I'm meeting with the King."

Gaius sighed, crossing his arms. "I assume this has to do with your trip to Nel'Oskow?"

"I found out more than we thought I would." Hayate nodded. "I'll fill you in later though."

"Very well, if duty calls. I have my own task to complete in regards to the King's approaching dinner party." Gaius clapped Hayate on the shoulder before bowing to Amy. "Perhaps after your business is done, you will allow me the honor of escorting you around the kingdom. Ithor is renowned for the beauty of its gardens."

"Yeah, I'll think about it," Amy responded, unsure of what to think about the smooth talking knight as he backed away. "He's a... confident fellow isn't he?"

"He's a good knight, shady, but a good friend." Hayate looked away from her and turned back to the door. "If you'd want, I could ask him to show you around later."

"No thanks." Amy shook her head and stepped over to his side. "I'd rather not wander around in a strange city with Don Juan. I'd rather stick with you, if that's okay?"

"Of course." Hayate smiled at her before nodding to the attendant, who opened the door with a bow.

A cathedral ceiling displaying well painted images of three moons, one of which had a reddish hue, sat over the spacious chamber. Paintings of landscapes hung in even spacing on the side walls while the third held mounted swords, shields, and a few axes. Two crescent tables covered by sky blue cloths sat a few feet away from an ivory throne atop three marble steps.

An older man, with graying hair and friendly eyes, sat on the throne, smiling as Hayate stepped forward and knelt. The man wore an elegant robe made from a bluish fur with white highlights and set his golden crown on the arm of his throne.

"Have I not told you to cease with such formalities?" The King rose and stepped down extending a ringed hand.

"Once more, as always majesty." Hayate stood and clasped his forearm.

"And who is this young woman you've brought before me?"

"King Ryoma, this is Amy Price." Hayate gestured toward Amy and waved her forward.

Amy stopped next to Hayate and forced a nervous smile as she greeted the King. "Hi."

"Welcome to Ithor my dear," Ryoma said with a nod then looked back to Hayate. "Not that the young lady's beauty is unwelcome in my hall, but I thought you were investigating Nel'Oskow?"

"I was, but there were some unexpected developments." Hayate explained how he had meet Amy and what happened on their way here.

"I see," Ryoma said after Hayate had finished. "Danothir plans to usurp the power of the Consortium?"

"That's what he said."

Ryoma arched an eyebrow. "And you believe that she is the Protectorate Goddess?"

"I do."

Ryoma nodded then glanced at Amy. "What is it that you want? If you are truly Araia's chosen one, then the fate of our realm sits in your hands."

"I don't know anything about your beliefs, and I don't mean to sound ungrateful," Amy held up her hands, hoping to avoid the topic of gods and legends. "I'm not who you think I am. I can't be responsible for an entire world. I just want to get home."

"Whether you are or not may be moot at this point. Danothir believes you are and he is well known for his barbarous pursuit of what he wants." Ryoma paused for a moment. "And from what you've told me, he is not the only one pursuing you."

"Do you think Lady Inara or the Sanada have joined Danothir?" Hayate asked.

"Lady Inara is far too conceited to work with anyone." Ryoma laughed, waving his hand. "And the Sanada, well, they are too difficult to read to even begin to guess why they have gotten involved."

"What can we do then?"

Ryoma stood in silence as he thought about the answer. "It might be best if I went to the Consortium to find out where they will stand in all of this."

"We should go with you," Hayate stated. "If they hear Amy's story firsthand, they might be more willing to help."

"True, but if I call this meeting, Danothir will be present. Having Amy there would only place her in jeopardy."

"Then at least let me accompany you."

"It's best that you stay with Amy. I will go and speak on your behalf," Ryoma asserted. "In the meantime, Ms. Price, you are welcome to stay as my guest for as long as you please."

"Thank you." Amy smiled.

* * *

Danothir adjusted his formal olive jacket as he walked through the well-lit halls of Hapes Cathedral, surprised to have received a summons three days prior. The cathedral sat in the center of Hapes Island, a few hundred yards away from the open roofed temple that housed the Gateway of the Gods. Meetings asking for the heads of the great Houses were called every few months. His being called now could only mean that the knight had reached Ithor and now sought to out his plans.

An edge of worry crept into the back of Danothir's mind as he passed expensive looking artwork on his way to the council chambers. Pausing to readjust his jacket again while a man in white opened the doors, he stepped into the domed room and found most of those present had taken their seats. Ivory desks—each bearing the sigil or crest of a different House or kingdom—sat on polished marble flooring and were arranged in a wide, broken, semi-circle. At the far end of the circle, a larger desk with two ivory chairs closed the ring.

"Welcome back Lord Borga," a deep-set voice said from behind. Danothir turned and saw a tall, dark skinned man with a light beard entering the chamber.

"It is good to see you again General T'Chello." Recognizing the Supreme Commander of Terra's army, Danothir forced a smile and shook the middle-aged man's hand. "Tell me General, why have we been summoned?"

"I am unsure of the details. I only know that the King of Ithor has called for this gathering." T'Chello adjusted his white military uniform, making himself look even more regal, much to Danothir's annoyance. T'Chello always managed to look so pristine no matter what he wore, almost as if he were dressed by the gods and sent to mock everyone else. Danothir longed for the day he would finally be able to tarnish the Generals perfect image and stain his uniform with his own blood.

"I see." Danothir smiled. It seemed his suspicions were correct, but if King Ryoma already spoke with the Chancellor and T'Chello knew nothing of it, then he had nothing to fear. It occurred to him that he had been *asked* to come, not ordered or taken by T'Chello's forces, which meant that the Chancellor did not believe the King.

A narrow door opened in the back of chamber and the Chancellor, Malik Shen, stepped in. Danothir stepped over to his desk and sat in a comfortable wooden chair. Glancing around the room, he noticed some of the Kings and Queens of the various kingdoms and dismissed them. As vast or powerful as the assorted kingdoms thought they were, they paled in comparison to the great Houses. He glimpsed Ryoma sitting opposite of him and smirked. A few seats to his left, Lady Inara sat impatiently tapping her slender fingers. Looking over to the right, he expected to see a member of the Sanada family but instead found a man in a black and red tunic.

"I thank you all for coming," Malik said after everyone settled into their seats. He stood behind the lager desk with T'Chello on his right.

"Is it not customary for the heads of each region to be present at such meetings?" Lady Inara asked. Her blonde hair reflected the light as she glared at the Chancellor with blue eyes that hid her true age. It amazed Danothir that the vain woman continued to retain the looks of a girl in her late twenties, but with a twenty-year-old daughter, the head of House Inara was much closer to his age if not older.

"You know that it is, Ritsuko," Malik replied.

Lady Inara gestured with her hand. "Then why is it that the Sanada are absent?"

The man in black gave a polite nod to the Chancellor before looking back toward Lady Inara. "Unfortunately, my masters were unable to answer your call to this meeting. I have come in their place."

"And who are you?" Lady Inara demanded.

"My name is Saskai Tri'on."

"You're Sanyoshu?" Danothir leaned forward. "A dog for the Sanada?"

"Yes." Saskai nodded, pride lining his voice.

"Please," Malik raised his hand to silence them. "I shall speak to House Sanada about this another time. We have come here today to hear from King Ryoma of Ithor." Malik nodded toward him and sat down.

"Thank you Chancellor." Ryoma stood and placed his hands behind his back. "As you all know, Hayate Thane was sent to Nel'Oskow to investigate recent thefts in the area. During his investigation, he found a young woman who emerged from the casket of Araia." He paused as everyone in the room began voicing their disbelief. "You all know the legends. I believe that this young woman may be the Protectorate Goddess."

35

"Preposterous," the King of Minolan spat. "What pretense was there?"

Ryoma shook his head. "I can offer little as proof at the moment besides her testimony."

"And where is this girl now?" Lady Inara asked, leaning forward on her elbows.

"I have asked that she remain within the safety of Ithor's borders." Ryoma glanced over toward Danothir. "She has learned of a plot to overthrow the Consortium, one crafted by Lord Borga."

Again the room filled with voices of disbelief. Danothir allowed himself a slight smirk before leaning forward on is desk, feigning outrage. "This is absurd. First you claim to have the Protectorate Goddess in your grasp, but offer us no proof. Then you accuse me of plotting against those in this room?"

"So you deny that you held the young woman?" Ryoma asked.

"I deny that she exists." Danothir glared at Ryoma. "There *was* a woman with your knight, but she was a criminal in my custody until your knight helped her escape." Glancing around the room, he got the impression that most believed his explanation. "I demand that you return her so that she may face the punishment of her crime."

Ryoma leaned onto the table, anger narrowing his eyes. "And what crime has she committed?"

"She conspires against my rule and incites the people to violence. The fact that you now make up such fantasies to protect a criminal, only shows how far Ithor has truly fallen."

"And how do you explain the crates of stolen Ithorian goods found in your warehouses?"

"Those crates were purchased through a seemingly reputable third party. I had no way of knowing if they were stolen or not." Danothir paused, displaying a look of sincerity. "Of course, any stole goods will be returned to Ithor."

Ryoma scoffed, rolling his eyes. "You have long been suspected of treachery, Lord Borga."

"The petty suspicions of a sad little King are beneath me," Danothir said coldly. "You accuse me of holding this woman wrongfully, and yet it is you who now hides her from us."

"If you believe she is in fact the one of legend, why not bring her here?" a woman, whose name Danothir forgot, asked.

"As I have said, I fear for her safety." Ryoma looked around the room. "At this time, she only wishes to return to her home realm."

"All of us here take the legend seriously." Lady Inara gestured around the room. "I would very much like to meet this girl, and if she is really Araia's chosen one, then we cannot dismiss her."

"I agree," Malik stated. "But before we can act, we need proof that she is who you claim."

"Why are you consenting to this?" Danothir spat. "The girl belongs to me."

"If she proves to indeed be the Protectorate Goddess, then we must do what we can for her," Malik replied. "But this matter between House Borga and Ithor does not fall into the jurisdiction of the Consortium. Therefore, it is up to the two of you to settle. I will consider what you have said, King Ryoma, but without any tangible proof there is nothing that I can do."

"Very well." Ryoma nodded before sitting down.

"I shall inform you all if anything new develops. Once again, I thank you all for coming." Malik stood, turning briskly, and exited the chamber through the door he had entered from, followed by T'Chello. Voices quickly filled the room as everyone began to stand, talking at once.

You're playing a dangerous game Ryoma, one that will leave your pathetic kingdom in ruins. Danothir stood and marched out of the chamber. Catching the sound of heels following after him, he peered over his shoulder to find Lady Inara walking toward him. "Something I can do for you, Ritsuko?"

"I'm just wondering what's in your head?" Lady Inara smiled, stepping close enough for Danothir to smell her flagrant perfume. "The Chancellor might have believed you, but I don't. You've been grabbing everything you can find about the old legends, not to mention that you've secretly been massing your forces."

Danothir cross his arms with a shrug. "There is no law against gaining a few troops."

"Perhaps, but it does call into question what you intend to do with them."

"I would mind my own affairs if I were you." Danothir let an edge creep into his voice. "Play with a knife long enough, and eventually, you get cut."

Lady Inara gave a pleasant smile, but her eyes held a dangerous look. "And if I were you, I'd worry less about the knife you see, and focus on the one you don't."

Danothir bit back a curse as he watched Lady Inara walk away laughing. He would have to deal with her as well as the Sanada, and she could prove almost as dangerous. His enemies will try to foil his plans to usher in a second renaissance and stand against his good works.

That was something he could not allow.

Chapter Six

Amy leaned against the metal railing on a small balcony overlooking the east side of the town. A cool breeze blew across her face, ruffling her hair. She spent most of the last few days with Hayate, touring the countryside. The day before, he took her to the kingdoms main library, so she could find some books about their history. The archeologist in her couldn't help being fascinated by the similarities to the cultures she studied.

According to what she read, the realm was originally divided into nineteen domains ruled, each ruled by different family, until a long and bloody war enveloped the realm three hundred years ago, leaving only eight of the Houses. The land that wasn't grabbed by the surviving Houses had become twenty one separate kingdoms, like Ithor.

A knock on the door brought Amy out of her thoughts as she turned and stepped back into the room provided to her. The room was spacious, with a soft bed on one side and a few bookcases next to a small timber desk. Five windows were spaced around the room, giving Amy a pleasant view of the castle and town. "Come in."

Hayate smiled and stepped into the room carrying two old looking tomes. "I brought you these. I figured since you've been reading our history, you might want to look through these."

Returning his smile, Amy took the tomes and set them on the desk. "Thanks."

"So how's you research coming?" Hayate asked after a moment.

"Smashing. Your history has some fascinating parallels to my own, as does your mythology," Amy replied. She looked at him for a moment then smiled again. "I was going to get some air out by the garden, care to join me?"

"I would."

They made their way outside and walked along a narrow path that led to the garden, passing many bushes with bright sunflowers, or rows of roses. Some of the trees had what looked like dandelions growing alongside the leaves. Other flowerbeds held exotic flowers or plants similar to ones found in many of the forests Amy had visited with her father.

Amy stopped at bed of flowers that grew out of bluish-green grass and marveled at them. "These are so beautiful." They looked very much like jasmines, but the buds were teal.

"You don't have flowers where you come from?"

Amy laughed. "Not like yours."

Hayate knelt down and pluck one of the delicate looking flowers. "Here." He placed the flower behind her left ear. "According to legend, Tai Re'l once used a flower like this to save her lover from death."

Amy felt a twinge of annoyance creep onto her face at the mention of more gods and legends. As much as she had enjoyed reading about this world's past, she had no intention of taking a place among any pantheon of deities; a fact that—despite her repeated efforts to convey—Hayate refused to accept. After a moment, she turned back and saw that he was staring at the sky.

"What's it like? Your world I mean." Hayate looked back at her.

"Well it's different from here. There's not as much open countryside and people are always rushing to do one thing or another." Amy paused for a moment. "Here it's more peaceful, serene."

They began walking again, talking about where they grew up and childhood memories. They spent almost an hour talking before they decided to head back to the castle. As they reached the gates, they saw an adolescent squire heading toward them.

"Sir Hayate, the King wishes to see you and Lady Price."

Feeling a surge of excitement at the thought of returning home, Amy followed Hayate as they hurried through the castle halls toward the throne room and waited until the squire showed them in.

"Your majesty." Hayate bowed.

Ryoma turned from the window, dismissing the squire, and stepped over to Hayate and Amy. "I'm afraid that, for the moment, the Consortium is unwilling to help."

"They didn't believe you?" Hayate asked.

"Some may have. They asked that I provide proof that Amy is truly the Protectorate Goddess before they could act."

"But how can we prove it?"

Ryoma shrugged, a somber look falling over him. "This is beyond my range of expertise. In fact, there is only one that I know of who may have knowledge we can use."

"Who?" Amy asked, unable to keep the disappointment from her voice. She didn't really want to find proof that she was a goddess, but if she disproved it, then maybe she could get home. "Could they help me find a way home?"

"The Sanada," Ryoma responded.

"Then I'll go ask them what they know," Hayate stated firmly.

"For the moment that is the only option open to us," Ryoma agreed. "But, you said you killed one of the Sanyoshu. They may seek retribution. Your life will be endangered along with Amy's."

Hayate straightened, tucking his hands behind his back. "I'll still go."

Amy felt a chill run down her spine. "No, there's no reason to risk your life. I'll go by myself."

"You have to understand." Ryoma turned toward Amy. "Once a knight of Ithor swears an oath, he is bound by the gods to uphold it. For him to give it to you means that he is prepared to do all in his power to aid you until he fulfills it or death takes him. The two of you must learn what you can from the Sanada. I will do what I can to defend against Danothir's treachery."

"Thank you." Amy smiled as Hayate bowed, thoughts of going home and arguing with her sister filling her head. But as much as she tried to hold on to those thoughts, she couldn't shake the feeling that something dark was coming.

* * *

Traveling on horseback by day and resting in small villages or camping under a shroud of stars at night, Amy and Hayate reached Austuria just before sunset. A vast sea of thick redwoods covered most of the region while undersized villages were sat in large clearings on the outskirts of the wooded areas. Closer inland, towns with more substantial populations appeared more frequently. Emerging from yet another patch of woods, they headed through a quaint town toward an inordinate palace near the edge of the area.

More prosperous than other towns she had seen, Amy admired the details of the buildings as they trotted passed. The look of most reminded her of ancient Japanese architecture, and the palace was no exception. Hand carved crimson mahogany lined the edge of roofing's, windows, and doors. The walls were made from a smooth, egg white stone. The blue-green lawn was vast and well maintained, with small tree's bearing bluish apples scattered about. Luminescent stones hung from short strings above a wide porch that wrapped around the entire palace. Small lanterns lined the cobblestone walkway leading to the elegant main entrance.

Reaching the main entrance, Hayate dismounted as a short man in reddish armor stepped forward to greet them. "We've come to speak with Lord Sanada."

A second man, a little taller than the first, stepped over and glared at them. "Who the blazes are you?"

Hayate returned the man's glare. "Tell your masters that a knight of Ithor is here."

The first man snorted. "Fine." He whispered something to the second man then looked back toward Amy and Hayate. "Follow me."

Hopping down to the ground, Amy followed a few feet behind the man and noticed a gold square with four lines etched on the back of the armor. "That's like the symbol the woman had in the forest."

"The lined square is the crest worn by anyone who works for the Sanada," Hayate replied quietly.

"So he's a Sanyoshu?"

"No, he's a regular in the Sanada army. The Sanyoshu all bear the crest but theirs is crimson, and only a member of the Sanada family bears the full serpent crest."

They were led into a large chamber with a small ivory table in the center. Intricate paintings hung on the walls, reflecting light from lanterns placed around the room to emphasize them. Two archways stood on the other end of the room, leading to other parts of the palace.

"Wait here," the man demanded before leaving, his boots echoing on the marble floor.

"Why were you so rude?" Amy walked around the room admiring the paintings. "We came here to ask for help didn't we?"

"Yes, but we'd just be wasting time with the guards." Hayate glanced in the direction the man exited. "Everyone knows that the *official* army of the Sanada is nothing more than a farce. Their real power lies in the Sanyoshu."

Amy nodded and went back to studying the paintings until the sound of footsteps entered the room. Looking toward the source, Amy saw a man in his thirties standing near the table, his black hair tied in low ponytail. He had a strong jaw line and a well-trimmed beard that gave him a stately look.

"So, who is it that demands an audience with me?" He spoke with a deep voice and was dressed similar to Yuki, only without the armor and loser fitting clothes.

"I am Hayate Thane of Ithor, and I wish to speak with all of the Sanada."

"Is that so?" The man crossed his arms, his eyes narrowing in annoyance. "And why should I grant this request?"

"Because it concerns the fate of our realm," Hayate replied.

"I was unaware that Ithorian knights had such dramatic flair." The man let out an amused laugh. "Follow me then."

"Who is he?" Amy asked.

"Genki Sanada, the head of the Sanada family," Hayate whispered back.

Following Genki, they walked through a series of halls that led outside into an open courtyard. The sounds of wood breaking and men crying out in pain emanated from behind a sliding door.

Stepping through the open doorway onto a crimson walkway about twenty feet above the rest of the room, they looked down at a man fighting four men armed with wooden swords. Various weapons, from swords to clubs, hung on racks on either side of the large, padded room.

The four men all charged at the single man, but in a motion too swift for them to avoid, he heel kicked them all on the jaw. He then alternated between punches and kicks to their face, dropping each in turn.

"Amazing." Amy stepped forward, leaning over the railing as a hint of awe rushed over her. "He looks like that Yuki woman."

"They should. Ikari's her twin," Genki answered.

"It seems we have guests." Yuki walked in and stood next to her older brother.

"This is…" Genki started.

Yuki turned her cold stare toward him. "Hayate Thane, wasn't it?"

"So you've met?" Genki laughed.

"What's all this?" Ikari looked up at the group.

"Come, join us and we shall all find out." Genki motioned for everyone to follow and started walking back inside the palace.

He led them into a spacious chamber with three large hand carved mahogany chairs sitting on a raised platform. A large window made up the wall behind the chairs, giving a clear view of the sun setting into the sparkling ocean. The image of a phoenix was painted on the wall to the left while the one opposite bore the serpent crest. Amy noticed that the ceiling had the golden symbol of the trickster god, Lorric, painted above the crimson thrones.

Genki sat in the center chair while Yuki took the one to his left. Ikari remained standing and walked over to his sister's side.

Yuki leaned back and crossed her legs. "So Hayate Thane, why are you here?"

"I assume it has something to do with her," Genki stated. "The alleged Protectorate Goddess."

"How did you know?" Amy asked.

"We make it our business to know these things," Ikari responded with a grin. "Ever since your King went to the Consortium, things have been rather chaotic."

"And I thought it was the little girl," Yuki chuckled.

"We've come to ask for your help," Hayate stated.

"How so?" Genki leaned to the side.

"We need proof that Amy is the Protectorate Goddess. You're the only ones I know of with any deep knowledge of the mystical arts."

Yuki's icy stare fixed on Amy for a moment, then shifted back to Hayate. "What makes you think we know any more than you?"

"You and your brother have both mastered the shadow arts of Alextien. Surely you've heard something regarding the legend?" Hayate stepped forward.

Yuki and Ikari glanced at each other and smiled before speaking in unison. "And?"

Amy saw the frustration wash over Hayate's face and put her hand on his shoulder. "We just want some information, that's all. I'm sure this whole goddess thing is a mistake, but trying to prove that I am her is probably the only way to prove that I'm not. After that, I can go back to my own realm."

Genki rested his bearded chin on his fist. "You seem to think I care, Ms... I'm sorry; I don't believe I caught your name."

"Amy Price."

"Well Amy, what makes you think I care?"

"Are you just going to sit back and let Danothir try to take control of the realm?" Hayate asked, anger reddening his face.

Genki waved a hand. "The petty concerns of petty men are beneath me."

"Besides," Yuki laughed. "He'll fail. He wants the power of the heavens but only has ambition to rule the realm? He lacks an imagination."

Ikari shifted his gaze to Amy. "What will you do if you are the one in the legends?"

"I, I don't know," Amy replied. She had spent a lot of time wondering that herself.

"You know, she could be the death of us all," Yuki alleged.

"What do you mean?" Hayate shot Yuki an incredulous look. "The Protectorate Goddess will save the people and make the realm a better place."

"That's the kiddy version." Ikari flashed a surreptitious grin. "The Protectorate Goddess will emerge welding the power of the gods."

"Yes," Hayate agreed. "She'll use those powers to protect the people of Terra."

"You see, that's were things get hazy." Ikari leaned against Yuki's chair. "There's always this one part that gets left out of these legends. The Protectorate Goddess shall emerge to *judge* Terra, and she will be given command of the war god's army. She *can* use the god's power to help, or she could summon Sha'Kring's army and destroy us all."

Amy felt her jaw drop as a wave of shock hit her like a brick to the head. How could they believe she had such power? Was she really supposed to be responsible for destroying a whole world?

Hayate too, stood in silence, stunned by the revelation. After a moment, he shook his head and glanced at Amy. "I believe in my heart that Amy is going to save the realm. Nothing you say is going to change that."

Amy gazed at Hayate, startled by the sincerity in his voice. Feeling her face warming, she looked away.

"Why don't you stay as a guest for the evening," Genki said after a moment. "It can be dangerous traveling at night. Allow us some time to consider what you've said."

"Very well," Hayate agreed.

Genki called for an attendant. "Take them to the guest rooms and see that they are comfortable."

As they followed the man out, Amy felt the cold stare of Yuki chilling her back, but at the same time, she felt as though something had shifted. Like a shadow in the room had brightened slightly.

* * *

Ikari stepped over to the window and gazed over the darkening ocean. Saskai had told him about Amy being protected by Ithor, and Yuki had also mentioned her encounter with Hayate a few days ago. But he didn't think that the source of all the recent commotion would come strolling to him like a gift from the gods.

"Remarkable," Yuki exclaimed.

"How so?" Genki shifted to face her.

"I had planned to track him down at one point, but now it seems that the gods had other plans."

"I am aware that he has killed a member of your sect, but now is not the time for retribution," Genki said plainly. "His death along with the girls will only bring unwanted problems down on us."

Yuki waved a reassuring hand. "Don't worry brother, I've no intentions on killing him yet, and I'll speak to E'Lan about the matter."

Ikari smiled, remembering the state E'Lan was in after she returned from Nel'Oskow and the fury that she radiated.

"What are you going to do?" Yuki asked.

"Nothing. Let the Consortium deal with this," Genki replied.

"Why waste an amble opportunity?" Ikari turned from the window with a mischievous grin, unsurprised that his brother had missed the obvious use the girl provided.

"What do you have in mind?" Genki looked toward him.

"The Consortium has been thrown into complete chaos since word of Amy's arrival spread. Some believe the legends are coming to pass, some don't. Danothir is beginning to make his move against the realm, and House Inara seems to be plotting something." Ikari smiled at the confused look on his older brother's face. "Why not use it? Let's stir the pot and add even more intrigue. Let's do what the Sanada have always done best; spin this to our advantage and ensure that when this storm passes, we're the only ones not caught in the rain."

"How?" Yuki stared at her twin, an all too familiar smile spread across her face.

"The first step just gave itself to us. They came looking for proof that she's the Protectorate Goddess so the Consortium can make a decision. All we gotta do is make sure they don't find any—one way or the other—until it's best for us."

Yuki laughed. "If we keep everyone in the dark long enough they'll end up killing themselves."

"And whoever is left standing will be crushed by the heel of the Sanada."

Genki stood and clapped Ikari on the shoulder. "Always the schemer, aren't you? However, there are some potential problems."

"Agreed," Ikari conceded.

"We'd need to keep an eye on the major players in this little game," Yuki stated.

"We'll have to keep tabs on the Consortium and Danothir." Genki glanced at Yuki. "As well as Amy herself."

"We also need to learn what exactly Lady Inara is planning," Ikari added.

Genki nodded in agreement. "I well see what I can do about hindering the Consortium's efforts. Yuki, follow Amy and her knight and keep them busy chasing the wind. I'll leave House Inara to you, Ikari, given Ritsuko's affection for you."

"I'll leave in the morning." Ikari walked over and sat in his chair. "But we need something to keep Amy and her knight busy."

"Like what?"

"The Roses of Tai Re'l?" Yuki glanced at Ikari.

"Perfect," Ikari responded.

"What are those?" Genki asked.

"An old legend Ikari and I picked up while we were in Alextien. According to myth, three crystal roses were used by Tai Re'l to find her missing lover. Supposedly, they can locate heavenly beings, among other things, in this case our alleged Protectorate Goddess."

Genki raised an eyebrow as he glanced at each of the twins. "And these roses are real?"

Yuki shrugged. "I didn't believe so, but you remember that box I took from Inara's men a while ago?"

"Yes." Genki nodded.

"A rose made from obsidian was carefully packed inside."

"I see," Genki laughed.

Ikari smiled, glancing up at the symbol of Lorric painted above. Deceit and trickery were the horned god's favorite pastimes, which was probably why he showed favor to the Sanada. A part of Ikari felt a hint of regret at the thought of using Amy for his own purpose, but, deceit and trickery were what he was best at.

Chapter Seven

Moonlight filtered through the faint layer of clouds hanging overhead as an icy wind swept through the empty garden on the north side of the Sanada estate. The soft sound of water hitting the shore and wind rustling through leaves gave the garden an eerie atmosphere. Amy leaned against a stone fountain and ran her finger over the top of the cool water.

Suspicious of the Sanada, Hayate had instructed her to wait while he checked to see how much freedom they were really given. So far, they had gone pretty much anywhere they wanted without much fuss from passing soldiers or workers. She remembered reading a little about the Sanada family before they left Ithor, but all she could remember now was some vague footnotes about some ancestors trying to rise in rank during the Great War. One thing that did stick out, however, was their name. Amy read a lot of various countries history and during Japans warring states era, a man named Yukimura Sanada was infamous for his attempts to kill the Shogun and take control of Japan.

The sound of footsteps caught Amy's attention. She turned toward the source expecting to see Hayate's warm smile, but was instead greeted by Ikari.

"Evening." Ikari gave a slight bow.

"Hello," Amy turned toward him. "What are you doing out so late?"

"I live here." Ikari smiled playfully. "What's your excuse?"

"I just wanted some air." Amy returned his smile. He had a cocky, boyish charm to him.

"I always found this place a little unsettling at night."

"It's a little on the creepy side." Amy laughed, finding herself put at ease by his playful attitude. "But all in all, it's a beautiful place. It must be nice to have all this and not have to worry about responsibilities or pressure from family to follow in their footsteps."

"You'd be surprised," Ikari smirked. "My family has a... interesting background."

"This whole world seems to. Everything here is so different from my home." Amy peered up at the clouds, thinking about her family. "Everyone seems to have these expectations that I can't fulfill. Expectations I don't want to fulfill. I'm grateful for everything Hayate is trying to do for me, but it's kinda overwhelming, you know?"

Ikari laughed softly. "No, but then people don't think I'm a god."

"Sorry, I didn't mean to go on like that."

Ikari shrugged, jumping onto the edge of the fountain. Amy was surprised that he didn't slip, considering the rim was barely an inch wide.

He began to walk around the rim and flashed her a warm smile. "Sometimes we're forced to play a role we might not want to. You can ether go along with it or try to fight it."

"What would you chose?"

"Me, I refuse to follow a fate I haven't forged for myself. I'd follow my own path, one that blends what others want with what I want. But, doing so is like walking a tight rope, one missed step and you fall, losing everything." Ikari let gravity tip him forward and stepped off the fountain.

Amy could almost feel his sincerity as she stared into his auburn eyes. After a few minutes of silence, Hayate returned and stepped over to Amy's side wearing a concerned look.

"Ah, just who I wanted to see," Ikari said with a nod. "I remembered something that might help you."

"What is it?" Hayate asked, enthusiasm pouring from his voice. "Any bit of information would be of great help."

"Have you ever heard of the Roses of Tai Re'l?"

Hayate nodded. "I read a little about them, why?"

"It's said that they can be used to identify heavenly beings."

Eyebrows furrowed in thought, Hayate glanced at Amy. "If I had those then the Consortium would have its proof."

"Yep." Ikari smirked.

"But who knows if they're real or not," Amy stated.

"Oh, they're real enough."

"But where would I find them?" Hayate inquired.

"There's this old man in Caladan who deals in ancient knowledge. He's the one to ask about these things." Ikari smiled then began to walk back inside. "If you'll excuse me, I need to go prepare for a trip."

Waiting until Ikari had left, Hayate turned back to Amy. "Are you okay?"

"I'm fine, we were just talking." Amy smiled reassuringly. "You act like you don't trust him."

"I don't, not entirely," Hayate admitted. "The Sanada are rather duplicitous by nature."

"I don't think Ikari was lying. I got the feeling that he wanted to help."

"It's irrelevant at this point anyway. Checking out this old man is the only lead we have."

* * *

Strolling through the hall's, Ikari smiled to himself. *Interesting, she doesn't really want be a goddess.* He couldn't help but wonder what her reason was for going off to look for proof of her godliness. What was she after? He was pondering the answers when he turned a corner and bumped into E'Lan.

"My apologies, Lord Ikari." E'Lan bowed her head.

"My fault. Wasn't paying attention," Ikari replied.

Leaning against the wall behind E'Lan, Yuki grinned at him. "Thinking about our guest?"

"Actually I was."

"She's pretty, but I doubt she's what you want," Yuki teased. "I saw that you two were having a nice little moment there."

"Ease dropping on me again, dear sister?"

Yuki shrugged her shoulders. "It's my nature."

"Well sorry to disappoint you, but she's nothing but a stone in my path." Ikari smiled playfully. "Shouldn't you be getting ready to leave?"

"I was just wondering when you'll get around to finding whatever it is your looking for." Yuki returned his smile.

Ikari let out an amused chuckle. "You're starting to sound like our master."

"He saw it too. That look you get in your eyes. You're always looking for something else."

Ikari raised an eyebrow. "And you think it's Amy?"

"No, but I know you brother, you're always skimming, always looking for a way to spin things your way."

Ikari laughed again. "It's my nature." Behind him, Ikari noticed a slight shadow bend around the corner. Recognizing the presence he felt trying to remain unnoticed, he looked over his shoulder. "You can join us Saskai."

Saskai stepped around the corner and stood by E'Lan. "I did not wish to intrude, my Lord."

"Perhaps you know what he's looking for?" Yuki looked over at Saskai.

"I do not, my lady."

Yuki shifted her vision to her right. "Care to take a guess E'Lan?"

"I, I would not presume to know the intentions of Lord Ikari," E'Lan replied, her voice low.

Ikari shook his head. Yuki was one of the fiercest fighters in the entire realm—far more brutal than he was in combat—but she always had the need to fix other people's problems, mainly his. "Not that this isn't fun, but I've got some things that need doing before I leave." He motioned for Saskai to follow and started down the hall.

"Lord Ikari," E'Lan called after him.

"Yes?" Ikari stopped and turned around.

"I just wanted to… to wish you well on your journey." E'Lan looked down at the floor, but Ikari caught a hint of her face reddening.

"See you when I see you." He started down the hall again.

"Oh I'm sure our paths will cross once or twice before this is over with," Yuki stated as he walked away.

"Probably."

* * *

Sunlight filtered through gray vapor as Amy walked along side of Hayate. They had left Austuria early in the morning after eating some kind of baked pastry that reminded her of crapes. Glancing up, Amy began to wish the she had an umbrella or at least a raincoat.

Hayate walked silently leading their horse by the reins while listening to Amy. She talked about some of the places she had traveled to with her father and growing up in London. It amazed her at how intrigued he was by simple things like cars or skyscrapers, but then, considering that he has never seen anything like them before, it was understandable.

"So you travel your realm studying the gods?"

"Yeah, as well as ancient cultures and civilizations," Amy replied. "I spent four years getting my degree. Well almost four, this was supposed to be my last semester."

"What will you do when you finish?"

"I'm not sure. My dad wants me join his team of archeologists, but truthfully, I don't think that's what I want to do."

Hayate gazed at her for a moment then looked back down the path they were following. "In Ithor, it's pretty common for a child to take over for their parents."

"It's not like I don't enjoy archeology, but he keeps pressuring me. I just need some time to figure things out."

"Maybe that's why you were brought here."

"How did you become a knight?" Amy asked, wanting to change the subject. "Was your dad a knight?"

"No, my mother was a shop proprietor and my father ran a small inn in Welend." Hayate reached into a pouch behind the horse's saddle and pulled out a small container filled with water.

"Do you get to visit them much?" Amy declined when he offered her the brown bottle.

"They died when I was a kid." Hayate took a sip of the water.

"I'm sorry." They walked in silence for a few minutes before Amy said anything. "How did you end up in Ithor?"

"King Ryoma found me working in a little tavern outside of Ithor. I guess he felt sorry for me and kept coming back. Eventually, he offered to make me a squire and I trained to become a knight."

"What made you decide that?" Amy smiled at him. Since they had first meet, this was the first time he really talked about himself.

"Part of the reason was to repay him. At the time, Ithor was in the throes of a depression. Economically, we were destroyed and are still trying to recover." Hayate put the water back into the pouch.

"What was the other reason?"

Hayate smiled and looked back toward Amy. "I wanted to make this a better world. I thought that if I could become a knight, a nobleman, then I'd be able to truly help people. I hopped to influence others to help rebuild things and improve the lives of the less fortunate."

Amy couldn't help but smile at Hayate's idealism. Continuing down the path in silence, Amy let her gaze linger on Hayate for moment before looking ahead.

* * *

Caladan was a small town near a range of small mountains to the north. The cobblestone streets were slick from rain and dark storm clouds hung overhead, blocking the sun. Many of the townspeople were hurrying to complete whatever they were doing and get inside before the rain started again. The few people Hayate and Amy passed seemed too occupied to notice the strangers.

Hayate had left their horse in one of the town's stables, paying the greasy looking owner more than he would have liked. Now, he and Amy were headed to the center of the town, where a few adobe inns and shops circled around the town square. Hayate had tried asking about any shops that sold antiques or mystical trinkets, but most people ignored him and pushed past. Eventually, one of the people he asked told him about a shop in the town square.

"Do you think this is the place?" Amy asked.

"I hope so. We've spent all day looking for it." Hayate opened the wooden door to the shop and followed Amy inside.

The shop was filled with worn wooden shelves and bookcases. Torch's mounted on squared pillars along the walls cast flickering shadows over piles of aged text. The scent of burning incense filled the room while the wooden floor boards creaked under their boots as they approached a shabby counter with more books piled on it.

"Certainly has a lot of books." Amy picked one up and thumbed through the pages.

After a few minutes, an older man with thin, graying hair, stepped out from behind a bookcase and walked over to them. Staring at them for a long moment, he ran his hand over his patchy beard. "How can I help you folks today, or night, whatever time it may be?"

"We heard that you're knowledgeable in ancient text," Hayate responded.

"Oh, that I am young man. I am Asano Terada, Caladan's foremost expert on the heavens."

Hayate and Amy shared a skeptical expression then looked back to the old man. He sounded like he had spent too much time reading books than living outside in the realm.

"Have you ever heard of the Roses of Tai Re'l?" Amy asked.

"Of course I have," Asano replied tartly.

"We're trying to find them. Anything you could tell us would be of help," Hayate said.

Asano stared at them for a long moment then nodded. "Follow me."

Asano led them behind the bookcase to a stairwell that Hayate failed to notice. The dark stairs took them up to a large room filled with more worn books and tattered scrolls lying around the carpeted floor. Glancing out one of the round windows, Hayate noticed that it had started raining again.

"Have a seat." Asano motioned to the small table centered in the room and sat on a shabby stool.

Hayate sat next to Amy on a wooden bench opposite of Asano. "What is all this?"

"My books." Asano gestured around the room. "My favorites. The more informative ones. Why do you seek the roses?"

"We need them to..." Hayate started to tell him why they had really come but thought better of it. "To identify some holy text for King Ryoma."

53

"Ah, I see." Asano nodded. "I've heard some interesting rumors lately. They say that King Ryoma and his knights protect a special girl, a girl hunted by Lord Borga."

"I don't know what you're talking about," Hayate lied. If word of Amy's appearance has already spread, then traveling unnoticed might become difficult.

"I think you do. I am not so old that I cannot see what is in front of me. Besides, some men from Nel'Oskow were here a day ago asking about the roses."

"What did you tell them?" Amy inquired.

"The same thing I'm going to tell you; that the roses can be found only by those chosen by the gods."

"Is there anything you can tell us?" Hayate asked.

"I can tell you that Lord Borga has been actively seeking the roses and anything mentioning the Protectorate Goddess, but lately, he seems to have hit a wall, so to speak."

"What do you mean?" Amy asked.

"Someone else seems to be searching for the same text and items. Only this unseen person is doing a far better job of it." A soft bell rang from downstairs, prompting Asano to stand and head toward the stairs. "Excuse me for a moment."

Someone else is looking into the legend, but who? As Hayate thought about the answer, the sound of falling books rose from downstairs.

"What was that?" Amy turned toward the steps.

Hayate stood and started toward the stairway, catching the sound of heavy boots hitting the wooden stairs. Hayate motioned for Amy to move out of sight and ducked beside the wall. Once the man reached the top of the stairs and stepped through the opening, Hayate saw that he wore the armor belonging to Danothir's soldiers and carried a crossbow.

Picking up a heavy looking book, Hayate quickly hit the soldier over the head. The soldier fell on his stomach and rolled, trying to get back to his feet, but Hayate stood over him and hit him hard on the temple, knocking him unconscious.

"Wait here," Hayate instructed Amy before he dropped the book and picked up the bow.

Hayate inched his way down the stairs, spotting two soldiers with their backs to him. He took careful aim and fired, catching the soldier towering over Asano between the shoulders. Hayate fired again, aiming for the other soldier, but his target managed to dive behind a shelf.

A trio of arrows peppered the stairway, forcing Hayate to jump back. After a second, he dived out and crawled behind another bookcase. Firing blindly at the soldier, he hastily searched for a better position and was about to roll behind a pillar, when the soldier leapt out, trying to run behind the counter. Hayate yanked the lever back, reloading the bow and fired, catching the man in the ribs as he ran.

Taking a long, calming breath, Hayate stood and ran over to Asano, who was slumped against the far wall. "Are you okay?"

"Just a bump to the head." Asano smiled up at him, but the smile faded as his eyes widened.

Alarmed, Hayate twisted around in time to see a middle-aged man in black with a lavender vest hit him on the face with the butt of his bow. He fell to the floor, questioning how he had missed the man when he noticed the crest on his torso, an inverted triangle with a pentagram in the center.

"Don't mind me. I'm just here for a bookkeeper." The man stepped over to Hayate and viciously kicked the downed knight on the side of his head.

A wave of agony shot through Hayate's body as darkness eroded his vision, leaving him with image of the man laughing over him.

Chapter Eight

Osaka Major was brimming with activity, despite the gloomy clouds hanging over head. The large city's streets swarmed with people hastening back and forth between the stone dwellings. Families crossed in front of extravagant carriages, hopping to escape the promise of rain the icy breeze carried over the general buzzing of the crowd.

Ikari leaned against a wall in a narrow ally observing the passing crowds, his well-trained eyes alert for any signs of danger. Wearing a dark cloak over his cloths, he looked like a typical merchant roaming the city. He had spent most of the day searching for information on the Inara family, but so far, had heard only second hand information he already knew.

Glancing across the street, he saw Saskai exiting a shop and heading toward him. "I'm afraid he didn't know anything of use," he said as he lowered the hood of his cloak.

"Not surprising," Ikari responded dryly. "People here seem to be blind about what's going on."

"Should we head back?"

"Not yet." Ikari shook his head. "But, we've spent a day asking around."

"Perhaps we are asking the wrong questions."

"No, I think we've been asking the wrong people. Since the aristocracy doesn't seem to know anything useful, we need to talk to the more sorted crowds." Ikari smirked and raised his hood. "We need to head to the poor side of town."

Saskai nodded then pulled his own hood up.

They walked across town unnoticed by the distracted people. Passing through the business district and ducking into a narrow ally, they reached an area considerably less maintained than the rest of the city. Painted walls were cracked and had a dense layer of dirt covering them. Even the air felt grimier due to the smoke from nearby factories that lingered overhead. Instead of the well-dressed upper class, a motley crowd of workers and peasants filled the uneven streets.

They wandered the streets for just over an hour before stopping outside of a large tavern named the Twilight's Swan. Stepping through the open door, Ikari was hit by the smell of smoke and ale. People sat around small triangle shaped tables, drinking or playing cards. A trio of half nude women sang a melodious song about an ancient warrior while a group of drunks sang along off key. A large circular stage was centered in the torch lit room, surrounded by a cheering crowd as two men grappled, each trying to knock the other off.

Ikari walked over to an empty table and smiled as he sat down. He had been to many places like this one over the years and they always had some scoundrel who knew too much for his own good. Now all he had to do was find him.

A short, plump woman waddled over to their table and flashed a practiced smile. "What can I get ya folks?"

"Two zoshi ales." Ikari returned the smile then watched her hurry away only to return a few minutes later with their drinks.

"Here ya are." She set the drinks down before hurrying to the next table.

Ikari and Saskai sat and observed the crowd, drinking the ale too slowly to feel its affects while giving the appearance of being two more drunks in a tavern.

The group around the stage erupted in applause as the shorter man pushed the other off the stage. Ikari chuckled to himself, watching the winner parade around, calling for more challengers. He was tempted to answer the man's challenge but dismissed the idea. That wasn't why he was here. Besides, beating that man would be like a dragon fighting a field mouse.

"There seems to be a lot of warriors here," Saskai observed.

"I noticed." Ikari set his ale on the table then stood. "Let's find out why."

They walked over and joined the group watching the short man battle a lanky, big headed fellow. After the short man won, Ikari made his way closer, ignoring the man's claims to be the strongest fighter in the realm, a title he intended to claim for himself one day.

"Who is he?" Ikari asked a bald man with stains on his shirt.

"I believe he's named Gaou. He's here for the big tournament tomorrow."

"Tournament?" Ikari raised an eyebrow.

"It is being held by Lady Inara in the grand arena. Warriors from around the realm have come in hopes of winning."

"And this tournament is open to anyone?"

"Yeah."

Ikari let a lopsided grin adorn his face as he made his way back to the table. Leaving three coins on the table, he turned and left the tavern, followed by Saskai.

"Did you find something?" Saskai inquired.

"I've just found my way into Ritsuko's court. I'll be entering that tournament of hers."

"Lord Ikari, is that wise?"

"It'll be easy. I just need you to go find me a suitable disguise."

* * *

Ritsuko Inara stood in front of a large jewel incrusted mirror, admiring how she looked in her long, lavender dress. Her long blonde hair hung over bare shoulders and covered most of her golden necklace. She smiled, pleased with her appearance, and slid two gold armbands bearing her families sigil over her elbows.

Turning around, she walked passed a small table covered with porcelain statues and stepped in front of a waiting aide. Ritsuko smiled again, and slowly paced around the man trembling in her study. The walls were lined with paintings, wall scrolls, or bookcases filled with worn tomes. A soft, burgundy carpet with the Inara family crest covered the hardwood floors.

"You may give your report now," Ritsuko whispered into his ear.

"We... we have learned the whereabouts of the box you were searching for."

"Where?"

The aide swallowed, his face growing paler. "The... the Sanada have it."

"Do they know the rose is in it?" Ritsuko felt her eye twitch as a flash of anger jolted through her.

"Probably, the lock wouldn't keep them from it if they wanted to open the box."

"I see." Ritsuko pushed back the urge to strike the man. "What about Danothir?"

"Your spies tell me that he is still looking for the girl, as well as clues on how to use her power."

Ritsuko had spies in all of the major Houses as well as in the minor kingdoms and the Consortium. Since she had returned from the meeting called by Ryoma, she had instructed all of her agents to give regular reports on anything interesting. "Have you found the girl yet?"

"No, my Lady." The aide kept his gaze glued to the floor. "But we are still searching. She was last seen in Austuria with a knight from Ithor."

Turning, Ritsuko slapped him across the face, drawing a little blood. "I already knew that!" She had been informed about Amy's visit to the Sanada days ago. So far, it appeared as though they weren't

58

interested in Amy, but Ritsuko knew better. Whenever the Sanada were quiet, that was when they were the most deadly. What angered her more was that her spies were too inept to learn anything of interest about what the Sanada were up to. "Where is she now?"

"I don't know."

"Where is Tres?"

"I sent him to Caladan." The aide winced as Ritsuko paused in front of him. "A man with considerable knowledge is said to live there."

Ritsuko nodded, resuming her deliberate pace around him. "Then my top concern is to retrieve the rose that your men lost."

"Lady Inara, perhaps you could simply ask the Sanada to return it since they don't seem to care about it."

Ritsuko felt her face burn red, but held back the urge to slap her aide. Forcing her annoyance back, she glared at the trembling man with a calm, cold, demeanor her daughter had labeled *the stare of death.* "You are as stupid as you are useless."

"Forgive me."

"Spare me your inane apologies." Ritsuko walked over to a glass case filled with expensive jewelry. Opening it, she pulled out an elaborate gold ring with a lavender jewel carved into a pentagram. "How long have you been my aide?"

"Just over two weeks," he answered in a shaky voice.

Walking toward the man, Ritsuko slid the ring over her right middle finger and spun the jewel to face her palm. "Sweet Liam." She circled around him once.

"It... its Leore, my Lady." He swallowed, sweat dripping from his brow.

"Whatever." She ran her left hand through his shaggy hair then grabbed a fistful, pulling him close. Ritsuko placed her ringed hand over his heart, focusing on the beating organ and the warm blood pumping through it. Extending her senses through his chest, she felt his body spasm a second before a flash of light pulsed from the ring, rupturing his arteries. An instant later, she felt his heart pop like an over filled bag and let his corpse fall to the floor. "Your services are no longer required."

She stepped back in front of the mirror and readjusted her dress and makeup. Many people had accused her of practicing the forbidden magic's over the years, and most met the same fate as her aide. The gods had made those arts available and she happily learned all she could. The gods gave her this power, which meant that all power was hers for the taking. If Amy Price was the Protectorate Goddess, then Ritsuko would take that power as well. The power of the heavens was her birthright and she wouldn't stop until she claimed it all.

Once again pleased with her appearance, she stepped passed the aide's body and exited the study. A young clerk stood outside and stiffened once he saw her.

"Where is my daughter?" she asked, while rotating the ring.

"Lady Alia is already downstairs waiting, my Lady."

"Have someone clean the mess in my study." Ritsuko started for the stairs without looking back.

Marching through the well-adorned halls, Ritsuko emerged in a large foyer and was greeted by her twenty-year-old daughter. Alia wore a tight, sleeveless black dress with long lavender gloves and gold bracelets on each arm. Her long blonde hair was tied back, save for a lock that hung over her youthful face and sea green eyes.

"Mother," Alia said, nodding her head.

"Come on, we mustn't be late." Ritsuko walked outside and stopped in front of a spacious carriage barring the family crest.

"Oh no, we can't have that." Alia rolled her eyes, stepping passed Ritsuko and into the carriage.

"Don't be snippy."

The driver closed the door after Ritsuko climbed in. A moment later, they started down the smooth road toward the arena. The inside of the carriage had silk curtains over the two windows. The floors were made from a reddish wood and the seats were covered with a plush, rose colored cushion.

"This isn't fair." Alia stared out the window, kicking a leg.

"What isn't fair?"

"This tournament of yours. I refuse to be a prize to some pig headed imbecile!"

"My dear Alia, I do this for you," Ritsuko stated softly. "I have spent my entire life building an empire worthy of our family, an empire that you will one day inherit. You will be a Queen revered across the realm."

"See that in a vision?" Alia sneered, referring to the dream quests Ritsuko often induced.

"Yes." Ritsuko let an edge creep into her voice. "You will be a beautiful, deadly Queen feared by all."

"Then why can't *I* choose who I marry?"

"Only one worthy of our family shall marry my daughter. Your husband must be a strong, capable warrior with no equal who can provide you with a strong daughter."

Alia scuffed, crossing her arms. "And you think one of those over glorified thugs is worthy?"

"Perhaps, these fighters come from many different lands, some from another realm. I am certain that a suitable man will be found."

"But I won't love him." Alia looked over and blinked back tears.

"Love is an indulgence." A bitter tone echoed in Ritsuko's voice. She leaned over and gently kissed Alia on the forehead with a reassuring smile. "I will ascend to my rightful place among the heavens and after me, you will take my place. The realms belong to us. I just want to ensure you are prepared to inherit them. Besides, after you have your daughter, you can always kill him."

Alia laughed. "It's amusing that you think you need to remind me as if I didn't know that already."

Chapter Nine

Ikari stood in front of the main entrance of the grand arena and watched as hundreds of people filed inside. Made from polished tanned stone, the arena stood six stories high with stadium style seats on the first two levels and the top three. The third level was reserved for those who could afford the overpriced and lavish private balconies.

Dressed in tan slacks, matching boots, and an oversized brown tunic with a large hood, Ikari walked past the four guards near the entrance, smiling through a black mask that covered his face from the nose down. Most people hardly looked twice at him as he headed toward the room assigned to the participants, and those that did, mistook him for one of many eccentric combatants filing in.

The outer section of the arena was filled with venders selling food or ale, and a thick layer of gray clouds hung overhead. Finding one of the many archways that led to the enclosed portion of the arena, Ikari stepped through and glanced around. Luminescent stones hung over the halls, providing light. Plush red carpet and matching tapestries with gold trim reminded him of an old opera house, which it was used as on occasion.

Ikari headed over to an attendant, inquiring about where to register his entry and was directed to a large oak door. It took him a few minutes to find, but once he did, he walked down the stairs into a small room lit by torches.

A bald man with double chins glared up and waved Ikari toward his small desk. "Your name, sir?"

"Mal Sounga," Ikari answered, pouring every ounce of arrogance he could into his voice. "The winner of this tournament."

"Yes, yes I've heard that before. You're in flight seven, number sixteen, got it?"

"Yeah."

"Good." The man rolled his eyes, pointing to the hall on his left. "Head down the hall and pick a tunnel, doesn't matter which one, and wait to be called."

Ikari started down the hall, and after a few yards, entered a tiny room with three tunnels, one on either side and one in front of him. He had seen enough arenas to know that they all went to three different waiting rooms on each side of the arena. Taking the tunnel to his right he walked down the narrow path until he reached a large room filled with other fighters. Some sat on weathered benches while others leaned against the walls. Many were bouncing back and forth trying to get loose before the tournament started. Peering across the chamber, Ikari saw the ramp that led to the field and stepped over to it. Looking up at the stands, he was unsurprised to find that they were almost full.

"Worried kid?" An older man with gray hair stepped over to him. Taller than Ikari by six inches, the man was in tremendous shape given his age.

"Hardly." Ikari poured bravado into his voice.

The man laughed, shaking his head, then asked, "What's with you kids today? This place is filled with some of the greatest warriors in the realm and you act like it's nothing. You come here with your little mask and act superior, but a boy like you has no idea what a real battle is."

"And you do?" Ikari mocked.

"I am Thade Folken. I've fought in many battles, and killed many men more skilled than you."

"Impressive." Ikari waved his hand. "Aren't you a bit old to be marrying Lady Inara's daughter?"

Before Thade could reply, a willowy man hurried into the room and called for everyone's attention. "Gentlemen, if you would please head up to the field."

Doing as he was asked, Ikari followed the others out and leaned against a wall. Two other groups filed out from the other rooms and did the same. Peering around the arena, Ikari's gaze stopped once he spotted Ritsuko and her daughter step onto their private balcony and motioned for the crowd to settle.

"Welcome brave warriors," Ritsuko shouted down to the gathered men. "As you already know, the winner will be given the honor of marrying my daughter. Fight well, for only the best of you will earn this right."

A low murmur rose from the fighters as Ritsuko sat next to her daughter. An official stepped onto the stage that would serve as the ring and began explaining the rules. "You will face each other in unarmed combat. You can either win by knockout, forcing you opponent to submit, or if you happen to kill him."

Ikari let out a surprised laugh hearing the last rule, but then, Ritsuko was known for being a bit blood thirsty, among other things.

"An elimination round will commence first," the man explained. "Each flight will enter the ring and face off in a battle royal. The last two men standing in each flight will move on the main tournament."

* * *

Three hours later, a bored Ikari looked up and found that Thade and a masked man had survived flight six's elimination round. The crowd, which hadn't quieted since the tournaments start, appeared to love every minute of the chaotic battles. Waiting for the ring to be cleared for the last flight, Ikari stood and stifled a yawn before the official called his flight to the ring.

The crowd continued its perpetual cheering as the final flight of fighters climbed into the ring. Making his way onto one of the corners, he heard a few of the men begin to exchange insults and stood with his hands in his sleeves, waiting until the official stepped out and raised his hand. The ring grew silent; its occupants tensing in anticipation of the officials signal to begin.

The official dropped his hand, and the ring erupted in flurry of motion as people began striking or pushing each other. In a matter of seconds, half of the fighters were pushed out of the ring or lying unconscious. A pair of burly men noticed Ikari and rushed toward him. Smirking beneath his mask, he leapt forward and kneed the first man on the face, then kicked the second on the temple before he touched the ground.

Just as the two men hit the floor, another took a swing at him. Ikari ducked, stepped behind him, and landed a kick to the back of his neck. Sauntering toward the center of the ring, he crouched, sweeping the legs of an older man, causing him to fall forward. Ikari let his momentum spin him around, uppercuting the man before his face hit the ring.

Glancing around, Ikari saw that only two other fighters remained standing. The tall bulky one grabbed the other and punched him in the ribs, then—grabbing hold of his collar and belt—threw him toward Ikari. Ikari spun forward and sent his foot crashing into the man's jaw, knocking at least one tooth loose and rendering him unconscious.

The crowd roared in thunderous applause while the bulky man and Ikari played to the crowd and stepped out of the ring to join the other winning combatants.

Ritsuko stood and signaled for the crowd to quiet. "Congratulations, you have advanced to the next round. Tomorrow you will face each other one on one to see who among you is truly worthy. Until then, I have provided lodgings for you not far from here and would like to invite you all to join me for dinner tonight."

Ikari peered up at Ritsuko and smiled to himself. *You're making this too easy.* With an invitation to the Inara estate, sneaking inside would be far less trouble than he had thought. *Time to find out what you're really up to.*

*   *   *

An icy wind swept passed Ikari as he walked along a damp path in the inn's garden. Ritsuko had reserved the entirety of the inn for the qualifying combatants and so far, seemed content to playing the generous host, but Ikari knew better. Ritsuko Inara was after something and this farce of a tournament was a part of it.

A trio of wagons had arrived about ten minutes ago to take the participants to the Inara estate, which was only a mile away. Ikari had ducked into an empty room while the others hurried off. Making his way to the estate, he worked his way through the garden and followed the dark alley's. Reaching the gate surrounding the lavish mansion, he began to search for a gap in the guard's perimeter.

"Lord Ikari." Saskai stepped out from behind a large tree hidden the shadows. The moon's light gave him an eerie appearance.

"Find anything useful?" Ikari stepped to his side.

"I'm afraid not. Getting inside unnoticed proved harder than I had anticipated, and once I got in, there were too many people wandering about for me to do any thorough searching."

"I imagine that everyone will be busy with dinner, so I should be able to move around easily enough."

"Shall I accompany you?"

"Nah, just hang around and keep an eye on things."

"As you wish my Lord."

"Where did you enter from?"

"Just around the southern gate, where the trees are thickest." Saskai pointed farther down the gate.

Ikari waved and headed to where Saskai directed him. Finding the grouping of trees, Ikari leapt onto a thick branch that hung over the gate. The trees would have been too high for an average prowler to navigate, but thanks to his training, he easily made his way across the spacious lawn. He paused once and waited for two guards to walk passed then continued until he reached main house.

Spying a darkened window two floors above, Ikari climbed as high as he could then jumped onto the balcony. He peered inside and found that the room was empty except for a few bookcases. Pushing open the large window, he stepped into the dark room and made his way to the wooden door, mindful of each step. As he got closer, he saw a series of shadows breaking the beam of light that shone beneath the door. Pressing an ear to the door, Ikari heard two maids complaining about Lady Inara's guests.

Nothing more fun than a room full of drunk, egotistical fighters.
Waiting until the women had left; Ikari opened the door and peered around. Seeing that the well-adorned hallway was clear, he made his way upstairs and began to search each room, working his way back down.

Ikari spent the better part of two hours searching the large, decadent mansion, ducking into rooms or leaping out of sight whenever someone passed by until he found his way to Ritsuko's office and picked the lock.

Ikari began looking through her desk, finding several invoices about excavations from different areas. He also found a cargo list giving detailed descriptions of dug up scrolls and jewels. Quickly glancing over the list, Ikari recognized some of the names from his studies and tried to remember what they were supposed to be used for. Making his way over to the bookcase, he noticed many books on ancient magic's or history and thumbed through a few.

He often heard rumors that Ritsuko practiced the forgotten magic's and had used them to solidify her power. Granted, he wasn't really in a position to judge. Ikari and his twin had spent years learning the shadow arts in Alextien causing many to refer to them as devils since most people wouldn't stand a chance against them in battle.

Setting the book back on the shelf, Ikari turned and walked over to a large glass case filled with jewels. He dismissed them at first, but caught sight of a silver bracelet with olive writing etched on it. Recognizing it from one of the books he had just flipped through, he grabbed the book and thumbed through the pages. He stopped at a section that told about how Lorric tricked the thunder god and stole his power, focusing on a picture of the silver bracelet.

Laughing in understanding, Ikari returned the book. Ritsuko wanted Amy's power, the power of the gods. Looking back at the case, Ikari began to wonder how long she had been searching for mystical items and how she had done so without his noticing. If all of those jewels were really items used by the gods, and he had little doubt that they were, then he would find a way to use them himself or destroy them.

The sound of people approaching dragged Ikari out of his thoughts. Deciding that he needed to come back to get a better look around, Ikari ran over to the window and jumped down to the next floor just as the door opened. He made his way back to the outer gate and vaulted over without breaking stride.

He was halfway back to the inn when he found Saskai waiting for him in the ally.

"Find anything useful?" Saskai asked.

"I think so," Ikari replied, considering his options. "Danothir just dropped a notch on my list."

"Lord Ikari?"

"I need to get back in there."

"It may prove difficult tonight. The other combatants have already returned to the inn."

"I'll have to wait until tomorrow then. Most of the house staff will be at the tournament, so getting in again should be easy." Ikari paused for a moment and pulled his mask down. "Go down to the warehouses and see what you can find there. Ritsuko is planning something big, and I wanna know what."

Saskai nodded then turned and headed off into the darkness. Ikari began to make his way back and pulled up his mask once he neared the inn. His mind kept running through the different scenarios that Ritsuko could be playing at, but they all ended the same. Lady Inara was making a grab for power and undoubtedly had her sights on ruling Terra, but he would put a stop to that.

The only ones destined to rule over the realm were the Sanada. Everyone else could either fall in line behind them, or be destroyed.

Chapter Ten

Listening to the sound of boots on wood and Asano's cries for help, Amy pressed herself against the wall, certain that the fighting had stopped. A lump of fear hung in her throat as she strained to hear any sign that Hayate was unhurt. After a few minutes, she heard one of the men order the others to drag Asano outside.

Waiting until the last of the men had left, Amy crept down the stairs, fear slowing each cautious step. Seeing that the room appeared empty, she peeked around one of the bookcases, praying that Hayate was still alive, and found him lying on the ground. Kneeling beside him, Amy shook him gently, trying to wake him and noticed blood dripping from a wound on his head. "Hayate!"

A soft groan escaped Hayate's lips as he slowly began to return to conciseness.

"Hayate," Amy repeated. She felt a relived smile spread across her face.

"Amy?" Hayate sat up, holding his head. After a moment he seemed to regain his composure and jumped to his feet. "I've got to go help him."

"What?"

"They took him, they took Asano." Hayate started toward the door but Amy grabbed him by the arm.

"Wait, you can't go running after them, you're hurt."

"I'm fine." Hayate pulled free from her grasp and stormed outside.

"You don't even know who took them." Amy followed him out into the rain, fear pouring over her.

"They were from House Inara." Hayate walked over to a woman and asked if she had seen anyone take the shop owner, but the woman only nodded no and hurried off.

Amy could feel his anxiety as she followed Hayate in search of any sign of Asano or the men who took him. They spent almost an hour scouring the town before giving up and started back toward the town square.

* * *

Yuki stared down at the rain slicked streets from her perch on the roof of a local bakery, watching with an amused grin as Amy and Hayate passed beneath her. She could have killed them at any time if she wanted, but doing so would not have served her propose, despite her boredom. She would have preferred to be elsewhere and leave her brothers to play their games of manipulation, but she was a good sister. And if that meant keeping an eye on Amy and her pet knight, then so be it.

Of course, there were other ways to have her fun. Her instructions were to observe and hinder, and so she would. The pair had spent the last hour wondering about the town because she spread the word about an Ithorian knight and a young woman to a few of Inara's men.

"Find them?" Yuki glanced over her shoulder as she felt E'Lan's presence silently approaching.

"They're holed up on the outskirts of town." E'Lan stopped next to Yuki. "They won't be much of a challenge for us."

"Oh, we're not going after them." Yuki again smiled. "Let the knight deal with them."

"So we're doing nothing?"

"For the moment. Since I can't run wild over the situation, I'll have to settle for being really annoying behind the scenes." Yuki turned and started toward the opposite side of the roof. "Keep an eye on the bookkeeper and make sure Inara's men don't take him outside the town."

"Yes Lady Yuki."

* * *

I really need to get that umbrella, Amy mused, glad to be out of the rain.

A short, plumb old man led Amy and Hayate to a small table near the back of a cozy little café. The scent of cinnamon lingered in the air and seemed to give the place a cozy atmosphere. Families ate exotic looking foods while laughing or telling stories around the square tables, while flames from lanterns and mounted torches lit the room.

"What'll you have?" The short man motioned toward the table.

"Something hot please." Hayate pulled out Amy's chair then pushed it in once she sat down.

Amy watched the man head off and took another breath of the sweet air. There was something about the little café that made her think of her grandmother's house. The smell of cookies or cakes baking always made her feel like a little girl again, anxiously waiting at her little plastic table with her sister.

Amy tried to push those sorts of memories away, but the more she tried, the more they entered her mind, and the more she thought about them, the more she began to fear that she might never get back home. *What if this becomes my life? Am I really going to end up stuck in this strange world?*

"Are you alright?" Hayate asked pulling her out of her thoughts.

Amy shook her head, clearing her thoughts and smiled. "I'm fine. A tad soaked, but fine."

"I, I'm sorry." Hayate stared down at a small glowing stone that sat on the center of the table.

"For what?"

"I've failed. I failed to protect Asano and now I might fail you."

"It's not your fault." Amy reached over and touched his hand. "You can't blame yourself for getting ambushed."

"I should have fought more, tried harder."

"They could have killed you." Amy squeezed his hand. "I'm sorry that he was taken and I hope that he's okay, but I don't care about finding proof or clues about some sodding legend. I'm just glad that you're okay."

Hayate looked up and smiled at her. "I didn't know I meant that much to you."

"Why wouldn't you? You're the only friend I have here." Amy returned his smile. They held each other's gaze for a few moments until the short man returned with two steaming mugs and sat them down. After receiving three coins from Hayate, the man hurried off to the other side of the room to welcome more customers.

"What is this?" Amy picked up the mug and swirled the lavender liquid. It had the faint scent of strawberries and looked a lot like syrup.

"It's wulong tea." Hayate took a long sip. "They make it from the sap of a wu-chen tree. I'm surprised they have it here though."

Amy brought the mug to her lips and took a hesitant sip. Finding it to her liking, she took another, longer, sip. "Why? It's really good."

"The trees are somewhat rare considering they only grow in Austuria."

Amy began to drink more of her tea when she noticed Hayate smiling at her. "What?"

"I... nothing." Hayate looked over at the crowed room.

With a smile, Amy started to drink the rest of her tea and glanced back toward Hayate, remembering what Mezza had told her. *Maybe she was right.*

Amy took another swig from the mug and dismissed the idea as silly. He was a brave, noble, and sweet knight. She was just a girl from London trying to find a way home. Besides, there was bound to be some princess or noblewoman somewhere that he had feelings for. Finishing the last of her tea, she looked back toward Hayate and noticed something held his attention. "What is it?"

"Over there."

Amy followed his gaze and saw three men dressed in lavender clothing with black armor. "They look like those guys that attacked us when we were with Bernard's family."

"They're also the ones that took Asano." Hayate looked back to her. "We can follow them; see if they lead us to wherever they're holding Asano."

"Hayate, maybe…" Amy let her sentence trail off. As she stared into his eyes, she began to feel his conviction and knew she wouldn't be able to talk him out of following them. Exhaling, she resigned herself to waiting and hoping that after this was finished, she might find a way home.

* * *

They waited for almost three hours before the soldiers finished their meal and left the café. The soldiers led them down the rain slicked streets and past various shop's that were closing up for the night. The glow from the two moons cast a pale light, while the damp night air added to Amy's apprehension as the three men entered a large barn with peeling paint and rusted doors.

Hayate lead Amy around the side of the barn until they reached a small window and Peered inside to find racks of tools sitting on the far wall. A large kettle was built into the wall to her right, as well as an anvil and a few large barrels. A middle aged soldier sat on top of a wooden desk playing with a knife. Glancing over, she found Asano bleeding and tied to a chair as the three soldiers passed him and strode over to the man with the knife.

"Has he talked yet boss?"

"No, but I ain't really been asking questions." The man with the knife laughed hoarsely then stood and stepped in front of Asano. "I'd love to cut everything this chump knows right out of him, but she said to bring him back alive. Now you bastards get some sleep. We got a long ride back to Osaka Major."

Amy forced the lump in her throat down as she ducked beside Hayate. "Who is that?"

"I'm not sure. He bears the insignia of House Inara, but he's dressed like a member of the Assassin's Guild." Hayate glanced through the window then ducked back down. "We'll wait until they've fallen asleep, then I'll sneak in and rescue Asano."

"Maybe we should get some help."

"I can handle this." Hayate smiled at her reassuringly. "Besides it's my duty."

Amy nodded, but couldn't push away the fear churning in her stomach. Waiting in silence for an excruciating twenty minutes, Hayate again peered through the window. After a moment, he started to make his way toward the rusty doors, but Amy grabbed his arm.

"Just... be careful, okay?" Amy watched as Hayate flashed another reassuring smile before opening one of the doors and crept in.

Hayate inched forward, watching the assassins for signs of discovery with each step, when Asano noticed him. Hayate quickly motioned for him to remain quiet and pulled a small knife from his boot to cut Asano's ankles and hands free.

"Thank you," Asano whispered while Hayate helped him up.

Hayate pulled one of Asano's arms over his shoulder and whispered a response, but he was too quiet for Amy to her. The two of them started back toward the door when a small object sailed across the room, cutting them off. With her breath caught in her throat, Amy watched as a silver knife pierced Hayate's shoulder.

"Hey kid." The man with the knives stood up and pointed one at Hayate. He spoke with a hoarse voice and had an unshaven jaw that emphasized his sneer and a scar on his left cheek. "Nobody gets that old man without paying for him."

Hayate let go of Asano and drew his sword, groaning in pain. "He's a person, not some piece of meat to be bought."

"That's all any of us are." The man laughed. "Walking, talking sacks of meat. We're all just meat here to be bought, or sold, cut and bled dry. I was paid quite a bit to pick up this piece of meat, and I mean to deliver."

"Who are you to decide if a man's life is worth a bag of silver?"

"Actually, he's worth two bags and the name's Tres, Ector Tres."

Before Hayate could respond, two of the soldiers rushed toward him. He pushed the first soldier into the wall behind him then ducked to his left to avoid the second soldier's sword. Amy tightened her grip on the door, watching Hayate and the soldier trade attacks. Just as Hayate seemed to gain the upper hand, the first soldier tackled him and struck him on the face. An enthused cheer slipped from Amy's lips as Hayate used his knife to stab the soldier in the neck and shove him off.

Asano staggered back a few steps while Hayate climbed to his feet and fought off the other two soldiers. Running into the barn without considering what she was doing, Amy grabbed Asano by the arm. "We have to get out of here."

She turned to lead Asano out, only to feel her wrist get squeezed, twisted, and yanked backwards. A fresh wave of terror washed over her as she was spun around and saw Asano fall to the ground, keenly aware of the sound of swords clashing, despite the fact that she was now inches away from Tres's scarred face.

"Like I told the kid," Tres whispered as he tugged her hair. "Nobody gets the old man without paying for him. Although, I'd be happy to take my payment out of you."

"Get away from me." Amy tried to hit him with her free hand, but he spun her around and wrapped his rough hand around her throat. Even as she struggled to get free, she heard one of the soldiers cry out as Hayate's sword sliced his stomach.

Still trying to free herself, Amy felt Tres's breath on her neck. "Keep moving around like that and I'll have to take you here and now."

Forcing away some of her terror, she pulled forward then slammed her head back into Tres's face. A sense of satisfaction weaved its way through her at sound of his pained grunt and his loosening grip. She tried to wrench herself free, however, Tres managed to fling her against the nearest wall.

A sharp pain shot through her body as her face bounced off the wall and she slumped to the floor. The edge of her vision began to blur, but she forced herself to stay conscious and turned around.

"Stupid bitch! After we're done with your knight, I'm gonna take my time with you." Tres smirked before moving toward Hayate, pulling another knife from his belt. The soldier and Tres began to slash or stab at Hayate, forcing him back bit by bit.

Amy pulled herself up to her feet, noticing a large hammer hanging on the wall next to her. Sliding it off the rack, she inched her way over toward the soldier. Once she was close enough, she lashed out, striking him on the back of the head. Just as he hit the floor, Hayate slashed Tres across the chest then kicked him back.

Tres staggered back a few more steps and looked over his wound. "You think a cut like this will stop me? Your little woman's going to be my plaything and you're going to die."

"Yield, you've already lost." Hayate stepped in front of Amy.

"Maybe, but you ain't really gonna call *this* a win, are you?" Tres pivoted to his left and sent his knife spiraling into Asano's chest. Eyes wide from terror, Amy saw the joy on Tres's face, even as he turned and sprinted out of the door.

Hayate hurried over to where Asano had fallen and dropped to his knees. "Hang on; I'll go find a healer."

"I, I am sorry I could not help you," Asano replied, his voice weak. Even as Amy knelt beside Hayate, she could smell the blood pouring from the wound.

"You need to save your strength." Amy held his hand. Already, she could feel the life draining out of him and see the color fade from his face.

"Go... go to Perukav, you can find..." Asano trailed off.

"Can what?" Hayate shook Asano's shoulder but got no response.

"He's gone." Amy placed her hand on Hayate's shoulder to comfort him and saw that the knife Tres had thrown was still there. "Are you okay?"

"I'll be fine." Hayate nodded and stood, pulling the small knife free. "We should go before Tres returns with more men."

With a nod, Amy followed Hayate out of the barn and back onto the street. The pit she felt in her stomach seemed to shrink the further they got from the barn, and more and more, Amy felt herself relax.

She stared to ask Hayate what they should do next but thought better of it. What could she say? On one hand, she was sorry that a man had died. He died because those soldiers wanted information about her. But on the other hand, the main thing that ran through her mind was the thought that maybe Hayate would give up on trying to prove she was some kind of goddess and she could go home.

Chapter Eleven

Children laughed and raced their way through the crowd swarming about the grand arena, ignoring the warnings of their parent's. The walls were lined with venders from different regions, selling mead or ale, while other's pedaled food or cheap toys. Guards were posted at each of the entrances and could be seen all through the halls. Granted, that wasn't much of a surprise considering the amount of people and the number of supposedly able fighters that were on hand, but there were far less guards than Ikari would have liked.

Still wearing his mask and cloak, Ikari ducked into one of the halls and weaved his way through the crowd. He had hoped that Ritsuko would have put more vigor into her security, but since she seemed to be a bit lax, he would just have to adapt his plans a bit. Rounding a corner, he squeezed between a pair of rotund guards and stepped into the stadium seating.

He made his way up the stairs and began to walk along the back row. The plush seating began to fade away as more and more people hurried to find seats. Strolling across the walkway, he could hear some of the men laughing and proclaiming how easy it would be for them to win, a boast he couldn't help but smirk at. It was always amusing to hear people claim to be the best fighters. Every one of the fighters here thought they could win. Ikari had little doubt that many of them were capable. A few might even be good. But none of them had spent years training in Alextien. None of them had been forced to survive tutelage under a man heinous enough to rival the great destroyer, Yun'Harrar.

Ikari stopped at a thin portion of the back wall that had a small crimson window in it and let his gaze travel down the stairs to a small railing about twelve feet above the grass field. Returning his attention back to the window, he saw that Lady Inara and had just entered the stadium and was talking to some well-dressed men. After a few seconds, Ikari turned and headed toward the nearest exit, deciding that he'd make one quick stop before joining the rest of the fighters.

Working his way back into the halls, Ikari found his way to a stairway and headed up, moving as fast as he could without drawing attention. Once he reached the top, he found himself in a well decorated hallway with soft brown carpet and luminescent stones hanging overhead, giving the ceiling the appearance of an open sky. Murals of men clad in armor, or blood, covered the walls. Some portrayed wild beasts stalking a wounded warrior, while other's depicted images of former heads of House Inara.

Spotting a door with the Inara family sigil, he stopped in front of it, testing the doorknob. He began to turn the knob but stopped, catching the sound of voices approaching from the opposite end of the hall. Ducking into the room and closing the door behind him, Ikari pressed his ear to the door and listened as the guards passed by.

Satisfied that they were gone, he turned and glanced over the chamber. A large table sat in the center of the room packed with vibrant colored fruits and roasted meats. Crystal pitchers filled with wine and other drinks sat amongst expensive looking glasses. To his left, he noticed a few bookshelves that stuck out from the wall. Across the room he spotted another, smaller desk with a large cushioned chair behind it.

Ikari moved toward the desk and saw a couple of old books on top along with a tattered scroll. He started to reach for the scroll but stopped when he noticed a blue book with the image of Sha'Kring, the slayer, on it. Flipping through the pages, he saw a passage about the war god's battle with a lesser god. He flipped through some more pages, pausing at a passage that had a small piece of paper in it to mark the page. It told of the war god's victory over his rivals and made a reference to some quest he had completed.

Why read this, Ritsuko? Ikari thought to himself, closing the book. He stood there for a moment pondering different scenarios when the scent of jasmine filled his nostrils. He started to wonder where the pleasant smell had come from, but the cold tip of a knife pressed firmly against the back of his neck gave him his answer.

"I'm impressed." Ikari chastised himself for letting someone get the drop on him. "Not too many people can sneak up on me."

"I'll be sure to have that carved on your tombstone," a young woman's voice replied. "So who are you? Are you some common thief, or are you just stupid?"

"Rest assured, there's nothing common about me."

"Then you must be the latter since you didn't see me hiding behind the bookcase."

"Now that stings." Ikari put a playful tone into his words. "Granted, that makes two mistakes."

"Two?"

"Mine, and yours. See, if you're going to hold a knife to somebody, you really shouldn't hold it that high." Dropping the book, Ikari spun on his heel, using his left hand to snatch the knife out of her hand while grabbing her neck. He let his momentum carry him around until her back was to the desk, and pushed her on top of it. "Makes it real easy for me to do that."

He loosened his grip on her neck and saw that she was Ritsuko's daughter. She wore an elegant lavender dress with black trim. A set of gold bracelets hung around each wrist and a silver pendent with a red gem fixed in the center hung from her neck.

"Let me go." Alia stared him in the eyes. He gazed back into her shimmering green eyes expecting to see fear or panic, but to his surprise, he found none. "All I need do is scream, and every guard here will rush through that door and kill you on the spot."

"You could, but I can't help but notice that you haven't yet." Ikari held her gaze for a moment longer before smirking beneath his mask and released her. Taking a nonchalant stance, he tossed the knife onto the desk next to her as she sat up. "Why is that?"

"Would you rather I did?" Alia flashed a coy smile, glancing at the knife. "What kind of thief gives a weapon back to a hostage?"

"One who's not worried." Ikari took a step closer and picked up the blue book he had dropped, amused that Alia had inherited her mother's talent for playing games. "What's with the books? Mommy dearest not planning on watching her own tournament and see who gets to marry you?"

"Please." Alia rolled her eyes. "The only thing that will come out of this farce of a tournament is me going to the trouble of poisoning the winner."

"A pretty girl like you doesn't want to get married?"

A slight smile spread across Alia's lips. "When *I* choose to marry, it well be with someone I find interesting."

"Well best of luck to you." Ikari waved with the book in hand and backed toward the door.

"Who are you?"

Ikari stopped by the table and let out a laugh. "You really shouldn't ask a masked man who he is. That would defeat the purpose of wearing a mask. I'm just a man, in a mask, who's taking a book."

"Yes, I can see that much, but what makes you think I'll just let you leave with my mother's book?" Alia jumped off the desk with the knife in hand and moved closer to him.

"Well for one thing, if you wanted me dead, you would have tried to stab me a while ago; and two, you were thinking about letting me go anyway."

"Am I?"

"It's becoming clear you don't want to see anyone win this tournament. So you figured, why not let him go. You'll wait a bit, then call for the guards, tell them about a prowler, and hope I put up enough of a fight to get this tourney stopped." He paused for a moment then inched forward as she lowered the knife. "That's a decent plan and all, but it's all contingent on how much ruckus I cause. So I'll make you a deal, you let me go without a fuss, I'll make sure this tournament is brought to a grinding halt."

"And you would do this because?"

"It suites my purposes; and frankly, the thought of being a thorn in your mother's side sounds kind of appealing."

Alia smiled seductively and leaned in close to him. "Is that all you find appealing?"

Leaning in close enough to feel the warmth of her breath, Ikari held her stare and grinned beneath his mask. "Do we have an accord?"

* * *

The gentle breeze swept through the arena and helped to carry the roar of the crowd from one end to the other. One section would stomp their feet as one fighter would build up momentum, but just like a change of the wind, momentum switched and the stomping was replaced with shouts of excitement or the occasional curse when a fighter was eliminated.

The stockier man fighting in the ring ducked to avoid a sloppy kick from his taller combatant then lashed out with a bloody fist, striking the other in the ribs. After another missed kick, the stocky man landed two wide punches on the jaw.

The morning sun radiated heat, warming the once cool wall Ikari was leaning against. Pulling up the hood of his cloak to help against the sun, he glanced toward the balconies and spotted Alia staring down at him. Since he'd first sat down during the opening match, every time he looked up, he found her gaze locked on him. Not that he minded being the object of her attention, but with her constant vision focused on him, it made sneaking off to break into Ritsuko's study a bit harder. Alia seemed content enough to let him be. Nevertheless, he didn't want to test how far he could push her.

What really baffled him wasn't how he would get in, but why she let him go in the first place. From what he had heard, Alia Inara was supposed to be a spoiled child playing with her mommy's money. He was surprised to find a woman who looked as if she'd do anything to get what she wanted, and was smart enough to find ways get other people to do it for her. Not to mention her mother, he knew about her practicing magic; however he wasn't expecting to find a study full of mystical artifacts. Once he got back to Austuria, he was going to have to devote a lot more time to looking into the affairs of House Inara.

To Ikari's surprise, the tall man was still standing, although blood poured from a nasty gash on his forehead. Punch after punch, the stocky combatant kept throwing bombs until his last shot curved short of its target, causing him to wobble for a moment before regaining his balance. The taller fighter grabbed the other by the sides of his head, let out a furious snarl, and thrust his knee into the man's face. No sooner did the man's unconscious body drop to the ground when, like a storm, the roar of the crowd flooded the arena.

"Finally." Ikari watched as the judge raised the tall man's hand. Two men in white rushed into the ring and carried the other man out of the arena.

"Yeah, that's what I'm talkin' 'bout," someone shouted to his right. Ikari glanced around and traced the voice back to its source. He recognized the man from the tavern fight a few days earlier, Gaou something. "This is what it's all 'bout. Two men just beating the brew right out each other."

"No fool; that is not what it's about." Thade made his way over to him, his posture as ridged and formal as one would expect from a soldier. "This is about life and honor. That feeling one gets when he faces an opponent, the hunger they each share, and the pride one knows when, with his own two hands, he fought and bleed and *earned* what he wanted. *That* is what this is really about. You and those like you who only see battle as a chance to win fame, will never know the taste of true victory."

Gaou spun toward the older man. "What are you sayin' old man?"

"He's saying you suck," Ikari interrupted. "Now sit down and shut up. You're giving me a headache."

Gaou took a few steps forward but a passing referee caught his attention causing him to pause. "I'll take care of your smart mouth later."

"You do that." Ikari stretched out his legs, rolling his eyes as Gaou stormed off. Across the arena he noticed a hooded man in brown robes passing out cups of water.

"And what is it you fight for?" Thade stood over Ikari, blocking the sun.

"Maybe I'm here to win Lady Inara's daughter." Ikari climbed to his feet and met Thade's stare. "Although she strikes me as being more troublesome than I'd originally thought; so maybe I'm here for the same reason you are, to see how good I really am."

"How then do you expect to bring honor to your family name when you hide behind a mask?"

"It's not about family honor or prestige. It's about being the best. It's about proving it to yourself and no one else," Ikari replied sincerely.

"It's about the moment." Thade seemed to accept his answer and nodded in agreement. "Well put."

"Besides," Ikari added. "I already know I'm going to win."

Another official stepped into the ring and raised his hands motioning for the masses to quiet. "The third match shall pit Thade Folken against Rngah Tolk."

"Watch this bout closely and you shall see the grandeur of a true warrior." Thade pivoted on his heel and marched into the ring. After a few minutes, his opponent joined him and began shadow boxing.

The pudgy official directed each of them to a corner then motioned to his left. "Rngah Tolk, are you ready?" He paused for a moment, putting on a show for the crowd, and then gestured toward Thade. "Thade Folken, are you ready? Then in the name of Lady Inara, I command you, fight."

A thunderous roar again filled the stadium as the two combatants rushed forward. Despite himself, Ikari looked on with his interest peaked. After all of the talking Thade had done, Ikari was glad to see that he wasn't just full of hot air. Tolk strung together a series of right jabs and left hooks, but none managed to find their target. Blocking a kick from Tolk, Thade landed a harsh blow to his sternum and followed with two swift shots to the jaw and went for a right hook, but Tolk countered with knee to the gut.

With each punch, the multitude of bloodthirsty spectators became more and more involved. Some cheered for Tolk, encouraging him to bludgeon his opponent without mercy; while others condemned Thade for his relaxed pace.

The pair danced back and forth across the ring trading punches. Tolk would push Thade back with a flurry of blows only to be repelled by a few hard shots. As the fight went on, most of the crowd seemed to be favoring Tolk. It appeared that Thade was at an extreme disadvantage due to the speed and frequency of Tolk's attacks, at least to the untrained eye. Ikari had been in enough fights to recognize when someone was being played with. A sense of amusement swept through him as he observed the two combatants. After another round of swift punches and hard shots, Ikari began to wonder how long Thade was going to keep up the games, but then he saw it.

It was only a slight shift, Thade had set his feet at a different angle, shifted his shoulders more, and at that moment Ikari knew the fight was over. Before Tolk could launch another assault, Thade blasted him with a ruthless blow to the jaw. A warm breeze seemed to steal the voice of every man, woman, or child as Tolk's motionless body bounced off the ring.

Shaking off his own astonishment, the official stepped back into the ring and raised Thade's hand. "The winner, Thade Folken." The crowd leapt to their feet and began to chant Thade's name as he pumped his arms in the air.

"Not bad," Ikari whispered as Thade and the official had exited the ring and walked passed. Leaning back against the wall, Ikari watched as more officials hurried over to clear the ring. A soft shuffling sound caught his attention and caused him to glance over and spot the man in brown robes making his way rounds. He moved with a slight limp and extended his shaking tray to each contestant he passed until he reached Ikari.

"Care for some water sir?"

"No thanks." Ikari waved a dismissive hand. The feeble man bowed then continued on his way. "Well, maybe I'll take a cup." He motioned for the man to stop but the man keep walking. Ikari followed him along the arena wall and down through one of the tunnels until he stopped in the empty waiting area underneath the stadium. "Nice touch, adding the limp."

The man rose a few inches as he straightened, turned, and pulled down his hood. "Thank you Lord Ikari," Saskai replied with a nod.

"Come to watch me fight?" Ikari teased. "Or did you sneak in just to catch a peek at Ritsuko's daughter?"

"No, my Lord. I attempted to enter the Inara estate but there were too many guards. Even with your skill, it will be extremely difficult to enter unnoticed."

"I was worried about that. Security around the arena isn't as tight as I thought it was going to be."

"What then will you do?"

Ikari crossed his arms, cycling through his options. He needed to get back inside Ritsuko's study but that seemed unlikely to happen. Too many people had begun to take an interest in him for him to disappear now. He could wait until later but there was no telling how long Alia would stay quiet. Besides, Ritsuko would notice the missing book sooner or later and start paying closer attention everything. The more he thought about it the more he came to realize that he only had one option left.

Reaching into his cloak, Ikari pulled out the blue book and handed it to Saskai. "Hold on to this. I took it off Ritsuko's desk this morning."

"Is this related to something you found last night?" Saskai tucked the book into a hidden pocket.

"That's what you're going to find out."

"Lord Ikari?"

"In about an hour I'll create a diversion around here and get our host to pull her guards from the estate. When I do, I want you to sneak in and take a silver bracelet from her study."

"How will you draw out the guards?"

Ikari turned and started back up the tunnel, waving over his shoulder. "Oh, I'm sure I'll think of something."

* * *

Ring attendants scurried back and forth, pushing brooms or dragging mops in preparation of the next round. A low murmur spread around the stadium since the officials had called for a brief intermission, giving many the opportunity to stretch their legs and return with overpriced food or watered down drinks.

Finishing their task, the workers vacated the ring and were replaced by a lanky man whose bald head cast a glare in Ikari's eye. "I call on Mal Sounga and Gaou Teushmit, please come forward."

After sitting around all morning and receiving a bye during the first round, Ikari had become a little antsy. Hearing his alias called, he jumped to his feet and hopped into the ring. He sauntered in the direction of the official with a slow pace, taking in everything around him. People rushed back to their seats not wanting to miss anything, even Ritsuko had finally returned and sat with her daughter, whose gaze was still fixed on him. Gaou had found his way in as well, and began pumping his fist in the air, playing to the crowd.

"My Lords and Ladies, to my left I present Gaou Teushmit." The official extended his hand, holding it in place.

"Yeah." Gaou bounced in place a few times and threw his arms up again. Receiving a long applause for his efforts, he turned, pointing a finger at Ikari and stepped closer. "I want you."

"At my right stands Mal Sounga." The official motioned toward Ikari.

Not wanting to be shown up, Ikari turned to face the masses. Letting his hood fall back, he slid his cloak off his shoulders, twirling it in an overly dramatic fashion as he whipped it around his body and let it fly out of his hand, and into Gaou's surprised face. "Oops." The audience burst into laughter while Gaou ripped the cloak off his red face and tossed it aside.

A hushed silence swept over the arena. Ikari tucked his hands into the opposite sleeve, awaiting the signal to begin. After a long moment, the official took a step back, clapped his hands, and shouted "Begin."

Gaou let out a wild snarl and rushed forward like a mad Kberos. Grinning beneath his mask, Ikari waited, then leapt forward and thrust his knee into his opponents face. Even over the endless cheering, Ikari could hear the snap of bone and felt the familiar warmth of blood on his pants. Gaou's head jerked back, causing him to fall, crying out in pain. Ikari landed on his toes, watching Gaou writhe on the ground holding his shattered nose.

Well that was disappointing, Ikari mused with a sigh. *I guess it's time to get to work.* Ikari stepped over Gaou and walked over to the center of the ring, pushing aside the official along the way. "Hey, Lady Inara," he shouted loud enough to be heard. "Let's save us both some time and just proclaim me the winner."

"Who are you to disrespect me in my arena?" Ritsuko responded, anger radiating from every word.

"I'm a man in a mask." Ikari noticed the amused smile Alia wore. "I'm the guy with the fiercest kick in all the realms. A man so brilliant, I rival the sun, and, I'm a man who's really bored."

"Leave my ring now and I shall let you live to tell this tale." Ritsuko leaned over the railing on her balcony. "Otherwise, I will have you beaten to death here and now."

"By who, these clowns?" Ikari laughed and walked around the ring. "Come on, I'd give a gold coin to any one of them who could hit me once."

"Enough." A heavy set man with thick arms stepped into the ring. "My Lady, please allow me the honor of silencing this fool as a show of loyalty to your grand House."

Ritsuko smiled, returning to her seat. "By all means."

The man bowed then turned and strode toward Ikari. Once he was close enough, the man tried for a roundhouse kick but Ikari easily avoided it. He followed with a swift punch aimed at Ikari's face, but Ikari ducked under the attack and stepped behind him. Ikari felt a sense of satisfaction as Ritsuko's face flashed with annoyance and the spectators demonstrated their delight. Pivoting on his right leg, Ikari shot his left foot straight into the man's chin as he tried to turn around. Blood, and what looked to be a tooth, flew from the man's mouth just before he dropped to the floor joining Gaou.

"Any other takers?" Ikari asked with a laugh.

"I will take you on." Looking over his shoulder, Ikari saw Thade striding across the ring. "I had thought that perhaps you were a kindred spirit, but now I see you are just another arrogant pretender disrespecting those around you."

Ikari shrugged his shoulders as Thade stopped about a foot away. "You know, I'm starting to like you."

They each stood still, letting a pleasant breeze waft over the ring. Many in the audience began chanting Thade's name or screamed obscenities. Even the other contestants gathered around the ring voiced their support; not that Ikari was surprised. From what he'd seen so far, Thade appeared to be man who valued honor and the worth of building up your own strength. A man like that could easily inspire those around him, winning them over to his side. Even Ikari had to admit to a certain amount of respect for the man.

Thade lashed out with quick right hook followed by two swift jabs, forcing Ikari back. Switching from right to left, Thade continued to attack. Still keeping his hands in his sleeves, Ikari danced around each punch, swaying one way or ducking in another and let everything fade from his mind, focusing on Thade. Aware of his position in the ring, Ikari started to duck under another punch but as he did, he felt Thade's foot catch his, causing him to stumble.

Faster than he expected, Thade plunged his right elbow into the side of Ikari's head. Caught off guard by the speed Thade now displayed, Ikari continued to stumble until Thade grabbed the side of his head and landed a solid blow to the face.

A sharp pain shot through Ikari as he staggered back a few feet. Vaguely aware of the crowd's sudden silence, Ikari flexed his jaw and looked at Thade with a grin. He had figured most of the fighters present would be easy pickings, but now he found himself face to face with someone with real talent. "You know, I think I underestimated your strength."

"I think you did." Thade smirked, raising his hand and letting a brown mask fall to the floor.

Ikari let his grin fade, kicking himself for not realizing he had lost his mask, which explained the stunned silence of the crowd. "Oh yeah, I definitely like you."

Chapter Twelve

A solemn young boy drove a well-decorated carriage down a desolate cobblestone road. Pale buildings with stained windows lined every street in the city, giving it the look of a crude maze. Beggars would hobble over crying for scraps of food or coin, slowing the carriage until the sound of the boys whip scared them away. Following the path, the carriage began to make its way up a steep hill that lead to the center of the city and to Lord Jamie Tarkin.

Danothir couldn't help but laugh as he looked through the carriage window at the impoverished city and then up at the lavish mansion coming into view. The Tarkin family was well known for their greed and the region of Hazgol stood as a testament to their folly.

Half the size it used to be, Hazgol had become so industrialized that the entire region had developed into one massive city. After decades of profiting from mining a rare ore, House Tarkin began to demand more and more taxes. They allowed themselves to be bribed by crime lords and watched as there land burned. Eventually, as is often the case with weaker Houses, the people revolted. They killed most of the Tarkin family and split the majority of Hazgol into tiny kingdoms ruled by tiny men.

The carriage paused for a brief moment while guards in dull armor opened a large iron gate that blocked the road. After another few minutes, the carriage stopped in front of the mansion and the boy scrambled to open the door.

Danothir stepped out and readjusted his coat. "Come, I want to be out of this god's forsaken place as soon possible."

"I have no intention of staying any longer than I need to either." Svipdag climbed out and stood just behind him. An old man hurried to open one of the two large, polished doors, letting them in.

"Go and fetch your master." Danothir brushed passed the old man and entered a cozy sized office to the left. A few expensive, but gaudy, portraits hung from hand carved walls. A small desk made from ivory sat on a light colored carpet with elegant chairs in front of it and one behind while a marble statue stood near a round window with silk curtains covering it.

"Not too shabby," Svipdag commented as he looked over a gold embroidered map that was displayed in a mahogany case.

"I spare no expense." Jamie Tarkin sauntered into the room followed by a man clad in dull armor. Tarkin was a heavy set man with graying hair and an uneven bread. Danothir rolled his eyes while Tarkin waddled his way over to his chair and sat, looking ridiculous in his green and yellow garments. "Well, what do I owe the pleasure to?"

"You know damn well why I'm here." Danothir slammed his fist on the desk. "Where is my cintas?"

"You know as well as I that it takes time to mine the ore."

"I paid you a considerable sum for large shipments that are made on time." Danothir locked his glare on Tarkin as he circled him and fought the urge to grab a pen from the desk and poke out an eye.

"It's, it's not my fault." A hint of fear crept into Tarkin's voice.

"Then whose fault is it that I now find myself sullied by the air in your House?"

"There was an accident in the mines," Tarkin answered, shaking in his chair. "I lost a lot of equipment and men. Perhaps with some more time and more money I..."

A bolt of rage shot through Danothir and he vented his fury by slapping Tarkin across the face. "You want more? The only reason you still have a House is because I pay you for the ore. I am the one who gives you enough to keep your land or buy your ridiculous art. I let you live comfortably while your House crumbles, and you ask for more?"

"Y... you can't talk to me like I'm some mongrel beast. Captain, arrest him, no... kill him." A look of sheer terror spread across Tarkin's face while Danothir smiled at the armored man, who stood motionless. "Captain, I order you to kill him. Now!"

"He won't be following your orders anymore." Svipdag stepped behind Tarkin, grabbed a handful of hair, and dragged his knife across his throat.

Readjusting his coat as Tarkin's body slumped to the floor, Danothir turned and headed toward the door. "I want every ounce of that ore, even if it kills every man, woman, and child in this city."

"As you wish," Svipdag replied just before Danothir stormed out slamming the front door closed behind him.

* * *

"What in the name of the god's are you doing here?" Ritsuko shot a fierce look down at the Ikari.

"I just came to say hi." Ikari waved, flashing the red faced woman an impudent smirk. Revealing himself to Ritsuko wasn't a part of his plan, but seeing the enraged look on her face made this minor inconvenience well worth the trouble. All he had to do now was keep pushing her buttons until, like a predictable tyrant, she lost her temper and played right into his hands.

"Today will be the last time you interfere with my affairs," Ritsuko spat, then shifted her gaze to the side of the ring. "Any man who kills him shall be proclaimed the winner of this tournament and can name their prize."

"This game ends now." Thade sped forward to attack, much to the delight of the stunned crowd.

Once he was in striking distance, Thade unloaded a solid punch aimed at Ikari's head. Ikari fell backwards, avoiding the blow, then handspringed off the ground, driving his heels into Thade's chin. Ikari could hear the thud as Thade's head slammed on the smooth ring floor, while he landed on his feet.

"Ordinarily, I'd love the chance to test my skill, but I don't think I'll be able to play with you anymore today." The sound of shuffling feet caused Ikari to turn around and spot a trio of the fighters headed his way. "Looks like I'm in for one wild party."

Figuring that he needed to buy more time, Ikari sprinted toward his attackers and punched the center most one on the face. Caught off guard by his sudden attack, the group barely had time to display their surprise before they were knocked out by a swift kick from Ikari or a well-placed punch. A short man in green tried to blind side him from the left, but Ikari dipped under the sloppy attack and chopped him on the throat.

Dispatching another pair of amateurs, Ikari began to smile. He had spent so much time seeking out strong opponents or sparing with his sister, that he forgot how fun it was to just cut loose and beat on weaklings. Each time he would take down a wave of fighters, the crowd seemed to cheer for him more and more. Dancing around the ring to avoid the varied attacks of the combatants, Ikari relished the sense of excitement that coursed through his blood.

One fighter went for a low kick, however, Ikari stomped on his foot and kicked him across the windpipe. Moving back toward a group near the ring's center, he dug his foot in one man's gut and used him to jump over another. Landing on the shoulder of a pudgy fellow, Ikari pivoted, kicking the back of his bald head.

Another man lashed out with a punch, hoping to catch Ikari while he was still in the air. Just before the punch made contact, Ikari grabbed the man's wrist, pulling him down and over with enough force to throw him into the last of the fighters.

The sound of applause filled his ears as he looked around the ring and saw that all of the fighters had been beaten. A hint of disappointment crept inside him but passed at the sound of swords being drawn. Ikari glanced over his shoulder to find a horde of Inara's soldiers rushing out one of the tunnels. "Fun's over I guess."

Sprinting out of the ring toward the south wall, he leapt up onto the railing and jumped into the crowd. Ignoring their shouts of surprise and bounding up the stairs three at a time, Ikari reached the thin wall he had stopped at earlier. Extending the fore and middle fingers of his right hand, he took a quick breath, channeling his energy into the tips of his fingers. Waiting until he felt the familiar tingle in his fingers, Ikari turned and flashed a smile at Ritsuko.

"You've been a lovely hostess and my thanks for such a wonderful time, but looks like I gotta go. Enjoy your tournament." He glanced at Alia for a moment, satisfied that he had fulfilled his vow and given Saskai the opening he needed, and then turned back to the wall. Slashing his fingers across the smooth stone, Ikari punched a large hole into the wall and leapt through leaving a screaming Ritsuko behind.

* * *

The streets of Osaka Major were abuzz with activity. Armed soldiers scurried about gathering up towns' people or anyone they thought to be suspicious. Others kicked in doors, hopping to flush out their quarry. Some of the populace began to protest but were quickly silenced by Inara's soldiers. The air reeked of fear, which brought a slight smile to Lady Inara's lips as her carriage pulled up to her estate.

The calm evening air did little to abate her anger as she stepped out and headed for her office. Stomping through the well-adorned halls, she brushed past several maids, catching sight of Alia following behind her. Bursting into her office, she stormed passed her Captain of the Guard, as well as her newest aid, and sat down behind her desk. "Where is he?"

"I, my men..." the Captain tried to reply but couldn't seem to stop quivering. "He's gone my Lady. We can't find him."

Ritsuko bit her lower lip in frustration. "I gave you the bulk of the estate guard and in all this time you can't find one man?" She forced herself to take a long, deep breath and regained her composure. There would be plenty of time to deal with his incompetence later. The important thing now was to retrieve the book Ikari had stolen, and to repay him for humiliating her in her own domain.

"Search every home. I want him dead, as in head mounted on my wall, dead." Ritsuko waved him off even though she already knew the outcome of the search. It had been noon when Ikari escaped the arena, and with the sun beginning to set, she knew that if her men hadn't found him by now then they weren't going to.

"Lady Inara, there is something else you need to be made aware of." Her aid motioned toward the display case.

"That being?" Ritsuko stood and moved over to see what he was talking about. Everything looked to be in order as she glanced over her varied assortment of mystical jewelry, but an empty space soon caught her attention.

"One of the workers spotted a hooded man jumping out from your window earlier in the day."

"Get out." A sense of panic raced through her as she realized what was missing.

That bracelet had been forged by the god Lorric and was a pivotal piece to her ascension. Now it was gone, taken by that impudent boy. Sitting back behind her desk, she ran her fingers through her hair, berating herself for playing into his hands. His disruption at the tournament was a farce to get her attention focused on him, giving a cohort, no doubt a Sanyoshu, time to steal what was hers.

Alia stepped passed the Captain as he hurried out the room. "Well mother, I hope you enjoyed the tournament as much as I did."

"I am not in the mood for childish games." Ritsuko felt her hand tense, as if she were about to claw someone's eyes out.

"Perhaps this was the work of Tai Re'l." Alia moved over to the display case.

"The goddess of love had nothing to do with this. Ikari Sanada is a devil whose favorite pastime seems to be annoying me. Every setback I've faced lately can be traced back to him." Ritsuko took another deep breath, forcing her anger to subside. Twice now the Sanada have stolen what was hers, and stuck their noses into her affairs. Worse, was the fact that he had taken her book right from under her nose while humiliating her at her own tournament. "I will make him suffer for this. I will retrieve my property and take my rightful place in the heavens, but not before I lay waste to Austuria and squash Ikari Sanada like a rat under my boot."

"I see he's left an impression, but if he's squashed, how will you mount his head?" Alia's voice held an amused tone. "I must admit he is rather intriguing. I've only heard a few rumors about him. Some say he fights like a demon, others claim he is the trickster god reborn."

Glancing over, Ritsuko held her daughters gaze for a long moment. "He seems rather obsessed with becoming the strongest warrior in the realms. Why the sudden interest?"

"He's just left an impression, that's all." Alia flashed a smile then turned and strolled out.

Ritsuko began to wonder why Alia seemed so interested, given that she rarely cared about anything that didn't concern her, but pushed aside her curiosity. Whatever Alia was thinking, she was sure to reveal it in time. In the meantime, Ritsuko had plenty to think about. Soon she would have everything she needed to complete her plan, but first she would have to get her bracelet back. *It's time the Sanada learned just how difficult I can be.*

Chapter Thirteen

Amy's hair whipped about her face as a warm gust swept through the valley. Riding behind Hayate, Amy glanced up at the high sun, wishing she had a glass of lemonade. *It's like being back in the Amazon.*

She began to think back to the last time she and her father were in Brazil. They had spent weeks looking for a temple that had been lost since the twelfth century only to find a rival archeologist had beaten them to it. She remembered the frustration they had felt after wasting her summer, but she also remembered how much fun they had working together. Amy closed her eyes, picturing the sound of her father's laughter or the smell of her sister's horrible cooking.

Pushing those memories back, she returned her attention to the long dirt road ahead of her. Large fields of lush grass stretched far off into the distance on either side of the road. Looking up ahead, Amy glimpsed the town of Perukav shimmering about five miles away. A little ways up the road, she noticed a wagon and two men riding on horseback. As Hayate steered their horse closer, Amy spotted a woman in a plain brown dress pressed against the wagon glancing up at the raggedy looking men.

"Thieves," Hayate muttered, with a sigh. She felt a hint of worry rise up as Hayate dismounted the horse. "Wait here while I go investigate."

"Alright, but be careful." Amy nodded. Hayate strode over to the wagon and stopped a few feet away from the men.

"Scram kid, this ain't your business." One of the men climbed off of his horse and started toward Hayate.

"Help me, please." The woman' eyes were wide with fear.

"I think it's time you left." Hayate glared at the two men.

"I thin' it's time *you* left." The man lashed out with a wide punch.

Parrying the blow with his left hand, Hayate struck the man on the jaw with his right. The first man fell to the ground just as the one still on the horse started forward. He pulled a long baton from his belt and swung violently at Hayate's head; however Hayate grabbed the man by the arm and yanked him to the ground. The man with the baton scrambled to his feet, attempting to attack again but Hayate drew his sword, slicing the weapon in two and pressed the blade against his neck.

"As a knight of Ithor, I'm placing this woman under my protection. Continue this meaningless fight and I will cut you down."

Backing away with their arm raised, the two men climbed onto their horses and turned to leave. "This ain't over knight." One of the men shot Hayate an angry look before riding off with his partner.

"Are you okay?" Amy hurried over to join Hayate, walking their steed.

"I'm fine." He smiled at her then looked back to the woman in the dress. "Are you hurt?"

"Thank ya stranger for the help." The woman smiled as she stepped over to him. "If I might impose one further request, would ya escort me into town?"

"It's no trouble, we were headed into town anyway," Amy replied. "What's your name?"

"Anna."

"I'm Amy and this is Hayate."

"A pleasure ta meet ya." Anna stepped back to the wagon and climbed on before offering Amy the seat beside her. "Least I can do is offer ya ride. What brings a knight of Ithor ta this speck of dirt?"

"We came here looking for a jewel shaped like a rose," Hayate replied.

"Haven't seen nothin' like that, but then bandits stole anythin' worth anythin' 'round here."

"What where they after?" Hayate hopped back onto his horse and trotted next to the two women as Anna started down the road.

"Those thieves were just after food and coin. Not anythin' new 'round these parts," Anna sighed. "Ever since that lousy Marzo come 'round, his thugs have been runnin' wild, lootin' or killin' as they would."

"Why hasn't anyone put a stop to it? You don't have sheriffs or anyone to help?" Amy asked as they reached the outskirts of town.

Lacking the crowds and lucrative shops of other towns Amy had seen, Perukav was considerably more run down than most. The small adobe houses had cracks ranging from minor to the absurd, with some missing entire walls. The few people walking the streets hurried along, avoiding eye contact as they went about their business.

"Law man 'round here got his head too full of Marzo's foul liquid to do his job," Anna spat.

"Liquid?" Hayate glanced at townswoman.

"Some kinda brew that sends a man's head off ta the heavens and give him vivid dreams, or terrible nightmares if he's unlucky."

"Taun." Hayate nodded, coming to an understanding Amy missed.

"What's taun?" Amy asked while the wagon turned around a worn building and started downhill.

"It's a narcotic that supposedly gives the user visions of the gods and lets them transcend this realm to walk in a higher plane." Hayate looked toward Amy. "It's also said that taun can affect the body, giving someone more stamina, strength, even help in healing, not that any of its true."

Reaching the bottom of the hill, Anna pulled the wagon into a small street filled with tattered tents and stopped in front of the second largest tent. "Welcome ta me home."

Amy smiled as two boys, no older the ten, ran out of the tent to greet Anna. Climbing down from the wagon, Amy glanced over the gray tents and found numerous people walking about in ragged clothing. The camp was filled with mostly women and children of varying ages. A few men working on the far side of the camp hammered away at what looked to be a house in construction. Others carried supplies or tools, pausing for a moment to glance at Hayate and Amy before continuing their work.

"You've all pulled together to make a camp?" Hayate walked his horse over to a wooden post a tied it in place.

"You kids hurry and unload the cart." Anna patted one of the boy's head before turning to face Hayate. "It's the only way we survived."

"What happened here?" Amy stepped over to Hayate's side, remembering some of the war torn villages she visited on some of her digs.

"A wild storm and Marzo hit." An older man, maybe fifty or so, strode out from the large tent and glared at the two newcomers. "Who are you and why are you here?"

"They're alright, Rohit, they helped with some bandits." Anna walked over and put a hand on the man's arm.

"Then they have my thanks, but they should still leave." Rohit peered down to Hayate's sword. "I don't want any trouble here because of them."

"With respect, troubles already found you," Hayate stated. "Those bandits probably won't stop until they've taken everything they can from your people."

"We've dealt with their like before. This town has been pillaged for all it has and in a short time, Marzo and his thugs will go." Rohit crossed his arms.

"And come back later to start again." Hayate stepped forward. "Let me help get rid of them."

Annoyed, but unsurprised by Hayate's statement, Amy put a hand on his shoulder, sensing his agitation. "Hayate, if they don't want your help, maybe we should go."

"Look kid, look around and tell me what you see." Rohit paused for a moment. "I got farmers who've seen too many winters, boys who've not seen enough, and women scared of being raped by Marzo's thugs. We ain't got the men to fight off Marzo and the law's no use."

"I can help you," Hayate pleaded.

"I don't care." Rohit waved his hand. "You helped Anna and I'm grateful. So you and you friend can stay the night, but I want you gone in the morning. Help yourself to some food, but we ain't got much."

"Sorry 'bout Rohit," Anna said following a few steps behind the older man. "Make yourselves comfy and I'll find ya in a bit."

Waiting until Anna and Rohit had disappeared into the tent, Amy stepped in front of Hayate. "Are you okay?"

"No, I'm not. Taun is…" Hayate turned away from her. "These people need our help. We have to find a way to convince them to fight."

"Hayate, they don't want your help. So let's just rest here tonight then leave." Amy let some of her growing aggravation at Hayate slip into her voice. "I get that you're a standup guy and all, but you can't stop to help every person you find. The world's problems aren't yours."

"I can't just sit back while people suffer." Hayate spun back to face her. "As the Protectorate Goddess, I thought you'd want to help them."

"I am not the bloody Protectorate Goddess!" Amy felt her face burn with anger as the words erupted from her mouth. "I'm not some divine being sent to save these people. I'm just a lost girl trying to go home. As much as I feel bad for these people and what's happened here, it's not my problem."

"I…" Hayate started but Amy cut him off.

"You dragged me here to find some damn rose, but even if we find the sodding thing, how does that help me get home?" Amy felt the corners of her eyes water, as she vented her frustration. "I'm tired of being chased by some mad man with delusions of grandeur. I'm tired of everyone planning my future. And I'm sick and tired of people calling me the Protectorate Goddess."

Hayate stepped forward and put a hand on her shoulder. "Amy, I know this must be hard for you, but…"

"I get that I'm being selfish and acting like a brat, but I can't help it. This is your world, Hayate. I just want to go back to mine." Amy wiped her eyes and turned away from him, heading toward the large tent. "I'm going to go ask Anna about some food."

* * *

Yuki crouched on the roof of a weathered inn that overlooked the camp her targets had taken refuge in. Too far to hear what Amy and her knight were talking about, Yuki began to wish she had spent as much time learning to read lips as Ikari did, like their master had instructed her. *Oh well.* Yuki glanced over her shoulder, feeling the presence of three of her subordinates joining her on the roof. "Did those bandits give you any trouble?"

"None, my Lady," E'Lan replied. "Their bodies were made to look as if they were slain by the knight's sword and dumped where they would be found easily."

"Good." Yuki smiled to herself. She had hoped to discover something useful from the bandits Hayate had run off earlier, but only learned that they worked for a man named Dhomas Marzo. Marzo was a petty dealer of narcotics and weapons, and had crossed paths with her a few times, usually to his dismay.

Yuki had many hobbies besides contests with her twin to see who could cause the most mischief, one of which was becoming the head of Terra's criminal underworld. It was a hobby that required her to annihilate anyone stupid enough to muscle in on her territory, including petty men like Marzo. "I'm going to have to pay a visit to an old acquaintance."

"Marzo won't take your presence well," E'Lan stated, more than aware of the past disagreements they shared.

"Of course he won't," Yuki laughed and turned away from the camp. "He'll think I'm here to kill him, which I probably will if he annoys me, but he could prove useful for the time being. I'll go and convince him that brave Hayate is a problem for him, and see how good of a distraction he can be."

"Is it wise to go to him alone?"

"He's only a man, E'Lan. The only danger I'll face is breaking a nail. Besides, I need to remind him that it's bad form to operate in *my* territories without paying up."

"What about the knight?" E'Lan inquired, a hint of anger creeping into her voice.

"Keep an eye on him." Yuki stood and started toward the far end of the roof. "But remember, you are not to kill him. Understood?"

"Of course, my Lady." E'Lan bowed her head.

"Let's see how much fun we can squeeze out of this town." Yuki leapt off of the roof with a laugh and started toward the center of town.

* * *

Finding her way to Marzo's dilapidated lair had proven far easier than Yuki expected. Located in the center of town, the shabby brown structure had two levels and took up half a block. Most of the windows were broken or stained by years of dirt and grime. Originally used for shipping, Marzo had converted the building into a crude forge for the weapons he sold. Deciding a direct approach in dealing with the small man would be easier; Yuki had strolled over to the front entrance and kicked in the large wooden door, demanding to speak with Marzo.

Allowing herself to be captured by his men, they now led her through a large chamber on the second level. Paying careful attention to the layout, and the number of men she saw, Yuki noted that the bottom floor held most of the forges and served as storage space for crates of what she assumed were drugs or weapons. The upper levels on the west side of the building served as quarters for the bandits. Hearing the sound of boiling water, Yuki glanced to her right and found a trio of men wearing cloth masks as they worked over a large iron pot, pouring ingredients in. Following her escort into a narrow hallway with peeling paint, she spotted more chambers similar to the ones she had passed.

As the hallway widened and turned to the right, they stopped at a generic looking door and paused while a tall man pushed it open and motioned for her to step inside. Doing as she was asked, Yuki entered the spacious office, trying to ignore the smell of mold that filled the air.

Mustard yellow flakes littered the floor where the unevenly applied paint had flaked off the wooden panels. A dirty cot was placed on the right side of the room, opposite from a large smeared window that overlooked a portion of the lower floor.

"My, what a lovely palace you've got." Yuki made her way to a large wooden table with two rusty chairs in front of it. A bowl of gray apples sat on one corner while various maps covered the bulk of the table. Sitting down in one of the chairs, Yuki grinned at the balding, pig nosed man sitting in front of her. "Marzo, you must be proud."

"Why the blazes did you bring her here?" Marzo Jumped to his feet, glaring at the men escorting her. Standing just over five feet, Marzo wore brown pants with a dark green tunic and a matching coat with gold trim.

"You told us to bring anybody snooping around to you," the man replied.

Yuki laughed and did her best to look as non-threatening as she could. "I'm only here to chat."

"Fine," Marzo huffed then looked back to his men. "But I want two of you in here and the rest outside the door." Marzo waited until his men had exited or taken up positions near the door before sitting back down. "Try anything and my men will cut you into tiny bits to feed the livestock."

"Relax. Even I would have trouble fighting all of your men." Yuki forced herself to keep a straight face, and leaned back. "I'm at your mercy."

"Get to the point."

"You've been busy since I last saw you."

"That's 'cause I'm a made man now," Marzo stated, fixing his collar. "Gone and gotten myself a respectable area and I got plans to expand my territory. Pretty soon I'll be the one controlling the tuan and weapons trade for this region."

"So you're suckling the teat of someone more powerful, huh? Is that why you've set up shop in my region?"

"Manners, little girl." Marzo shook his head. "You might control the black market east of Hapes, but Perukav is fair game."

"I am the black market east of Hapes, but that's not why I'm here." Yuki reached over and grabbed one of the apples before leaning back and putting her feet on desk. "I'm here to help you."

"Unlikely."

Yuki held up a hand. "I couldn't help but notice the people camped out on the edge of town."

"Lousy chumps have been holed up for weeks now, holding out on me." Marzo ran a hand over his head as if he still had hair to smooth over. "They even gone and hired themselves a knight to help them. Bastard killed two of my men."

"Really? How unfortunate." Yuki took a satisfying bite of the apple. "I've been following that knight for a while now. He's pretty good, skilled enough to hold his own against me." Yuki paused, giving

Marzo a second to let his imagination help her achieve her goal. "If he can slow me down, you might have a bit of a problem on your hands."

"I doubt that. What's he to you?"

"Nothing but a pain. I'm more interested in his lady friend." Yuki took another bite and continued with a mouth full of apple. "You help me get the girl from the camp and I'll help you deal with the knight."

"You... help me?" Marzo raised a suspicious eyebrow.

"Believe or not, I want that girl more than I want you out of my territory. Help me grab her and I'll let you have the region all for yourself."

"Interesting proposal," Marzo said after a long minute. "Let me think it over." Marzo stood and sauntered over to the door before pausing to smirk over his shoulder. "Enjoy the fruit."

"I will." Yuki smiled, imagining what orders Marzo was giving on the other side of the door.

Chapter Fourteen

The sound of wings fluttered through the calm air as nocturnal birds took flight in search of food. The night sky held an abysmal look with dark clouds mirroring Hayate's confusion as they blocked the light from the moons. Taken aback by Amy's earlier outburst, he had spent the afternoon helping the men build the house while enduring the teasing of some of the children at his poor construction skills. As concerned as he was about Amy, he felt it was better to give her some space and resisted the urge to go and find her. Not that he knew what he could say to make her feel any better.

Hoping to find her during dinner, Hayate weaved his way through the mass of people who now gathered around a large fire near the edge of the camp. People joked and laughed over plates of roasted meat and creamed soup despite the hardships that had befallen them. An older man sat on the far side of the fire telling stories meant to scare some of the children.

Taking a bowl offered to him from a tall boy he had met earlier, Hayate thanked him and sat down on a dusty bench, hoping to spot Amy. "Have you seen my friend around?"

"Ya mean the pretty girl who yelled at you?" The boy sat next to him and began to slurp down his soup. "I think she's with Anna doing girl stuff or somethin'."

"I see." Hayate laughed.

Stirring his own soup with a wooden spoon, he noticed the faint sound of hooves and looked around at the camp. Seeing nothing unusual, he went back to eating his dinner only to catch the familiar click of a crossbow bolt locking into place. Looking back into the darkness, Hayate spotted a flash of metal reflecting the light from the fire, and instinctively dropped to the ground, pulling the boy down with him, and tipped the bench to its side.

"Get down!"

Just as the words left his mouth, a barrage of arrows flew over overhead, some hitting the wooden bench while others found refuge in the sides of unsuspecting townspeople. Screams of terror filled the air, matched by cries of pain as men and women fell to ground while others scattered to avoid getting hit.

Hearing the frightened cries of the boy beneath him, Hayate pulled his sword free, anger washing over him like a wave on a beach. "When I tell you, run and find someplace to hide, got it?"

Waiting for the hail of cease, Hayate peered over the bench and found three bandits reloading their weapons a few yards away.

"Go." Hayate Scrambled to his feet, picking up the bench, and hurling it at the closest bandit.

Sprinting forward as the bench knocked the man over, Hayate brought his sword to his side and slashed the second bandit across the gut. Spinning to face the third man, he swung his sword downwards, smashing the man's bow as he tried to block. Not allowing the man to draw his sword, Hayate slammed his shoulder into his chest, knocking him back before killing him with a backhanded slash across the neck.

Taking notice of the sounds of swords clashing, Hayate turned back toward the first man and swung his weapon upwards, blocking the bandit's blade. Blocking another attack, Hayate stepped forward, using the pommel of his sword to strike his opponent's forehead. Staggered by the blow, the bandit lashed out blindly with a high attack. Hayate ducked under the arching sword and rushed forward, driving his own blade into the man's stomach.

"Amy?" Concern furrowing his brow, Hayate wrenched his weapon free and let the man slump to the ground, searching for Amy. The sounds of steel clashing could be heard even over the frightened shouts of women and children, while men sat on horseback across the camp barking orders. Making his way through the camp, he spotted two bandits stepping out from the largest tent followed by Rohit, who held Amy by the arm as he dragged her out. "Amy."

"Let go of me." Amy struggled to pull free from Rohit's grasp and spun to face him. Kneeing him just below the waist, she slipped free a moment before one of the bandits clubbed her on the back of the head, knocking her to the ground.

Fear racing through him, Hayate dashed toward Amy—sword held ready to strike—when a faint motion to the left caught his attention, causing him to dive to the right just as a silver blade swung for his head. Hitting the ground on his shoulder, Hayate rolled into a low crouch and spotted a pair of bandits stepping out from between two tents.

"What's da rush, huh?" one of the bandits' sneered while his partner drew two knives.

"You two." A tall man on horseback motioned toward Hayate while two men lifted an unconscious Amy onto his horse. "Deal with him."

Rohit struggled to climb back to his feet. "Wait, what about our deal?"

"We have the girl; you dogs can go back to your scraps." The man with Amy turned and rode off, followed by most of the bandits.

Growling in anger, Hayate tried to run after the man, but the two remaining bandits jumped in front of him, attempting to cut him down before he could follow. Hayate jumped back, avoiding their initial attacks and began to inch backwards, swaying around or parrying their continued assault. Instinct guiding his counterattack, he felled one of the bandits with a low slash and managed to trip the second before finishing him off.

His mind swimming with fear for Amy, he started toward his own horse when Rohit moved to block his path. "Move."

"Let the girl go." Rohit waved his hand. "They only wanted her. As long as they have her, then they'll leave us in peace."

"You gave her to them?" Hayate clenched his teeth, feeling his anger boiling over into fury. "You sacrificed her to save yourself?"

"Of course," Rohit replied, stabbing a finger in the direction the bandits had taken. "Better she dies than one of us. If you'd been less concerned about one girl, you might have saved the lives of the people killed tonight."

"If you had listened to me in the first place and fought, all of this could have been avoided." Hayate forced his hand to stop shaking and sheathed his sword. Focusing his thoughts on finding Amy, he pushed passed Rohit and mounted his horse. "You're a coward. These people died because of your cowardice, but I won't allow Amy to die because of it." Hayate turned away from Rohit, and began to gallop up the dark road that led to the center of town.

Riding as fast as he could through the empty streets, Hayate found himself approaching a large building that served as the bandit's base. Smoke rising from chimneys or from fires burning on the far side of the edifice gave the abandoned homes, piles of rubble, and the fields of dead grass surrounding the place an unwelcoming look.

Angry and disappointed at himself for not protecting Amy better, Hayate pulled back on the reins, slowing his horse to a trot while dismounting far enough away from the structure to remain hidden by the shadows. He found a small house a block away from his goal with one of the walls missing and—after insuring that the dwelling was empty— left his steed to continue on foot. Creeping along the walls of any remain homes or buildings, he worked his way toward the main entrance at a cautious pace.

Hayate reached the last of the houses and peered around the corner to find four bandits sitting in front of a large iron door. Listening to their conversation for a moment, he quickly realized that they were not planning to leave any time soon, and figured fighting his way through wouldn't be his best option. Opting to find an alternative entrance, he made his way to the east side of building, pushing back his growing apprehension. Reaching an open field, filled with piles of debris and empty crates, the sound of something hitting the ground behind him caused Hayate to spin around and duck behind a large crate.

Hands moving to his sword on instinct, the young knight scanned the rooftops of the structures he had left behind. Noticing a flutter in the shadows, he held his gaze for a long moment. *Probably nothing.*

Hayate turned back to the building in front of him, dismissing the shadow. Even if someone had spotted him, they would have sounded an alarm or moved to attack him.

Certain he had remained unseen; he noticed a flickering light coming from an opened chamber of the rundown building and moved to get a better look. Ignoring the voices coming from inside, he pressed himself against the wooden wall and inched over to the open double doors to peer inside.

Spaced wide enough to reveal archways that led to other sections of the bandits base, stacked barrels lined each of the walls of the chamber. A few tables, covered with papers or vials of muddy liquids, were scattered around the torch lit room. As curious as he was about the barrels, what caught his attention were the six female Sanyoshu moving about the chamber and the bodies of dead bandits whose blood oozed over the dirt covered floor.

Recognizing one of the women as E'Lan Barda, Hayate's mind began to run through reasons for her to be here when the cold tip of a steel blade brought his mind to a halt.

"Wha..." Hayate traced the blade to another Sanyoshu standing behind him. "I guess that was you I saw?"

"Move." The woman gestured toward the chamber. "E'Lan, guess who came snooping."

Turning away from one of the tables, E'Lan flashed an unnerving grin at Hayate as the woman pushed him forward. "Sandra, what's he doing here?"

"Some of the bandits attacked the camp while you were gone and took the girl," the woman behind him replied. "He came to find her."

"He's late then," E'Lan shrugged. "How lucky for me."

"What are the Sanyoshu doing here?" Hayate glanced around, searching for an opening to escape. "And what do you mean I'm late?"

"I'm here to tie up a loose end with Marzo, and, it seems that the gods have graced me with an opportunity to tie up our loose end as well." E'Lan motioned toward some of the other Sanyoshu, who began dumping barrels while another picked up one of the lanterns sitting on a table. "As for your little friend... well, she's gone, just as you're about to be."

Sandra stepped forward, shaking her head. "But Lady Yuki instructed us not to kill him."

"She said not to kill him. She never said anything about not letting him die." E'Lan drew her sword and glared at Sandra, her eyes burning with anger. "I'm not about to let him interfere with our operation here. We burn this place as planned, only now, he can burn along with Marzo's taun, and our comrade—whom he killed—will be avenged."

"Not tonight." Shoving Sandra into one of the Sanyoshu, Hayate sprinted to his right. Grabbing a lantern from a small table, he hurled it at E'Lan, causing her to roll to the side as he darted through an archway.

"Light the rest on fire and move to the next area." E'Lan ordered running after him. "I'll deal with the knight."

Emerging in another chamber, this one fairly empty and dark, Hayate scanned the room hoping to find his way into the main sections of the building and to Amy. Spotting an open door, Hayate started toward it when the sound of E'Lan's furious cry stopped him in mid step. Spinning to face his pursuer, Hayate blocked her opening attack, but was pushed back by her momentum. Orange light from the fire burning in the room he had just exited flickered across the open chamber while E'Lan continued her assault, slashing or stabbing with fluid, dance like motions.

Blocking and evading as best he could, Hayate anxiously searched for a way to end this fight, desperate to find Amy and make sure she wasn't hurt. He had to make sure she wasn't dead. A flash of light, reflecting off of E'Lan's blade as it missed his forehead by a narrow margin, pulled his thoughts back from his growing fear.

Pushed back, Hayate felt his foot hit the wall while batting aside another attack. E'Lan sneered, seeing him out of room to retreat and lunged forward, intending to impale him. Adrenalin surging through him, Hayate dropped to one knee, feeling the air zip by as he evaded her weapon, and pushed forward. He slammed his shoulder into the woman's gut, pushing her back before standing straight and rammed the crown of his skull into her chin.

Stunned, E'Lan staggered back, holding her jaw when a loud rumbling shook the room. An instant later, a second explosion blasted through the wall of the blazing chamber, knocking both combatants to the floor. Bits of burning wood and clouds of smoke filled the room while streams of dark colored liquid led trails of flame across the floor.

Ears ringing from the blast, Hayate scrambled to his feet and started toward the opened door when two bandits burst into the area.

"What in the…"

Shoving passed the surprised bandits, Hayate found himself in a small galley that reeked of smoke and booze. The galley was mostly empty, save for two short benches to the right and the three shouting bandits drawing their weapons.

"I don't have time for this." Hayate blocked a downward strike and pushed the man back, happy to see him trip over the bench, before kicking the second bandit in the ribs. The third stepped forward, swinging his curved knife with a violent snarl, but missed as his target parried the assault.

Catching the knife wielders ankle with his foot while he stepped to the left, Hayate drove his sword into the man's torso as he stumbled forward. Kicking the slain man into the first, knocking him back over the bench, he glanced at the doorway and found that E'Lan had killed the two men near the door and charged after him.

Readying himself for her assault, a wave of relief fell over him at the sight of the second bandit moving to intercept her. Killing the man with a string of swift cuts, E'Lan swore, forced to block an angry attack from the remaining bandit.

Leaving E'Lan and the man to fight amongst themselves, Hayate found an open archway and hurried through it, all thoughts returning to Amy.

* * *

Yuki swallowed the last piece of her apple with a grin while staring out the large window at the pillars of smoke rising into the night sky. Still sitting in Marzo's office with her feet on the desk, the sound of the double doors creaking open jogged her from her half sleep. "I was beginning to think you forgot about me."

"I had a surprising opportunity fall into my lap, one too good for me to let pass." Marzo strolled into the room holding a curved knife and wore an ecstatic grin as if he'd just won a fortune in silver. "You understand."

"Of course." Yuki gave a pleasant smile, balancing the apple's core on one finger. "Any thought on my offer?"

"I've decided to pass."

"Oh? Why is that?" Yuki asked, already knowing the answer.

"Because I've finally beaten you at your own game. I had my men grab that girl you're so keen on getting. Right now, they're loading her up for a trip down south. I know a few unsavory gents who'll pay a fair sum for her."

"My, I'm shocked by this sudden and unforeseen turn of events." Yuki rolled her eyes and sat up in her chair. "Let me guess the rest. You were going to wait for that knight I mentioned—whom I'm guessing you avoided killing—to arrive, blame me for it all, and let me and him fight it out until you kill the winner. And with me gone, you'd be in position to steal my territories, right?"

"Pretty much."

"That's a rather pathetic plan." Yuki glared at Marzo, letting a threatening look gloss over her eyes. "Besides, in your haste to outwit me, you failed to account for two things, little man."

"And what's that?" Marzo motioned with his free hand, signaling the guards meant to kill his guest.

"One, I've always been ten steps ahead of you and you're far too easy to manipulate. And two..." Yuki paused for a moment, enjoying the irritate look on Marzo's face, when a loud explosion shook the building. "...Your place is on fire."

Springing to her feet, Yuki kicked the chair behind her, sending it flying into the closest guard. Clutching the apple core in one hand, she nailed Marzo with a right hook and let her momentum spin her around until she was facing her attackers.

Yuki found one of the men knocked flat by the chair and shifted her gaze to the chubby bandit to his left, hurling the remains of the apple at his head. Hearing a shuffle from behind, Yuki ducked under an attack meant for her head and drove her right heel into Marzo's gut, forcing the air out of his lungs. Yuki snatched the weapon out of the air as it slipped from his hand and sent it flying toward a bandit near the doorway.

Sprinting forward with a smile as the knife found its mark, she hopped over the man knocked over with the chair as he rose. The bandit she had hit with the apple snarled, raising his sword for an overhead strike before swinging it downward with a vicious shout. Relying on her speed, Yuki grabbed the rising man and spun him to her left, placing him in the path of his compatriot's sword.

Darting around the dead man, Yuki hit the third bandit with a harsh uppercut, relishing the feel of his chin connecting with her fist, before whipping around and planting a high kick into his exposed throat. The last of Marzo's guards stood frozen, his sword shaking in his hands, amusing Yuki enough to flash him an evil smile.

"Don't worry little boy, you won't feel a thing." Yuki dashed forward, vaulting as high as the roof would allow. Landing with her hands on top of the man's head, Yuki gripped the sides and twisted her body, snapping his neck before landing on her feet. "Now Marzo, you're going to tell me where you sent the girl so I can continue playing with the knight."

"You're crazy. Even you can't fight your way passed all of my men." Marzo tried, and failed, to keep the panic out of his voice as he backed away trembling.

Yuki stalked forward with a slow, deliberate pace that matched Marzo's retreat. "Assuming E'Lan hasn't killed them all already, I only have to fight my way passed a dozen or so of your poorly trained morons. Now unless you want a face full of glass when I throw you out that window, I suggest you tell me what I want to know."

A pleased smile spread across Yuki's lips as Marzo began to blurt out the information she wanted while pleading for his life. Not that she really had any intention of sparing him. As soon as he finished talking, she fully intended to remind him who ran things in this region by seeing how far she could throw him out that grimy window.

* * *

The sound of glass breaking and a man screaming caught his ear as Hayate fell through a wooden door and into a vast open roofed cavity of the burning building. Ignoring the pain from E'Lan's kick, he forced himself to his feet, curious about the source of the loud thud that echoed off the walls. Smoke filled the sky while fire danced in the distant portions of the complex, fueled by the dried out wood and accelerated by barrels of flammable liquids. Hastily scanning the room, Hayate spotted multiple fire pits set up as well as other equipment used to forge weapons scattered around. An open door to his left led into a dim hallway while the other archways ran upstairs or into chambers that were probably on fire by now.

Returning his attention to the door he had fallen through, Hayate found E'Lan charging toward him. Swords clashing as they renewed their deadly dance across the dusty floor, he noticed a movement from across the room. Hayate managed to block each of E'Lan's attacks with more success and began a slow shift from defense to offense. Lungs burning from exhaustion and smoke, he deflected a wide slash, tipping her balance, and aimed a blow at the woman's legs. Anticipating the attack, E'Lan managed to jump back, but not before his sword grazed her thigh. With her face twisted in pain, Hayate pressed his attack, and sent her tumbling over a table filled with unfinished swords.

Using one hand to leap over the table, Hayate went to finish her off only to strike the floor as she rolled out of the way. He started after E'Lan, hopping to prevent her from getting back to her feet, when a pair of hands grabbed him from behind. Surprise flushing over him, he felt himself fall backwards while the foot of his unseen attacker dug into his back and kicked him over the table.

Hayate landed hard on his back, losing his grip on his sword while the air rushed out of his lungs. Reaching for his weapon, Hayate tried to sit up when a boot pressed down on his neck, preventing him from doing so.

"Now, now, play nice." Yuki leaned forward, putting a little more pressure on his throat. "I'd have thought you'd be off saving your dear Amy."

"Why are you here? What have you done with Amy?" Hayate struggled to free himself.

"Calm down and you'll live to find out." Yuki kicked his weapon away then stepped over to pick it up. "E'Lan what is going on here?"

"Forgive me, Lady Yuki." E'Lan limped over to Yuki's side and knelt on one knee. "I... I let my anger cloud my judgment and went against your wishes."

"Meaning?" Yuki raised an eyebrow.

Hayate climbed to his feet holding his throat. "She tried to kill me."

"Did you?" An irritated look fell over Yuki. "I'm fairly certain I told you not to kill him, or am I mistaken?"

"I did not intend to kill him per say." E'Lan lowered her head. "I planned to leave him here to burn with the bandits. Lady Yuki, I acted alone. The others have carried out your orders as instructed. I am the only one to blame for what has happened."

"Tell me what you've done with Amy." Hayate started forward, but a glare from Yuki caused him to stop.

"She's gone," Yuki replied with a shrug. "Taken south to be sold as a slave or so Marzo claimed."

"If it hadn't been for your games, I could have saved her before they ran off." Furious at the two women for their part in Amy's kidnapping, Hayate clenched his fist, ready to attack when Yuki tossed his sword at his feet.

"You can kill her if you want." Yuki smiled. "She did disregard my instructions, marring an almost flawless record."

Hayate stared at the smiling woman for a long moment, surprised by her offer, and picked up his sword. Glancing over to E'Lan, he considered taking up the offer, but decided against the idea. "Knights don't kill needlessly."

"How generous of you, or naïve." Yuki looked down at her subordinate. "Well since the chivalrous Hayate decided to spare your life, I guess I can find it in my heart to forgive you this one trespass."

"My Lady?" E'Lan looked up, eyes wide with surprise.

"You are my best Sanyoshu after all." Yuki let a dangerous look wash over her. "But if you ever countermand my wishes again, I'm going to have you flogged. I'm not sure if I'll ever have them stop."

"I understand. Thank you Lady Yuki."

"As for you." Yuki looked back to Hayate. "I suggest we discuss the location of your missing friend someplace a little less on fire."

"Why help me now?" Hayate asked while Yuki turned and started toward the darkened doorway on the far side of the room. A moment later, E'Lan picked up her weapon and followed after her.

"Call it an apology. Besides, I can't have your quest coming to an end, can I?" Yuki shrugged.

"Sure." Hayate sheathed his sword and followed the two women into the hallway. Feeling confused and angry, Hayate bottled up his fears about Amy, determined to find her no matter what game Yuki Sanada was playing at.

* * *

"Gentlemen, I've asked you here tonight because we all have something in common." Ritsuko leaned against a round wooden table in the center of a circular room located under the east wing of her estate.

Large luminescent stones hung from the ceiling, casting an eerie grayish light over the chamber. Shelves filled with text acquired from across the realm lined the wall to the left of the stairway leading back to the main house. A long curved table filled with vials of colorful liquids and glasses of foul smelling slime sat on the right side of the room while a wide rack of various implements was placed opposite of the stairway.

"We have all been humiliated by Ikari Sanada," Ritsuko continued, glancing over the three men standing before her. "I chose you three because during my tournament, you showed the most promise. You were also the ones who lasted the longest against Ikari."

"What is it you want from us?" the man standing on the right asked, clearly off put by the menacing tools hanging behind her.

"I want to give you all the chance to avenge the humiliation visited upon you by Ikari Sanada. He bested you because of his training in the shadow arts. He used an unfair advantage and annihilated each of you." Ritsuko paused letting her words stir their anger. "Here, I can give you what you need to level the playing field."

"Truly?" the older man in the center asked. "I would give anything for the opportunity to fight him on even terms."

"Glad to hear it." Ritsuko glanced at the man, her favorite of the fighters gathered at her tournament and the one who fought the best against Ikari. "Thade, right?"

"Yes, my Lady."

"You once fought for the honor of my House as a soldier in my armies. I'm pleased to see your loyalty has not ended with your retirement." Ritsuko turned, picking up a silver tray with three small glasses filled with a lilac colored fluid and handed each of the men a glass before setting the tray aside. "If you want the power to regain your honor, if you want to serve my House and reap the rewards, drink this and swear fealty to me."

"For you Lady Inara, for your House, and for the glory of combat, I pledge myself to your service." Thade raised his glass to his lips, but Ritsuko put a hand on his arm to stop him.

"Not you," Ritsuko stated while the other two men swallowed theirs and fell to the floor convulsing in pain. "They'll be fine, after a while. The metamorphoses can be a bit... taxing."

"I will endure what I must to reclaim my honor." Thade stood ridged, his head high and eyes unwavering, despite the cries of pain from his compatriots.

"I'm sure you will, but I have an additional gift to give you first, one that will enable you to surpass Ikari Sanada and anyone else who would stand against me." Ritsuko walked over to the rack of tools and picked up a foot long iron brand that bore her families sigil then stepped over to the table on the right side of the room a grabbed a vial of crimson liquid.

Pouring the liquid over the brand, she smiled seductively at Thade as the metal instrument began to glow as if it had been pulled from the fires of the underworld, and made her way back to him. "Serve me well and the power I give you tonight will pale in comparison to the rewards of my service."

"My body and spirit are yours," Thade replied.

Ritsuko ran her hand across his broad chest before taking the glass from his hand. Smiling at the fearless, blind loyalty Thade radiated from his eyes, Ritsuko stabbed the ancient brand into his chest, just over his heart. Ignoring his pained scream, she dug the smoldering piece of metal further into his skin as it burned through cloth and flesh, and caused him to fall to his knees, crying out in agony.

"Of course they are." Ritsuko let out an amused laugh while a familiar lavender light and howling wind swept through the chamber and she began to pour the liquid down the screaming man's throat.

Chapter Fifteen

"Morning sir. Interested in buying some fish? I have the finest seafood in the land."

"No thanks." Ikari strolled down the busy cobblestone streets of the market district, waving off the various people as they tried to sell their goods. "I forgot how crowded Osaka Minor was."

"Is it wise for us to remain so close to Lady Inara's domain?" Saskai asked.

Osaka minor, a small kingdom ruled by a distant cousin of the Inara family, was half a day's travel from the much larger Osaka Major. Known throughout the realm for being a major trading city, one could find anything from exotic foods to people, if you knew where to look.

"We should have some time before Ritsuko's goons think to look here. Besides, we won't be long." Wearing a dark green robe over his clothing, Ikari pulled the book he had stolen from Ritsuko out of a side pocket and thumbed through it again. As much as he tried, he still couldn't make out what language it was written in, much less what it meant, which is what brought him to Osaka Minor in the first place. He had hoped to find someone in the sea of shops, stores, and traveling carts that could at least point him in the right direction.

They reached a large crossroad and stepped to the side to allow a rose colored wagon to pass, followed by a group of kids throwing a crescent shaped disk back and forth. Turning to the right, Ikari and Saskai started down a wider street. Stables filled with horses and other livestock lined both sides of the street while a gust of cool wind blew through the roadway, clearing the morning haze to reveal a blue sky.

"Lord Ikari." Saskai stopped and glanced across the road toward a crowded booth.

Tucking the book back into its pocket, Ikari followed his gaze and found a group of sleazy looking nobles eyeing the young women being marched out in front of them. "Indentured servants, if they're lucky. Playthings if they're not. Not that uncommon in this region. Either way it doesn't matter to us, or are you getting soft on me?"

"It's not that, my Lord." Saskai nodded toward a wagon pulled to the side of the booth and the man dragging a shouting girl out of it.

"Interesting," Ikari replied, spotting what had drawn his attention. A flush of surprise washed over him as he watched the man drag Amy Price out of the wagon.

"What should we do?"

Ikari considered for a moment, torn between choices. On the one hand, he had his mission to complete. Sifting out what the book and bracelet he had taken from Ritsuko were going to be used for, as well as what she had planned was his primary objective, and stopping to help the girl from another realm didn't really benefit him in any way.

But on the other hand, he abhorred what passed for legal slavery, hated how snobbish, unimaginative fools with delusions of real power acted as if they could own the realm. To his surprise, he found a small part of himself wanting to help Amy, but helping her now would not serve the cause of the Sanada. And Ikari was born to serve the Sanada.

"Leave her." Ikari turned and continued down the street, forcing himself to remember why he was there to begin with. "If she disappears into the darkness of this city, it makes no difference to us. Besides, keeping an eye on Amy is Yuki's job."

"As you wish, my Lord."

They walked the next few blocks in silence, avoiding a handful of armored soldiers as they passed by. Making their way into an older part of the city, they spent an hour hopping from one store to another, questioning dealers of antiques, or keepers of the cities libraries about the book with no luck.

Growing frustrated, Ikari tracked the royal historian down to a small brick building. Leaning against a chipped counter, he ignored the commotion coming from outside and allowed the pudgy man to flip through the book, absentmindedly waiting for the man to say "Sorry son. I haven't seen anything like this before."

"No one has," Ikari let some of his irritation slip into his voice and slipped the book back into his robe. "Thanks anyway."

"Where should we look now?" Saskai asked from the doorway.

"I'm fresh out of ideas. Maybe we should just look for a sign from the..." Ikari pulled open the narrow door and stepped outside, noticing a series of shouts coming from his left. He glanced toward the source just in time to see Amy crash into him. "...gods."

"Ikari?" Amy scrambled to her feet, holding a large piece of wood in one hand. "I could really use your help."

"Interesting," Ikari muttered while three men and a lanky nobleman came running up. "Can I help you gentlemen?"

"My gratitude for stopping the girl, sir," the lanky man said between breaths. "I'll take her now."

Amy took a step back and held her piece of wood at the ready. "Touch me again and I'll cave your skull in."

"Seems she's not interested." Ikari flashed his best, cocky grin and shrugged. "Guess she comes with me then."

"Nobody gets the girl without paying for her," one of the other men shouted.

"Come with me girl." The nobleman stepped forward and waved her over. "I bought you and I can make your time with me quiet rough or pleasurable."

"Piss off you stupid sod." Amy swung her weapon, catching the lanky man's arm.

"Just grab the bitch." The first man started forward, reaching for a knife on his belt, when Saskai shot through the door. Moving in one swift motion, Saskai drew his sword, slicing off the man's weapon hand. He then moved to intercept the other two thugs, and easily dispatched them with a trio of swift slashes.

"I really hate slavers." Ikari stalked over to the trembling nobleman and grabbed him by the shirt before spinning him in front of Amy. "I think you should apologize to the lady, and to me, for the annoyance."

"Never." The nobleman tried to pull free.

"Apologize to us or say hi to my friend over there." Ikari pointed at Saskai as he finished off the wounded thug. "Your choice."

"I apologize for my unfavorable behavior," the nobleman stated with a defeated sigh.

"Bugger that." Amy darted forward, clubbing the man across the jaw and knocked him out before dropping the piece of wood. Looking over to Ikari, she smiled. "Thanks."

"Glad to help," Ikari returned her smile. "I'm a bit surprised to find you here. I thought you were off with your knight."

"I was, until they grabbed me. Where am I anyway?"

"Osaka Minor." Saskai wiped the blood from his blade before sheathing his sword. "Perhaps we should leave before any more attention falls on upon us."

* * *

Finding a populated section of the city near the northern edge, Ikari sat across from Amy, listening intently as she told the story of how she had ended up running into him. A string of carts selling noodles and other foods, were set up to their right while a group of minstrels played a melodious tune to the applause of the crowd. Finishing her story, Amy drank the mug of water sitting in front of her.

"So what coincidence brought you way out here?" Amy set the mug down.

"I'll get us some more water." Saskai stood and headed over to one of the venders.

"I'm not much for coincidence actually. Providence, but not coincidence," Ikari replied remembering his master's constant lecturing. *There is no coincidence, only providence and preparation. No matter how chaotic things appear, there's always a plan to be sniffed out.*

"I was in the area investigating House Inara." He recounted parts of the tale that led him to her, careful to leave out the bit where he intended to leave her to her fate. "It looks as if the gods planed different though."

"Tsh... gods." Amy rolled her eyes and leaned forward on her elbows. "I'm so sick of hearing about gods."

"I take it your time with Hayate hasn't gone as you'd hoped."

"Don't be daft, I love getting chased all over an alien world with everyone telling me what my destiny is and deciding my fate for me."

"I can relate." Ikari leaned back in his chair. "From the moment I was born, my family has laid out the path I'm supposed to follow, whether I wanted to or not. My life is to serve the will of the Sanada, and achieve the family's destiny."

"Sucks, huh?" Amy smiled. "You told me you'd forge your own path. How do you do it with so much being dropped on you?"

"It's all about knowing what you want. Once you know, all you have to do is go after it with everything you got. Of course, it helps if your goals mesh with those planned for you."

"And if they don't?"

"Well, I refuse to follow a fate I haven't forged for myself." Leaning forward, Ikari was surprised to find himself identifying with Amy. "I'll use whatever assets I need to in order to achieve my goals."

"That's a pretty cruel way of seeing things."

"It's the way of the world. Everyone uses someone for something. Kids use parents for food and shelter, Kings use subjects for power or influence, and you and I use what we can to handle our families. To get what we want, it's only natural that someone gets used." Ikari paused for moment. "The question is, what do *you* want?"

"I want to go home."

"Then why travel with Hayate, whose obvious goal is to prove you are the Protectorate Goddess?"

"I was hoping that following him would ultimately prove that I'm not." Amy let out a sigh and ran her fingers through her hair. "Every time we meet, I seem to end up talking about myself. How about you tell me what you want?"

"At the moment?" Ikari pulled the book out from his robe and handed it to Amy. "To find someone who can read this."

Amy looked the book over and ran her fingers over the inscription on the cover. "It looks kinda familiar."

"Really?" Ikari paused for a moment, glancing over toward Saskai. "Hold on for a second. I'll grab us those drinks." Joining Saskai over by the cart, Ikari took the mugs of water and leaned close enough to avoid getting overheard. "Change of plans."

"My Lord?"

"I've decided to stick with Amy for a while." Ikari handed him the stolen bracelet and instructed him on what to do next. After nodding in understanding, Saskai headed north, disappearing into the crowd. Walking back to the table, Ikari sat down in the chair next to Amy before handing her a mug.

"What happened to your friend?"

"He's incredibly shy around pretty girls, so he decided to run off before he embarrassed himself." Ikari smiled.

"You're lying." Amy returned his smile

"What makes you say that?"

Amy shook her head with a shrug. "I dunno, gut feeling."

"I sent him to run an errand for me." Ikari eyed the young woman, curious about why she was questioning him. Seeing that she was satisfied with his answer, he nodded toward the book. "You said you recognized the language?"

"Yeah. It looks like some kind of journal." Amy thumbed through some of the pages. "These look like notes on something while other sections seem to tell a story."

"How do you know the language?"

"I'm not sure." Amy shrugged, closing the book. "Must be some ancient dialect my dad taught me as kid."

Ikari raised an eyebrow with a grin. "You know, I think there's a way for us to help each other."

* * *

D'Gust Svipdag strolled along the Cliffside, looking down at the water crashing against the rocks of the Austurian beach. Ignoring the lavish estate of the Sanada family to the far right, he uttered a silent praise for the gods, grateful that the rain had ceased. He had spent most of his time whipping the mines in Minolan back into shape and executing anyone who refused to work. Satisfied that Lord Borga would be pleased with his results, Svipdag had traveled to Austuria, where he spent the night wooing a mildly attractive maid who worked in the Sanada estate.

Dressed in the attire of a statesman and carrying a large jug of ale, Svipdag ignored the young maid, whose full name he hadn't cared enough to remember, as she prattled on about life working for the Sanada.

"And every so often, we spot the Sanyoshu wandering around," Mwenda stated in an excited tone. She slowed her pace, allowing Svipdag to catch up before looping her arms around his free limb. "So tell me again about your business travels."

"Like I said the other day…" Svipdag took a sip of the ale before playfully pouring some into the maid's egger mouth. "…I'm traveling with the statesmen visiting Lord Genki. But rather than spend all my time with work, I thought I'd see for myself how friendly the famed land of Austuria was."

"And do you find it to your liking?"

"Maybe." Svipdag kissed Mwenda, sharing the mouthful of ale with her.

"And did you mean what you told me? About taking me with you when you go and letting me work as your aide?"

"Of course." Svipdag suppressed a chuckle as he put an arm around her shoulder and turned her toward the water. "I couldn't leave such a fair lady like you to waste away as a mere maid. Of course, I have to finish my business here first."

"Then hurry."

"You could help me. Lord Genki recently procured a jewel shaped like a rose. If you could sneak it to me, so I can get a grasp of the tastes of your Lord, it would help me with my trade arrangements."

"I'm not sure…"

Svipdag dipped his middle finger into the ale then slowly brought his hand over to her mouth, letting the dark liquid drip onto her lips. "No one needs to find out. I just need to learn if I have anything Lord Genki would value. Once I've seen the rose, you can take it back with no one the wiser."

Mwenda smiled, buying into his kind words and story, and licked the ale off of his finger. "Okay, if it'll help."

"Good girl." Svipdag pulled Mwenda down to the ground and kissed her, deciding that as long as he was in Austuria, he might as well enjoy himself.

* * *

"I forgot how crowded Osaka Minor was." Yuki let out an irritated sigh as she stared down at the busy streets from a large hill to the north of the kingdom. "I hate crowded cities. All that sneaking around you have to do drives me insane."

"Shall I begin searching for the girl?" E'Lan asked from her side.

"I suppose. Hayate should be here soon anyway." Yuki turned around, milling over how to delay the knight's quest further when she spotted Saskai standing a few feet away, causing her to reel back from surprise.

"Lady Yuki." Saskai bowed.

"Damn it Saskai, I thought I told you never to do that again. I don't care if my brother lets you pop up out of nowhere, it creeps me out when you do that." Yuki forced herself to take a deep breath to slow her racing heart.

"I apologize, Lady Yuki." Saskai glanced at her for a moment, choosing his next words carefully. "Lord Ikari instructed me to continue to do so. He said it was... amusing."

"He's going to pay for that." Yuki moved the lock of hair hanging over her eyes and smiled, plotting her revenge. "But don't tell him I said that. So, what does dear Ikari have to say?"

"Lord Ikari has decided to follow Amy Price for the time being."

Yuki raised an eyebrow. "Really? I thought that was my job?"

"It seems she can be of use to him in learning about a book he acquired from Ritsuko Inara. He has instructed me to ask you to switch duties for now. He will stay with Amy and Hayate while you investigate the intentions of House Borga and House Inara."

"I knew it," Yuki laughed. "He has a soft spot for the girl. Tell him I'll do as he asks."

"I cannot. After I've spoken to you, I am to report back to Lord Genki."

"Alright, you can go." Yuki waved him off. "E'Lan, make your way down to my brother and tell him I'll play his game. And if you can, try to scare him out his skin, see if he likes it."

"As you wish, my Lady." E'Lan stepped over to her side as Saskai disappeared over the hill. "I'll try to match Saskai's ability to appear around Lord Ikari."

Yuki glanced over at her subordinate and raised a curious eyebrow. "Are you smiling?"

"N...no, my Lady." E'Lan clamped down her smile but failed to hide the red on her face. "I wasn't..."

"Speak your mind."

"It's just... I've always found your brothers games to be... charming."

"Charming, really?" Yuki teased, more than aware of E'Lan's secret crush on Ikari. "I never knew you shared my brother's childish sense of humor. Maybe you can clear his mind of that Amy girl."

* * *

Night began to descend over Osaka Minor as people swarmed the streets, some looking to buy whatever goods they needed, while others glanced over the various diners and cafes deciding on where to eat for the night. Hurrying through the bustling streets at a dead run, Hayate made his way toward the northern edge of the city.

It had taken him longer to arrive in Osaka Minor than he would have liked, and even longer to track down the bandits who had abducted Amy. After spending hours searching for them, he had found two of them dead. Witnesses had claimed that a girl matching Amy's description was sold to some nobleman but ran off with two men who had killed the bandits. After asking around, Hayate had been told that the trio was seen in the market area, so he hastily worked his way there.

Finding the crowded market, Hayate scanned the assembly, slowing to a walk while stepping through spectators who laughed or sung along to a trio of minstrels. The thickness of the crowd mirrored his rising anxiety as he pushed through people and his own fears. Emerging from the crowd into an open area filled with wooden tables and families watching the performance or eating roasted meats, Hayate peered over the tables and felt a flush of relief as he spotted Amy laughing.

"Amy?" Hayate started toward her table, but a jolt of alarm shot through him once he saw who was sitting next to her.

"Your knight in less than shining armor finally joins us." Ikari smirked, closing a blue book and slipping it into a pocket in his robe.

"If you've hurt her, I swear I'll kill you," Hayate stated, surprised by the anger in his voice, and stood ready to draw his sword.

Amy rose to her feet and stepped in front of Hayate before smiling reassuringly. "It's okay. He helped me get away from those bandits."

"Then he did it for some ulterior motive," Hayate replied, not taking his eyes off of Ikari. "We should leave, now."

"Calm down." Amy put hand on his arm. "Ikari isn't an enemy, he's a friend. One who might be able to help."

"Help how?" Hayate felt himself calm a bit from the warmth of her hand and let the edge fall from his voice. "They say you should be wary of a Sanada bearing gifts."

"Now that stings," Ikari replied, his voice dry. "You're on a quest to find mystical items and the Protectorate Goddess, which I'm extremely knowledgeable on. I'm on a mission to find out what House Inara and House Borga are up too, which effects the both of you. And Amy's on a quest to get back to her homeland, a goal I may be able to help her with. Our three goals are complementary, and helping you is the best way to achieve all three."

"And what do you gain in return?" Hayate asked.

"I help Amy find a way to where she belongs—" Ikari gestured at Amy then back to himself. "—and she helps me with some translations and research."

"I'd prefer to pass on your kind of help, and your sisters."

"She's not so bad, once you get to know her." Ikari laughed and leaned forward. "I'm a lot nicer than she is. Besides, with me around, you don't have to work as hard to protect Amy."

"I'll protect her..." A bolt of anger shot through Hayate.

"Enough," Amy growled a moment before grabbing Hayate by the arm, pulling him away from Ikari. Stepping passed a woman in a lavender cloak, Amy led him a few yards away from the table to a quieter area of the square and turned to glare at him. "What's with you? Ikari saves me and agrees to help us, and you thank him by threatening him?"

"I don't trust him."

"Why not?"

"Because he's a Sanada." Hayate waved his hand in anger. "Whatever reason he has for offering to help, it's only for own purposes. He's just using you."

"Everybody uses someone for something." Amy paused, and let out a long breath. "I get that you're worried about me and I appreciate everything you've done for me, but if he can help me get home then I can't say no just because his family has a bad reputation."

"I just don't want to see you get hurt," Hayate responded, letting his own anger fade. "But if he's anything like his sister..."

"His sister is... scary, but I don't think he's a bad guy." Amy smiled. "Besides, I know what it's like to get held in a bad light because of a sister."

"I promised to help you, so if this is what you really want, I'll be with you every step of the way." Hayate returned her smile, unable to retain his frustrations.

* * *

Ikari watched as Amy dragged Hayate off, amused by Hayate's responses. He knew Hayate wouldn't like him joining their quest, especially if the knight had already crossed paths with Yuki, but what did surprised him, was the fact that he wanted to help Amy. Why, he wasn't sure. But there was something about her that resonated with him. However he would have plenty of time to ponder his reasoning's after he learned about the book.

Leaning back in his chair, Ikari spotted a woman in a lavender cloak walking toward him. The woman sat down in the seat next to him, filling his nostrils with the scent of jasmine.

"You are very true to your word, Ikari Sanada."

"And you are?" Ikari asked, surprised to hear his name. The woman pulled back her hood and smiled as her blond hair fell over her shoulders. "Alia Inara?"

"You seem surprised. Don't tell me I managed to get the drop on you a second time?"

Forcing any astonishment from his face, he flashed a smirk and glanced around, searching for any threats closing in on him. "How did you manage to find me?"

"You can relax, I came alone." Alia leaned forward. "Your little display in the stadium did its job. Mother is furious, the dimwits you defeated are steaming, and I no long have to worry about choosing a husband."

"Happy to help."

"As you should be. I was so impressed by your skill that I've decided to take *you* as my husband."

"Say again?" Ikari returned his attention to Alia, nearly choking in shock.

"My family has a tradition, only the most skilled and worthy man may marry a daughter of the Inara family. I usually balk at tradition, but I have never seen anyone with your abilities. You're one of the best warriors in the realm, and your mind is almost as sharp as mine. Plus, marrying you would really anger my mother." Alia reached over and took his hands into hers. "I thought Tai Re'l had forsaken me, but I realize that the goddess of love sent you to me. You and I will be glorious together, and our love will dominate the realms."

"I'm... flattered. Really, but I'm fairly certain that wasn't in our agreement." Ikari pulled free from her warm hands. "So, as tempting as marriage sounds, I'll think I'll pass."

"What?" The inviting sparkle that shown in Alia's eyes changed into an icy stare. "I'm offering myself to you. I'm more powerful than my mother, or at least I will be soon. They say you want to subjugate the whole realm. I'm offering you more power than even you can dream of."

"I can dream pretty big." Ikari grinned. "Sorry. You're a bit too far south of sane for my taste."

"You're rejecting me?" A confused, hurt look fell over Alia's face, one that was quickly replaced by one of fury as she jumped to her feet. "No one rejects me."

"Then it's my pleasure to be the first." Ikari also stood, half expecting an attack. Keeping one eye locked on her, he couldn't help but notice how much like her mother she looked.

"You can't reject me. The gods have ordained our love."

"So insanity does run in the family," Ikari quipped.

Alia dug her nails into the top of the table, her face turning a shade of red Ikari had never seen before. After a moment, her body straightened and she regained her composure, returning the seductive smile she had worn when she first sat down to her lips. "You will be mine, and if that means I have to drag you back to Osaka Major and force you to marry me, than I shall."

"How romantic."

"If this is a test from the heavens, then I will overcome it." Alia returned her hood to her head and turned to walk away. "And you will learn that I am not so easily scorned. I *always* get what I want. I will see you again, soon."

Ikari watched while Ritsuko's daughter walked away, unsure of what just happened. "She's going to be problem." Mind racing from questions about why she had fixated on him, how she had found him in such a crowded area, and why he found her attractive, he barely noticed Amy and Hayate step over to him.

"Friend of yours?" Amy asked.

"No, but I get the feeling I'll be seeing her again." Ikari forced his trademark grin to his face. "We should probably leave by morning. This place doesn't seem so friendly anymore."

Chapter Sixteen

A temperate breeze blew over the Consortium controlled province of Remus, carrying the sounds of heavy traffic underneath the afternoon sun. Carriages and wagons rolled past each other on wide stone roads while people clothed in a wide variety of colorful garments went about their daily routines, hurrying across the streets or marching along on sidewalks. The city was filled with elegant buildings of varying heights, many of which were made from white or tanned stone with marble pillars bearing elaborate carvings, while others had decorative fountains placed near their entrances.

Sitting in the back of an open wagon next to Hayate as it rolled down the smooth road, Amy half listened while he tried to explain the history of province. Not large enough to be considered a House like Austuria, and with no official ruler to make the city a kingdom, the province of Remus had fallen into the direct control of the Consortium itself, with members of the Consortium electing a Governor every few years to act as city administrator.

According to Hayate, the city had at one time served as the capital of the realm, before the Consortium moved to Hapes Island, and had been known as the city of walls. Although little evidence of the walls that once ringed the city remained, Remus was the original site of the Gateway of the Gods and other ancient museums that claimed to have housed mystical items.

Despite her initial disinterested in traveling north to Remus, Ikari had convinced her it could be worth going after a few days of helping him translate his book. Even though they had just finished the first quarter of the book, Ikari seemed focused on a section that mentioned some museum. Hayate and Ikari were both interested in searching the city, despite their constant bickering, and after considering that this was the original home of the gateway that let people travel from one realm to another, she concluded it could lead to a way home.

Amy glanced toward the rear of the wagon and grinned. She found Ikari lying with his hands behind his head pretending to sleep, wearing his usual black and red clothing. Unsure of how she knew he was pretending, Amy returned her attention to the city, wishing Hayate and Ikari would get along.

"So where am I dropping you folks off?" the boy driving the wagon asked.

"Good question." Amy looked from the boy down to Ikari's book, which sat on her lap, hoping for an answer.

"We should start our search in the city's library." Hayate glanced at Amy. "They're bound to have records of the old museums and other artifacts found in the area."

"We should hit the local taverns," Ikari replied without opening his eyes.

"A bit early for a drink isn't it?" Hayate shot an annoyed look at Ikari. "We came here to learn something."

"Exactly. We're here to figure out why Ritsuko is interested in the city."

"If she's as interested in Amy as you clam," Hayate scoffed. "Then she probably read that book of yours for the same reason you stole it. She's after a clue about the Protectorate Goddess."

"I agree."

Hayate let out an annoyed growl. "Then why go to a tavern? What possible use could that be?"

"Ritsuko had that book for a while, and knowing her, she probably already read it twice. Therefore, we have to assume she's already been here. That means she's a step ahead of us. And since she's not an idiot, it's safe to assume she's already checked out the obvious places, libraries, city records, all of that." Ikari sat up, flashing a grin at the knight. "I want to go to the taverns for same reason you wanna go to a library. They're both full of information if you know where to look."

"The Consortium built one of the realms biggest libraries here. I say it's the best point to start from," Hayate replied.

"I agree with Hayate," Amy stated, hoping to end the argument. "I think the library is a good place to start. When I was reading the book, I ran across a passage I recognized from a scroll I glanced over back in Ithor, and I want to check it out. I'm at my best when I'm buried in a book anyway."

"Well, if I'm outvoted..." Ikari trailed off, lying back down with a mock-defeated sigh.

"We can always try it your way later." Amy dropped the book on Ikari's stomach then turned back to the boy. "I guess we're going to the library."

"Sure thing lady."

Reaching their destination a short time later, Amy and the others found their way up a wide set of stairs and through the entrance of a three story building. Boots echoed off the painted cathedral ceiling as they walked across portions of the marble floor not covered by carpet. Bioluminescent stones fixed with elegant glass casings were mounted on the walls and placed on top of mahogany tables. The outer portion of library held newer scrolls and periodicals, while the inner portion looked more like a labyrinth of eighteen-foot tall shelves, each filled with worn tomes and dusty books.

After talking to one of the librarians, the trio was led to the second floor, where most of the ancient records of the city were stored. The second floor looked similar to the first, except for being less cramped and having more tables and desks to work at.

"This place is amazing." Amy bounced from one shelf to another. "There's so much history here about your whole world. It's an archeologist's paradise. I could spend years studying in a place like this."

"Given the amount of books in this place, we might be here for that long." Ikari started toward the stairs. "I'll go see about getting some snacks while we work."

"I'll go with you." Hayate glared at Ikari before looking back to Amy. "I shouldn't be gone long."

Amy stepped over to another shelf and pulled a copper colored book out. "I'll be fine. Who'd try to grab me in a public library filled with people? Just try to get along with Ikari."

"No promises." Hayate laughed.

* * *

Hayate followed Ikari as they made their way outside and began walking down the busy streets and turned onto a less crowded road. Ignoring the sounds of the city or the people they passed, Hayate began to wonder if Ikari knew where he was going or if he was just arbitrarily turning down different streets to annoy him. Dismissing the thought as they walked into a large square with parked carriages and greenish blue bushes along the road, Hayate tried to push aside his anger, considering his words.

"Well?" Ikari stopped in the middle of the square and peered over his shoulder.

Hayate stared at him for a moment, surprised. "What?"

"You obviously have something to say, so what is it?"

"Why are you here?" Hayate let his annoyance add some venom into his words. "Why are you helping Amy?"

"I told you. My mission and hers..."

"What are you really after?" Hayate interrupted, tired of his games. "You and your demon spawned sister have been toying with us since we left Austuria."

"You're so hung up on Yuki. I'm guessing E'Lan tried to kill you. But since you're here, it looks like she failed. That's... very rare. Whatever happened between my sister, E'Lan, and you has nothing to do with me. She has her operations and I have mine."

"And what do you get out of this?"

"I get to mess with Ritsuko and make sure her plans fall apart."

"So you're using Amy as a piece in a game." Hayate took a step forward, trying to hold back his anger. "You're risking her life."

"Like you haven't?" Ikari spun around and glared at Hayate, a dangerous look narrowing his eyes. "You've dragged her halfway across the realm selfishly trying to prove she's a goddess just to make yourself feel better about your beliefs. You made her a target for Danothir. The only reason she's here for me to help is because you failed to protect her from some pathetic bandits."

"My goals are not selfish."

"You can act as righteous as you want, but you're using her just like me. The only difference is, while I'm doing it, I'm trying to help her find a way home."

"I will help Amy. No matter what she..." Hayate started, surprised by the anger in Ikari's voice and wondering if it was genuine or not, when something caught Ikari's attention and caused him to turn away.

"Quiet." Ikari held up a hand.

Feeling his face flush with anger, Hayate reached for Ikari with one arm while clenching his fist with the other. "Don't..."

"I said shut up." Ikari grabbed Hayate by his tunic and spun him toward a narrow street with three men walking their way, each with long black cloaks draped over them. "Someone wants to say hi."

"Who are they?" Hayate let his anger disappear and brought his left hand up to his sword. "I don't suppose they're friends of yours."

"Yeah sure, if by friends you mean guys I humiliated and beat the stuffing out of." Ikari laughed while the three men stopped a few yards in front of them. "The tall one in the center is Thade Folken, a stuffy but entertaining fellow. I forgot the other two guy's names, crappy fighters."

"Don't mock me." The man on the right shouted, pointing a finger at Ikari. "You know ya remember the name of the man who nearly stomped you."

"Of course. You're Paou... something, right." Ikari grinned.

"Gaou! My name is Gaou..."

Ikari rolled his eyes, letting out an annoyed sigh. "I don't really care what your name is."

"You are as disrespectful as before, I see." Thade let his cloak fall to the ground to reveal the blackish purple leather pants and shirt he had on. A dark red blood stripe ran the length of his leg while the crest of the Inara family adorned his crimson vest. The sleeves of his leather shirt also bore the slanted strips of a general.

"And I see you whored yourself to Ritsuko. Too bad, I thought you had pride," Ikari replied.

Hayate glanced at each of the three men then back to Ikari. "We should end this quickly and get back to Amy."

"Agreed," Ikari responded without looking away from Thade. "I can handle these three. Head back to Amy, but don't take the same route we used. There may be more of Inara's goons around."

Hayate shot Ikari a quick glare. "I can take care of myself."

"I don't care about you." Ikari smiled. "I just don't want you leading them back to Amy."

Leaving Ikari to deal with the three strangers, Hayate turned to his right and sprinted down a narrow alley while trying to avoid the few pedestrians that were in his path. Emerging in a wider alley—this one much cooler than the street due to the buildings blocking the afternoon sun—Hayate ran, figuring that the alley would serve as adequate cover while he found his way back to the library. Veering into another wide alley, he heard the familiar whoosh of an arrow shot passed his head while rounding a corner and spotting three men with crossbows chasing after him.

Returning his attention forward, Hayate found another set of men charging toward him. He drew his sword, bringing it up to strike, but noticed he was approaching a side alley and ducked into it. Half as wide as the last, he slid to a stop, cursing as four more men advanced on him. Standing ready to fight, Hayate glanced around searching for another way out of the alley when a middle aged man leading the men spoke in a familiar, horse, voice.

"Surprise, surprise. If I knew it was you, I'd have thrown you a better welcome." Tres sneered at Hayate while playing with a curved knife in his right hand. "What brings you to my little city, meat?"

"Out of my way." Hayate poured force into his voice even though he knew he was moments away from being surrounded.

"What's ya hurry? You and me, we got some catching up to do before the boss lady gets here."

"Lady Inara is here?" Hayate asked, dread beginning to crush any hope he had of escape.

"She'll be here shortly." Tres motioned for his men to take Hayate. "She only gave orders about your friend, so hopefully she ain't too interested in you, and then you're gonna be all mine."

* * *

"Shall we pursue him?" the man to Thade's left asked in a calm, emotionless voice, his face pale and angular.

"No, Zenon. Ikari Sanada is our target." Thade crossed his arms behind his back.

"You're all pretty confidant you can take me considering how badly I trashed you last time we met." Ikari eyed Thade carefully. He knew enough about the older man to know that he was a tad on the arrogant side, but then, most skilled fighters were. He also knew that as dense as Gaou may be, Thade wasn't stupid enough to challenge him unless something had changed. Whatever that something was, Ikari knew there was only way to sniff it out. "Come on fella's; let's see if you can last a little longer this time."

"Take him." Thade nodded, sending Gaou charging forward while Zenon circled to the right.

Ripping the cloak from his shoulders to reveal a uniform similar to Thade's, Gaou unloaded a flurry of strikes, all aimed at Ikari's head, forcing him to step back as he evaded the attacks. Ikari grinned, recognizing the attack pattern and ducked under a right hook, planning to knock the bruiser out with a single kick as he did during Ritsuko's tournament.

This time however, as he stepped behind the taller man, Gaou twisted, nailing Ikari with a back fist to the temple that sent him stumbling to the side. Surprised by both the amount of pain shooting through his head and by how fast Gaou had moved, Ikari failed to block his follow up jab. Ikari swayed to avoid another hook then stepped closer to Gaou and hit him with a trio of rapid strikes to his ribs before capping his attack with jumping heel kick to the jaw.

Landing ready to attack again, Ikari felt his eyebrow rise as Gaou staggered back a step instead of falling like he had hoped. Ikari stepped forward to press his attack when his legs got kicked out from under him. Cursing himself for losing sight of Zenon, Ikari rolled to the side in time to see the stoic fighter spinning out of his sweep and land a kick to the sternum. Tumbling backwards, Ikari rolled to his feet and took a defensive posture trying to figure out how he failed to sense the man's approach.

"You guy's been working out?" Ikari sneaked a glance at Thade and found him standing where he had left him.

"You will find we are not the same as when you defeated us in Osaka Major." Zenon rose to his feet and let his cloak fall to the ground. Zenon, like Gaou, was dressed in a dark lavender body suit made from leather, and wore long dark brown boots. Unlike his compatriots, Zenon's uniform was sleeveless, and revealed long azure veins that ran up his left arm and ended just passed his ear on his bald head. "Just as you will find that you cannot achieve victory."

"Not if this is a whose face can scare the most kids contest." Ikari forced his voice to sound jovial, despite the apprehension that flowed through him as Zenon renewed his attack with a string of fluid kicks.

Letting his instincts guide him, Ikari ducked or blocked as many of the kicks as he could. He ignored the sting of each blocked attack while backing toward a parked wagon and managed to parry a high kick. Seizing the opportunity, Ikari threw a set of punches followed by a trio of rapid kicks. Zenon skillfully blocked each of his attacks, but in doing so, he gave Ikari enough time to backflip onto the wagon.

Welcoming the space to maneuver, Ikari somersaulted over Zenon just as he attempted to kick his legs out from under him. Ikari landed on his hands, curled close to the ground then sprang up and backwards, driving his heels into Zenon's shoulder blades, knocking him into the wagons side.

Rolling to his feet, Ikari spotted Gaou rushing toward him and flipped sideways to avoid getting tackled. Pleased at the sight of Gaou smashing into Zenon, Ikari had just landed on his feet when Thade flew toward him and slammed his shoulder into Ikari's chest. Ikari gasped as the air rushed from his lungs and he fell backwards. Stopping him mid-fall, Thade grabbed him by the collar and hammered him with a shot to the face. Crying out as pain racked his body, Ikari felt a knee crash into his gut followed by another painful punch to the jaw.

"I've seen your type before." Thade attacked again before turning around and threw Ikari across the square. "You like to toy with your opponents, using your agility to wait for an opening and pick them apart. Smart, but you won't have the chance if you can't breathe."

"True," Ikari gasped as he struggled to climb to his feet while Zenon and Gaou did the same. "Don't suppose you'd consider a five minute respite?"

"Your only option is surrender," Zenon stated while circling to the left.

Gaou began circling to the right, flexing his arms, ready to attack. "That's right you foolish... fool. Stop movin' so I can pound you into pudding."

"Well, with such a clever turn a phrase like that, how can I possibly win?" Ikari wiped some of the blood from his lip and glanced around. "Of course, I do have one option left."

"That being?" Zenon inquired.

"This." Ikari spun on his heel and sprinted down a narrow alley.

Running passed a pair of kids hiding behind a stack of crates, Ikari turned into a wider backstreet, and glanced over his shoulder to see Gaou and Zenon chasing after him. Turning into another alley, Ikari ran through and emerged on a heavily crowded street. Eager to put distance between himself and his pursuers, Ikari hastily made his way into the crowd, wondering how Thade, Gaou, and Zenon had managed to become so much stronger and what other surprises Ritsuko might have for in store for him.

* * *

Light from two of the three moons gave the streets of Austuria an eerie look as night began to fall over the region. Sticking to the backstreets, a young maid made her way toward her destination, a gleeful smile plastered on her face. She carried a foot long wooden box with a plain looking lid under one arm and smoothed out her dress with her other. Dreams of living in lavish mansions or exotic villas with servants of her own filled her head as she thanked the gods for the good fortune that had led her to meet such a kind man.

Hurrying passed a cozy diner, Mwenda spotted Svipdag leaning against the side of a closed shop and waved at him, overflowing with happiness. Svipdag smiled and motioned for her to follow as he walked between the shop and another building. "I can't wait for you to take me away."

"My work is almost done." Svipdag put a finger under her chin as she joined him. "Did you bring it?"

"I have it here." Mwenda handed him the box. "As long as it's back by midnight, no one will notice it's gone."

"That won't be a problem." Svipdag opened the box and picked up the crystal rose that sat inside it. "Beautiful, they even kept the scroll with it."

"Do you know what it is?" Mwenda asked, happy to see that Svipdag was pleased. "Lord Genki was very curious about it."

"It's a gift from the gods, according to legend." Svipdag returned the rose to its box then motioned for someone to come. A second later, a man in brown clothing took the box. "We're done here. Get ready to return to Hazgol."

"We are to leave now?" Mwenda stared at Svipdag, confused.

"I am." Svipdag laughed. "You've been very helpful. The hospitality of Austuria is all they say it is."

"What about me? I must return the rose…"

"Don't worry about the rose." Svipdag grabbed her by the hair and pulled a knife from his belt.

Filled with fear and forced to turn around, Mwenda felt his course hand cover her mouth an instant before she felt the cold steel of the blade cutting into her throat. Then she felt nothing.

Chapter Seventeen

"Lot of guards standing around for such a calm night." Yuki leaned against a stone pillar and stared at the large building swarming with men armed with bows and hiding in the shadows. The single story building was located on the eastern edge of Remus and was surprisingly well maintained for a lair of cutthroat assassins.

"The guards will make sneaking in difficult," E'Lan stated, keeping herself in the shadows of the pillars.

"It would, if we were planning on killing him." Yuki gave E'Lan an admonishing look. "We came here to follow up on a lead on Borga. Even though Ector Tres and I are competitors for control of Terra's criminal empire, we've never actually crossed paths. There's no reason he can't give us a little information."

"I would feel more comfortable if some of the others were here to provide support."

"Their time is better spent investigating Borga in Nel'Oskow." Stepping into the light from the moons, Yuki started toward the entrance of the building, walking slow while keeping an eye out for any sign of danger. "Still, stay sharp."

"Of course, my Lady."

They stopped a few feet away from a stone archway and waited for a man in leather clothing to step toward them. Eyeing the two women over, he waved his right hand, undoubtedly signaling guards hidden out of sight to aim their bows. "You got business here?"

"I do." Yuki glanced around and spotted three men perched on the surrounding rooftops aiming their bows. "But not with you."

"Deal with me or leave," the man spat.

"Fetch your master," E'Lan replied with a hint of annoyance. "Tell him…"

The sound of the metal door opening in the archway cut E'Lan off and a short woman, dressed similar to the guards, emerged and pushed the man aside. "Have your men come back inside. I'll assist our guests."

"The boss's orders were…" the man started.

"Orders change. Get inside and shut up or I might just let these Sanyoshu kill you." The woman waited for the man to comply with her orders then turned to face Yuki and E'Lan. "Apologies, my name is Lydia Zora, and I will take you to see Tres."

"Finally, someone with sense." Yuki forced a pleasant tone into her voice, deciding to let E'Lan play the part of an angry guest. Stepping into a sparse lobby, Lydia led them through a dark colored hall lit by the bluish glow of the luminescent stones mounted on the bare walls. They passed an archway that led into a large chamber filled with weapons and turned into a wider hall.

"Is this how you greet all of your guests?" E'Lan asked.

"Not at all. It's just... you are Sanyoshu. We don't see many of you in this region," Lydia replied. "Plus, we are expecting an important guest later this evening."

E'Lan shot Lydia an annoyed look. "You're not supposed to see us, unless we want you to."

Amused at how well E'Lan had kept Lydia's attention, Yuki slowed her pace, taking in the layout of the building as they weaved their way through, noting rooms of interest or where guards were posted.

"If I may, what business do you have with Tres?" Lydia led them into a sizeable circular chamber filled with men and women sparing or maintaining their weapons.

"I'm hoping to learn something," Yuki answered.

The chamber was lit by the same stones as the hallways but with a few extra torches scattered around. A set of wooden tables sat between a dozen or so stools on the left side of the room along with an archway that led further into the compound. A plain looking door that led to a small office with darkened windows was on the far wall, flanked by racks of spears and swords. Near the wall to right, Yuki spotted a middle-aged man sitting on another wooden table, playing with a short knife.

"Your guests." Lydia walked them over to the man then smiled at the women before leaving.

"Well, you're obviously Sanyoshu." The man leaned forward with a twisted grin. "And you have the family crest so you're either one crazy broad, or you're Yuki Sanada."

"And you must be Tres." Yuki laughed, surprised that he recognized her. "Not exactly the handsome rouge I heard about."

Tres let out an amused grunt. "And you're *exactly* the aggravating bitch I heard you were. So why are you in my city?"

"Nothing you need to get worried over. I came to investigate a rumor about Danothir Borga. Word has it that he's moving a sizable army into the area."

"That why you're here?" Tres glanced at his office for a second then looked back to Yuki. "To look into a thug with his own House?"

"Why lie about it?"

"You have a reputation in our circles as a cutthroat bitch."

"One I rather enjoy." Yuki let her voice sound jovial, but wore a stare that made it clear she was serious. "I only want to know if you've heard anything about Borga. If you haven't, E'Lan and I will leave."

"No, no... stay. It just so happens that I do know a little about Borga. He hired one of my guys to do a job in Ithor." Tres motioned with his free hand and the room fell silent.

"How cute, you trained your monkeys to do tricks." Yuki glanced around, taking quick count of how many of Tres's assassins were in the room.

"We can't all turn tricks." Tres smirked.

"Show Lady Yuki respect." E'Lan stepped to the side to gain room to maneuver, while looking as if she was only focusing on Tres.

"You're going to tell me what you know." Yuki glared at Tres.

"I would, 'cause I have no love for House Borga, but I don't like you either, and my long-standing employer would just hate it if I let you go without some form of molestation." Tres stood up on top of the table. "And, I have more guys than you."

"True, but if you know of my reputation, then you know E'Lan and I can slaughter your gaggle of moronic men."

"Yeah, I heard about those shadow arts you and that pest of a brother of yours learned. Rumor has it that you can even smash through stone with your fingers." Tres jumped back and landed on the stone floor, prudently putting the table between himself and Yuki. "Not someone I'd want to fight."

"And yet here we are, you and them all about to piss away your meaningless lives," Yuki stated. "Why is that?"

"Because I told him to," a woman's voice answered.

Yuki turned to her left and saw a blond woman in a black and lavender dress step out of the office followed by three men. Surprised that she didn't sense their presence, Yuki barely noticed the sound of the Tres's men rushing forward.

"Take 'em," Tres ordered.

E'Lan drew her sword, turning to fight off the initial surge of assassins, but was pushed back. Yuki shook off her alarm, and swept the legs of the first opponent that reached her. Dancing around the skilled attacks of the assassins, Yuki rolled to the right before vaulting over a charging woman.

Searching for the fastest way out of the room, she landed on her feet, but just as she did, the oldest of the three men flanking the woman in black grabbed her from behind and threw her into the cold wall.

"Gaou, Zenon, leave her to me. You two subdue the other one."

"Understood, Thade." Zenon nodded before moving toward E'Lan.

"Judging by the clothing, I'd say you're with House Inara. Thought I recognized the loin-spawn of Ritsuko Inara." Yuki shot forward, unloading a volley of kicks aimed at Thade's head. Understanding why Tres had sounded so confident, Yuki continued her attacks while Thade evaded each kick.

"You seem to be as disrespectful as your brother." Thade parried a kick and began his own assault, throwing a series of punches and forcing her to block. Arms aching from each blocked punch, Yuki tried to dart to the right but, to her dismay, Thade matched her maneuver and scored with a shot to her ribs. Blinded by pain for a moment, she felt him grab her by the collar an instant before he flung onto one of the tables. "And you're fighting styles are similar."

Instincts and training guiding her body, Yuki rolled to her feet and back-flipped just as Thade split the table with an axe kick. Yuki sprang off the wall, twisting head over heels, and drove both feet into Thade's face before kicking off and landing in a low crouch. Dashing forward, she pressed her attack with a string of blows to his midsection as he stumbled back.

Impressed that he remained standing, Yuki aimed a high kick at his temple, however, Thade managed to catch her foot and nailed her with another shot to the stomach. Air rushing out of her lungs, she spun around, reeling from a forearm blow to the jaw, when she felt his arms wrap around her waist. Elbowing Thade in the ribs, Yuki tried to free herself when he lefted her over his head and drove her into stone floor. She struggled to rise to her hands and knees, her head pulsating waves of pain throughout her body, while she resisted the darkness edging her vision.

"You fight similar to him, but you seem to prefer moving in for the quick kill." Thade grabbed her by the tunic and tossed her into the nearby wall.

"More fun to kill than to toy with." Yuki slumped against the wall and spat out a mouthful of blood. Noticing how quiet the chamber now was, she peered around and saw Zenon and Gaou standing over E'Lan's prone body.

Tres sauntered toward Yuki waving one of his knifes. "I like both."

"Tres." Alia stepped out of the doorway and glared at the older man. "I told you I wanted them alive."

"Right, except I want her dead." Tres returned Alia's glare. "Just like I want that knight dead. Don't forget, I may serve House Inara, but your mother's orders supersede yours."

"As long as you serve my House, you'll do as I say. So long as we have her and the knight, Ikari will have to come to me," Alia replied. "When he does, you can take the girl for my mother. I'll even let you keep Yuki and Hayate, but only after I have Ikari Sanada."

"Fine," Tres relented after a moment.

"All this for my brother…" Yuki asked between labored breaths. "…and that meaningless girl?"

"Just for Ikari." Alia smiled down at Yuki. "I couldn't care less about the Protectorate Goddess. Lock her and the Sanyoshu up with the knight."

"This had best work." Tres stepped over to Yuki and grinned. The last thing she saw was his boot rushing towards her face.

* * *

Amy sat at the edge of one of the library's tables reading a journal written by a girl who survived a raid on the city decades ago. Half distracted by sounds of people exiting the building in anticipation of the library closing for the night, Amy looked up at the stairs hopping to see Hayate and Ikari walking up. She leaned back in her chair, wondering what was keeping them, and glanced out one of the large windows. A ping of uneasiness tugged at the back of her mind, although she no idea why.

"About to graduate from college, lost on another world, and I still end up spending my nights alone in a library." Letting out a tired sigh, Amy returned her attention to the pile of books scattered across her table, when a soft whistle caught her attention.

"Amy."

Turning in her chair, Amy found Ikari standing in the shadow of one of the aisles, waving her over.

"Ikari?" She moved to join him, surprised that he had gotten passed her without her seeing, when she noticed blood on his lip. "What happened? You're bleeding."

"Really?" Ikari wiped the blood from his lip with a grin. "I think I've finally found someone enjoyable to fight."

"What's going on? Where's Hayate?" Amy peered around, ignoring the excited tone in Ikari's voice.

"He's supposed to here." Ikari's smile faded. A sound coming from the stairway grabbed his attention, prompting him to pull Amy behind one of the bookcases.

"What is going on?" Amy whispered while Ikari peaked around to see the librarian announce that the library had closed.

"Come on." Ikari led Amy along the back wall until they reached an open door hidden behind a large shelve. Closing the door behind Amy, he clicked the metal lock in place before starting up the dark wooden stairs.

"Where are we going?"

"To the roof," Ikari replied over his shoulder. "I couldn't risk leading them to you, so I sneaked in through the loft from the roof."

"Where is Hayate?" Amy stopped just as she reached the top of the stairs, and let her eyes adjust to the dim moonlight being filtered through grimy windows.

Used for storage purposes, stacked chairs and empty crates were scattered across the dusty room. Piles of unused wood sat near an open window, and a few cobweb covered painting hung on the walls or sat on top of the single table near the back of the loft.

"If he's not here, we have to assume he got grabbed by the guys that attacked me." Ikari turned to face her. "We ran into some old acquaintances of mine who've apparently joined up with Ritsuko."

"So what do we do?" The ping of apprehension Amy had felt began to grow into dread.

"Smart play is to cut and run."

"We can't ditch Hayate like that." Amy glared at Ikari. "I won't. Everyone says you're supposed to be this great fighter. There has to be a way to help him."

"We're outnumbered and have no idea how many men Ritsuko has in the city. I know they want me dead, and they probably plan to sell you to Danothir, assuming Ritsuko doesn't have something else in mind for you." Ikari turned away from her as a look of guilt flashed over his face. "I'd love to charge into their camp and take them head on, actually, I'd enjoy the challenge; but those three guys I mentioned aren't the same pushovers I fought in Osaka Major. I had my hands full fighting them off alone. I can't fight them if I have to watch out for you too."

"I can handle myself," Amy stated. Her mind swimming with emotions, she stepped closer to Ikari and was surprised to feel a sense of confliction as he raised an eyebrow at her. "Okay, maybe I can't. But I still have to try and help him. I get that he's not your favorite person, but I really need your help to save him."

"I don't like him." Ikari stared at her for a long moment before letting out a long breath and his eyes softened. "But you, you're starting to grow on me."

"Thanks."

"Don't thank me yet." Ikari walked over to the open window and climbed onto the roof before looking back at Amy. "Even money says he's already dead."

"He's not." Amy marched over to the window and climbed out. "I can tell."

* * *

The streets of Remus were quiet and still. A few drunks leaving the local taverns or lovers too blinded by romance to heed the dangers of the night, hurried through the city streets on their way home. A cool breeze swept over Ikari as he and Amy crept toward the edge of the roof they had climbed onto.

They had spent almost an hour searching for signs of Hayate. Ikari could have easily covered more ground if he left Amy on the roof of the library, but she had insisted on coming along. Lacking his prowess for sneaking across rooftops and leaping building to building, Amy still managed to keep up with him as they weaved their way through the alleys of the city to avoid getting noticed by Thade or anyone else looking for them.

While making their way through the business district, Ikari had spotted a man positioned on one of the roofs. After taking out the would-be look out, Ikari spotted two more men on different building and dispatched them with ease, piecing together what they were up to.

"You really think we'll find whoever those guys were watching?" Amy whispered.

"They used a triangle pattern to keep eyes on their target." Ikari glanced at Amy, wondering why he had given in to Amy's request. He didn't need to save Hayate for his scheme to stall the search for the Protectorate Goddess to succeed. Hayate dying would actually benefit his plans, but somehow, he found himself going out of his way to help the knight. "Based on where they were positioned, whoever they were protecting should be down there."

"I take it you do this sort of thing a lot?" Amy glanced at him for a moment before looking over the edge of the roof.

"Everyone needs a hobby." Ikari crouched close to Amy, making sure they were both still hidden in shadows, and peered down into the silent square. A few tables and wooden benches were scattered around the open area, but what caught his attention was the young woman sitting alone in the square's center. "Not exactly who I was expecting."

"Who is she?" Amy asked in a hushed voice.

"That would be Ritsuko Inara's bratty daughter, Alia."

"And she's the one who took Hayate?"

"Apparently."

"What's that song she's humming?" Amy tilted her head as if she was straining to hear. "It sounds... familiar."

"What song?" Ikari looked from Alia to Amy, wondering what it was that had drawn her attention. "I don't hear anything."

"I know that song. It's the same as before..."

Ikari stared at Amy for a long moment, concerned over the vacant look that fell over her face. He started to reach out to her when she let out a long breath and returned to normal. "Wait here and say out of sight."

"Where are you going?" Amy asked.

Ikari flashed a smile and took a few steps back. "She's waiting for me. It'd be rude to keep a lady waiting."

Walking to the opposite side of the roof, he found the metal banister they had used to climb onto the building and slid down to the ground. Keeping to the shadows, Ikari made his way around the buildings surrounding the square in silence, alert for any other soldiers posted nearby.

Satisfied that there were no other threats lurking about, Ikari found an alley that led back into the square and hurried through. Approaching from Alia's right, he peered up to the roof and found Amy perched where he had left her.

The scent of jasmine filled his nostrils, while the cool breeze carried the faint sound of an ancient tune. *How could... it's not possible she heard this from up there.* Confusion swirling up inside him as he stepped closer, Ikari glanced up at Amy, recognizing the song Alia was humming. The song was an ancient, slow paced hymn, fabled to be sung by the goddess Araia. As pleasant as the song was, it was one rarely heard due to its association with the destruction of the realm.

Close enough to grab her, Ikari set aside his thoughts about Amy and focused on Alia. "You know, if I wasn't such a nice guy, I might find you following me from Osaka Minor a little off-putting. Or are you always this forward with men?"

"Only with the ones I find interesting." Alia turned to face him with a jubilant smile on her face. "Don't tell me you find me boring."

"I find you… surprising." Ikari chuckled while scanning the area for any threats. "Didn't expect to see you again."

"I'm a girl who gets what she wants. And if I want *you*, I'll have you."

"I'm not some horse on a pasture to be bought. I have feelings," Ikari replied with a mocking grin.

"On the contrary, you're going to be my prized stud. One I intend to ride for the rest of our days." Alia's smile widened at the sight of him wincing. "Your metaphor, not mine."

Walked right into that one. Ikari suppressed a smirk; surprised to see she had a sharp wit. "So what, besides my dashing good looks, are you after?"

"I wanted to let you know that I'd be happy to allow you to escort me to the Chancellors ball in a few days. It would be an appropriate place to announce our engagement, and it would really upset my mother."

"As tempting as that last part sounds, I still have to pass."

"I can be very convincing." Alia's smile shifted into a twisted sneer. "For example, your knight friend…"

"He's not my friend," Ikari interrupted.

"Give yourself to me and I'll let him go."

"Bit of advice. If you're going to force someone to do what you want, you should probable try using somebody they actually care about. It's is all about leverage."

"I agree. You might not care about the knight, but I'm sure the girl he travels with does. I'm also sure that she would like to have him returned with his organs on the inside."

Ikari raised an eyebrow, wondering how much about Amy she actually knew. "Still not interested. Amy's worth a lot more than one knight." Tired of playing her game, Ikari turned and started toward an alley on his left.

"Amy huh?" Alia snickered. "I have your sister; her and that unsociable E'Lan woman."

"Unlikely." Ikari froze in mid-stride, questioning how else Alia could have known E'Lan's name.

"Still not interested?" Alia smiled again as he turned around. "I've been reading up on you. People say you and your sister are close. Twins are always close, I suppose. I never had a sibling so I wouldn't know."

"You expect me to believe you captured the second best fighter I know of all by yourself?" Ikari asked, more to convince himself than out of disbelief.

"You've met Thade and his two flunkies? Mother sent them after you, and I volunteered to help. Whatever she did to them... well, they're more than a match for you and your demonic sister." Alia locked her gaze on Ikari as she leaned forward. "I have proof."

She slid her hands over her long dress before slowly lifting it up to reveal her shapely legs and a black and red short sword strapped to her right calf. Laughing as she removed the weapon from her leg, Alia let her dress fall back to her ankles before tossing Ikari the sheathed sword.

"Yuki's sword." Ikari stared at the familiar weapon in his hands, stunned that Alia had managed to capture Yuki.

"Surrender yourself and the Protectorate Goddess to me by dawn, or you get to learn what it's like to be twinless." Alia hopped off the table and stepped passed him. "The choice is yours. I'll be waiting for you on the southern edge of the city, by the old stadium."

Waiting until Alia had disappeared down the main path out of the square, Ikari anxiously made his way back to the roof he had left Amy on. Scaling the building with the help of the metal banister he had used earlier, Ikari hopped onto the roof and spotted Amy as she moved to join him. "We may have a slight problem."

"I know, I heard," Amy replied, ringing her hands. "We have to find a way to save Hayate from that beastly woman."

"You heard?" Ikari raised an eyebrow. *You just keep getting more and more interesting.*

"Does it really matter now?" Amy began to pace in front of him. "If I turn myself over to her, would she really let him go?"

"Noble of you, but I doubt it." Ikari forced a calm tone into his voice, running through his options. "She's just as likely to kill us all."

"So what do we do? She said she'd kill Hayate and your sister." Amy stopped and turned to face him, her eyes narrowing. "Or were you really going to just walk away and let him die?"

"You have to be cruel to be kind." Ikari looked up into her upset eyes. "The more someone knows you care about the people they're holding, the more power you give them. Of course, if they grabbed your sister, it's pretty much assumed that you care anyway."

The anger on Amy's face softened and she shook her head. "Sorry. I didn't mean to snap at you."

"Don't worry about it."

"So what now?"

"Since we have a while before dawn, I say we follow Alia back to wherever it is she's holed up in. We find where she's hiding…"

"And we find where Hayate and your sister are," Amy finished.

"You're learning." Ikari motioned for Amy to follow as he started toward the next building over.

Forcing himself to set aside his growing curiosity about Amy, he felt a wave of apprehension wash over him. He bottled up his concern for Yuki and E'Lan, not wanting Amy to pick up on it, but failed to clamp down on the grin that spread across his face. As concerned as he was about facing Thade again, a part of him felt excited. Excited over the prospect of finding someone that could push his skills.

Someone fun to fight.

Chapter Eighteen

"So... you do, do this a lot?" Amy crawled across the top of a high wooden shelf that overlooked a small storage space filled with bottles of wine or some other kind of berry smelling liquids.

"Once or twice," Ikari replied a few feet ahead of her. "Sneaking into places I'm not supposed to be tends to go along with being an information broker. Besides, it's kinda fun and I'm really good at it."

"Back home we call it stealing secrets, and it's illegal." Amy watched as Ikari dropped down to the floor. Crawling to the edge of the shelf, she swung her legs over before letting herself fall. Stumbling as she landed, she felt Ikari catch her with an arm around her waist.

"Would you rather we let Alia capture us?" Ikari smirked and let go of Amy before stepping over to a closed door and cracked it open. "We all have skills we're good at. You're naturally curious about different cultures so you study the ones of the past. Hayate lets his naiveté lead him on a quest to save everyone from everything. And me, I spin things to my advantage and get what I need from an asset in the name of the Sanada."

"Is that what you really want?" Amy stepped over to his side, sensing a hint of regret from him.

"Kitchens clear." Ikari pushed open the door and hurried over to an empty counter.

"You think this is where Alia is holding Hayate?"

"We spent half an hour following her across the city to get here. Odds are this is the place."

Staying close behind him, Amy followed Ikari through an archway on the right side of the kitchen and into a darkened hall. They worked their way through the building in silence, ducking into empty rooms or darting out of sight to avoid the occasional assassin that strolled passed. After passing a few empty rooms, they found a large study, lit by a sizeable glowing stone fixed to the manila colored ceiling. Two tables sat in the center of the room on top of a dirty brown carpet while a few pictures hung on walls and a small crate filled with books and torn scrolls sat next to a dark archway.

"I wonder what they're doing with these books." Amy stepped over to the crate.

Ikari shrugged with a grin. "Looking for something."

Amy turned to face him and noticed a second hallway through an open door behind him. "Looking for what?"

"Not sure. But they have maps of every inch of the city." Ikari handed Amy one of the maps as she joined him by the tables. "Some of these were drawn over fifty years ago."

"I never was able to find any useful maps while I was at the library earlier."

"If the Assassins Guild is working for Ritsuko, they could be the ones gathering up mystical items for her." Ikari looked up from the tables, sniffing the air as he scanned the room. "Do you smell that?"

"Smell what?"

"Smells like… jasmine." Ikari spun toward the archway, a wave of alarm radiating off of him. "Damn."

Surprised by the agitation in Ikari's voice, Amy followed his gaze only to find Alia strolling into the room, flanked by three men in lavender clothing, and a dozen armed men. "Oh… bugger."

"I see you couldn't wait for our date. I guess you like me after all." Alia smiled and stopped a few feet away from Ikari. "And you brought a friend. Too bad I'm not the sharing type."

"Nice to see you again, Thade, Zenon, third guy." Ikari smirked, while the assassins circled around him and Amy.

"I told ya my name is Gaou. Gaou!"

"Whatever." Ikari looked back to Alia. "Were you waiting for me?"

"After Thade failed to capture you earlier, I knew you'd sneak off somewhere and we'd never find you." Alia turned and started down the archway, motioning for him to follow.

"Do you have to provoke the guys ready to kill us?" Amy whispered, alarmed as one of the men pushed her forward. Staying as close to Ikari as she could, Amy followed him down the hall; now brightened by a series torches.

"I figured that the only way to find you was to let *you* find *me*," Alia continued as they emerged into a large chamber filled with tables, weapons, and a small office along the back wall. Tres and a few more of his men were standing in the center of the room. "I knew you'd go looking for whoever attacked you, so I had some of Tres's men follow me while I waited for you."

"Clever," Ikari laughed. "You figured I'd find you then follow you back here, so you left your men waiting to grab me as I did. But given that I already took out three of them, I guessing you changed plans."

"Not at all. You're too good to be spotted by Tres's idiots," Alia stated.

"Watch your mouth," Tres snapped, glaring at Alia.

Ignoring the middle-aged man, Alia continued. "You took them out thinking that they were supposed to follow you and then came here to free your sister."

"So you let me sneak in and waited until we were far enough inside before saying hello," Ikari finished Alia's story.

"Impressed?"

"Surprisingly, yes," Ikari replied. "I'm curious, how did you manage to hide all of them from me? I'm usually good at sensing people approaching."

"The girls quiet the skilled little witch, just like her mother." Tres stepped over to Alia. "If you're done flirtin', I have a job that needs doing."

"Take the girl if you want." Alia waved at Amy before turning toward the hall opposite of the office. "Take Ikari up to my room."

"Take him." Tres nodded at two of his men then flashed a sinister grin at Amy. "Lady Inara will probably want you alive, but she ain't gonna mind a little damage though. You, me, your knight, and a whole lot of knives are gonna have a real ball tonight."

"Stay away from me." Amy tried to back away, but one of the men grabbed her by the back of the neck.

"Holding a guy's arm's behind his back is a good strategy, save for the fact that it can leave you vulnerable." Ikari swung his head backward, slamming it into the nose of the man holding him. He then kicked the man's knee, breaking his leg before pulling himself free and catching the second man with a trio of swift punches. Darting toward Amy, Ikari kicked the man holding her neck an instant before he threw him into Tres.

"Thanks," Amy said, wishing her heart didn't feel like it was ready to explode.

"Take this." Ikari handed her his sister's sword. "Go back to the study and through the second door. Whatever Alia did to mask people's presence seems to have worn off. Hayate and Yuki should be close by."

"But..." Amy started but Ikari rushed forward attacking a wave of assassins.

"Get going!"

"Grab her," Tres shouted angrily.

Holding tight to the sheathed sword, Amy sprinted down the hallway. Fueled by adrenalin and fear, she burst into the manila study and ran through the dim hall, all too aware of the men chasing after her. Rounding a sharp corner, Amy found a closed wooden door, locked from the outside. She slid the bolt back with shaking hands and pushed the door open as she stepped into the cool room. The chamber was about twenty yards wide, and just as long, with walls made from a dull grey stone and lit by hanging torches.

"Hayate." A jolt of alarm and relief shot through her as she spotted Hayate sitting in the center of the room, his arms chained to the ground. "Are you okay?"

"I'm fine." Hayate jumped to his feet, eyes wide with surprise. "What are you doing here?"

"I gotta get you out of here." Amy pulled at the chains.

"We're fine too by the way." Startled, Amy looked over to her left and saw Yuki and E'Lan chained to the wall, each with their hands over their heads.

"Sounds like you have company following." Yuki motioned toward the door. "Maybe you should unchain us."

"Forget about them. We can't trust them." Hayate tried to point toward the door. "The key is hanging over there."

Spinning on her heel, Amy spotted the key and yanked it off of the nail it hung from. Running back over to Hayate, she frantically tried to release the lock on his chains. "Got it."

"Look out." Hayate shoved Amy to the side as the chains fell from his wrists and two men charged in.

Tackling the first man as he raised his sword to attack, Hayate punched him once before grabbing the arm of the second man and nailed him with a blow to the jaw. Still holding onto the man's arm, Hayate punched him again before kneeing him in the stomach and landing a blow to the head. Hayate wrenched the man's sword free as he fell and used it to block an attack from the first man as he rose.

"Unchain us," E'Lan shouted.

The sound of more men rushing into the room caused Amy to look back for a moment, unsure of what she should do. Fighting off another opponent, Hayate kicked one of the men in the gut, pushing him toward Yuki while Zenon entered the room.

"We can help you." Yuki leaned back against the wall and kicked the man that stumbled toward her. "Or would you rather watch your dear Hayate die?"

"Alright." Amy ran over and unlocked Yuki's chains. "We need to help Ikari too. He's fighting who knows how many of them on his own."

"Stay out of the way." Yuki snatched her sword from Amy's hand and tucked it behind her hip. "And free E'Lan."

"Where is Lord Ikari?" E'Lan asked while Amy hurried over to her, and Yuki shot into the fray, attacking anyone who came near her.

"In the exercise room." Amy slid the key into place, unlocking E'Lan's restraints.

"E'Lan." Yuki grabbed one the men by the wrist and drove her palm into the back of his elbow, breaking his arm an instant before she kicked another attacker in the throat. Turning away from E'Lan, Yuki kicked one of the swords that had fallen on the floor back and into the air.

E'Lan charged forward, catching the sword in mid-air, and parried the attack of an axe wielding woman. Keeping as far from the fray as she could, Amy watched while Hayate, Yuki and E'Lan finished of the remaining assassins.

"Most impressive." Zenon stepped forward. "This should prove most invigorating."

"Enjoy it while you can." Yuki stood ready to fight. "E'Lan, go and assist Ikari."

"Understood." E'Lan glanced from Yuki to Zenon then ran out of the room.

"We need to get out here." Hayate grabbed Amy by the hand and moved toward the door, his vision locked on Zenon as he and Yuki began to circle each other like two hungry wolves.

"Alia has maps of the city." Amy ran behind Hayate once they entered the hall. "I think she knows where the museum is."

"Then we need to find Alia." Hayate ran into the study just as a boot to the ribs blindsided him, knocking him to the right.

Amy reached the doorway a second later and turned toward Hayate when a sharp pain shot through her head as someone grabbed her by the hair and spun her around, shoving her away from Hayate and into the wall. Leaning against the wall, Amy spun around and spotted Tres stepping toward Hayate, with a sword in one hand and a knife in the other, while Alia hurried out of the room carrying a large book and some maps, shadowed by Gaou.

"Ain't either one of you leaving tell I had my fill of your guts drippin' off my knives." Tres lashed out, forcing Hayate to defend as he scrambled to his feet.

"She's got the maps." Amy pushed off the wall and sprinted down the archway, ignoring Hayate's cry for her to wait. She knew that she wouldn't be much help to Hayate in a sword fight, but she *could* help by getting the maps back from a spoiled rich girl like Alia.

* * *

"Gaou, stay with Lady Alia," Thade ordered while Tres chased after Amy. "I will defeat Ikari."

"If that is your wish Thade." Zenon started toward the archway Amy had ran into. "Allow me to retrieve the girl."

"Let's see what you got, old man." Ikari punched one of the assassins on the jaw an instant before he rushed forward to meet Thade head on.

Excitement and fear mixed together as Ikari opened with a flurry of punches. Continuing his assault, Ikari buried his concern about Amy and Yuki, ignored the whispers of Alia and Gaou as they walked off, and focused on the man deflecting his strikes. He strung together another series of punches, all the while watching Thade's movements, the placement of his footing, and the angle of his shoulders; waiting for that subtle shift he'd make before switching from defense to offense.

A sly smile spread across Ikari's face as he spotted Thade shift his stance and set his right foot. Ikari stepped forward, throwing a high kick aimed at the bridge of Thade's nose, but to his surprise, Thade spun around his kick and caught him with a fist to back of the head. Reeling from the blow, Ikari felt his opponent's large foot crash into his back, causing a surge of pain to shoot up his spine.

Stumbling toward a pair of armed men, Ikari rolled under their swinging blades and nailed one with a kick to temple as he rose. Ikari twisted on his toes, catching the second man with a roundhouse kick, and found a wave of their compatriots swarming around him.

Dancing around their attacks, Ikari glanced to his right keeping an eye on Thade as he stalked forward. "What happened to taking me on alone?"

Ikari ducked under an axe aimed at his neck and swept the legs out from under two of his attackers. Taking advantage of the opening he had created, he darted through before flipping onto one of the tables.

"If you feel slighted in this contest, draw your blade," Thade replied.

"Thought you knew by now, mine is a style that doesn't use weapons." Ikari glanced over the room, taking a quick count of his enemies.

Eight assassins remained on their feet, all of which he could deal with, if he didn't have to worry about Thade. *I gotta figure Zenon and Gaou might join in the fight. Not to mention however many more guys Tres has in the building.* Whatever magic Ritsuko had used on them, they were definitely not the same men Ikari had beaten in Osaka Major. Unless he found a new weakness to exploit, there was a good chance that he might lose this fight.

Unable to keep the enthused smile from his face, Ikari surveyed the room. "Only three people have ever forced me to draw my sword, and you're nowhere near as good as them."

"Arrogant to the end?" Thade paused as he waited for the remaining assassins to regroup. Moving at once, the assassins rushed forward, their angry cries filling the room.

Ready to meet their charge, Ikari felt a familiar presence and smirked. He waited until they were parallel to the archway, then vaulted off the table and landed, forcing them to turn toward him just as E'Lan shot into the room. Moving with the fluidity and deadly precision Ikari would expected from Yuki's top Sanyoshu, E'Lan cut down two of the men before the rest knew to defend. Her sword flashing as it connected with enemy steel, E'Lan continued her macabre ballet while Thade dashed toward her.

Grateful for the assistance, and happy to realize that Amy must have succeeded in freeing Hayate and Yuki; Ikari caught Thade with a blow the chest. Ikari nailed Thade with a side kick, followed by two high roundhouse kicks. The first found its target, but the second was blocked with one arm while Thade used his other to throw an angry punch. Allowing himself to fall backwards to avoid the attack, Ikari rolled to his feet in time to block Thade's follow up attacks.

Evading a knee aimed at his face, Ikari spun low and swept Thade's leg. As Thade tried to catch himself, Ikari grabbed him by the shirt for a throw, however, he countered with an elbow to the jaw and a throw of his own. Sailing over the bodies of dead assassin's, Ikari turned his head, twisting in midair and took control of his fall.

Sliding to a stop, he found that E'Lan was finishing off the last of the men, and that Gaou and Alia were hurrying across the room toward the back office, carrying a large book and maps tucked under her arm.

"E'Lan, stop Alia." Ikari glanced over again and noticed Amy chasing after Alia. "And protect Amy."

"But my Lord..." E'Lan stared.

"Do it!" Ikari turned back to Thade in time to see another fist flying toward him, and smiled.

* * *

Fists flew passed the evasive head of Yuki Sanada like stones from a sling, driving her back. Each step brought with it another barrage from Zenon's well-trained fists, and each backwards step forced her to continue to block or parry. Grateful for the protection the light forearm guards provided her sore arms; Yuki ducked under a wide attack and began her own assault, stealing the momentum. Zenon began to step back, blocking each of her punches, and causing a pang of annoyance to shoot through her.

Slipping a strike passed his defenses, Yuki aimed a roundhouse kick at his shaved head. Her kick blocked by Zenon's left arm, she threw another only to have it blocked as well. Egger to take his head off, Yuki feinted a punch to the stomach but before her leg had come down to the floor, she shot it forward and went for a side kick.

Clearly anticipating the maneuver, Zenon blocked the kick an instant before he nailed her with a punch to the stomach. Not giving her time to recover, Zenon scored with a spinning kick to the chest as she stumbled back.

Yuki grimaced, trying to force air back into her lungs, while her lanky opponent surged forward to press his attack. Sidestepping to the left, Yuki grabbed his extended arm by the wrist and pulled it down then back, causing him to flip over. Turning to keep Zenon in her field of vision, Yuki let out an irritated growl as he rolled through his fall and picked up a set of steel hatchets dropped by one of the dead assassins lying on the stone floor.

"I am pleased to see the vaunted legends of the Sanada fighting prowess are more than mere rumor." Zenon turned to face her, twirling his weapons as he took a low attack stance. "Killing you will be a most illustrious honor."

"As if I would ever allow myself to be killed by a man like you." Yuki let her anger over his calm demeanor fuel her attack as she renewed their dance. Missing with a pair of swift kicks, Yuki threw a punch aimed at Zenon's chest but he deftly crossed his weapons to block and pushed her back.

"You speak as if the choice was yours." Zenon rushed forward, unleashing a torrent of rapid, twisting attacks, all intended to hack her into chunks of meat.

Adrenalin and the bitter taste of fear pumped through Yuki as she put all of her energy into evading the flashing blades. Twisting around a horizontal slash, she felt the air shift as one of the hatchets narrowly missed her nose. Zenon followed her movements and swung both arms downward, forcing her to step forward or let him sheath his miniature axes in either side of her shoulders. A sharp pain shot through her shoulder an instant before she realized that Zenon had used the hatchets as hooks and yanked her forward. Elbowing her in the face, Zenon attempted to plant a hatchet into her stomach, but she managed to roll free from his grasp and escaped with only a painful slash along her side.

Rolling to her feet near the wall she had been chained to, Yuki Jumped up, over a slain assassin, and kicked off the wall. Twisting as she did, Yuki scored with a harsh kick to Zenon's temple, causing him to stagger back. Seeing her chance to finish him, she bounced off the ground, vaulting over him and landed in a handstand on top of his head.

Just as she landed, however, Zenon let her weight push him over and rolled back as the two fell. Caught by surprise by his counter, Yuki felt the heels of his boot slam into her stomach just before he hit the ground, and sent her tumbling over the corpses of his allies. Yuki climbed to her feet slowly, using every moment before Zenon attacked again to catch her breath, and noticed a discarded sword sitting in front of her.

"You surprise me." Yuki watched while her opponent rose and turned to face her, and began to focus her ebbing energy. "Not many men have the stamina to keep up with me in a fight. You've even managed to earn your way into a rare category with me."

"That being?"

"Men I respect," Yuki replied, trying to keep him talking. Her training in Alextien had taught her many unusual skills, one of which was how to sense the strength of her opponents. She could feel how much vigor Zenon had left in him and knew if she wanted to see him dead at her feet, she would have one chance. "Besides my brother and my master, no one has pushed me this far before."

"Rest assured, I will see that respect reciprocated. That said, I believe this dance of ours has reached its conclusion."

"I agree." Yuki let a smirk she usually shared with Ikari slip to her lips, and let her energy flow through her. "It's time you died."

Zenon twirled his blades, taking up an attack stance. "Know that after you are slain, I will see to it that you receive a funeral befitting a warrior of your caliber and perform the rites of The Slayer. I pray the war god welcomes you into his camp."

"Let's see whom The Slayer favors." Yuki shot forward, pouring her energy into her legs and kicked the dead assassin's sword, sending it spiraling toward Zenon's chest. Batting aside the sword with his left hatchet as he lunged forward, Zenon attacked with his second, intending to spill her intestines across the floor in one violent slash.

Willing herself to move faster, Yuki spun around his attack, ignoring the pain from the hatchet as it grazed her side, and drew her own weapon. Letting her momentum add to the force of her right arm, she felt her sword slice through Zenon's windpipe as she drove it through the back of his neck.

Leaning close enough to whisper in Zenon's ear, Yuki let a warm sense of satisfaction wash over her while blood gushed from his throat. "Fight well at the sword of Sha'Kring."

She pulled her sword from his neck and lowered his body to the floor. Taking a moment to inspect her own wounds, Yuki stepped into the dark hallway, noticing the all too familiar sounds of swords clashing and started toward the study.

* * *

Hayate ducked under a wide ark from Tres's sword and went for a lateral strike of his own. Pressing forward, the young knight alternated from left to right, attacking with a zeal brought on by concern for Amy. His arms beginning to feel the strain from the lengthy duel, he ignored the ringing in his ears from the clang of their swords and looked through their bright sparks in order to pursue his foe. Hayate stepped ahead, swinging the unfamiliar sword he wielded down toward Tres's collarbone, but the cagey man parried his attack and attempted to slash him across the belly with his knife. Jumping back to avoid the cut, Hayate was forced to block a series of ferocious assaults.

Evading Tres as best he could, Hayate felt his back hit the table in the center of the room just as he deflected another attempt to find his neck. Hayate kicked Tres on the chest and rolled over the table, but not before Tres managed to plant a gash across his leg. He suppressed a painful groan as he came to his feet and looked up in time to see Tres hurl his sword at his head. Diving to the side, Hayate rolled to his feet with his weapon ready to defend.

"You cost me a lot of time, boy. After the boss lady is done with your girly friend, I'm gonna enjoy taking it out on her. 'Course 'fore that, I'll be using your guts as a garter." Tres pulled a second knife out of his belt.

"Interesting idea." Surprised, Hayate glanced to his right and found Yuki strolling into the study. "Maybe I should cut your balls off and wear them as a necklace. But, then I'd have to touch you."

Ignoring Yuki for the moment, Hayate returned his attention to Tres. "Surrender now or you die."

Tres glanced from Hayate to Yuki as a frustrated look fell over his face. "Another time." Letting out an irate growl, Tres hurled one of his knives at Yuki's face an instant before he threw the second one at Hayate.

Instinct guiding his arms, Hayate stepped to the left, batting the knife to the side, only to find Tres sprinting out of the room.

"Look at him go." Yuki stepped over to Hayate, smiling at the knife sticking in the wall behind them before motioning to the archway that led to the training chamber. "Shall we?"

"Why should I trust you?" Hayate turned to glare at the woman. "Or am I supposed to forget about what happened in Perukav?"

"Besides the fact that I just helped you," Yuki replied in an annoyed tone. "What other reason could there be for us to work together?"

Hayate glared at Yuki for a moment before realization smacked him in the face and he spun around. "Amy."

* * *

"Hey." Amy slid to a stop a few yards behind Alia and her heavily muscled bodyguard. Realizing as they turned to face her, that as determined as she was the get the maps and book away from them, she had no idea how she was going to accomplish that task. "Um… give me the book."

"And how do you propose to take it?" Alia sneered at Amy.

"Okay, this might not have been my brightest idea, but I can't let you get away with that book. It could lead to a way home."

"It's hard to believe that Ikari would choose you over me," Alia replied. "I wonder why, considering you're not that bright."

"Maybe it's because I don't come off as a loony tart," Amy retorted.

"He can't choose you if you're dead." Alia turned toward Gaou. "Kill her."

"Aren't we suppose ta turn her in to Lady Inara?" Gaou asked.

"I don't care what my mother wants. Kill her, now."

"Ya got it." Gaou started forward with a twisted grin on his face.

Fear swelling inside her as she backed away, Amy started to turn to run, when she saw E'Lan rushing past her. Forcing Gaou to pull his outstretched hand back as she aimed her sword at his elbow, E'Lan stepped between him and Amy, and began a fervent assault. Ducking or swaying to avoid her skillful sword, Gaou rolled to his right before getting pushed back by a kick to the face.

Turning away from E'Lan and Gaou's battle, Amy darted toward Alia and grabbed hold of the large book. Hopping to simply grab the book and run, Amy tried to wrench the hardback free, only to have Alia pull back on it.

"Let go," Alia hissed, struggling to keep the tome from Amy.

"Piss off!" Amy pulled back on the book then reached back and punched Alia on the cheek. Stepping back as Alia fell over, Amy tucked the book under her arm and rubbed her fist, surprised by how much it hurt. "Ow."

"You dim little tramp..." A livid look washed over Alia's reddening face as she pulled a dagger out from under her dress and scrambled to her feet. She took a step forward when the sound of Hayate's voice caused her to pause.

"Hayate." Amy felt herself smile as she looked over and saw him running toward her.

"Thade!" Alia scooped up the maps she had dropped and began to back toward the office. "Gaou. We're leaving."

"Why?" Gaou swayed to avoid getting stabbed by E'Lan then nailed her with a kick to the side an instant before he landed a harsh punch to the face. "No way these chumps can defeat us."

"I said now!" Alia reached behind her and opened the door.

"Understood," Thade replied from further down the chamber. Pulling a large weight off a fallen rack, he hurled the metal disk at Ikari—who backflipped to avoid getting hit—before turning and sprinting over toward E'Lan. Thade hastily grabbed E'Lan by her tunic, spun, throwing her into Hayate and Yuki before they could reach Amy. He then pushed Gaou toward Alia and scanned the room as the two reached her.

"Why run when we're winning?" Gaou asked.

"Because, you egregious fool, I have the information Ikari and the girl came to find." Alia backed into the office. "There's no need to continue this, since I know where they'll be later."

"We will meet again, Ikari Sanada." Thade waited until Alia and Gaou had disappeared into the office before following them in and slamming the door shut.

"We can't let them escape." Hayate sped past Amy, chasing after them, but just as he started to open the door, it slammed closed. He began to push against the wooden door and was joined a second later by Ikari. "Something's blocking it."

"Don't leave now, the fun just started." Ikari kicked the door then let out a long breath.

"Shouldn't we go after them?" Amy stepped over to Hayate as he leaned against the door, breathing heavily.

Ikari shook his head, sucking in air. "Just because you can chase someone doesn't always mean you should."

"He's right," Yuki agreed. "Unless *you* want to do all the fighting for a while?"

"What about Tres's flunkies." Amy looked from Ikari to Hayate.

"Probably already fled when Tres retreated." Hayate stepped closer to Amy. "Are you okay?"

"I'm fine. I'm more worried about you right now."

Yuki stepped over to the office wall and slid to the floor. "I guess the question is what to do now?"

"We need intel," Ikari replied.

"Lady Yuki, Lord Ikari." E'Lan stood near the center of the room and looked down at the bodies of some of the assassins. "This one still lives."

"Ask, and the gods provide." Ikari smiled.

Chapter Nineteen

"Any luck with the tunnel?" Yuki laid on top of a wooden table in the center of the blood stained training room, kicking her leg over the edge.

"Nope." Ikari shook his head, walking out of the back office carrying Hayate and E'Lan's swords in each hand. After he and Hayate had smashed their way into Tres's office, he found the narrow tunnel Alia had used to flee but was unable to pick up her trail. Whatever spell Alia used to mask the presence of Thade and company during her ambush, had been employed to aid in their escape. "You?"

"Nothing I hadn't already known." Yuki rolled to face Ikari. "Before Alia Inara showed up, Tres mentioned something about sending an assassin to Ithor for Borga."

"Interesting. Don't tell our knight friend about this, he might run off and do something... annoying. It's better to keep him chasing after the Protectorate Goddess for now."

"I was planning to check out Tres's story anyway. I'll deal with the Ithor situation."

"Try not to kill too many people while you're there. Ryoma can be a bit of a pain when he sets his mind to be." Catching sight of E'Lan as she entered the chamber, Ikari smiled and handed her weapon to her. "Find anything useful?"

"No, my Lord." E'Lan bowed as she took her weapon and returned it to her back. "A few of Tres's men remained, but they were easily dealt with."

"I doubt Alia would have left anything too obvious for us to follow. She is pretty smart," Ikari mused, but a raised eyebrow from Yuki caused him to suppress a smile. "For a spoiled brat, I mean. Get anything from the assassin?"

"Our dear and earnest Hayate is with him now," Yuki replied, rolling her eyes. "You can imagine how well that's going. Are you sure you wouldn't rather kill him. I'm sure E'Lan wouldn't mind."

"Tempting, but as annoying as Hayate is, he has his uses." Ikari started toward the hallway that led deeper into the complex.

"Like giving you an excuse to follow Amy?" Yuki teased, following a step behind him. "Or did you go through all of this due to some misguided belief in the Protectorate Goddess."

"She's a girl, not a goddess." Turning down the corridor into a wider hall lit by torches, Ikari recalled his curiosity about how Amy could hear him when he was talking in the square with Alia, or how she always managed to know when he was lying. "It's all in the name of the Sanada."

"Smart play would have been to cut and run. You chose to help her... or to see Alia Inara, since you find her *interesting*. I'm not sure which is more disturbing."

"Of two of us, who is it that got themselves captured by a spoiled rich girl?" Ikari flashed Yuki a mocking grin as they worked their way through the halls. "Or would you rather you stayed in that cell?"

"I only got caught in a trap meant for you," Yuki replied with a defensive tone. "And don't change the subject. I know the smirk you keep trying to hide. It's your, *I find something really fascinating smirk.* Now, as your dear and loving sister, I demand to know what's in your head."

"And here I thought you could read me like a book?"

"I can... usually, and it saddens me to think you're interested a dull little wench like Amy. You can do so much better, right E'Lan?"

"Um... I," E'Lan stuttered from behind.

"You're not exactly the person I'd go to for relationship advice." Ikari stopped in front of a wide oval shaped door and turned toward Yuki. "Given the fact that every man you've ever seen has ended up sliced into tiny chunks and fed to wild boars."

Yuki frowned, waving a dismissive hand. "It's not my fault that most men are simpering idiots. And I didn't kill all of them. One lived."

"My sister, the great and merciful." Ikari laughed, seeing the irritated look on Yuki's face then pushed the wooden door open and stepped inside. "So... how's it going?"

"He isn't talking." Hayate stood in front of the surviving assassin, who was tied to a burgundy chair in the center of the room. Eight yards long and just as wide, the room was devoid of any decorations and lit by a trio of torches as well as light from one of the moons that shone through a high window. A small table sat on the left side of the room, a few feet away from the diminutive bed Amy sat on.

"I bet I can help with that." Yuki flashed a twisted smile at the bound man. "I remember you. You're that rude little man that greeted us at the door. I'm just going to refer to you as door guy, if that's alright."

"He's a trained assassin," Ikari replied, looking toward Hayate. "He's not going to talk simply because he's captured."

"Then what do you propose?" Hayate shot Ikari an annoyed glare as he stepped to his side.

"Just give me a knife and half an hour, and he'll spill his guts," Yuki laughed, circling around the sweating man like a predator stalking its prey.

"You can't torture him." Amy rose to her feet and walked over to Hayate.

"Why not?" Yuki raised an eyebrow.

"Because it's wrong." Amy turned toward Yuki. "Even if he is an enemy, he's still a human being."

"Amy's right," Hayate agreed. "Knights don't torture their prisoners to get what they need."

"I'm not a knight," Yuki retorted.

"And I won't allow you to…" Hayate started, before Ikari waved a hand to cut him off.

"Relax. We aren't going to torture him. As my sister is well aware, torture only gets the fastest answer to end the pain." Ikari glanced at Yuki for moment then back to Hayate and Amy.

"So what do we do?" Amy asked.

"Interrogating a trained operative to reveal what he doesn't want to takes a certain amount of skill. You have put them into a fragile state of mind." Ikari paused, noticing that Yuki had sat on the man's lap and began whispering into his ear.

"Get this crazy witch away from me." His face turning pale, the assassin tried to pull away from Yuki. "I'll tell you whatever you want, just get her away."

"Fortunately," Ikari continued. "Fragile states of mind happen to be one of my sister's specialties."

"What… what did she say to him?" Hayate stared at Yuki for moment.

"Trust me." Amy swallowed. "You're happier not knowing."

"Start talking." Yuki hopped off the terrified man's lap and stood next to E'Lan near the doorway. "What's Tres's relationship to House Inara?"

"The boss has been working for Lady Inara for years. She had us searching the realm for any magical trinket we could find, especially anything involving ascension."

"Why would she care about ascension?" Hayate pondered aloud. "Legends about ascension are always tied to the Protectorate Goddess."

"I'm guessing Ritsuko's interested in rising to heavens." Ikari frowned, recalling some of the odd items he had seen in her personal study.

Hayate raised an eyebrow and glanced at Ikari. "And do what; steal the power of the gods?"

"I read a passage in that book you wanted me to translate, about items that were said to transform a person into *a pool of luminous light*." Amy looked at Ikari. "And there were a few passages that talked about methods to access higher plains of existence."

"She wants to become a god herself," Ikari stated.

"Is that possible?" Hayate stepped away from Amy and peered out the window.

Ikari nodded. "Ritsuko is as skilled in dark magic's and forbidden sorcery as Yuki and I are in combat. And it explains her sudden interest in Amy."

"How?" Amy glanced at Ikari with look that told him she didn't really want to know.

"She believes you're the Protectorate Goddess. In her mind, that makes you the closest being to the gods."

"Reaching a level on par with the gods isn't like hopping on a wagon going into town," Yuki stated in her usual, cold tone. "The gods choose who gets to walk among them."

"If Ritsuko can steal your... essence, or whatever it is about you that makes you capable of becoming a goddess, then..." Ikari trailed off.

Hayate turned back toward the group with a grim look. "Then Lady Inara becomes a goddess instead of Amy."

"Danothir wants Amy to gain control of the war god's army." Ikari laughed, understanding exactly what he had found in Osaka Major. "I doubt Ritsuko will be that short sighted, or as kind. Especially to me."

"I guess you can reach the gods by wagon." Yuki shot Amy a twisted smile. "And you're the wagon everyone wants to ride."

"Thanks," Amy replied and stepped over to Hayate. "That makes me feel so much better."

"Yes, well, all this talk about the Inara's is starting to bore me." Yuki turned away from Amy and flashed Ikari a grin. "I'll leave Ritsuko and her daughter to you. I have better things to do than chase after my brothers crazed admirers."

"Yes dear sister, go butt into someone else's business for a while." Ikari returned her smirk, knowing she was heading off to Ithor.

"Lord Ikari." E'Lan bowed before following Yuki out of the room.

"That woman could chill the spine of Yun'Harrar himself." The man tied to the chair let out a relieved breath.

"No kidding," Amy whispered.

"Shut up." Ikari kicked the chair over, knocking the man to the floor. "I can always call her back. Now, about those maps Alia took with her?"

"All I know is that she and the boss were looking for some old building," the assassin stated.

"And she found it." Hayate stepped over and lifted the chair back into a sitting position. "She must have mentioned something. A name, district, something."

"The boss was happy to find that book. He said something about it being written by some high society woman, but that's all I know."

Ikari stared at the trembling man for a long moment before letting out a disappointed sigh. "He's empty."

"You're sure?" Hayate asked.

"He's telling the truth about not knowing anything." Amy turned and started for the open door. "Maybe we can figure out where the museum is after we've gone through the book. I might know what woman he's talking about."

"What about him?" Hayate nodded toward their captive.

"Leave him." Ikari turned to follow Amy. "E'Lan tied him up well enough, but given that he's a trained assassin, I'm sure he'll manage to free himself... in a day or so."

"What woman was he talking about?" Hayate closed the door behind him as he followed after Amy and Ikari.

"While I was waiting for you guys back in the library, I came across an old article about a woman, Nadine Valmont I think." Amy hurried around the corner and led them into the study where she had left the book she had gotten from Alia. "Anyway, she and her husband owned a lot of land in the city and were big on altruistic gestures."

"I don't see what that has to do with the museum we're after." Hayate stepped close to Amy as she opened the large book sitting on the table, and smiled slightly as their shoulders touched.

"The Valmont's last recorded donation to the city was to build a new museum. I couldn't find out where it was built, but while I was thumbing through this earlier, I noticed a few inventory reports." Amy turned page after page scanning the text when a pleased smile spread across her lips. "Here, it's a shipping manifest."

Ikari stepped over to the table and glanced over the page trying to figure out what Amy had seen. "It looks like crates and lumber. The Valmont's owned a quarter of the city, those could have been shipped anywhere."

"I'll wager a Pharaohs ransom these went to the museum," Amy replied confidently.

"How can you be sure?" Hayate looked up at Amy, his smile growing just enough for Ikari to notice.

"Spend your life around archeologists and you'll end up in a museum often enough to recognize an order for more shelves and displays. Plus, look at the index numbers on the crates. This might be another world, but I know a cataloging system when I see one."

"That's great. Does it say where any of the shipments were delivered to?" Hayate looked back at the book. "Wait, this says a shipment was delivered near Oolan Field."

"Where's that?" Amy inquired.

Hayate shook his head, staring at the page. "I have no idea. There is no Oolan Field anywhere near the city."

"Not now anyway." Ikari smirked, remembering one of the maps he had seen sitting on the table before Alia had escaped. "Years ago a quake hit the city devastating enough that scribes had to redraw their maps of the area. Oolan Field was buried under what is now the Dai Vox Canyon."

* * *

Cool air drifted over the dusty trails that led through the canyon while light from two moons began to fade as dawn crept closer. The climb down to the canyon floor had proven to be easier than the high ledges and jagged rocks would lead one to believe, much to Amy's relief. Trying to ignore the anxiety floating around in her mind, she followed a few steps behind Ikari, content to let him lead Hayate and her to the mouth of the large cavern a dozen yards ahead of them. As they crept closer to the opening, Amy noticed large piles of dirt and rocks to the right and rows of shovels and pick-axes to the left.

Dad would love a site like this. Plenty of places to search and no clue what he'd find. Amy bit back the urge to drift off into memories, willing herself not to feel quite so homesick; an effort that, so far, had failed.

Sensing a ping of confusion from Ikari, Amy looked over and found him hunched over the ground, staring at footprints. "Something wrong?"

"I wouldn't say wrong. Odd, but not wrong." Ikari glanced over to the cave then scanned the area around them.

Hayate knelt down next to Ikari and looked over the tracks they had been following. "They don't lead inside?"

"They do..." Ikari shook his head and pointed to a set of footprints. "But *these* don't belong to Alia or Tres's men."

"Workers maybe," Hayate responded.

"Workers stop digging at sundown, and with the wind blowing as constant as it is, their tracks would be more obscured." Ikari pointed in the direction they had come from. "Alia's group came down the same trail we did and headed straight into the cave. These other tracks came down a different path, and they don't match any of Tres's guild buddies."

"Any chance it's just some kids wandering around?" Amy asked, picking up a hint of concern from Hayate.

"Could be, but either way we still need to follow Alia inside." Hayate waited for a nod from Amy and Ikari before jogging into the cave.

Finding more digging equipment laying against the cave walls, Amy noticed a wide opening at the far end of the cave. Walking over to it, they stepped through and found themselves heading down a narrow, sloping tunnel, lit by a flickering torch at each end. They reached the end of the tunnel and found a large hole that dropped down into a darker tunnel.

After checking to see if anyone was waiting to hack them into tiny pieces, Hayate jumped down first then caught Amy as she followed. Waiting for Ikari to join them, Amy glanced around and noticed that the floor and walls of the tunnel were smoother.

"I think this is the place." Amy knelt down and dusted a portion of the floor to reveal dark tiles. Making their way through the hall, they emerged in a stuffy chamber with knocked over display cases and a badly damaged ceiling. "I'm surprised there's any light down here."

"As long as there's heat for the luminescent stones to absorb, they can glow for almost a thousand years." Hayate walked through an opening to the left that led to a similar chamber. "Did any of those books you read say what section of the museum the rose might be in?"

"Not really." Amy shrugged as they passed through an archway held up by two stone columns, and waved away some of the dust falling from above. "It's your world... realm, whatever; if you found a magical rose of the gods, where would you keep it?"

"Magical jewels weren't really my focus of study." Ikari stepped over to a display of stuffed animals. "Could be in a display dedicated to Tai Re'l, or with rare jewels, or it could be buried under rubble."

"What's that sound?" Amy turned toward another, smaller chamber and hurried to a set of open doors.

Staying behind one of the doors, Amy peered down a flight of stairs and into a large and well lit chamber. Patches of marble floor could be seen through the layers of dirt. Displays of varying sizes were scattered across the room, some remained standing while others were lying broken on the floor. Standing in the center of the room, with Thade and Gaou at her side, Alia watched as Tres and his men searched for the rose.

"Guess we found them," Ikari quipped from the second door.

"We should take them now, before they find the rose." Hayate looked toward Ikari, who shook his head in response.

"Too many." Ikari scanned the chamber. "Tres and his goons are annoying enough, but dealing with Thade and Gaou in a building that might collapse on top of us if things get rough isn't likely to end well."

Hayate let a mocking smirk flash across his face. "I thought the Sanada were all fearless battle nuts willing to fight anyone for the challenge?"

"I am." Ikari shot the young knight an irritated look. "I may be a bit overzealous when it comes to a fight, but that doesn't mean I don't have a healthy respect for a strong opponent. Thade was good the first time I fought him. Now, thanks to Ritsuko's sorcery, he's a whole lot better. And since knights of Ithor have the fighting skills of hyperactive toddlers with a pointy stick…"

"This isn't helping, boys." Amy raised her hand to cut them both off. Ignoring the sounds of Alia's men, she stared across the chamber at a darkened doorway, catching the faint sound of a familiar humming voice. "We still have to get in there and across the room. I think the rose might be in that smaller chamber ahead."

"This place is pretty big, it could be anywhere." Ikari looked back over the room then returned his curious stare to her. "What makes you think in there?"

"I don't know… gut feeling I guess." Any shrugged, trying to force the faint humming out of her head. "But I'm pretty sure it's there."

"I believe you." Hayate smiled at Amy. "Ikari and I can deal with them while you wait here."

"What part of *there's too many to fight* did you miss?" Ikari asked.

"We don't have to fight and *win*. We just have to distract them long enough for one of us to get in and out of the room." Hayate smirked.

"That's a lot of people to distract for one person," Ikari retorted.

"I'm not some dainty bird incapable of taking care of herself. I can help..." Amy trailed off, not wanting Hayate or Ikari to shoulder all of the danger. "I can find the rose."

Ikari glanced at Amy for a moment then let out a defeated sigh. "Assuming Alia doesn't have anyone else lurking around, you could follow the wall to the right and use the debris and cases to sneak passed."

Hayate put his hands on Amy's shoulders. "I'm supposed to protect you. I'm not about to let you risk getting hurt."

"But its okay when I watch you get hurt protecting me?" Amy looked Hayate in the eye, angry and determined to do whatever she needed to in order to end their quest and get back home. "I can do this."

"Amy..."

"Give it up Hayate. You're not changing her mind." Ikari chuckled as he reached to the back of his hip and drew his sword. Flipping the red and black weapon around his hand, he handed it to Amy handle first. "Still, it might be better if you had this. Just in case."

"Won't you need it?" Amy reached for the handle.

"In case you haven't noticed, I tend to fight unarmed. It's how I was trained, and more fun." Ikari flashed her a reassuring smile then looked to Hayate. "I'll sneak down first and get their attention. I'm sure Alia is smart enough to see through a distraction, so after a minute you come rushing in. Do try not to get bogged down fighting a single guy. This'll work so much better if you hit and run."

"I know what I need to do," Hayate replied with a growl.

"I'm just saying, nothing distracts a guy in a fight like some annoying witty banter. You should try it. Might help get that stick out your backside." Ikari grinned as he slipped through the doorway and bounded off the stairs and to left, landing lightly and rolling behind a large display case.

"I think I'm starting to hate him." Hayate drew his own sword and turned back to Amy.

"He's not so bad." Amy smiled and took Hayate's free hand as she peered around the door.

Amy watched as Ikari made his way to a ten-foot tall oval case and leapt on top of it. "Alia, I pictured you as more of an art kind of girl than ancient history. And it's so nice of you to bring the kids along."

"Ikari." Alia spun to face him as everyone in the room stopped. "How very unsurprising. You do realize that you can't beat Thade and Gaou, and you won't stop us from finding that rose?"

"What can I say?" Ikari shrugged. "It's my hobby to stick it to House Inara whenever I can."

Alia smirked. "Well, you can stick it to me whenever you like."

"I walked right into that didn't I?" Ikari let out a sigh.

"You did." Alia's smile broadened.

"Enough." Tres pulled a knife from his belt and gestured toward Ikari. "Everyone shut up and kill him."

"'Bout time." Gaou charged forward, smashing through Ikari's wooden perch.

Ikari flipped sideways off the display case and landed in a low crouch before rolling to evade a knife thrown by Tres. "You know, if you guys don't play nice, I might revoke your museum privileges."

Growling angrily, Thade stalked forward radiating resentment. "You cannot match me. That you have seen for yourself, but you still mock us? Does your arrogance know no bounds?"

"No, not really." Ikari danced around a trio of armed men, flipping and rolling to keep them off balance. "I mock. I'm chatty. It's part of my charm."

"This ain't a spectator's sport people," Tres barked. "Kill him!"

"Wait." Alia raised a hand, holding back a group of assassins. "He's baiting us."

Suppressing the urge to feel amused as Ikari enticed Tres and his men's anger, Amy let go of Hayate's hand and tried to keep the worry from her voice. "Be careful, okay."

"You too." Hayate held his gaze on her for a moment longer before readying his sword and sprinting down the stairs.

"There." Alia spun toward Hayate. "Ikari was a distraction. Kill the knight."

Amy held Ikari's sword tight in her left hand and waited while Hayate drew attention away from the stairway. Finding her opening, she hurried down the flight of stairs and dashed behind a fallen pillar. Moving along the right side of the chamber with caution, she caught glimpses of Hayate fighting off one of the assassins before evading the next. The sound of swords clashing filled the air along with angry voices from Alia and Gaou, while Ikari continued to maneuver around.

A cloud of dust and dirt began to form, stinging Amy's eyes as she scrambled over smashed shelves and piles of debris.

Reaching the door and at a run, Amy entered the room and paused, letting her eyes adjusted to the lack of light. Able to make out a few tables and display cases, many of which were little more than rubble on the floor, she glanced around, noticing for the first time that the humming in her mind had shifted into a soft singing voice. Amy started toward a larger bookcase, feeling drawn to it, just as she had been drawn to the portal that had brought her to this world.

"Stop… stop singing." Amy shook her head, trying to forget the voice ringing in her ears.

Reaching the overturned bookcase, she knelt down and pushed it aside as best she could. A warm glow began to pulse through the pile of books, dirt, and whatever else had fallen out the case, causing her to shift through it. Tossing aside a mask of one of this world's gods, Amy let out a relieved laugh as the singing faded and picked up a sapphire rose about the size of a baseball.

"At least I didn't get flushed down some magical loo this time." Picking up Ikari's sword, Amy noticed that the sounds from Hayate and Ikari's fight had stopped, and hurried to the door.

Wondering for a second if her friends might have been killed, she quickly dismissed the thought, realizing that she would have felt something if they had. What struck her as odd was the overwhelming sense of surprise she felt not only from Hayate and Ikari, but from everyone else in the chamber. Stepping through the door, Amy almost tripped over herself as she gazed around the chamber and found the source of everyone's surprise.

A woman in black clothing with a gray chest plate and a matching cloak, sauntered down the stairs at the far side of the chamber while a horde of similarly dressed men—each armed with crossbows and swords—lined the walls and surrounded the shocked combatants. Ikari and Hayate each began to back toward Amy while Thade, Tres, and their group flanked Alia.

"Who are they," Amy asked, wishing she had stayed in the dark room.

"Those would be the extra foot prints we spotted." Ikari kept his voice calm and almost cocky, but Amy could feel the apprehension bubbling within him. "Looks like Yuki was right about Danothir having troops in the city."

"How can you tell?" Amy stared at the woman.

Hayate gestured toward the woman. "The pin on her collar has his sigil."

Stopping in the center of the chamber, the tall, dark skinned woman scanned the room before letting a tight lipped grin adorn her scarred face. "Since I already have your attention, I'll be brief. Hand over the rose without incident, and I no longer have a reason to kill all of you."

"No chance. Ain't no way some woman is going to stop me." Gaou started forward only to get pulled back by Thade.

"Who're you?" Tres demanded.

"At the moment, I'm the person who'll decide if you journey to the domain of Ako'Reah or not," the woman responded in a calm, smoky voice.

"And what's to say me and my men don't send you screaming into her arms first?" Tres motioned for his assassins to ready their weapons.

"And how do you propose to do that?" the woman countered. "I clearly have you outnumbered. Even if Sanada and the knight decided to help you, my comrades have plenty of arrows and excellent aim."

"What do you want?" Alia stepped in front of her allies, signaling them to stand down.

"I only came to collect the rose. You, Lady Inara, and your people are of little interest to me. Therefore, I am willing to make this offer once. Take your men and leave now, or chose a chamber to act as your tomb."

Alia glared at the woman for a moment before glancing over her shoulder as Thade whispered his support of accepting the offer. Waving off Tres and his protest, Alia returned her vision forward.

"It seems I'm left with little choice. We'll take our leave." Nodding to Thade, who barked the order to retreat, Alia turned toward Ikari as she began to back out of the chamber. "Do try to not die, Ikari. I'm sure that Tai Re'l will guide you to me another time."

"Why? Have I angered her somehow?" Ikari held his arms out, acting as if he was confused.

"What does the goddess of love have to do with you and her?" Hayate raised an eyebrow at Ikari.

"Don't ask." Ikari shook his head.

"It's such a shame to see young lovers separated by death." The woman turned to face Ikari and the others after watching Alia depart. "Now, Lord Sanada, the rose."

"Don't suppose you're willing to give us a pass as well?" Ikari inquired.

"My orders are to retrieve the rose. Killing you and disposing of your bodies is a superfluous task I don't need. However, I am getting tired of asking. Hand it over or die."

"No." Hayate stepped in front of Amy, readying his sword and drawing the attention, and aim, of the surrounding soldiers. "We can't let Danothir get the rose. I won't..."

"Be smart," Ikari interrupted. "I'm fast, but even I can't dodge that many arrows, nor can Amy. But if you think you take them all... be my guest."

"He's right." Amy step forward and put her hand on his shoulder. "Live today, and you can always fight tomorrow."

Letting out a defeated growl, Hayate sheathed his sword. Squeezing his shoulder for a moment longer, Amy handed Ikari his weapon and stepped over to the smiling woman, handing her the jewel rose.

"Smart girl." The woman snatched the jewel from Amy's hand. Admiring the rose in her left hand, she raised her right to eye level and snapped her fingers. "We're done here, comrades. Let us depart."

"What does Danothir want with the roses?" Hayate asked over the sound of boots hitting the tiled floor.

"After you dig yourselves out, you can travel to Nel'Oskow and ask him yourself."

"Dig ourselves out?" Amy looked over at the woman as she started up the stairs behind the last of her men.

"She intends to collapse the entrance into the museum," Ikari stated.

"Of course." The woman paused at the top of the stairs. "I said I'd let you live and I will be true to my word. However, as kind as I am, I'm not foolish enough to leave a Sanada a clear path to my back. Collapsing the entrance to the next room will slow you down just long enough for me to fade away like the morning fog."

Standing in panicked silence, Amy watched as the woman disappeared into the darkness of the next room. "Shouldn't we try to—I don't know—stop her?"

"Why, nothing's changed." Ikari returned his sword to his hip before stepping over to a fallen pillar and sat down.

"He's right." Hayate wiped some of the dirt off his face and turned toward Amy. "If we chase after them now, they'll kill us. Our best chance is to wait and dig our way out."

"Assuming she keeps her word," Ikari added.

"I'm willing to trust the word of a fellow knight on the battlefield," Hayate replied. "Not that we have much choice."

"About that..." Amy glanced back to the stairs, recalling the feeling she got as the woman spoke her last words. A moment later the sound of crashing rocks and falling dirt momentarily drowned out Hayate and Ikari's argument. "I'm pretty sure she lied about simply slowing us down."

"So much for the vaunted valor of a knight," Ikari scoffed.

Blocking out Hayate and Ikari, Amy forced herself to take a long breath, bottling up the fear that pulsed through her veins with every beat of her heart. Years ago, she had been trapped in a cave-in and escaped to tell the tale. Of course, at the time, her dad had been by her side, and together they had found another way out. She just had to keep her composure, like her father had done, and treat the current situation like any other problem.

Her anthropology professor would often state that a rational mind can solve any problem. *All I have to do is think it through, remember my research, and...* Amy spun toward her friends, mentally kicking herself for not remembering earlier. "Guys."

"It was your idea to surrender," Hayate stated, ignoring Amy.

"Guys."

Ikari rose to meet Hayate's glare. "It was that or find out how many arrows will fit into our chests before we hit the ground."

"So you traded one death for another?" Hayate retorted.

Ikari shrugged. "Maybe, but I traded an immediate death for a later one. It was the smart play."

Waving her hand in annoyance, Amy walked back into the room she had found the rose in and looked around. Scanning each of the walls, she spotted a pile of shattered display cases and what looked like a broken column blocking a doorway into another chamber.

Yes. Smiling to herself, Amy twisted around on her toes and hurried back to find Hayate and Ikari still arguing. "Hey guys."

Hayate glared at Ikari, clenching a fist. "Forgive me if I'm not as self-serving, jaded, or opportunistic as you."

"Self-serving?" Ikari stared at Hayate. "I'm here because I was foolish enough to let my emotions get the better of me and agreed to help Amy. All I've done since I met you is help."

"All I wanted was advice on where to begin looking into the legend. Or is your idea of helping sending your maniac of a sister to follow us?" Hayate waved his arm. "I never asked, or needed your help."

"Amy did," Ikari responded; his usual calm tone replaced by one of anger. "I'm here for her, not you."

"Will you pair of wallys shut your gobs and turn it in already!" Amy marched in between the pair and pushed them apart. "You're acting like pair of unruly kids. Now if you're done arguing about who's helping the most? Maybe you two can help me get us out of here."

"How?" Hayate asked after a moment, his face reddening from embarrassment.

Clamping down on the urge to smile as both Hayate and Ikari forced themselves to regain their composure, Amy pointed at the room behind her. "I spent hours going over everything we could find about the museum. One of the books I read had the floor plan of the building. If you two can help me clear a doorway, I can get us back to the hallway we climbed in through and back out into fresh air."

Chapter Twenty

The kingdom of Ithor was known for its lush country sides, beautiful gardens, and for surviving a long depression made worse by the attempts of its enemies to seize control from its much loved King. Even the castle in which King Ryoma ruled was an intriguing sight.

Made from a dark stone, the castle was an elegant, and aesthetically pleasing, structure designed to ward off the fiercest of enemies, but at the same time, its construction and decor were rather inexpensive. The halls were well decorated and filled with plenty of light from the afternoon sun, and even the servants seemed happy enough as they scurried about their business. The only room that bordered near decadence was the banquet hall. A fact not unexpected considering his evening plans.

King Ryoma sat back in his throne, leaning on one of the arm rests while one of his advisors prattled on about requests being made by some of the statesmen invited to the dinner planned by the King. A knight dressed in tan pants with a dark gray tunic and brown cloak stood near the advisor.

"These guests are an awfully demanding bunch," the knight stated.

"And considering the purpose of this dinner it's in our best interest to indulge them, Sir Gaius," the gray haired advisor retorted.

"And I have my concerns over the security of this dinner." Gaius gestured toward the servants setting up the tables inside the vast room.

"It'll be fine Gaius," Ryoma stated. "It's not as though we've invited enemy warlords to dinner. This is just a gathering of the regional governors."

Maids scurried about dusting or polishing any metallic surface, while others wiped down tables and placed intricate cloth coverings and napkins. Dressed in a handmaidens clothing, E'Lan went unnoticed as she folded her napkins, listening to every word spoken. Both she and Lady Yuki had spent the morning searching for any signs of the assassin hired by Borga only to find that their prey was smart enough to stay hidden. Figuring that the only way to catch their target was to stay close to the King himself, Yuki had instructed E'Lan to disguise herself as a handmaiden and learn what she could.

Gaius rolled his eyes. "Yes, because politicians are such an unscrupulous bunch."

"Majesty, I do wish you would reconsider the dinning arrangements," the older advisor said. "A King should be seated on his throne, not in a wooden chair, fine as it may be. You must consider the message it sends."

"I have." Ryoma shot the old man an annoyed glare. "I am hosting this dinner because I have need of the governors support, the same governors that represent the people I reign over. What kind of message would I be sending if I waste funds on needlessly extravagant dinners and expensive décor? Is that the message you want conveyed from your King after enduring costly wars and an economic depression?"

"No, of course not, majesty."

"I thought as much." Ryoma glanced over the room. "I have conceded enough to make our guests happy."

"Will this help?" Gaius gestured toward the table E'Lan was working at.

"I hope so. Danothir has been speaking against us ever since Hayate helped Amy escape from Nel'Oskow." Ryoma paused, causing E'Lan to wonder if he might already know about Borga's plot to kill him. "He's growing bolder in his efforts to find her and he knows she travels with Hayate. It's only a matter of time before he moves against us, and when he does I want our people to be ready."

"And the Consortium has done nothing?" Gaius asked.

"What can they do? I have done what I can to stall him, but without proof of his treachery there is little more I can do without starting a war. The other concern I have is with House Sanada. Genki has gone out of his way to make sure neither Danothir nor myself gains any momentum in convincing the Consortium."

"You think he's up to something?"

"I know he is. Genki Sanada is not nearly as clever as he thinks he is." Ryoma laughed, rising to his feet. "Regardless, we need this dinner to go well if I hope to convince the governors to support a war with House Borga, so I'm counting on the two of you."

"Yes, majesty." Gaius and the advisor both bowed while Ryoma started toward the door.

"I'll see to greeting the guests." Gaius followed after the King.

Folding the last of her napkins, E'Lan waited until Ryoma and his knight had left before heading out the door herself. Turning right, she made her way through the halls, passing a few servants or knights as they went about their business. After a few minutes of navigating the corridors, E'Lan spotted a woman dressed in a similar brown and white dress through an open door and stepped inside the modestly furnished bedroom.

"May I assist you?" E'Lan stepped over to the woman, who was busying herself by making the bed for one of the evening's guests.

"Thank you, E'Lan." Yuki smiled up at her beneath her bonnet. "How was Ryoma fairing?"

"I found no sign of our target." E'Lan took the sheet out of Yuki's hand and began to unfold it. "The King is planning a large dinner party tonight in order to garner support against House Borga."

Yuki nodded. "I see. Then in all likelihood, our target is already here someplace."

"Should I search the grounds again?"

"No." Yuki shook her head. "All of the extra servants and dinner guest roaming around have made it easy for us to go unnoticed, but that will also be true for our assassin. Besides, I may know how to find him."

"How?" E'Lan continued to make the bed, noticing the sounds of two squireswhistling as they passed by the door. "I will be glad to leave this place."

"Why?" Yuki laughed, waving at the boys as they passed by. "You seem to be quite popular. You should wear a dress more often."

"Please don't tease, my Lady."

"You'll never get my brothers attention covered up in battle armor."

E'Lan finished tucking in the corners of the sheets and looked up at Yuki, noticing that her face suddenly felt warmer. "Really? You... you think he might..."

"I think we should check the kitchen." Yuki stepped over to the door. "With all the extra guests, I'm sure security around the King will be fairly heavy. If I wanted to kill him, poison would be an easy way. Well... if I wanted him dead, I'd play in his blood first, but then I've always been more hands on."

"Of course, my Lady." E'Lan nodded, trying to hide the discomfort of Yuki's joke from her face, and followed her back into the halls.

* * *

"Marie, hurry up with the wine."

E'Lan pushed passed the shouting, plump woman and tried to drown out the constant clattering of pots or the clang from plates getting stacked and wheeled out as the servants prepared dinner. She and Yuki had spent most of the afternoon searching through two of the three kitchens in the castle and found nothing but flustered servants scurrying back and forth. Finishing her sweep of the bustling room, E'Lan paused next to an unmanned counter covered with spices and herbs layed out, and let out a tired sigh. Taking in the scent of the tasty smelling herbs, she glanced around and spotted Yuki walking toward her.

"Remind me to never visit Ithor again. This kingdom and its people are far too dull for my liking." Yuki stood next to E'Lan, gazing over the kitchen. "This annoyance had best be worth the trouble. I assume you found nothing."

"It seems our prey has immersed himself well." E'Lan looked down to the counter, feeling hungry after wandering through kitchens all afternoon, and picked up a thick bluish gray herb.

"Tres's man has to be around some place. If he intends to poison the meal, he'll have to make his move soon."

"Should we recheck the other kitchens?"

"I'm almost tempted enough to let Ryoma die. Ikari was the one who wanted me to come here. I hope it wasn't out of concern for that girl and her feelings toward Ithor. Either way, this is turning into more work than I had initially planned. What do you say E'Lan, should we cut our losses, find the local tavern, and avail ourselves with the local cretins; or just get back to tracking Danothir's movements?" Yuki smiled, letting out an amused laugh. Questioning how serious her comment was, E'Lan lifted the herb to her mouth when Yuki grabbed her by the wrist. "I wouldn't eat that."

"Lady Yuki?" E'Lan noticed the surprised look on Yuki's face as she glared at the herb. "I don't understand, its only allium-prasum."

"No, it's not. It looks like it and it smells like it, but it's not. Allium-prasum has four leafs, this has three." Yuki took the herb from her hand and held up the side with the leaves.

Nodding as understanding sunk in, E'Lan looked back to the counter and found two bags of the herbs waiting to be sliced. "Poison?"

"Indeed." Yuki tossed the herb into a nearby fire. "Allium-donna, a very poisonous and extremely rare herb. It looks like our assassin has a decent amount of cleverness in him after all. Not many people would notice the difference since allium-donna only grows in Alextien." Yuki stepped over to another workstation and tapped the cook on the shoulder. "Who is working this station here? I have an order change to give them."

"I believe that's one of the guest's cooks. Zhim... I think it was. I forget his name but he went to finish unloading his cart."

"Thanks," Yuki replied, looking back to E'Lan for a moment. "Burn the bags."

Spinning back to the counter, E'Lan grabbed the two bags and tossed them into an empty fire pit before closing the metal cover and flipping the in use flag. She quickly caught up to Yuki as she sped through the narrow hall that led to a small loading bay.

E'Lan scanned the area, noticing that the sun had finally set, and searched for anyone holding a bag similar to the ones she had burned when she spotted a man with blond hair carrying a bag of allium-donna.

"Lady Yuki." E'Lan nodded toward the man dressed in a pale tunic.

"If he runs, kill him." Yuki stepped over to the man, wearing a disinterested look on her face. "Zhim, right?"

"Yes, why?" Zhim stopped a few feet in front of Yuki.

"I have an order change I'm supposed to give you."

"Talk to Pierce about it. I just prepare spices and seasonings." Zhim started to push passed Yuki, but she put a hand on his shoulder to stop him.

"Not that order." Yuki looked him dead on, letting her eyes convey her seriousness for a moment. "And you know how the boss gets when things get messed up. He'd have my hide if I didn't deliver the message."

Zhim stared at Yuki for a long moment before nodding and motioning for her to follow. "Let's talk some place quieter."

E'Lan waited for a moment before falling in line behind Yuki and Zhim. They walked across the loading bay in silence, ducking into a small storage room about twelve yards wide and just as long. Closing the door behind them, E'Lan took note of the few crates in the room and the empty shelves along the back wall.

"So, you said the boss sent you?" Zhim turned to look the two women over with a suspicious eye. "Both of you?"

"Who would think to question two handmaidens?" Yuki smiled. "Especially on an evening like this."

"It's nice having a guy or two on the inside to keep an eye on things." Zhim returned Yuki's smile. "Although I was told that we'd have no contact with each other."

"What can I say, the situation has changed."

"How's that?" Zhim glanced from Yuki to E'Lan and folded his hands behind his back. "You of course have the authorization word?"

"Of course." E'Lan nodded, keeping her eyes on his hands. Yuki motioned for Zhim to step closer, but as he did, he pulled a curved blade out from under his tunic.

Instinct taking over, E'Lan shot forward, blocking his downward attack an instant before she twisted his arm around and forced his own knife between two of his ribs. She quickly covered his mouth with her free hand, to stifle any cries of pain, before pushing him down to the ground.

"Thank you E'Lan." Yuki stepped over the man and dropped down on his chest, using her legs to pin his arms down and wrapped her fingers around his throat.

"Who are you?" Zhim gasped between labored breaths.

Smiling, Yuki waved a finger in front of his face while keeping pressure on his throat with her right hand. "I'll ask the questions if you don't mind. Now, you mentioned having a man inside the castle. I'd love to know who that is."

"You really expect me to talk?"

Yuki wore a cold smile, looking down at the scrowmming man. "No, not really. I can guess your backup plan. The only real question is how much fun I can have killing you versus the amount of noise you'll make."

"If the guild has a second man inside, they would most likely have stayed near the King." E'Lan looked over to Yuki, wondering how they could track the second assassin down.

"I agree." Yuki let an ecstatic grin spread across her lips as she tightened her grasp on Zhim's throat, cutting of his ability to breathe as he began to struggle beneath her. "The second assassin is bound to notice dear Zhim's departure. He'll have little choice but to assume the operation has been compromised and resort to killing the King himself."

"But how do we find him before that?" E'Lan asked.

"We'll have to wait until he makes his move." Yuki paused, locking her eyes on Zhim's as the last convulsions of life faded from him. "Which unfortunately means you'll have stay close to the King. Enjoy the dinner party."

"Yes, Lady Yuki." E'Lan let her shoulders drop as she tried to keep the disappointment from her voice.

"Buck up." Yuki flashed her a playful smile as she stepped off of Zhim's body and dragged it toward one of the crates. "Maybe you'll meet a knight and he'll fall deeply in love with you."

"Please don't tease."

* * *

"More wine, majesty?" E'Lan filled Ryoma's glass, yearning for the assassin to reveal himself and kill a few of the pompous, corpulent pigs that passed for noblemen. Of course, she had always viewed the noble class with distain usually reserved for sewer dwelling vermin, the Sanada family being the only exception.

Lady Yuki and Lord Ikari had always earned the respect and loyalty of their followers through their actions while other nobles simply demanded it. Lady Yuki was cruel, but she was also kind. She would slaughter anyone foolish enough to stand in her way, inflict horrors that could make the gods cringe, but she would also fight and die for what she wanted and the ones she cared for. That was why E'Lan would follow her to the depths of the underworld, and that was why she would endure the infectious stupidity of Ithor's noblemen.

"Thank you," Ryoma replied over the noise of multiple conversations that filled the banquet hall while servants made their way around the crowded table, refilling glasses and plates.

Continuing her round of the table, E'Lan again took note of people while Ryoma called their attention to continue talking. Five servants, including her, moved about the room and security was much lighter than she would have expected given the nature of the dinner. The only visible security was the knight sitting to Ryoma's right. Of course, having spent the day sneaking around the castle, she knew that Gaius, or whatever his name was, had insisted that a pair of guards be stationed outside the chamber and a small contingent were posted in the next room.

"We understand your concern over this matter, majesty, but you must also understand that we have our concerns as well," a balding, lanky noble stated. "Even if Lord Borga is plotting against us, you have little proof. If we begin amassing an army now, that may be interpreted as an act of aggression. We cannot risk war with House Borga."

"I am not asking you if we should go to war with House Borga. I am asking for your support in preparing for one Lord Borga will start." Ryoma sat his drink down and glanced around the table. "He has been stealing our supplies for months now. He feigns compliance with the Consortium just enough to keep them from allowing me to investigate further."

"I assume this stems from the report Sir Hayate made?" another nobleman asked. "Has he sent back any news of his quest?"

E'Lan ignored Ryoma's response, noticing the casual gaze of a servant holding a tray of desserts as he made his way toward the head of the table and scanned the room. Moving as fast as she could without drawing attention to herself, E'Lan spotted the familiar point of a dagger as the assassin worked it out of his sleeve. Realizing that she wouldn't make it around the table in time, E'Lan hurled the pitcher of wine at the man's head while leaping onto the table.

She lunged at the surprised man, silencing Ryoma in mid-sentence, and nailed the assassin with an elbow to the chin as her momentum knocked him over. Rolling clumsily to her feet due to the long dress she wore, E'Lan found that her opponent had already gotten to his feet and was charging toward Ryoma. Alarmed, she shoved Ryoma to the side with one hand while grabbing a tray off the table in order to block the attack.

"Guards!" Gaius shot to his feet and moved to the King's side.

"Damn." The assassin hurled his dagger at Ryoma and turned toward the door, but E'Lan managed to deflect the blade with the tray. The assassin pushed passed a pair of stunned noblemen and pulled a second knife just as the guards opened the doors. Maintaining his stride, he slashed the throat of the taller guard before disappearing down the hall. E'Lan started after the assassin, but found the doorway cut off as more guards poured into the room.

"Your majesty, Are you alright?" a guard asked.

"I'm fine." Ryoma started toward E'Lan but Gaius blocked his path.

"You three, detain that woman." Gaius jammed a finger at E'Lan. "Captain, lockdown the castle. No one gets out until the assassin is found. The rest of you come with me."

Ryoma stormed after Gaius as he started toward the door. "Do you really intend to arrest the woman who saved my life?"

"I intend to hold her until we find out who she is and what she's doing here, majesty." Gaius paused and took the Captain's sword as he ran past. "Sire, she is obviously not a maid in your service, so until I am certain that she is no threat, I strongly suggest that we lock her up."

"Fine, but put her in one of the guest rooms," Ryoma relented before Gaius hurried out of the room. "I'm not so ungracious that I'll throw my savior in a dungeon."

"You're too kind." E'Lan resisted the urge to break the first guards arm as he reached over to grab her.

Allowing herself to be led out of the room, she glanced over her shoulder and found the other two guards trailing behind. Waiting until she and the first of her escorts rounded a corner, E'Lan kicked the side of his knee, causing him to cry out and release her arm before she threw him over her hip. Drawing the fallen man's sword, she spun on her heels while ducking low and slashed the second guard's leg just as he rounded the corner. She then surged forward, catching the last guard by surprise as he tried to ready his weapon, and plunged her sword through his left shoulder until it hit the wall.

"You're fortunate that I was ordered to avoid killing any of you." E'Lan turned back toward the hallway she was being led through and sprinted away from the guards, relieved that she no longer had to play handmaiden. All she had to do now was find the assassin, assuming Lady Yuki hadn't already killed him.

* * *

"Search that way, we'll go this way."

"Fools keep yelling and I'll get away perfectly," the assassin whispered to himself as he worked his way down a narrow alley that led away from the castle.

"I agree." Stepping out of a darkened archway, Yuki grabbed the man by his collar and pulled him into the alley between a pair of one-story buildings. Slamming him into a cobblestone wall, she grinned as he turned to face her. "Clearly the knights of Ithor are ill-equipped to handle a member of the Assassins Guild. Unfortunately for you, I am."

"Good for you." The assassin aimed the blade of his dagger at Yuki's neck, but she blocked his attacked with ease and grabbed his weapon hand. Holding him by the wrist, she pulled his arm straight before slamming her free palm into his elbow joint, breaking his arm.

"I don't suppose you'd consider telling me everything you know?" Yuki laughed as he howled out in pain, but to her surprise, the man managed to fight through it enough to throw a punch with his good arm. Ducking under the swing, she let some of her energy flow into her fist before striking him in the gut, taking care to hit him just hard enough to crack his ribs. "Was that a no?"

"What are you?" Spitting up blood, the assassin's eyes widened with fear an instant before he turned to flee.

"If you run, you'll only die tired."

Yuki let him get back into the alley she pulled him from before dashing after him and shoved him face first into a stone wall. Spinning the assassin around, she grabbed the top of his head and his chin and paused just long enough for him to figure out what she was about to do, before twisting her arms, snapping his neck.

"See." She let his body crumple around her feet and turned to leave when she felt the approach of one of Ryoma's knights. Putting on a welcoming smirk, she turned to face the knight as he stepped toward her. "Evening, Sir Gaius."

Gaius glanced down at the body before looking back to Yuki. "You did this?"

"I did," Yuki replied sensing the approach of more guards.

"Who are you?" Gaius asked, confusion lining his face.

"Let's just call me a concerned citizen."

"I'm sure you are, but you're going to come with me. I have a few questions I need answered." Gaius held his sword at the ready.

"Sorry, you're not my type."

"Sir Gaius," one of the knights shouted from an alley over.

"Over here." Gaius peaked over his shoulder, searching for his men, a distraction Yuki gladly took advantage of and disappeared into the night.

* * *

Music filled the lower level of the Harkon Inn while men and women danced to an odd, but pleasant melody. A small orchestra sat on the far right of the vast room, playing flutes, stringed instruments, bongos, and one instrument Amy could only describe as a crazy looking bagpipe. Sitting at one of the many tables placed over the wooden floor, Amy took another sip of the teal drink in her mug, enjoying the sweet taste and music spinning around her.

After spending hours digging a way out of the museum ruins, Amy was glad that Ikari had found the inn and was willing to pay for a room so they could rest. He had even bought her the colorful dress she now wore since all of their clothes had been covered in dirt and grime. After crashing out on a soft bed, and enjoying a long bath, she had wandered downstairs to get a bite to eat. It wasn't long after ordering her food that a somewhat attractive man had approached her to dance and bought her first drink, but he disappeared after she told him she was waiting for someone.

Peering over the moderately lit room, Amy spotted Ikari walking down the stairs and waved him over with a broad smile. "Over here."

"You seem to be in a good mood." Ikari sat in the chair next to her and glanced at her plate. "You mind?"

"Go ahead." Amy looked around expecting to find Hayate walking over. "Where'sss Hayate, I want to dance."

"Dance?" Ikari looked up at her after taking a bite from her roll. "Hayate's up taking a bath. You want to dance?"

"Yeah sho?" Amy took another swig from her mug. "Cant a girl dance? They have music, and I see people dancing, sho I wanna dance."

Ikari glanced at her with a suspicious eye. "I'd have thought you'd be worried about what you're going to do next."

"I was, but after eating, and drinking whatever this stuff is, I have decided to shimply relax and enjoy the evening. I don't wanna think about how unlikely it ish that I'll ever get back home. I don't wanna worry about being shome dumb goddess everyone sheems to want to depend on. I wanna drink this blue stuff, it's really good, and I wanna dance."

Ikari stared at her for a long moment before leaning over and smelling her mug. "How much of that have you drank?"

"Five, shix, I lost count."

"Well, that's called an Azure-Rez, and you are very, *very* drunk," Ikari laughed, leaning back in his chair.

"I am not," Amy replied indignantly, trying to stand only to find that the floor had started rocking and fell back in her seat. "I think I would know if I were banjaxed. You should know I'm a college girl. I knows how to handle liquor. Besides, I don't taste any alcohol, and I'm not even shlurring. Did I jush shlur?"

"Most people don't notice; it tends to creep up on them. It's a blend of various drinks, but the rez root gives it the teal color and masks the alcohol."

"If Hayate isn't coming down then I'll dance with you. I assume dancing is a skill useful even to spies."

"As flattered as I am to be your second choice, you'll find I'm not much for dancing. I'm sure someone here would like to take up the offer though." Ikari took a strip of meat from her plate while acting hurt by her comment.

"You know, five guysh tried to pick me up while I was eating."

"That dress does show off your..." Ikari paused for a moment, and Amy caught him staring at her chest. "...eyes."

"I'll bet. Can I ask you shomething?" Amy leaned forward, steadying herself with the table and forced the smile from her face. "Why did you agree to help me?"

"Being friends isn't enough?"

"No... I mean yes, but... it's just that with Hayate, I get why he's with me. He wants me to become the Protectorate Goddessh so I can save the realm or whatever I'm supposed to do. King Ryoma helped me because he's almost as chivalrous as Hayate. But you are harder to figure out. There are moments when I feel like you're completely open, and there are times when I feel like you're holding back."

"I live a complicated life." Ikari laughed halfheartedly, mulling some thought over. "I spend most of my time training, or stealing secrets. Not that I'm complaining, mind you. I love fighting and I love the art of information gathering, and I excel at both. I do it because I have to, because no one else in my family can." Ikari finished the roll he was eating and leaned back. "In a way, I'm a little jealous of Hayate. He knows exactly what he wants from life and has found something he can pour his heart and soul into. I'm stuck playing the same part I always have—the one my family chose for me—until the day I find something worth giving myself to. So I become who I need to be to complete my mission, and sometimes that means holding yourself back, even from a girl from another realm."

"Maybe the best way to find whatever it ish you're looking for is to stop holding yourself back from your friends. You know, I think you're lonely. That'sh why you wanted to come along with Hayate and me."

"Is that a guess, or are you saying you can sense whatever feelings I've kept buried?"

"I'm not shure, it's hard to tell right now. I may be a little tanked up at the moment." Amy took a long drink from her mug, finishing the last of the beverage with a smile. "Plus, I think you like me."

"Do I?" Ikari laughed. "Well, you're certainly not dull, but my interest lay elsewhere."

"Oh, I forgot. You and that crazy Alia woman have been flirting pretty heavily," Amy laughed. "I agree, she's cute, a bit off her nutter, but cute."

"Gee thanks," Ikari chuckled sarcastically. "What about you? I'd say you liked me a little."

"Nope, not in the least. Okay, you are kinda cute in a roguish, shcoundrel kinda way, but you're not my type."

"I suppose I'm not. It's hard for a simple guy like me to compete with a knight in less than shining armor."

"You think I like Hayate?"

"It's a little obvious." Ikari smirked. "Granted, I don't think he's noticed."

"You... you think he likes me?"

"For a girl so adept at sensing others feelings, I'm surprised you can't tell something as apparent as that." Ikari paused for a moment nodding toward the stairs. Following his gaze, Amy spotted Hayate and felt her smile broaden. Pushing his chair back, Ikari rose to his feet and smiled at Amy. "I'm sure the two of you will work it out."

"Where are you going?"

"Home, I need to take care of some things."

"What about that book? I haven't finished reading it yet." Amy stood, ignoring the wobble of the floor.

"Keep it. I got what I needed from it. Maybe it'll be of more use to you." Ikari flashed a sly smile as Amy stepped over and hugged him.

"So this is goodbye?"

"Nah, I'll see you around." Turning away from Amy, Ikari whispered something to Hayate as they passed by each other before clapping him on the shoulder. "Ta."

Amy watched for a moment as Ikari disappeared into the crowd before looking over to Hayate. "What did he say?"

"Nothing important." Hayate shook the confused look off his face and smiled at Amy. "Would… would you care to dance?"

* * *

Confusion, disappointment, and exhaustion roamed free through Ryoma as he made his way through the halls. Relieved that the last of his guests had departed, he let out a tired breath, hoping to at least slow the questions swarming around his head, the least of which was who had tried to have him killed.

Adding more mystery to the evening was the body one of the cooks had discovered in the loading bay. A body that none of the noblemen or servants could identify. The only lead they had was the unknown woman who had saved him earlier, but given that three hours had passed since her escape, he had little hope of getting any answers from her. To make matters worse, the attempt on his life had interrupted him before he could convince all of his guests to support him against Danothir.

Turning down another hall, Ryoma spotted Gaius heading toward him and greeted him with a nod. "Judging by the look on your face, I take it my would-be assassin managed to elude you."

"Depends on your definition, sire." Gaius bowed before moving to walk alongside the King. "We did find him…"

"Then why the annoyed face?" Ryoma continued down the hall.

"We found him dead; killed by a handmaiden."

"My mystery savior I suppose? I wondered where she had run off to."

"She escaped?" Gaius looked over to Ryoma, surprise furrowing his brow. "The woman that killed the assassin was different from the one at dinner."

"I see." Ryoma stopped outside of a mahogany door the led to his personal study and noticed the guard standing to the right.

"I am aware of your distaste for these things, but given the evenings events, I thought it wise to post a guard at your study and bed chambers for the night."

"I'd argue about it, but somehow I doubted I'd win."

"It's a knight's duty to protect his King." Gaius smiled. "If everything is in order, majesty, I'd like to continue my search for the two women."

"Do you honestly think you'll find them?"

"No, but I'll feel better trying."

"Goodnight then." Ryoma waved as Gaius headed back down the corridor before opening the door to his study. Stepping inside, he was surprised to find that the room was completely dark except for the moonlight that shinned through the glass ceiling. "Guard, who doused the lights?"

"I don't know, sire. As far as I knew..." the guard started as he stepped into the doorway but Ryoma raised a hand to cut him off, noticing, the woman sitting behind his desk on the right side of the room.

"Never mind, I think I have an idea." Ryoma stepped into the center of the room, certain that the woman at his desk was the one that saved him earlier.

"King Ryoma, we need to talk." The woman shifted her gaze to the doorway. "In private."

The guard drew his sword, moving toward the desk. "On your feet."

"It's alright; we're just going to have a conversation." Ryoma held his arm out, blocking the guard's path.

"But, your majesty," the guard protested.

"Its fine," Ryoma retorted, putting a little force into his voice. "If she was a threat, she would have let me die during dinner. Return to your post, and close the door behind you."

"Yes, your majesty." The guard bowed before stepping out of the room and pulled the door closed.

Returning his attention to the woman, Ryoma stepped over to his desk and turned on the lantern sitting on the corner. "You know, some consider it rude to go breaking into other people's homes. How did you manage to get back in here anyway?"

"Your security is utterly pathetic, Ryoma, at least for someone with E'Lan's skills."

Ryoma spun around, startled to hear a woman's voice coming from behind him, and nearly jumped back as the familiar woman stepped out of the shadows and flashed him a sadistic smile. "Yuki Sanada. Which means the young lady at my desk is one of your Sanyoshu."

"And they say Kings aren't very bright." Yuki stepped passed him and sat on the edge of the desk.

"And how are you involved with this?" Ryoma kept his gaze on Yuki.

"I'm your guardian spirit, sent by the goddess Araia to watch over you."

"I find it more likely that the trickster sent you with all manner of mischief in mind." Ryoma glared at the dangerous woman, wishing he had let the guard stay.

"Is that anyway to talk to the women who saved your life?" Yuki glared at Ryoma, the flames from the lantern giving her eyes a demonic gleam. "I find your lack of gratitude rather disheartening."

"And why did you go to all of this trouble to help me?"

"Because now you owe your life to the Sanada, and we enjoy having favors owed to us." Yuki paused, picking up a letter opener from the desk. "Don't get me wrong. I would love to see you castrated and beheaded while your sad little kingdom burns in the wake of Yun'Harrar. However, it was felt that keeping you alive would be to our benefit, so I was overruled."

"What am I to the Sanada? Your family has never cared about Ithor before."

"You're a thorn digging into Danothir's side and that suits us."

"So I've been spared only to be used as a pawn by the Sanada." Ryoma let out a laugh, trying to figure out what possible motive Yuki and her brothers could have for getting involved with Danothir. "I'm *so* grateful."

"You should be." Yuki shot to her feet and grabbed him by the collar an instant before she swept his legs out from under him and slammed him onto the wooden floor. Suppressing the urge to grunt from pain as his head hit the floor, Ryoma looked up to find Yuki leaning over him, holding the letter opener an inch above his left eye.

"Impressive, most men would be whimpering like babies or calling for help by now, but you seemed to have kept your composure."

Ryoma forced a confident smile onto his face, surprised, and relieved, that he managed to keep his uneasiness from showing. He had, on occasion, dealt with Yuki during meetings of the Consortium, and learned enough to know that she could be like a rabid bloodhound. Any sign of weakness on his part, and he felt certain that she would kill him herself just for the pleasure of it. "Well, you've made it clear that you want me to live. And I don't like to be intimidated."

"Still, you need to realize something. I am not the merciful one in the family. My brother Genki may only kill those that stand in our way, and Ikari avoids killing when he can since he finds it troublesome, but I don't. My brothers won't kill what they can use, but I find I rather enjoy squashing weak little bugs. Actually, I like it a lot. Between you and me, it makes me all warm and tingly inside, but I digress. The point is, you do not want to play with me. You're not up to the challenge." Yuki held her stare for a long moment before tossing the letter opener aside and stood up. "By the way, you're right about Danothir preparing for war, but you've failed to see the bigger picture. It's not just Ithor he's moving against but the Consortium as a whole."

"What?" Ryoma climbed back to his feet with caution.

"He's been slowly positioning his troops all over the region for weeks now. He's also the one who hired the two assassins to kill you. You seemed to have really gotten under his skin." Yuki motioned toward E'Lan, before stepping over to the door. "Just thought you'd like to know. Have fun at the next Consortium meeting."

"What do you expect me to do with that information?" Ryoma turned to watch her as she opened the door. "I can't exactly go to the Consortium with this."

"The information is yours to do with as you please. You're a bit more clever than most men, I'm sure you can find some way to use it." Yuki waved over her shoulder while stepping into the hall and out of sight. "Goodnight, your kingliness."

* * *

Ritsuko stood inside of her study, admiring her reflection in an elegant mirror when the sound the door opening drew her out of her thoughts. Taking one last look at herself, she glanced at the door as Alia and Tres stepped through. "At the risk of ruining an otherwise productive evening, would either of you care to explain why Ikari is still alive with my book?"

"I would have had him if Tres and his band of thugs hadn't proven to be so completely ineffective." Alia shot Tres an annoyed look before dropping down into one of the chairs.

"Don't go penning this on me girl," Tres retorted. "If you had let me kill them instead of playing with them, they'd be dead."

"I told you, Ikari is mine," Alia spat. "I won't allow him to be killed by the likes of you."

"Enough!" Ritsuko looked from Alia to Tres.

"Either way," Alia continued. "We would have at least gotten the worthless rose if not for Borga's men."

Ritsuko looked back to Alia. "What do you mean?"

"We found one of the roses you had me searchin' for, but got ambushed by a gang of soldiers claiming to be from House Borga," Tres answered.

Ritsuko crossed her arms, scowling. "So Danothir is after the roses as well."

"Let me get back to my mission, my original mission. The one that didn't involve babysitting your brat of a daughter and those mystical freaks you conjured." Tres stepped closer to Ritsuko. "I'll find you your magic trinkets then take back the rose that got took."

Ritsuko stepped behind her desk and pulled her chair out. "I've already located the next rose and you are ill-equipped to retrieve it, so I'll be sending Gaou along with you."

"That dim brained freak couldn't handle wiping shit from his ass on his own." Tres walked over and stood next to Alia.

"Stop talking." Ritsuko let her growing annoyance creep into her voice. "I have something far more important for you to do before you leave. I'm putting you and Thade in charge of the army I've gathered. I need you to begin preparation for war."

"What about that book Sanada stole?" Tres inquired.

"I don't need it to complete *this* stage of my plans, although it would have made things far easier. For now, it will have to wait." Ritsuko sat down in her chair and waved at the door. "Now get out."

"As you command." Tres turned, pausing long enough to glare at Alia before exiting the room.

"Now Alia," Ritsuko looked to her daughter. "Why did you countermand my orders to kill Ikari?"

"Isn't it obvious mother?" Alia leaned back in her chair, gazing out the window. "Because I intend to marry him."

"You what?" Ritsuko felt her face flash red as anger rushed through her.

"You told me I had to marry the winner of that asinine tournament of yours, and he was obviously the winner."

"If this is some game…"

"It no game, mother," Alia interrupted. "You are always going on about how we have some great destiny given to us by the gods. It was you that taught me that only the strongest, smartest, most worthy man is fit to marry a daughter of House Inara, and you were right. The gods led Ikari to me and I have gladly claimed him as my own."

"Ikari Sanada has made it his life's mission to get in my way." Ritsuko leaned forward, trying to force herself to calm down. "What bizarre fate could possibly lead you to choose him?"

"I find him interesting. He has a mind so similar to my own, it's as if Tai Re'l herself made him for me. Angering you is simply a charming hobby of his. There is no one more worthy of my love than Ikari Sanada." Alia smiled.

"And you really think that man could ever love you?"

Alia narrowed her eyes. "I will *make* him love me."

"You know I will never allow this." Ritsuko laughed, too furious and surprised to do anything else.

"I don't see how you have a choice," Alia replied in a calm tone Ritsuko had heard often when she was growing up. It was the boastful, unconcerned manner she spoke with when she knew she was going to get what she wanted. "Not if you want to finish the army you planned to use when you ascend or whatever it is you call it."

"What do you mean?"

"I mean the bracelet Ikari stole from you. The one you need to fully enhance your mystical army. Without it you can only give them a fourth of the power you intended and hope you can still maintain control over them."

"That power stems from a source thousands of years old." Ritsuko eyed her daughter carefully, wondering what she was getting at. "A fourth should be enough to defeat my enemies."

"But not enough to *slaughter* them. It's really too bad you can't get all of that power." Alia paused for a moment, playing with one of her bracelets. "What if I could get it for you?"

"How?" Ritsuko asked, disbelieving what she had just heard. "You're no sorceress."

"Just because I've never been interested in following your footsteps, doesn't mean I haven't been paying attention. I've picked up many skills you failed to notice. I know exactly what was in that book Ikari took and what we need to access every bit of power you planed on." Alia's smile widened as she leaned forward on the desk. "I will help destroy your enemies and ascend to the heavens, but in return, Ikari Sanada is mine to do with as I please."

Ritsuko leaned back in her chair, swallowing a lump of anger while her rage shifted to pride. She had begun to think her daughter was too weak to take her place as head of their House, but now she saw that there was more to her whining and bratty attitude than she had thought. Alia was proving to be a calculating, manipulative, uncompromising woman she could proudly call her daughter. "It looks as if I have no choice."

Chapter Twenty-One

Light from the morning sun filtered through the tinted windows of the Sanada estate. Making his way through the familiar halls, Ikari spotted Saskai waiting for him and waved. "Morning."

"Lord Ikari." Saskai bowed before walking alongside Ikari. "I apologize for not returning sooner, but Lord Genki instructed me to lead the investigation."

"Investigation?" Ikari glanced at Saskai. Since returning to Austuria late last night, Ikari had opted to go straight to bed rather than hear Saskai's report of the last few days. One of two decisions made in the last couple of days that he now wished he could change.

"One of the maids was found murdered. Lord Genki will explain, he's asked to see you and Lady Yuki."

"Yuki's back?"

"She returned a few hours after you did."

Turning down a narrower hall, Ikari and Saskai stepped through a sliding door and onto a small bridge that overlooked one of the gardens. Cutting across the training room, they stepped back into the corridors when Ikari felt his sisters approach and let a mocking grin decorate his face. "So, how was Ithor?"

"Thank you so much for sending me to such a dismal little land." Yuki stepped into the main hall, followed by E'Lan. "After playing dress up for Ryoma and his plump, idiotic noblemen, we were denied the simple pleasure of hearing the assassin's screams."

"So he got away?" Ikari paused as they reached the archway to the throne chamber.

"No, he's dead. He just died far too quickly for all the trouble E'Lan and I went through." Yuki returned his mocking grin before stepping through the archway. "I should have you flayed for that."

"If it makes you feel any better, I was buried alive in an old museum," Ikari laughed, stepping over to Genki, who was holding a white flower.

"It doesn't." Yuki sat down in her chair.

"This was waiting for you." Genki handed Ikari the flower, which he now recognized as a jasmine, and a folded piece of paper. "I was hoping you could explain, although the note doesn't say who it's from."

"I can guess." Ikari opened the paper and read it aloud. "See you there."

"Ikari, have you been keeping secrets from me?" Yuki raised an eyebrow, snatching the note and flower from his hand. "A woman's handwriting? I don't recall meeting anyone good enough to court you."

"Rest assured dear sister, when I do meet someone, I'll be sure hide her from you to spare me your meddling." Ikari glanced at the flower, wondering how Alia could have known he would be here to receive her message. "That's just a reminder of a reoccurring pain."

"It sounds as though you two had an interesting journey." Genki smiled at his younger siblings while E'Lan and Saskai stood to the right of the three chairs. "And what happened in Ithor?"

"Don't worry about it." Yuki leaned to the side and kicked her legs over the armrest. "That pathetic little King owes us a favor. Two, if you add in the fact that I didn't kill him myself. So brother, what is it you wanted to see us about?"

"We've had a theft that has me concerned." Genki stepped over to the glass wall and stared at the morning sky.

"I assume this has something to do with the dead maid Saskai mentioned?" Ikari asked, wondering what he had missed while helping Amy.

"Yes, we believe so," Genki replied. "From what he's been able to piece together, the maid was hired by someone pretending to be a statesman and stole a particular item from us before getting killed."

"Serves her right," Yuki stated in a bored tone. "What was taken? I assume it's something more valuable than money."

Genki nodded. "She took the box containing the crystal rose you acquired and the scroll Ikari took from the shipment heading to Nel'Oskow."

"Any idea of who hired her?" Yuki asked.

"I can guess." Ikari crossed his arms, looking from Yuki to Genki. "Smart money says it was Danothir. He's the only one who knew we had the scroll and the rose."

Genki turned away from the window, scowling. "He risked an awful lot to steal a mythological rose. Why now?"

"Assuming the stories about it *are* a myth," Ikari replied, surprised that he had even considered that there might be some truth to the legends about the roses. "Either way, Danothir seems to think they're not. We know he's planning to overthrow the Consortium, but even he isn't stupid enough to think his army would be enough to defeat T'Chello or the combined forces of the other Houses. In his mind, he needs to get all three roses and usurp the war god's army if he wants to win."

"I don't suppose you picked up some magical trick to stop him?" Genki inquired.

"What about that book you took from Inara?" Yuki peered over to Ikari. "Maybe we can use something from there."

"Sorry, I forgot it back in Remus." Ikari shrugged, wondering how Amy was doing on her search. "There was nothing useful to us anyway."

"You forgot it?" Yuki stared at Ikari for a long moment, the look in her eye making it clear that she didn't believe a word he had said. "How uncharacteristic of you."

"Do you think it's actually possible for him succeed, that the legend of the Protectorate Goddess is true?" Genki turned to look at Ikari.

"You mean do I think Amy is the Protectorate Goddess?" Ikari asked, thinking about his time with her.

"Of course she's not." Yuki waved a dismissive hand. "She's just some brat that we probably should have killed to end this annoying debate."

"She's just trying to go home," Ikari stated, reminding himself of what he already knew. "And we don't need to kill her."

"It would make things far simpler." Yuki sat up in her chair. "Or are you starting to care about what happens to her?"

"No..." Ikari looked back to Yuki and forced his voice to return to its usual cocky tone. "Not at all. I just think she still has her uses."

"How so?" Genki stepped back over to his chair.

"Danothir still needs her to gain control of Sha'kring's army, and Ritsuko needs her to steal her power and ascend. So long as we keep track of Amy, we can anticipate everyone's moves."

"But for how long?" Yuki leaned back. "Danothir has one rose already, and according to my spies, he's already positioned his forces to attack Hapes Island."

Ikari let out a disappointed chuckle and sat in his own chair. "Actually, he has two roses. While I was in Remus, Hayate, Amy, and I managed to find the second one but we got ambushed by a squad of Danothir's men."

"It seems things are progressing faster than we thought." Genki paused, pacing in front of the twins for a moment. "Our window to take advantage of the situation is slipping by us."

"Not necessarily," Yuki shook her head. "Ikari is right about Amy being useful, for the moment anyway. Since Danothir is so bent on fighting the Consortium, why not let him? T'Chello and the other

House's either kill him, or he'll weaken himself fighting for a costly victory. Either way, we should let them kill each other and then slip into the winner's bed chambers and slit their throats as thanks."

"We need to see how close everyone is to going to war, before deciding anything," Genki stated. "Still, not a bad idea."

"So how do we pick the brains of the Consortium?" Yuki asked, playing with the flower still in her hand.

Ikari let a grin return to his face as he stood and turned to Genki. "That should be easy enough. Every major player in our little game will be at the Chancellor's ball. It's the perfect place to feel out what's in their heads."

"But you hate those parties slightly less than I do. Why go now?" Yuki glared at Ikari.

"Because this one might prove interesting." Ikari smiled and plucked to flower from her hand.

"Forgive my interruption," Saskai said. "But, is it wise for you to go alone, considering Ritsuko's desire to kill you?"

"I'll be fine," Ikari replied. "Given all the security that the Chancellor puts in place and T'Chello's zero tolerance of violence, the party is probably the safest place in the realm."

Yuki hopped up off her chair and took back the flower. "I agree with Saskai. You really can't go to a party like that alone."

"Why not?" Ikari arched an eyebrow, wondering what Yuki was getting at. "Genki was going to go alone."

"Actually, I was planning on taking the Duchess of Chulan," Genki responded.

"Oh." Ikari and Yuki both rolled their eyes.

"What?"

"Nothing." Ikari shook his head while glancing at Yuki. "She has a wonderful... a... a wonderful personality."

"Betrice is an exquisite woman," Genki retorted.

"Sure, for a shallow, transparent, amateur manipulator." Yuki shrugged.

"And she's kinda dull," Ikari added.

"And spoiled," Yuki pointed out.

"And not that bright, really."

"Definitely inept."

"And she never shuts up."

"And talk about piss poor taste in clothes."

"Alright." Genki waved his hands. "I get it, you don't like her."

"Not really," Yuki and Ikari replied in unison.

"Wait a minute." Ikari let his grin fade and turned toward Yuki. "How come whenever I see a woman you don't like, you never stop meddling, or trying to fix me up with someone you picked out, or trying to kill her? Why don't you ever pester him?"

"Because as much as I dislike the duchess, she suites Genki well enough."

"Thank you... I guess." Genki stared at Yuki for a moment, unsure of what to say.

"Besides, it's a sister's right to help her brother find a worthy woman." Yuki tossed the rose to E'Lan. "I would expect the same from you."

"Except the last man that came to call on you ended up splattered all over the floor," Ikari retorted, recalling the scene.

"And the walls." Genki smirked.

"And the rafters," Ikari added. "Not sure how you actually managed that though."

Yuki shot to her feet, glaring at her brothers. "Don't swing this to be about me. You're one who's not going alone."

"And who exactly should I take?" Ikari asked, curious about what the answer would be.

"Isn't it obvious?" Yuki flashed an amused grin and sauntered around Saskai and E'Lan before pushing her forward. "You should take E'Lan."

"E'Lan?" Ikari repeated, unable to hold back his laughter.

"Yes, E'Lan. She's actually a wonderful dancer, and more than capable of watching your backside... incase anything should happen." Yuki shifted her eyes to E'Lan. "Plus I'm sure she'd love to go. Wouldn't you, E'Lan?"

"Um... if... if that is what you wish, my Lady." E'Lan bowed, trying to hide her reddening face.

"It is." Yuki smiled before looking back to Ikari. "Of course, since I'm lending you E'Lan, it's only fair I take Saskai for a while. So long as he doesn't do that creepy pop out of nowhere thing."

"Don't worry about it. I'm sure he'll stop." Ikari turned to face Saskai, mouthing for him to keep doing it.

"I heard that." Yuki punched Ikari on the arm.

"I guess that's settled." Genki clapped Ikari on the shoulder before starting toward the archway. "We should leave within the hour if we want to make it to Jadzia in time for the ball."

"It's your lucky day, E'Lan." Yuki stepped over to E'Lan, her smile growing while E'Lan's face turned into a dark shade of red.

"Looks like my brother is finally going to want to get you out of your clothes… and into a formal dress."

"Please don't tease." E'Lan followed Yuki out of the chamber.

* * *

"So we're riding through the swamp, not that we were lost." Gaius stated in a less than convincing voice while placing a stack of books on a corner of the hexagonal table Amy was sitting at. "I was fairly certain I knew which way to go."

"I'm sure you did." Tuning out his story, Amy looked from the large, worn tome sitting in front of her to the book Ikari had left her.

She had spent most her time since returning to Ithor reading everything she could find relating to travel between the realms. Set up in the castle archive hall, which had a high, elaborately painted cathedral ceiling, she was surprised to find such an extensive collection. Of course, given the importance the people of this world place on mythology and magic, it shouldn't be too surprising to find plenty of material on their lore. The only problem was, she had little interest in their religions or history. Her only concern now was trying to find a clue that could give her what she wanted.

Amy let out a long breath and pushed the large book aside before reaching for another, one of many that she had covering the polished wooden table. Reading a passage about a distant country described as the land veiled by the gods and a man's search for it, a nagging voice in the back of her mind kept pulling at her as if she'd read about the story before.

Turning the page, she noticed a pause in Gaius's story and nodded. "Oh yeah?"

"Yes, and that's when we were attacked by slobbering stuffed flowers and a horde of purple, one winged birds."

"That's good," Amy replied, trying to remember why the story sounded so familiar.

"And you're not paying attention, are you?" Gaius stepped over to her side and picked up the book she was reading. "I'm not boring you, am I? That would sting my ego far deeper than any blade."

"I was paying attention. You said something about slobbering flower birds…" Amy reached for the book but Gaius pulled it away. "Wait, did you say slobbering flower birds?"

"You have been buried under these books since you returned and I feel it is my duty as a knight to rescue you from such tedium. Why don't we enjoy the morning with some fresh pastries in town? We can explore the fields under the afternoon sun, and then see the traveling performers show under the evening's starry sky."

"As fun as that sounds…" Amy again reached for the book only to have pulled away again. "…I need to get back to work."

"A beautiful girl like you shouldn't spend her days buried in books. What are you reading anyway? Hayate said that you didn't have any clues about the next rose's location." Gaius scanned the page before letting out a laugh and closed the book. "The tale of Lord Arulius?"

"Why does that name sound so blooming familiar?"

"It's a widely known story." Gaius laughed and leaned against the table. "He wasted his life searching for the land veiled by the gods, which of course doesn't exist, until he died a bitter old man."

"That's right." Amy felt her head snap up and shifted through the pile of books, searching for one she had read earlier. "The stories say he had a key that could open the path to… to…"

"The key of Arulian would reveal the land of Gaia." Gaius rolled his eyes. "What utter nonsense. Every child knows the place is nonexistent."

"It's not." Amy grabbed the book Ikari had left, remembering a passage she had read in Remus. "Thousands of years ago Gaia was another name for Earth."

"Don't tell me you actually believe the story? It's a myth. A tale to warn against obsession."

"And a month ago, I would have said the same thing." Amy glanced up at Gaius. "But here I am, on another world, in a castle ripped from the stories of Camelot, where magic and gods are believed to be real."

"I see your point, but…"

"I read a passage a while ago about this story, but I never did learn where the key was supposed to be." Finding the page she was looking for, Amy stood to show Gaius. "It says the key was left with Arulius in his final resting place, wherever that is."

"Some claim it was in the hills of Khampf."

"I know that name." Amy felt a sense of excitement building as she flipped through the book again and found a picture of a faded map. "You're a genius."

"Yes, I know… but what did I say?"

"I know where I have to go thanks to you." Amy closed the book and hugged Gaius, unable to restrain her exhilaration. "I could kiss you."

"Feel free." Gaius smiled and leaned forward, but Amy turned away and started toward the oval doorway.

"Where's Hayate? I have to tell him."

"He should still be in the terrace with the King." Gaius spun toward her. "About that kiss?"

"Thanks." Heart pounding with excitement, Amy sprinted out of the chamber. Apologizing to anyone she bumped into as she hurried through the corridors, Amy let thoughts of her family drift into her mind, hopeful for the first time that she might be able to see them again.

Finding Hayate and Ryoma talking on the southern terrace, Amy slid to a stop in front of them and tried to force enough air back into her lungs to talk. "Sorry to interrupt, but I have something to tell you."

"Is everything alright?" Ryoma asked.

"Smashing." Amy stood straight, finally catching her breath. "I found something."

"A clue about the second rose?" Hayate stepped over to her side.

"No, something better. I might have found a way to get back home."

"What... really?" Hayate's face flashed a moment of disappointment before morphing to confusion. "How?"

"The answer was right in front of me in that book of Ikari's, I just couldn't figure it out until Gaius mentioned Khampf." Amy flipped open the book. "According to the text I've been reading, the key to get me home is in Alextien."

"Alextien?" Hayate and Ryoma repeated in unison.

Amy nodded. "Yeah. I figured we could check it out..."

"We shouldn't." Hayate shook his head. "Alextien is too dangerous."

"If it gets me home, than I'm willing to risk it."

Hayate again shook his head. "No. I won't let you let risk your life for something that might not be real. I'm sure we can find another way."

"But I can risk my life helping you find some bloody rose? I helped you search for those stupid roses despite the fact that I never wanted to and have abso-bloody-lutely no intention of fulfilling whatever legend you all think I am." Amy let her growing anger creep into her voice. "I thought you'd be happy for me. I may have finally found the one thing that I've actually wanted since I fell out of that casket, and now you don't want to help me?"

"Of course I want to see you happy. I'd do just about anything for you," Hayate retorted equally impassioned. "But I don't want... I don't want to..."

Clearing his throat, Ryoma stepped over and put a calming hand on each of their shoulders. "If you two calm down for moment, I think you'll both agree that you're letting your emotions get the better of you." Pausing for a second, Ryoma looked at Hayate. "I can see how much you care for Amy, but if going home is what she wants, then we are honor bound to assist her in whatever way we can."

Hayate let out a long sigh before nodding in agreement and looked back at Amy. "You're right. I swore I'd help you no matter what."

Ryoma shifted his gaze to her. "But, Amy, I don't think you realize what and where Alextien is."

"It's some town Ikari trained in isn't it?" Amy looked away from Hayate, feeling a wave of dejection washing off of him.

"It's not a town, it's another realm." Hayate stepped over to the stone railing and stared down at the garden.

"One known for attracting the must unsavory sort of men and women from any of the other realms," Ryoma added. "Even the hardened villains of this world get swallowed and devoured by the beasts that dwell in that pit. Legend says that Yun'Harrar, drunk on blood and wine, laid siege to the realm for forty years."

"Why?" Amy glanced from Hayate to Ryoma, surprised by the unease they both radiated.

"Because he could," Ryoma answered with a humorless laugh.

"Look, if Alextien is that dangerous then I won't ask you to come with me," Amy stated solemnly. "But it's probably my best chance to get back to my own realm."

"I won't let you go alone." Hayate turned to face her. "I'll stand by your side no matter where that leads us."

"For the record, I'm against you going." Ryoma held up a hand to cut off any rebuke before Amy or Hayate could speak. "But since I'd simply fail to talk you out of this, there is little I can do. However, Alextien is too dangerous a place for you two to travel alone. You'll need a guide, someone who knows the realm and the terrain."

"Ikari does, doesn't he?" Amy felt her sense of hope returning, albeit diminished. "I'm sure he'd help."

"I doubt that," Hayate scoffed. "Not unless there's something in it for him."

"He's not the evil mastermind everyone thinks he is. Well, he's not as bad as everyone thinks he is." Amy glanced at the book in her hand as Ikari's last words to her rang in her ears. "He'll help."

"I can find out tomorrow night." Ryoma flashed Amy a reassuring smile. "I'm sure at least one of the Sanada will be at the Chancellor's ball. I'll ask on your behalf."

* * *

Twin moons floated over the star lit backdrop of the night sky covering the small city of Jadzia. Located just west of Hapes Island, the diminutive city was pleasant, although lacking in the extravagance that characterized other cities run by the Consortium. The only reason anyone bothered to learn the name of the city was the fact that Chancellor Malik Shen was born there and that the city was host to the yearly ball thrown in the Chancellor's honor.

Walking with E'Lan on his arm and his brother a few steps ahead, talking with the Duchess about the cathedral's decor, Ikari took note of the buildings layout, marking the position of each sentry they passed out of habit.

"Security is tighter than I imagined." E'Lan took in their surroundings as they followed a portly man in green down a long, well decorated, hall.

"T'Chello is different than most of the overstuffed generals in command of vast armies." Ikari smirked, picking up the hum of the multiple conversations reverberating out of the large room up ahead. "He's actually competent."

"I hate these formal parties," E'Lan grumbled while smoothing out her long red dress. "These clothes are so impractical. How is anyone expected to fight in something like this? I do not understand why Lady Yuki insisted I wear this."

"I don't think fighting was what Yuki had in mind." Genki flashed a grin at Ikari while adjusting his jacket. Both he and Ikari wore a formal red and black suit with gold trim, a traditional ensemble worn by the Sanada family.

"You look fabulous darling," Betrice stated. "It's about time I saw dear Ikari with a girl. I was…"

"One moment my Lords and Ladies." The man escorting them to the party chamber held up a gloved hand. Stepping over to a small set of stairs, the man rang the small bell placed on a pedestal. "Introducing Lord Genki Sanada accompanied by the Duchess of Chulan, and Lord Ikari Sanada and his escort, E'Lan Barda."

A sense of amusement fell over Ikari as the chamber quieted for a moment and everyone glanced at the newcomers before resuming their conversations. "You'd think they'd never seen me at party before."

"They probably haven't," Genki laughed. "You do tend to spend most of your time fighting or sneaking about. Since you already have everyone's attention, I'll leave you to enjoy the party while I get what we need."

"How very kind of you." Ikari watched as Genki and Betrice walked down the stairs and disappeared into the crowd. "Shall we?"

"As you wish my Lord." E'Lan took his arm as they descended into the bustling party.

Paintings lined the bronze and gold walls of the chamber, each lit by a small triangular glowstone. Larger luminescent stones mounted on the walls or hanging from chains attached to marble pillars, cast the chamber in a warm light while soft music played by an orchestra filled the room. Tables with delicious smelling food were set up near the back and side walls, and servants worked their way through the crowd, carrying trays of snacks and drinks.

Greeting a few of the other guests as he passed by them, Ikari spotted the Chancellor talking with Ritsuko. Taking a pastry from a passing waiter, Ikari looked over to E'Lan. "Why don't you see if you if can't wrangle a little information out of the other guests. I'm going to go be distracting for a while."

"I am afraid I'm not very good in these sorts of situations. I wouldn't know where to start." E'Lan glanced away from Ikari, eyeing the crowd. "Also, Lady Yuki instructed me not to let you out of my sight. Actually, she instructed me to remain on your arm for the duration of the evening, but I am reasonably certain that she meant it in jest."

"I'm sure." Ikari smirked, wondering what other meddlesome orders Yuki might have instructed E'Lan to follow. "Don't worry, you'll do fine. A beautiful woman like you should have no problem getting into a conversation." Backing away from E'Lan, Ikari stepped over to the Chancellor and Ritsuko with a wide smile. "Chancellor, how nice to see you again."

"Ikari, it's been too long." The Chancellor returned his smile and shook his forearm. "I trust you're enjoying yourself."

"Your hospitality is awe-inspiring." Ikari held up his pastry. "As is your taste in food."

The Chancellor pointed to a small table a few yards away. "You should try those little cakes imported from Osaka Major."

"I do intend to try something from Osaka." Ikari turned his smile to Ritsuko. "Lady Inara, you're looking quite lovely, despite your years."

Ritsuko forced a pleasant smile to her face as her gaze shifted from the Chancellor to him. "Lord Sanada, it's nice to see that the burden of maturity hasn't weighed you down any."

"You'll have to excuse me." The Chancellor nodded to Ikari and Ritsuko. "I should probably mingle a bit more."

"I understand," Ikari replied.

"May your reign continue to bring posterity." Ritsuko lifted her glass as the Chancellor left.

"So, Ritsuko, I heard you had a little tournament a while back. How'd that work out?"

"Fine, until an irritating pest fouled things up." Ritsuko let her disingenuous smile fade into a look of contempt. "What do you want, or did you travel to Jadzia just to pester me?"

"Not *just*." Ikari took a bite from his pastry. "I heard there'd be snacks. Oh, and I want to know what you did to Thade and those two goons you sent after me."

"You're not concerned are you?" Ritsuko laughed. "The great Ikari Sanada worried about a washed up General and a fool for a subordinate."

"Despite my often jovial attitude, I actually had some respect for Thade. Whatever you did to him isn't natural, and anything that lets him increase his power that much and that fast is going to have a large string attached."

"I gave Thade exactly what he wanted. And with that gift, he is going to drag your bloodied, jovial, body to my feet so I can dig my nails through your chest and feel your heart burst in my hand."

"Nice to know I've been on your mind."

"You have. I had a special set of jewelry enchanted just for you." Ritsuko smiled, this time with genuine delight and malice. "The thought of killing you makes me absolutely giddy."

"I'm flattered really, but I'm not into older women." Ikari let his smile fade and glared at Ritsuko. "Especially one stupid enough to think she has a chance to best me or believes for one second that I would allow her to gain the power of a goddess. You should know by now that the divine right to rule belongs to the Sanada. Everyone else gets crushed beneath my heel."

"I'm glad to hear it," a familiar voice stated from behind Ikari, carrying the all too familiar scent of jasmine.

"Alia." Ikari turned to face the younger Inara, who wore an elegant, and flattering, black dress.

"Now that you're here, let's dance." Alia grabbed Ikari's hand and pulled him toward the orchestra, but paused long enough to shoot Ritsuko an irritated look. "Mother."

"Enjoy the party Ikari." Ritsuko smiled again, but her eyes held the same dangerous look. "We'll just have to wait and see who the gods favor in the race to rule."

* * *

"General T'Chello." Ryoma lifted his expensive glass of Calodian ale, smiling as he approached the well-dressed General. "My compliments on another well planned banquet."

"Thank the regional governor and her aids, they planned the whole thing." T'Chello nodded. "I merely followed orders and stayed out of their way."

"Still, this one could prove superior to last years." Ryoma laughed. "If you have a moment, there are a few things I'd like discuss with you."

"Splendid party, General." Genki Sanada stepped passed Ryoma with a woman on his arm. "You do the Chancellor proud."

"Thank you," T'Chello replied with a stiff nod. "But if you'll excuse me, I'm told the cakes are too good to be passed up."

"Oh?" Genki's date Smiled as she followed after T'Chello. "Then I must have one."

"Hurry back darling." Genki smiled, watching her leave, before turning back to Ryoma. "So, how are things in Ithor?"

"Well enough, but I'm sure you already know exactly what's happening in my court."

Genki feigned concern. "You sound vexed."

"And you know why." Ryoma let the false pleasantries fade from his voice. "As grateful as I am for your sister's help, I don't appreciate your family using my kingdom to play your games."

"I heard Yuki paid Ithor a visit," Genki laughed while grabbing a glass from a passing waiter. "But whatever games she plays in her free time are not of my making, nor are they my concern."

"It seems rather clear to me that you and your siblings share in my desire to see Danothir's plans put to an abrupt end. Or has your fledgling support of my arguments been a coincidence?"

"Is it so hard for you to believe I've been swayed by your argument?"

"Yes," Ryoma replied plainly. "If you are just playing the political angles, Ikari wouldn't be involved and he wouldn't have helped Amy Price. And we both know how your sister feels about politics. You want Danothir stopped just as I do, so why not openly stand against him? You, or Yuki, obviously have more information than I do."

"What I do, I do for the name of the Sanada. If not standing against Danothir benefits me, then that is exactly what I'll do. House Borga will be swept aside when I deem it advantageous." Genki glared at Ryoma.

Ryoma let out a breath. "If you won't stand with me, perhaps you'd consider helping in a smaller capacity?"

"That being?"

"Amy believes she might have found a way to return to her realm thanks to the book your brother gave her."

"He gave her?" Genki repeated with a surprised look. "What does this have to do with me?"

"Not you. The key to getting Amy home may be in Alextien." Ryoma took a sip of his drink. "Given Ikari's familiarity with that realm, I hopped he might be willing to guide them."

Genki glanced to the side, thinking over the request when the orchestra began to play a waltz. "As simple of a request as that is, Ryoma, I'm going to have to refuse. That girl you're helping is too valuable to let her disappear into whatever unknown realm she appeared from. She still has a part to play."

"You mean helping her isn't to your benefit? She is not some token on a board to be played and discarded." Ryoma let his growing anger creep into his voice. "If you have no intentions of helping at all, why have Yuki warn me about Danothir's movements? Why have Ikari help Amy and Hayate find the rose?"

"As I said, my sibling's games are their own." Genki's pleasant smile returned as the Duchess returned with a small plate. "We'll have to talk again, perhaps at the next meeting of the Consortium."

"Of course." Ryoma nodded, swallowing his frustration. "Until then."

* * *

"I hope you are as skilled on your feet while dancing as you are when fighting." Alia extended a gloved hand as the orchestra began to play an ancient waltz.

Ikari smiled, taking her hand and pulled her close as each started to move along with the music. "I'm curious, how do you keep finding me?"

Alia smiled, locking her gaze onto his eyes. "I'm sure you've noticed the scent of a room when I'm around."

"Jasmine?"

"That's more than just perfume. I told you I'm just as skilled in magic as my mother, but I have a particular fondness for potions, and poisons. Did you know that some plants and insects attract potential mates through scent?"

"Through the use of pheromones. Nifty skill, one people don't share. And as near as I can see, or feel, you're not a talking flower sprouting pedals." Ikari twisted Alia around before letting her pull him into her. "Or are you hiding another set of legs under that dress of yours?"

"Have you been using this dance as an excuse to feel my body?"

"Merely returning the favor."

Alia smirked. "I found a way to replicate the process in myself. I find it makes dealing with people easier, especially the simplistic cave dwellers my mother wants me to marry."

"So I'm under your thrall?" Ikari stared into her eyes, already knowing the answer.

"I dosed you the moment you walked into mother's study in the arena." Alia ran her fingers along his face. "Most men would be drooling lumps of mush by now, but not you. I'm sure you might have felt the effects for a short time, but you proved to be immune. Whether it's because of your training or the will of the gods is irrelevant at this point. It's just another sign that you and I are destined to be together."

"You are an interesting girl, but that doesn't answer my original question."

"Isn't it obvious? You're immune to my glamour but the pheromones inside of you are a mystical part of me." Alia stepped around Ikari with a seductive smile, dragging her hand across his chest. "I'll always know where to find you."

"What makes you so sure I'll marry you?"

"Because Tai Re'l has told me you will." Alia swung back in front of Ikari, drawing a smile from him. "And the fact that you will never meet anyone more suited for you. Not to mention how much mother hates that I've chosen you."

"That last bit always tempts me," Ikari laughed, surprised to find himself enjoying the moment. "But I prefer to travel down my own path. Not one laid out for me, even if it is by the gods."

"And that is exactly why I love you."

"You're just going to have to except that I'm not the marrying type." Ikari slid his hands back around her hips with a flirtatious grin as the orchestra neared the end of the song. "Plus there's no telling what Yuki would do if she found out about you."

"You'll be mine, 'cause you already are." Alia wrapped her arms around Ikari's neck and pressed her lips onto his. Forgetting about the crowd around him and the fact that the song had now ended, Ikari closed his eyes, returning her embrace. After a long moment, Alia pulled away from him and flashed him her familiar smile before stepping past him. "If you happen to end up in Alextien, do try not to die before we meet again. Ta-ta"

"See you around." Ikari smiled, watching her walk away. *Well, this wasn't part of my plan.* Stepping back into the crowd, he began to search for E'Lan when Alia's last words popped back into his mind. *Alextien?*

* * *

Festive music from a few isles over radiated over the grass field the traveling festival was set up in. A gentle breeze blew over the field, carrying the sound of laughter as well as the scent of roasting candies and treats. Children of varying ages ran up and down the aisles, playing with newly won prizes from one of the booths or shouting for their parents to hurry to the next game. Lanterns hanging from decorated posts gave the bluish-green grass an almost magical glow, while light from the twin moons shined clear and bright.

Strolling down a wide aisle, and ignoring the encouraging shouts to try their hand at winning another prize, Amy held up the large stuffed creature Hayate had won for her and smiled.

"I stand corrected and in awe of your prize winning abilities." Raising an eyebrow at the six-limbed creature, she couldn't help but think it was the mutant offspring of a lion and a wild boar. "What is it?"

"It's a cathla," Hayate replied.

"Yes, I had one of those but the wheels fell off." Amy glanced back at Hayate to find him staring at her with a confused look. "Sorry, where I'm from that's a sarcastic reply that means I have no idea what you're talking about."

"I sometimes forget you're from another realm." Hayate smiled.

"I see. So would you rather I was like the women from Ithor?" Amy lowered the stuffed animal and glanced at a woman dressed in a long flowing gown and another knight she hadn't met. "Some fair maiden groomed to be a princess, acting all dainty and proper."

"Honestly, the women here are a bit pretentious. I'd much rather spend my time with you. You're strange, but you're fun."

Amy looked away for a moment, trying to hide her satisfied smile, before looking back toward him and giving him a playful shove. "What do you mean strange?"

"Not strange, I meant different... unique." Hayate turned down another aisle, and almost tripped over a running child. "It's... it's just that I've never met anyone like you before. You're fun, you're smart, prettier than most women in the court, I'm just glad I met you, and you're playing with me again aren't you?"

"A little." Amy laughed, nudging him with her shoulder. Walking close enough for their arms to brush against each other, they started toward the edge of the festival. "Good answer though."

"What about you? I'm sure Gaius has asked to accompany you to the festival, and you two seem to get along. Would you rather he came along with you? Or Ikari?"

"Gaius can keep asking all he wants, and Ikari and I are just friends. There's no one else I'd rather be with besides you." Amy glanced at Hayate and found him smiling at her. A warm sense of contentment swirled around her as they reached the edge of the festival. For the first time, Amy felt happy to have been brought to Hayate's realm despite her desire to return home. "Where are we going anyway?"

"Over there." Hayate pointed to a small grassy hill a few yards ahead. "I figured it would be the best place to watch."

"Watch what?"

"The festival travels through Ithor every year." Hayate led her to the top of the hill and motioned toward an open field behind the festival as he sat down. "They're particularly known for their..."

A thunderous blast from overhead drowned out Hayate's last words, causing Amy to turn and find an explosion of color lighting the night sky. Bursts of red and blue flared brightly, only to fade an instant before silver and gold swirls took their place.

"...fireworks."

"Wow." Amy curled up beside Hayate, forgetting about her fear of never getting home and the machinations of those that sought to use or kill her, and let herself enjoy the moment. Taking Hayate's hand as they pointed out favorite designs made from the fireworks, Amy leaned her head on his shoulder, enjoying the warmth from his body. "Thanks for this."

Chapter Twenty-Two

"One of these days, your majesty, I'm going to have to attend one of those balls. An elegant affair such as that seems incomplete without my glorious presence," Gaius stated, nodding at Hayate and Amy as they entered the King's study.

"Majesty, Gaius." Hayate greeted both of them, sneaking a glance at Amy's smile as she did the same.

"Well, don't you two look happy." Gaius stepped over to the small window and leaned against the paneled wall. "Of course, I would be too if I'd had the honor escorting Amy to the festival. I'm deeply wounded by not receiving an invitation."

"I'm sure you'll recover." Hayate patted Gaius on the back.

Amy stepped in front of the small desk Ryoma sat behind. "How did it go with Ikari? Is he going to meet us?"

"I'm sorry Amy," Ryoma replied. "I spoke with Genki about assisting us, but he was adamant in his refusal. It's unlikely that they will help again."

"Typical of the Sanada." Gaius shrugged. "They never do anything unless it's to their benefit."

"I'm sure Ikari will help me." Amy shook her head. "Maybe if I asked him myself?"

Ryoma let out a sigh. "Genki made his position clear. He wants to keep you here so he can use the confusion of the legend to his advantage. He won't send Ikari to help."

Amy turned away from the King with an angry gesture. "I don't give a damn about Genki Sanada."

"Amy." Hayate reached over toward her, wishing he knew what he could say that would comfort her.

"You're the one who told me that Genki was just a figure head." Amy spun toward Hayate. "So who cares what he said. I know Ikari. He left that book for me knowing I'd find the passage about Arulius."

"You can't know that for sure," Hayate retorted.

"Does he really seem like a guy who'd steal a book from House Inara just so he can give it away?" Amy looked at Hayate, her eyes pleading.

"If he knew about the passage, why didn't he just tell you about it?"

"That I don't know." Amy shook her head. "But I do know he'll help if I ask. And I'm going to ask him, even if I have to go Austuria on my own to do it."

"You won't go alone." Hayate smiled; glad to see her frustration fading. "I'll do whatever I can to help you, even if that means going back to Austuria."

"Thank you."

Ryoma let out an amused, but defeated sounding laugh. "I won't bother to continue trying to talk you out of going. So I'll simply wish you both good luck."

"Three, your majesty," Gaius corrected.

"I can't ask you to come with us." Hayate turned toward Gaius, surprised to hear him volunteering. "You know how dangerous going to Alextien is."

"I do, but I would be forever bereft if I let you shoulder the perils of that realm alone." Gaius stepped over to Hayate and Amy with a cocky smile. "My very knighthood would be cheapened if, by some inaction of my own, any misfortune befell our dearest Amy. Besides, I've never been to Austuria. They say it's quite lovely."

"You practiced that, didn't you?" Hayate laughed.

"I haven't the faintest idea of what you mean," Gaius responded. "So when do we leave?"

* * *

Traveling by horse, Amy and her two companions reached the picturesque home of the Sanada after three days. Eager to begin searching for the key that might lead her home, Amy followed Hayate as he tied their horses in the stable while Gaius spoke with the stable boy. They then followed a wide path up to the main entrance where they were greeted by two armed guards.

"Be nice this time." Amy nudged Hayate with her elbow.

"We're here to speak with Ikari Sanada," Hayate stated before the guards could ask what they wanted. "Please."

"Better." Amy snickered.

"Follow me." One of the guards turned and headed inside.

Gaius let out a soft whistle as he trailed behind the others, slowing every now and then to admire a vase or piece of art as they passed through the halls. "Say what you will about the Sanada, but they do have excellent taste."

"Say whatever you like, so long as you're respectful, knight," E'Lan stated from further up the hall, striding toward them.

"Wait... I know you." Gaius stepped up to Hayate's side. "You're the woman from the dinner party, the handmaiden."

"Yes," E'Lan replied. "State your business and leave."

"We came see Ikari," Hayate retorted.

E'Lan glared at the young knight for a long moment before shifting her gaze to Amy and Gaius. "Come with me." Dismissing the guard, E'Lan turned and started back down the corridor.

"I'm sensing a bit of animosity here." Gaius glanced at Hayate.

"You should feel what I'm sensing." Amy kept her gaze on E'Lan, who radiated a cloud of anger and loathing thick enough to block the afternoon sun. "I don't think she likes us very much."

"You remember the Sanyoshu I told you about?" Hayate whispered.

"Yes." Gaius nodded.

"That's her."

"Ah. Judging by the look in her eyes, I'd say she aims to fulfill her promise." Gaius clapped Hayate on the back. "I will morn your loss. I don't suppose you know if she's seeing anyone?"

"Really?" Amy raised an eyebrow while looking over to the flirtatious knight.

"A beautiful girl like her, who happens to be skilled in battle, is a rare find." Gaius flashed a smile at Amy. "Unless you're so overcome with jealousy that you simply must have me here and now."

Amy rolled her eyes and looked away, recognizing the section of the house. "I'll try to restrain myself."

"Wait here." E'Lan shot Gaius an irritated glare a moment before stepping through an open archway.

"I think she heard you." Hayate smirked at Gaius then looked over to Amy. "Do you really think you can convince Ikari to help?"

"Yeah, I do." Amy nodded. E'Lan stepped back into the corridor and motioned for them to enter the chamber. Filing in behind Hayate, Amy saw Yuki slouching on the chair to the far left with Genki standing a few feet away. "Where's Ikari?"

"Thank you E'Lan." Yuki dismissed the Sanyoshu with a wave.

"We came to speak with Ikari," Hayate stated.

"I know why you're here." Genki shot an angry glare at each of them. "And my answer is the same as the one I told your King."

"With respect, Lord Genki, we're not here to ask *you* anything." Hayate returned the glare.

Genki let out a long breath and began to pace around the set of chairs. "As a knight that follows the orders of his King, I'm sure you understand that as the head of House Sanada, I speak for those within. I have no reason to aid you any further than we already have, and I certainly have little reason to see Ms. Price depart our realm. At least, not until her usefulness has ended."

Hayate clenched his fist. "I won't let you, or anyone, use Amy like a tool."

"Forget it Hayate." Gaius motioned toward the archway. "They obviously won't help."

"No, it's more than that." Amy stepped forward, picking up on the silent communication between the siblings. "It's not that they don't want to help, they just don't want Ikari to help. Why? Why won't you let us talk to him about Alextien?"

"Because you're dangerous." Yuki straightened, keeping her icy stare locked on Amy. "Ever since Ikari met you, he's been off his game, conflicted. For whatever reason, he seems to be drawn to you. A fact I find more and more abhorrent. You're a distraction he doesn't need. A cause not worth his time to fight for, and he knows this, but he keeps helping you anyway. Why is that?"

"Because I can," Ikari's voice rang from behind.

Amy spun around, surprised to see Ikari standing in the archway. "Ikari?"

"Hey." Ikari strode passed Hayate and Gaius and stopped next to Amy. "I do what I do because *I* choose to."

"And I assume you're going to choose to assist them again," Genki stated angrily.

"Of course I am." Ikari shrugged, staring at Genki for a long moment.

Yuki held her gaze on Ikari for a long moment before turning to Genki. "I suppose we have no choice then. It's not as if we could stop him."

"Fine," Genki growled. "I was planning to leave for Hapes this afternoon. They can ride along."

"Perfect." Ikari smirked as he looked over his shoulder. "Saskai, keep Amy and her friends entertained for a few minutes."

"Of course, my Lord." Saskai stepped into the chamber.

"Thanks." Amy smiled at Ikari.

"What are friends for?" Ikari nodded a second before Amy and the others followed Saskai out of the room.

"Well, that was interesting," Gaius laughed from the back of the group.

* * *

"Why are you wasting more time with them?" Genki turned toward Ikari with an angry look on his face.

"Because I choose too, and because it's to our benefit," Ikari replied. "You're not seeing the bigger picture."

"What picture would that be?" Genki dropped down into his chair. "The only picture I see is one I care little about. Danothir, Ritsuko, and the Consortium are poised to wipe each other out, which is what we wanted. Helping that girl now is a waste of time."

"That's where you're wrong," Ikari stated.

Yuki stared at Ikari for a long moment before raising an eyebrow. "You don't actually believe she's the Protectorate Goddess, do you?"

"Of course not. But whether she is or isn't, is irrelevant at this point. She's still our best asset to gain information on Ritsuko and Danothir." Ikari circled around to his brother's side, considering his words. "Everyone we've been watching in this game is about to make their move, but we're still playing catch up. Back at the Chancellor's ball, Alia mentioned something about Alextien. At the time I didn't know what to think about it, but now, we have Amy and her knight wanting to go. You know how I feel about coincidences. Something is happening in Alextien, and it's in our best interest to find out what."

Genki raised a skeptical eyebrow. "And you really think it's worth the trouble?"

"Information is what we live for. If you want to control the game, we need to know all the possible moves."

Genki crossed his arms, thinking over what Ikari had said. "What do you think, Yuki?"

"He's right. He usually is. We can't let ourselves fall behind everyone else." Yuki glanced over toward Genki. "Besides, Alextien is a dangerous place. I'm betting on Amy and her friends dying after a day."

"Alright," Genki laughed as he stood and started toward the archway. "We'll do things your way."

"Have I ever let you down?" Ikari grinned as Genki exited the chamber, pleased that he had managed to sway his decision.

"You know you can't fool me." Yuki slid out of her chair and stepped over to Ikari.

Should have known she wouldn't let it go that easy. Ikari flashed a smirk, knowing she'd see through it anyway. "Meaning?"

"Genki is willing to believe you because he can't see things the way we do, but I always know when you're lying."

"And you knew I'd find out Amy was here but you still tried to hide her from me. Why?"

"I wanted to see how you'd react." Yuki shrugged and sat down on the floor, crossing her legs under her.

"Another test?"

"I was concerned. That girl has gotten in your head and I don't understand why."

"I can relate to her." Ikari laughed as he sat next to Yuki, surprised to find himself having a conversation like this with her. "Honestly, you wouldn't understand."

"I'm your twin, I get everything about you."

"Almost everything. You and I are the same in a lot of ways, but we're also different. You were made for the lives we live. You like being the thing in the shadows that makes people afraid at night."

Yuki pointed a finger. "So do you. I've seen the delight that lights up your eyes when you fight. You love it as much as I do."

"I do, but I also want more. I want to be a part of something bigger than *who's the greatest warrior* or who controls the criminal underworld." Ikari laughed, unsurprised by the confused look on Yuki's face.

"And you think that girl can lead you to that something?"

"Don't know, maybe... but I know that something's coming. I can feel it, and when it gets here, I'm going to be right at the front of it."

"And if this something is a threat?"

"Then I'm going to annihilate it." Ikari felt himself smile. "Either way, I'm going to be part it."

"I get it. I've always known you've been waiting for... whatever it is you're waiting for." Yuki returned his smile with smirk of her own as she pressed her forehead against his. "So I'll play your game and leave the girl alone. It is a sister's duty to see her brother happy after all."

"I actually expected a little more meddling before you let it go." Ikari rose to his feet.

"As long as your heads clear, I'm content. And I don't meddle. I simply suggest... strongly." Yuki took Ikari's hand as he pulled her to her feet. "Besides, I'm more concerned about your interest in Alia Inara."

Letting his head fall with a laugh, Ikari started toward the archway. "E'Lan said something?"

"E'Lan knows something? I had to force it of that dimwitted Duchess." Yuki chased after Ikari, clearly enjoying herself. "Did you dance with E'Lan?"

"We were working."

"You danced with Alia."

"Let it go."

"How can I let it go?" Yuki cringed with a shiver. "That's just weird."

* * *

A cool breeze blew over the large port, carrying the scent of the river that surrounded Hapes Island. Standing out over the smaller structures that littered the island, the grand hall that housed the Consortium sat near the southern edge of the isle. Well maintained stone roads allowed access to every portion of the island. Further inland, statues of various gods or ancient heroes decorated the streets, giving anyone passing by something to admire besides the elaborate, but typical, column-heavy architecture that the Consortium favored.

Riding in the back of a horse pulled rickshaw, Ikari glanced over the crowded street, ignoring the conversation between Hayate, Gaius, and Amy. "I know it's been a while since I was here, but is it always this crowded?"

"You noticed it too." Yuki sat across from Ikari, peering over her shoulder. "And the port heading for Hapes?"

"A lot of ships just sitting there." Ikari let his mind wander for a moment, considering the implications. The rickshaw driver pulled to the side as they reached their destination, thanking Genki after receiving his pay.

"It's probably just merchants unloading their goods." Genki climbed out of the rickshaw.

"Maybe." Ikari flipped sideways and landed lightly on the ground, while everyone else clambered out.

E'Lan stepped over to Yuki's side, followed by Saskai. "Perhaps I should investigate."

"I had intended to accompany Ikari to Alextien," Yuki sighed, nodding to E'Lan. "But I guess it's best if I stayed to check things out a bit."

"I still think it's nothing, but do as you will." Genki started up a stone path that led to the grand hall. "I have a meeting to attend. Try to keep out trouble."

"Come along E'Lan. With any luck, we'll find someone to play with." Yuki flashed an evil grin.

"You'd better go with her." Ikari turned to Saskai.

"My Lord?"

"Those two and high-society noble types aren't the best mix." Ikari paused glancing at the path Genki had taken. "And keep an eye on Genki."

"Understood." Saskai bowed before disappearing into the crowd.

"Something wrong?" Hayate stepped over to Ikari.

"Nope." Ikari nodded. "Just playing a hunch. Let's go."

Amy stepped over to Hayate's side as they started toward the center of the island. "I know it's probably a silly question, but what's Alextien like?"

"Some say the air stinks of death," Gaius responded. "That the realm is so foul, even the sun refuses to shine upon it."

"Really?" Amy shook her head.

"It's not so bad really." Ikari flashed a grin, while stepping around a fountain standing in the plaza in front of the large temple that housed the Gateway of the Gods. "There's not much vegetation, not like here, and what little remains is often poisonous. It's a realm covered in dirt that looks like it's been scorched by the flames of Yun'Harrar. And the sun does shine there, it's just blocked by a layer of smoke and black clouds that refuse to dissipate despite the night winds. And the sandstorms—there's a lot of deserts in Alextien—they can strip the flesh right off your bones."

"It can't be that bad." Amy stared at Ikari for a long moment. "You're just joshing me, right?"

"Yeah," Ikari smiled. "It's just like any other realm, only a bit less cheerful."

"You're lying." Amy shot Ikari a playful look.

"Why would you think that?"

"For one," Hayate interrupted as they reached the temple steps and walked in through the large opening. "You lack credibility."

Ignoring Hayate's comment, Ikari glanced around the cream colored temple and spotted a few of the staff scurrying about their business. Built mostly for show rather than function; the temple was little more than an extravagant wall built around the Gateway. Murals of the gods hung from some of the walls, while others held paintings of different landscapes from the various realms. Light gray columns with plaques containing information about traveling held the cathedral ceiling overhead.

"This is amazing." Amy stopped near one of the decorative columns and ran her fingers over the engravings. "It's similar to the temple my dad found in Belize. The architecture of this place, of the whole island, looks like it's been influenced by the Greco-Roman culture, while places like Ithor are Arthurian and Austuria is more pre-shogunate."

"I have no idea what any of that means," Gaius laughed. "But I do enjoy the excitement in your voice."

"I don't really understand the significance either," Hayate admitted.

"Where I come from, those are three worlds separated by thousands of miles and hundreds of years. This suggests that at some point, those cultures and our two worlds were somehow connected." Amy glanced at each of them, remembering that archeology wasn't really a field studied in their world. "I'm an archeologist. This kind of thing excites me, okay."

"We can tell." Ikari turned to his right, noticing the sound of footsteps approaching, and saw the familiar face of the temple mistress. "Lucilla."

"Lord Ikari, it's a pleasure to see you again." The middle-aged woman curtsied, wearing a long white and gray dress. "What brings you back to Hapes?"

"Traveling to Alextien," Ikari replied a moment before she slapped the back of his head. "What was that for?"

"Were you raised a heathen boy? Introduce me to your friends." Lucilla slapped him again.

"Hi, I am Amy."

"And that's Hayate and Gaius. Those two aren't friends." Ikari rubbed the back of his head while the two knights greeted Lucilla. "You know, you hit hard for a woman with brittle bones."

"Don't be a baby. That wretch of a master of yours still owes me money." Lucilla motioned for them to follow as she started toward the Gateway.

Gaius let out an amused laugh. "So, the great and powerful Ikari Sanada is afraid of a sweet old woman."

Lucilla spun around with an annoyed look, slapping Gaius across the face. "Watch your mouth boy. I ain't no old woman yet."

"Perhaps sweet is not quiet the right word," Gaius muttered, rubbing his cheek.

"I like her." Amy smirked.

Stepping through a wide corridor, they emerged in a large, open courtyard that made up the center of the temple. A stone walkway led from the corridor to each of the five archways that stood on the far side of the square. Lush grass grew within the sections marked off by the pathway, and a three-foot stone pillar sat a few yards away from the centermost Gateway.

"Are you sure you want to take a lady like her to Alextien?" Lucilla stepped over to the pillar.

"It'll be fine," Ikari answered.

"Alright." Lucilla slid the yellow stone into position and laid her left hand on top of the teal crystal at the pillars center. An instant later the archway on the far right filled with a think orange liquid that began to rippled inward. "And tell that wretch to pay me."

"No sooner said than done." Ikari bowed before stepping over to the Gateway with the others. Peering to his left, he noticed Amy staring at the shimmering liquid, her breathing heavy. "You sure you want to do this?"

"I'm sure." Amy shook her head. "It's just... the last time I went through one of these, I ended up trapped in a casket."

"I'm not going to let anything happen to you." Hayate gave a reassuring smile. "We'll go together."

"You're sweet." Amy bumped him with her shoulder before taking his hand. "Through the looking glass?"

"Looking glass?" Ikari and Gaius shared a confused glance as Amy and Hayate stepped through the archway, disappearing into the glowing liquid.

"She is a strange one, isn't she?" Gaius asked following after them.

"She's not dull." Ikari smiled.

* * *

Danothir marched through the lavish corridors of the Consortium's grand hall, enjoying the sound each boot made as they hit the polished marble floor. A jolt of, what he could only describe as a moment of perfect contentment, surged through him, adding a spring to each step that he hadn't enjoyed since he seized control of House Borga so many years ago. Years of careful planning, of forcing himself to be patient, had led him to this moment; the eve in which he finally took what the Chancellor and the chaos-inducing Consortium were too inept to use properly. Power.

Turning into the large hall that led to the meeting chamber, Danothir spotted Lady Inara talking to a tall man clad in black and purple clothing. "Ritsuko."

"That'll be all for now, Thade." Ritsuko motioned for her lackey to leave. "But don't stray too far. I may have need of you later."

"Yes, my Lady." Thade bowed before exiting the hallway.

"New toy?" Danothir asked making no attempt to hide his dislike for the woman as he stepped past her.

"In a manner of sorts." Ritsuko returned his glare. "You seem to be in a surprisingly good mood today. Could that have anything to do with the ships in the harbor?"

Danothir paused. "I'm sure you have a point somewhere in all of this, but I'm not in the mood to play games with you."

"Good, then allow me to cut to the point. I know that almost every single ship in that harbor belongs to you and that each is filled with your best and brightest troops to sack this island." Ritsuko paused as the pleasant feeling Danothir had been enjoying turned to a growing anger. "Or do you still wish to play the fool."

Danothir spun on his heel, shooting the smug woman a fierce look he wished would bore a hole straight through her face. Forcing the anger from his burning face, Danothir let his mind wander, trying to figure out how much she really knew. In all the years he had known her, he had never known Ritsuko to be one for simply bluffing an opponent. "What makes you think you know anything about my plans? Or has Ryoma Ashok's endless accusations finally found someone gullible enough to listen?"

"I have my ways, and many resources the Consortium does not. You're not nearly as careful as you think you are. Now you can stand here and pretend to be as ignorant as you wish, but if you do, I'll have little choice but to tell the Consortium everything I know."

"Even if you knew anything, you have no proof."

"So far as you think, and even if I don't, all I need do is lend my support to that idiot Ryoma and things for you will get very uncomfortable."

"So why haven't you spoken with the Chancellor?"

"Because, I find myself in the unpleasant situation of needing something from you."

"That being?" Danothir let the edge slip from his voice, surprised by her comment.

"You have at least one of the Roses of Tai Re'l in your possession, and reports say you've already taken the second one from the Sanada. I'll soon have the final rose, but I need the other two to complete my plan."

"Ah, and I'm to give them to you, foregoing my own plans, or you go to the Chancellor."

"Like it or not, we have common goals," Ritsuko snapped. "We both want control of the realm so we might as well work together, for the moment."

"You're proposing an alliance?" Danothir let out an amused laugh, remembering the sense of enjoyment he had felt earlier. "That tight little dress of yours must be cutting off the blood in your brain. You have nothing to offer me."

"You really are that short sighted aren't you?" Ritsuko mocked. "As vast as your forces have grown, you still won't be able to defeat T'Chello, Ithor, and everyone else."

"Once I have the final rose, I'll be able to take control of the war gods armies…"

"And how do you propose to accomplish that?" Ritsuko interrupted, waving a hand. "Were you a practicing sorcerer? Are you even remotely familiar with the ritual to summon the slayer's army? Because I am, and I can assure you that if you're not, you'll fail."

"I'm listening."

"I will help conjure a force capable of laying waste to anyone standing in their path, in addition to lending you my own sizable army, and together, you and I will take control of the realm. In return, you will give me the roses so that I can achieve ascension."

"Ascension?" Danothir crossed his arms. "That's a myth, just another word synonymous with dead."

"Believe what you want. That just means that the realm will be all yours when I ascend." Ritsuko stepped over toward him and smirked. "So Lord Borga, do we have an accord or do we not?"

Danothir stared at Ritsuko for a long moment, considering whether choking the life out of her would be simpler than working with the woman, but decided against it. As infuriating as she was, she did raise a few valid points. If she was really set on chasing an impossible notion like ascension, then he saw no reason not to accept an offer that would more than double his forces. "I believe we do."

"Good." Ritsuko smiled again, nodding toward the doors at the end of the hall. "Shall we? You know how the Chancellor hates to start late."

"He won't have to worry about that for much longer." Danothir laughed. "By the way, you might want to have your ship ready to depart the island. You never know when a storm might hit."

Chapter Twenty-Three

"After passing through that... quaint little field a few miles back and viewing the lavish splendor of the countryside, I can honestly say that Alextien is everything people claim it to be," Gaius stated from the back of the group as they followed a dusty path surrounded by dry, dead looking trees.

"You actually lived here?" Amy waved her hand in front of her face while another gust of arid wind blew over the landscape.

"For almost eight years," Ikari replied, spotting the rustic village he and Yuki had spent most of their time in when they weren't training. Dark, charred looking dirt covered the ancient stone roads, giving the tan colored buildings a clean appearance despite the layers of grim caked onto them.

Hayate coughed, waving off another cloud of dust carried by the dry wind. "On purpose?"

"Hey, show some respect." Ikari glanced over his shoulder as they neared the village. "I have a lot of fond, painful memories of this place, and I'm not about to let you or anyone else insult my master's home."

"You must care about him a lot." Amy glanced at Ikari. "I've never felt such a sense of fondness coming from you."

"There's not too many in the realms that I respect, but he's on the top of that list. He's the greatest warrior I've ever seen, and by far the most evil and cruel. He makes my sister look like a merciful saint."

"There's an unsettling thought," Hayate whispered to Gaius.

Ikari stifled a laugh as they reached a large oval shaped wagon being loaded by two kids. A few villagers, dressed in the usual brown and gray clothing of the region, stopped to glance at Ikari and the others as they passed before scurrying off to whatever it was they were doing. "Also, he can kill you with his mind."

"You really think he can help us with our search?" Amy asked.

"If there's anything worth knowing in these parts, I guarantee he'll know about it. Only trick is getting him to share the information with a minimal of hoop jumping. Either way, it should only take us an hour or so to walk to his valley. We can hit the mountains by nightfall."

"This is daytime here?" Amy stopped for a moment, peering up at the shadowy sky. "That's just depressing."

"If we're going to be traveling all day, we should get some food" Hayate stated.

"There's a tavern down the road with decent food," Ikari replied, surprised by the number of wagons rolling through the village.

After a few minutes, they reached a building with an oval shaped swinging door and stepped inside. Noise from dozens of conversations filled the air along with the smell of roasting meat. Shouts of excitement mixed with disappointed moans erupted every few minutes as groups of people gathered around various tables, playing the game of their choice. Following behind the pair of knights as they found an empty table, Ikari caught a brief flash of a familiar presence and glanced around the crowd trying to find the source.

"Nice little pub. It's very... shady." Amy leaned closer to Ikari. "I think I understand why no one wants to come here, and you're not paying attention. Ikari?"

"Damn." Ikari let out an annoyed breath and spun around only to find a gloved fist flying toward his face.

Swaying to avoid the attack, Ikari smiled as he blocked a second volley of strikes before returning the tall, middle aged man's greeting. Catching sight of Hayate and Gaius reaching for their swords while the man evaded his attacks, Ikari pushed the man back and held up his hand to stop the knights.

"Come on Ikari boy, who taught you to watch your back?" The man, dressed in dark green and gold robes with a scar on his unshaven cheek, stepped forward with a grin and embraced Ikari.

"Another friend of yours I assume?" Hayate shifted his gaze to Ikari.

"This is Master Neit Balor Segomo," Ikari responded after stepping back.

"Ah, the infamous instructor of your shadow arts." Gaius stepped over to Neit and extended his hand only to have it pushed aside.

"And who's this pretty thing?" Neit moved closer to Amy, bowing his bald head.

"I'm Amy, Amy Price."

"So what brings my favorite student back to Alextien with a pair of Ithorian knights and a girl as obviously out-of-place as you?" Neit turned toward Ikari. "Let me guess, you're here for a trip to the Khampf mountains."

"That's too good for a guess," Hayate replied with a suspicious tone. "How..."

"Because you're not the first to ask about them." Neit sat down at the empty table a moment before everyone else did the same.

"Who else asked?" Ikari leaned forward, pushing back his surprise.

"A while ago, some short godless son of a pig with an affinity for knives came to me asking for a guide through the mountains," Neit answered.

"Tres," Hayate groaned.

"And you helped him?" Amy looked over to Neit.

"Of course. His coins spent just like any others."

Gaius crossed his arms as he leaned back in his chair. "That puts a wrinkle in our plans, if he already has what we came for."

"We'll have to find a way to take it from him before he gets back to Terra," Hayate replied.

Neit waved his hand dismissively. "Won't be easy. That Tres fellow brought a horde of lackeys with him to dig up every bit of shine they could from that mountain, including a hulking chap with an ill, yet dim, look about him."

"That would be Gaou." Ikari let out a laugh, surprised that Thade wasn't leading the party.

"Crossed paths with that one have you?" Neit raised an eyebrow at Ikari. "It's odd, that Tres fellow dug up all kinds of shine only to turn around and sell most of it. The only thing he kept was a box with some inscriptions about the goddess Araia. It's interesting, 'cause not long before they came here, I happened to hear a rumor about a girl falling out of a casket. You wouldn't happen to know what all that is about would you?"

"Do you know where Tres has the box now?" Hayate leaned forward on the table.

"More or less." Neit stood and nodded toward the barmaid behind the ivory counter across the room. "But first, why don't you buy me a drink, Ikari boy."

"Master, we're in a bit of..." Ikari trailed off, knowing that his words were wasted.

"We don't time for this," Hayate stated.

"No choice." Ikari followed after Neit and leaned against the smooth counter.

Ordering some ale from the young woman serving the drinks, Neit sat on one of the raggedy stools before looking over to Ikari. "So what's with the girl? What's the angle?"

Ikari hung his head with a sigh. "Why is it so hard for anyone to accept that I might be helping her out of the goodness of my heart?"

"Well, maybe it's 'cause you're Ikari Sanada. You don't do anything unless it's to your benefit." Neit paused to drink from his mug.

"I've already heard this speech from Yuki; I really don't need to hear it again." Ikari glanced over at Amy as she smiled, holding Hayate's hand. "She's a friend, and I relate to her situation."

"Heard you call a lot of people a lot of things, but friend is new. So you're really here because of her?"

"You know that I am."

"And do you know what it is she has you chasing?"

"She was looking for a way home." Ikari turned back to his master only to find the playful smile he had a moment ago replaced with a somber glare. "Or is there something I should know."

"You and your mates should let this one go."

"So we're clear, the knights aren't included in the friend category. And what do mean?"

"You wanna help the girl, fine, but stay away from Gaou. He's not one I like you fighting."

"Gaou's like a giant trained monkey, only lacking the previously mentioned training. Even with the enchantments Ritsuko gave him, I can take him. Not saying it'll be easy, but doable."

"Listen Ikari boy, he's not enchanted, he's infected."

"With what?"

"Gods only know, 'cause I couldn't tell you, but I've seen it before. I once fought a man like him, smarter, but infected just the same. He had the same off blue scars lighting up his body. First time I fought him, he killed four of my pals. I fought him thrice more and each time he kept getting stronger. I can't say as to how it happened, but I know that as strong as I was, it took me and three others to bring him down. This path you've chosen for yourself is a dangerous one. How would it look if my best student got slaughtered in my own town?" Neit shook his head, downing another swig on his drink. "And I've just gone and gotten you excited havent I?"

"It's not like I have much choice." Ikari felt a slight smirk spread across his face. "You trained me to be a warrior. You made me a monster most people can't compete with, so I seek out the ridiculously strong to fight. Gaou has something I need. I'm gonna take it."

"You really are a battle nut aren't you?"

"It's a gift," Ikari laughed. "Now are you going to tell me how to find Gaou, or do I get to spend all day scouring the village?"

"Alright." Neit's playful smirk returned as he finished the last of the ale. "Go and get your friends and I'll get you on your way. But don't expect me to help."

Ikari laughed while backing away from Neit. "I never do, master."

"Ikari." Neit waited for the younger man to stop before rising to his feet. "You keep going down this path and you might not like what you find along the way."

"Maybe." Ikari shrugged. "But it's still the path I chose to follow."

* * *

Brownish light from what Amy assumed was the afternoon sun filtered through the layer of thick clouds that hung over the village. Crouched between a pair of shoddy looking buildings behind a pile of broken furniture waiting to be hauled off, Amy watched as Tres barked orders at his men loading the large wagon.

After getting the information they needed from Neit, Ikari and the others had made their way to a rundown factory to find it swarming with assassins. Leaving her to hide in the alley, Hayate, Gaius, and Ikari had decided to scout the area and find a way inside.

"I hate when they make me wait on the sidelines." Amy let out an annoyed sigh and peered around the pile again.

"So you'd rather be risking your neck with the rest of us?" Startled, Amy spun around and found Ikari kneeling behind her.

"It's not like my neck's not already on the line." Amy slapped his shoulder. "Besides, I'm actually getting used to the danger."

"It does get a little fun." Ikari nodded. "Surprised I managed to startle you given your unusual ability to sense people's emotions. You're gonna have to teach me that skill one day."

"I can't really control when I do that." Amy shook her head. "Not yet anyway."

"Not yet?"

"I'm kinda getting used to that too. And I'm getting better at it. I can read Hayate like book, and I can read you a lot easier than before. Gaius is kinda hard. I don't get much from him."

"Do me a favor. If you're digging around in my head, don't dig too deep. Guy's got to have secrets." Ikari grinned. "So what's our assassin friend been up to?"

"Still loading whatever's in those crates."

"Least he's not ready to leave yet."

"Won't be long before he is." Gaius made his way toward Amy, followed by Hayate. "Another wagons load of crates and he'll be on his merry way."

"What's he loading?" Amy asked.

Hayate crouched next to Amy. "I only caught a quick glimpse, but it looked like it's nothing but food and provisions. But it's more than his band of assassins would need."

"Assuming it's for him." Amy shrugged. "Isn't he working for House Inara?"

"You think he's shipping supplies back to Osaka Major?" Gaius looked over toward Amy.

Hayate peeked around the pile of furniture for a moment before looking back to the group. "What else could he be doing with them? And even if he's not, we can't let him keep all that."

"I'm up for anything that might annoy Ritsuko, but that's not why we're here." Ikari motioned toward the factory. "Tres has our magical box under guard inside. But there's no way we can fight passed them all and make it back out."

"So how do we get the box?" Hayate followed Ikari's glance.

"I can get their attention for a while and draw Gaou, and whoever else might be lurking around, away while you guys sneak in and grab it."

"What about the wagons?" Hayate inquired.

"Leave them to me," Gaius replied with a nod. "And I'll see what I can do about slowing down their pursuit when they come after us."

"Just make sure you two get in and out quietly, and we'll be home for dinner." Ikari smirked and started down the alley to the left.

"Here's hopping." Amy returned his smile before following after Hayate.

Staying within the shadows of what passed for Alextien's sun, Amy and Hayate followed the winding alley until they were across from the western wing of the factory. Out of sight from Tres and the main entrance, they hurried across the empty field, before darting behind a worn shed. Keeping close to Hayate, she peered around the shed and found a group of assassins rounding the corner at the far end of the factory.

"Ikari better give us a good distraction or we won't make it far." Hayate peaked around the shed.

Noticing a plume of smoke rising from across the factory, Amy chuckled as the sound of shouting caused the patrolling group to run out of sight. "I think he just did."

"What's with the Sanada and burning factories?" Hayate scoffed a moment before taking her hand and running over to the far corner of the building. Pressing his back to the wall, Hayate peered around to the back of the complex before looking back to Amy. "Ikari must be doing his job, there's only two guarding the door. I think I can reach them before they call for back up."

"Or?" Amy flashed him a reassuring smile an instant before she ran around the corner. Stopping after twenty yards, she spotted the two guards standing near a staircase that led to a narrow doorway. "Hey, either of you sodding muppets still looking for me?"

Waiting just long enough to hear their response and see them start after her, Amy spun on her heel and sprinted back the way she came. Sliding to a stop well behind Hayate, she turned in time to see the first guard slashed across the chest. Hayate wasted no time in dispatching the second guard, who tried to evade his attack only to catch the tip of Hayate's sword with his throat.

"That was reckless." Hayate glared at Amy after scanning the area.

"I told you before; I'm not some dainty bird who can't contribute anything." Amy nodded toward the door. "Shall we?"

"Yeah." Keeping his sword in hand, Hayate led her up the stairs and slowly pushed open the door.

After making sure that there was no one in the immediate area, they dashed inside and began to work their way toward the center of the factory. The sound of excited shouting reverberated throughout the dull corridors as enemy soldiers rushed toward the commotion outside. Darting past a dirt covered window, Amy caught sight of Ikari eluding a group of bow wielding archers in the courtyard below, when she felt an odd hum buzzing in the back of her mind.

"Hayate, wait."

"What?" Hayate stopped a few feet ahead of her and turned around.

"I think we should go this way." Amy pointed at a narrow archway to her left and started through it, letting the singing in her mind guide her. Turning down another corridor, she spotted a wooden staircase and hurried down, ignoring the concern in Hayate's voice as he asked her where she was taking them.

Reaching a wide door marked as a loading bay, Amy pushed it open with a grin and stepped into a large room with a broken down conveyer line and multiple doors that led to the courtyard and other parts of the factory. A few windows of varying size were scattered along the wall providing enough light to make out the writing on some of the crates lying about. Amy walked over to a small crate sitting on the conveyer belt and tried to lift open the led only to find it nail closed. "Here it is."

"How could you know that?" Hayate looked at Amy, confusion lining his face.

"I can feel it, like I did in Remus." Amy shook her head, realizing that some outside force had once again driven her actions. "I don't know how I do this. I don't want to know. It kinda scares me when I think about it. I'm starting to think I'm not even a person anymore."

"We'll figure out what's happening with you. Whatever it is, you know I'll help you get through it." Hayate stepped over to her side and squeezed Amy's hand before giving her a reassuring smile.

"Promise?" Amy returned his squeeze, taking comfort from the warmth of his hand.

"My word as knight." Hayate held his smile for a moment before turning to the crate and using his sword to pry it open. Returning his weapon to its sheath, Hayate pulled a cloth covered box out of the crate and set it down.

Feeling drawn to the square box, Amy quickly unwrapped it to reveal a small polished chest made out of a burgundy colored wood. The domed cover had a golden inscription painted on it, which Amy recognized as ancient Terran. "Wow, not exactly what I was expecting."

"What's it say?"

"You shall know pain as well as joy, for you are beloved by the goddess, whose gifts are everlasting," Amy read.

"That's a passage from the Book of Tai Re'l."

"The second line says that Arulius placed the love of the goddess within the box." Unsure of what to think about the inscription, Amy opened the lid and felt a wave of surprise and disappointment wash over her. Looking over to Hayate, she picked up the crimson colored jewel and held it for him to see. "It's a rose."

"That would explain why Tres is here."

"It's a bloody rose. We came all this way for another sodding rose?" Amy tried to force back her frustration while looking over the

228

chest, hopping for something more when the sound of breaking glass filled her ears. Spinning around, she saw Ikari fly through the window and crash onto the stone floor with a groan. "Ikari?"

Rolling to his side, Ikari wiped away some of the blood that trickled down his face while climbing to his feet. "We should probably go now."

"This way." Amy spun back to the door she and Hayate had entered, clutching the rose tight, and started toward the exit only to slide to a halt as Tres sauntered into the loading bay. "Or not."

"Don't leave now; we've *so* much catchin' up to do." Carrying a sword in his left hand, Tres pulled a silver dagger from his belt and waved it mockingly. "Had this made special just for you."

"Shame you won't be using it." Hayate pulled Amy back while standing ready to attack. "Amy, get to the courtyard and make a run for the alley."

"What about..." Amy started, but let the sentence drop as Hayate pushed her back just as Tres lunged forward.

"Go." Hayate blocked Tres's initial attack, only to be put on the defensive by a torrent of fevered slashes.

"You heard the knight." Ikari charged forward, kicking an assassin back out the window as he tried to climb through. "We're right behind you. And watch out for Gaou, I think I made him mad this time."

"Yeah, right." Running to the wooden door at the left end of the room, Amy swung it open and sprinted down the wide hall. Adrenalin flooding her body, she burst through the door at the end of the hall, emerging into the open courtyard. *Got to find a way out of here.*

Amy hastily glanced around and spotted of group of soldiers, and Gaou, pouring onto the loading bay through the hole Ikari had made. Ignoring the clashing of steel she knew belonged to Hayate's sword, she made her way around a cluttered patio. Following along the buildings wall for a few hundred yards, Amy found the second, burning, loading bay, and frantically looked over the area.

"Grab the woman." Two assassins stumbled out one of the smaller doors, along with a fresh plume of smoke.

Rushing toward Amy, the first assassin grabbed her by the left wrist as she tried to spin away and yanked her back. Biting back the pain that shot through her wrist, Amy let her momentum from the tug add to the swing of her right arm and nailed the man on the jaw with the crystal rose. Ignoring his cry of pain, she poured all of her strength into her leg, kicking him between his legs. She wrenched her arm free as the moaning man slumped to the ground and turned to face the second man, but found him falling to the ground while Gaius pulled his sword out of the dead man's back.

"You really aren't the damsel in distress." Gaius flashed her a smile before stepping over to the garage sized door and unbolted the lock. "Still, not very sporting kicking man like that."

"I don't give a piss about sporting." Amy kicked the first assassin in the face as he tried to climb to his feet. "We need to get the blazes out of here, now."

"That thought was not lost on me. That's why, when I was setting fire to the place, I saved this." Sliding the door open with a shove, Gaius revealed a small wagon and led the horse pulling it outside. "Your carriage, my Lady."

"I could kiss you." Amy climbed into the back of the open wagon while Gaius took the driver's seat and started back for Hayate and Ikari.

"Let's consider that a reward for getting out of this alive." Gaius glanced over his shoulder. "Is that a rose?"

"Let's just get Hayate and Ikari and get out of here."

"Yes, of course." Gaius nodded as they neared the courtyard.

Pushing back a growing sense of danger, Amy peered over Gaius's shoulder and found Hayate fighting off Tres and a pack of his men while Ikari used his acrobatic skills to evade the attacks of the assassins and Gaou. "Guys, come on," Amy shouted while Gaius stopped the wagon thirty yards from the fight.

* * *

Somersaulting over a low kick from Gaou, Ikari rolled under the blade of another soldier, before kicking him into a snarling Gaou. "Your stooges have gotten better, Maou. I'm actually breaking a sweat."

"That why you're constantly running away?" Gaou shoved the soldier aside and renewed his attack.

"No. You just have really bad body odor, and you're leaking. It's kinda gross." Ikari smirked, referring to the strange glowing blue liquid that dripped from his scared face.

Parrying a wild punch from the brawler, Ikari retaliated with a trio of kicks aimed at the taller man's head, but Gaou managed to block each of them. Ikari vaulted sideways to avoid an attack from an overzealous soldier, and landed a few feet away from Hayate as he leapt through the broken window, followed closely by Tres.

Aching from the blows Gaou and his men had landed, Ikari searched for a way to put some distance between himself and the assassins, as they swarmed after him. To his right, he caught the sound of Hayate's sword clashing with Tres's.

"Don't know how you ended up in a dump like this, but I'm glad you did." Tres waved his dagger for a moment before renewing his attacks. "I've been waitin' for a chance to slide this into your gut."

Blocking a strike from an axe wielding assassin, Ikari caught sight of a wagon sliding to a stop and heard Amy's shouts. Ikari swung the axe wielder by the arm, using him as a makeshift shield while nailing another attacker with a kick to the jaw. Twisting back into the axe wielder, Ikari used the man's arm as leverage, and threw him into another pair of assassins before turning towards Hayate. "Time to go."

Hayate parried a thrust from Tres before following up with a punch to the face and a kick to the stomach, which caused the older man to stumble a few steps. "I know."

Blocking the eager blade of another soldier, Hayate pushed him into Ikari, who leapt onto his back before rolling backwards and launched the surprised man toward his comrades. Ikari let his momentum carry him back to his feet and turned to follow Hayate as he sprinted toward the wagon.

"We ain't done yet," Tres shouted behind them.

Moving as fast as they could, two assassins attempted to block their path, but Hayate slashed the first across the chest as he ran while Ikari slid under the second's horizontal strike and sweep his legs before spinning back to his feet.

Close enough to make out the panicked look on Amy's face, Ikari noticed her pointing behind them when a flash of silver whizzed past his head. Following the whirling flash, he realized too late what had almost nicked his ear just as Hayate cried out in pain while falling forward.

"Hayate." Amy started to jump out of the wagon but Gaius grabbed her arm.

"Stay there." Ikari waved her back while stooping down and pulling Hayate's arm over his shoulder, careful to avoid the silver dagger sticking out of his back. Running as best as he could with Hayate barely able to stumble along and a pack of assassins a moment from slicing them up to feed the native dogs, Ikari reached the back of the wagon and shoved Hayate into Amy before diving in himself. "Going now would be good."

Not needing further encouragement, Gaius whipped the reins of the horses and pulled off, coaxing as much speed as he could out of them. "I hope you have a way out of this."

"Head to the Gateway." Ikari forced air back into his lungs and peered back to find Tres and Gaou barking orders. "Won't be long before they come after us."

"A... Amy," Hayate tried to push himself up only to have his arms give out and fell on his face.

"Don't move." Amy kneeled low enough for him to see her while caressing his head. "We're going to get you help. He's going to be okay, right?"

"Tres missed his heart, but it's in pretty deep. Hold him down." Ikari motioned toward the dagger and waited for Amy to comply before pulling the weapon out. Ignoring Hayate's cry of pain, Ikari stared at the blade, noticing an odd, greenish substance covering it in addition to the knight's blood. "Poison."

"What?" Amy looked up at Ikari with tears in her eyes.

"A present from Alia, I'll bet." Ikari tossed the dagger to the side just as Gaius drove them passed the edge of the village.

"So what do we do? We have to help him."

"Nothing we can do." Ikari shook his head, unable to glimpse at the pained look on Amy's face. "Not until we get back to Hapes."

"Assuming he can last that long," Gaius muttered, steering the wagon around the curving road as they entered what passed as a forest.

"He'll make it." Amy shot Gaius a furious look before returning her attention to a moaning Hayate. "He has to."

"At least we don't have Tres and his goons to deal with," Gaius replied over his shoulder.

"I wouldn't be so sure." Ikari glared down the road, sensing the pursuit of Gaou and a troop of soldiers. "I thought you were going take care of their means of pursuit?"

"I did," Gaius spat. "Or did you not notice the fire."

"Obviously you missed a wagon or two."

"How can you be sure they're following? I don't see anyone." Gaius turned in his seat to look back, but a glare from Ikari answered his question. "Right, so what's the plan, *my Lord*?"

"Working on it." Ikari turned to check on Hayate when the wagon made a violent jolt, as if they had just run over a large rock. Searching for the cause, Ikari saw a wooden arrow sticking out of the neck of their horse an instant before the animal slumped to the ground causing the wagon crash into its corpse.

Flying out of the wagon along with the others, Ikari landed hard on his injured side and winced as a jolt of pain shot through him. He rolled onto his back, still disoriented from the crash, and scanned the area searching for the source of the attack when he noticed the all too familiar clash of swords. Following the sound to its source, he saw Gaius pushing back an assassin with a bow slung over his shoulder. Gaius ducked under a string of attacks before killing the assassin with a thrust to the lower stomach.

"What happened?" Ikari climbed to his feet and stepped over to Gaius.

"Damned assassin was waiting and took out our horse." Gaius shifted his gaze toward the front of the wagon and hurried over to Amy and Hayate. "We need to get going before the rest catch up."

"Help me carry him." Amy struggled to lift Hayate up, a trickle of blood running down her forehead.

"We still have close to a mile before we reach the Gateway, and that's a long run on foot." Gaius stepped closer, letting the edge fall from his voice. "I'm sorry… but we can't take him with us. We try and we all end up dead, and he's going to die anyway."

"We are not leaving him here." Amy glared at Gaius, her pale face twisted with grief and anger.

Gaius put a hand on her shoulder. "It's my duty to get you and the rose back home. It's what Hayate would want."

"We're not leaving him to die," Amy shouted, slapping his hand away.

"Amy, He's right. You'll never make back dragging Hayate." Ikari stared at Amy for a long minute, surprised by the aura pulsing off the crying woman. Swallowing back any remnants of pain or doubt that still lingered in him, he turned to face the road behind them and started forward. "Not unless someone holds them back."

"What? No, that's crazy. You can't fight them all yourself." Amy tried to go after him but the weight from Hayate stopped her. "You can't sacrifice yourself for me. We can all get out of here together."

"Who said anything about self-sacrifice?" Ikari paused and turned, flashing Amy a cocky smile. "I'm going to kill them all."

"Ikari…"

"This is the path I chose to walk. So go, and follow your own. I'm curious to see where it takes you. Besides, it's not in my nature to run from a good fight." Ikari shifted his gaze to Gaius and let out a determined breath. "Get them home."

"Good luck." Gaius nodded, moving to help Amy carry Hayate.

Watching as Amy and Gaius carried Hayate off, Ikari turned back toward the village, letting the sense of excitement he usually felt before a fight wash over him. *Good thing Yuki's not here to see this. I can only imagine the lecture I'd get.* Ikari laughed to himself as he spotted Gaou and his troops riding on the back of a wagon and sprinted forward to greet them.

"Looks like I'm in for another wild party."

Chapter Twenty-Four

"What exactly are you getting at?" the Chancellor asked, leaning forward in his chair.

As pleased as he was with how the meeting had started, Genki had to force the scowl from his face while Ryoma made his surprisingly convincing argument against Danothir. Despite his efforts to hamper the Ithorian's progress, Ryoma had laid out a riveting tale about Danothir's alleged attempts to undermine the kingdoms. He had even managed to sway some of the other Kings and Queens to his side.

"I can prove that Lord Borga was behind my near assassination," Ryoma continued, holding his stare on each of the gathered nobles just long enough to gauge their position on his accusations. "I can prove that Lord Tarkin was murdered by his second in command, and if given proper time, I will prove that he is even now positioning his troops for a coordinated attack on the kingdoms."

"I'm curious." Genki shifted in his seat, wearing a well-practiced look of doubt. Despite his general dislike of Ryoma, he had to admit to a begrudging respect for the man and the way he handled himself. Anyone else would have crumbled from the pressure Danothir put on Ryoma, as well as the pressure about Amy, and the discrete pressure from Genki himself. "You seem to have pieced a lot together since our last meeting. I'm wondering how you learned of this plot?"

"I have been investigating this since I first sent Hayate Thane to Nel'Oskow." Ryoma let a slight smirk slip through his calm demeanor. "I am not without resources, one of which has requested that she remain anonymous."

"These are serious accusations Ryoma," the Chancellor stated. "But if you can prove any of this, I will take action."

"I would think it wise if we conducted our own investigation before we jump to conclusions." Ritsuko leaned forward, speaking for the first time. "After all, Danothir is not the only one who has forces roaming about."

"What do you mean?" The Chancellor turned toward Ritsuko.

"What I mean is, I have confirmed reports of a certain knight running amuck in Osaka Minor," Ritsuko replied.

"Hayate is helping to find the proof about the Protectorate Goddess that you *all* demand." Ryoma turned to Lady Inara, letting a hint of anger line his voice.

"Enough." Danothir slammed his fist onto the table as he jumped to his feet. "Do you have any idea how tired I am of listening to all of you?" Letting an uncomfortable silence fall over the room, he began to walk around the table. "I have sat here and listened to this pathetic little man accuse me of treason, and watched as you all bicker about it and do nothing.

"But that's all any of you do, isn't it? You sit here and bicker about every little problem and nothing ever gets done. But when I take action, when I do what is necessary, I'm plotting. Well, if that is the charge against me, then I stand guilty." Danothir paused as he reached Ryoma, pondering something before continuing his purposeful walk. "This Consortium of fools has weakened our realm. Chaos looms at our heels and you do nothing. Tarkin was weak. His weakness led his House to ruin, but I will not allow that to happen to the realm. I killed Tarkin because he was weak, just like you're weak, Chancellor."

"I'd choose my next words carefully Danothir." The Chancellor rose to his feet, glaring at Danothir, who stopped in front of him. "You're admitting to murder and are inching dangerously close to high treason."

"*I'm* not the one guilty of treason," Danothir spat, anger turning his face a dark shade of red. "Your weakness betrayed our realm. Your pointless meetings, and your never ending bureaucracy... No, you, and them, your all to blame for everything. I'm not betraying the realm, I'm saving it. I will do what you could not, what they cannot. I will unite the realm and usher in a new era of greatness. The right to rule—and I have chosen my words Chancellor—that divine right, is mine."

"Guards!" T'Chello jumped to his feet.

The Chancellor stabbed a finger at Danothir, his face red and twisted into a snarl. "Danothir Borga, you are hereby bound by the authority of this Consortium. You *will* submit to that authority and stand trial for murder and treason. You will..."

"To Yun'Harrar with your authority!" Danothir lunged forward, pulling a slender dagger out of his suit pocket and plunged it hilt deep into the Chancellor's throat. Snarling as he ripped the bloody weapon free, he stabbed the gagging man in the chest, before letting the Chancellor fall to the floor.

"You..." T'Chello dropped to the floor next to the Chancellor's blood soaked body, pain twisting his face. "Guards!" T'Chello looked toward the entrance as five guards burst into the room. "Arrest him, now."

"Please." Danothir turned away from the fuming general and stepped over to the large window that overlooked the island, wiping his bloody hands on his suit. "As Ryoma has pointed out, I've been planning this for years."

Caught off guard by what he had just witnessed, Genki found himself staring wide eyed at Danothir, when he spotted clouds of smoke rising over the island. Forcing himself to regain his composure, he stood, noticing for the first time the faint but excited cries from outside. "What have you..." Genki started only to get cut off as a loud explosion shook the chamber.

"Did you really think I'd be unprepared? It took some doing, but I've managed to work some of my own men into your precious guardsmen." Danothir turned back to T'Chello for a moment before sauntering to the entrance and the guards. "Kill them all."

Well played Danothir. Genki watched as the guards moved to attack the unarmed nobles while Danothir disappeared into the hall. The panicked protests of frightened of the room's occupants began to fill the room as they backed away from the advancing guards. Searching for his best option for escape, Genki cursed himself for not having the foresight to conceal a weapon of his own. Refusing to allow himself to be killed by Danothir's goons, he kicked the expensive chair he had been sitting in at the closest guard, causing him to trip.

Seizing the opening, Genki lunged forward, nailing the axe wielding guard with a right hook. He followed up with a blow to the stomach, when he caught sight of a second guard moving toward him. Trying to avoid getting gored by the second guard's sword, he dove to the side, but still felt a sharp pain shoot through him as the cold steel cut into the flesh of his arm. Genki let out a pained grunt as he hit the floor and rolled onto his back in time to see the attacking guard raise his sword to finish him off. A wave of panic churned his core as the guard swung his arms, but to his surprise, Ryoma tackled the guard, knocking him to the ground.

Catching the clang of swords clashing, Genki looked to his left and saw that T'Chello had managed to get his hands on a sword and was fighting off one of Danothir's men, while Ritsuko sprinted out of the chamber. Returning his attention to his own troubles, he spotted another guard rushing toward him and rolled to the side, evading a broad sword meant to impale him. The guard hoisted his weapon, snarling as he prepared for a second attack, only to be stopped short as Genki's foot crashed into his groin.

Satisfied by the pained wheeze the guard made as he doubled over, Genki coiled his leg before launching it forward, scoring with a savage kick to the face. Staving off panic, Genki climbed to his feet, surprised to see that Ryoma had punched out his opponent, and found the first guard he had tripped running toward him. Ducking under a sloppy high attack, he landed a solid kick to the man chest just as he turned to face him. Genki started forward, eager to press his advantage, but stopped, noticing the blade of a sword sticking out of the guard's torso.

Letting out a chuckle as the guard slouched to the floor, Genki nodded while Ryoma recovered the bloody sword from the dead guard. "Didn't know you knew how to use one of those."

"I was a knight before I was King." Ryoma smirked, tossing the weapon to Genki. "Sword?"

"No, thank you." Genki tossed the sword back to Ryoma, noticing the relative quiet of the chamber and the guard he had kicked crawling toward a dropped sword. Finding what he was looking for, Genki picked up the axe the guard had dropped and stepped back over the crawling man. "I've always been partial to axes." Looking away from Ryoma, he raised the heavy weapon before driving it in-between the guard's shoulder blades. "More heft."

"I see." Ryoma grimaced, turning to face T'Chello. "I know it's in poor taste, but, it seems I was right after all."

"Noted." T'Chello stepped over to the main entrance and peeked into the hall.

"Any ideas on how to get out of this little trap?" Ryoma asked. "Danothir is bound to send more men to kill us. Especially you General, given that you've just inherited the Chancellor's duties to rule."

"I'll see his corpse ravaged by wild dogs for this treason." T'Chello marched over to the wall behind the Chancellor's seat and opened the private door. "We'll go this way. Danothir left archers in the hallway."

"Doesn't this lead to the Chancellors chamber?" the King of Fero asked. "Won't they be waiting for us?"

"There is a secret passage in this hall that will take us outside. I doubt Danothir would have learned of its existence." T'Chello motioned for everyone to follow before stepping inside.

Waiting for everyone else to file into the narrow corridor, Genki stepped through the door and pulled it shut behind them when he noticed Ryoma glaring at him. "Yes?"

"I was just wondering if this was enough to get you to actually help me with Danothir, or were you going to keep playing games?"

"I havent decided yet." Genki held up his wounded arm. "But they did ruin my favorite suit."

* * *

Ikari vaulted forward, leaping over the horse pulling the wagon, and crashed feet first into the face of the soldier holding the reigns. Counting seven soldiers baring Inara's crest, in addition to Gaou, Ikari rebounded off the man's face and landed in low crouch on the horses back.

"Fella's." Flashing Gaou a taunting smirk, Ikari drew his sword and flipped sideways, slashing the galloping steed across the neck. Just as his feet touched the ground, he rolled to avoid getting hit by the crashing wagon and spun to face it as it slammed into a charred tree. Twirling his sword to remove some of the blood from the blade before sliding it back into its sheath, Ikari stalked toward the cursing men as they recovered and pulled their own weapons. "That wasn't a rental, was it?"

"You're gonna get squashed like a little annoying bug," Gaou growled, causing the azure scars on his face to pulse with light. "You're dead You're gonna die feeling my boot on your face like a... a... a bug gettin' squashed."

"Squash the bug, squash the bug," Ikari mocked, hoping to goad the man into fighting him rather than chasing after Amy. "Don't you ever come up with anything a bit more witty? Or is Ritsuko not paying you to have an actual thought of your own?"

"I'm paid to snap you like a small stick," Gaou spat.

"So that's a yes?"

Gaou grabbed two of his men and shoved them up the path. "You two go get the girl. The rest of you, kill him."

"Don't leave now, party's just getting started." Ikari started after the two departing soldiers but a sword wielding man darted in front of him, cutting him off with a surprisingly efficient attack. Ducking to avoid the attack, he spotted two more soldiers leaping over him and landed with their swords ready to strike.

Rushing toward him in a coordinated attack, the two soldiers unleashed a string of fluid slashes, forcing him back into the remaining two guards. Shocked by the soldiers skills, Ikari swayed to avoid a stab from the first soldier and hooked his arm, punching him across the jaw before shoving him toward two of his compatriots.

"What happened to all your smart comments, huh?" Gaou laughed while Ikari backed away.

"Your guys have been working out." Ikari took up a defensive posture, scanning each of the soldiers for an opening to attack, when he noticed their eyes. Each of the soldiers circling around him had a fierce glare, a focus he had never seen in simple swords for hire before, yet alone anyone working for House Inara. These men had the eyes of a true soldier. A soldier that believed heart and soul in what he was fighting for. And each of them had a single, unnatural, grayish blue eye. "This is new."

"What'd ya expect?" Gaou smirked. "The boss lady done to them what she did to me and Thade. 'Cept they ain't got the good stuff like we did, but it's more than enough to finish a punk like you."

"You guys do realize that Ritsuko infected you with some sort of mystical disease that will probably end with your deaths don't you?" Ikari raised an eyebrow, when he sensed a movement from behind him.

Ikari twisted to avoid a vertical slash and let himself roll backwards, pushing off the ground with his hands, and drove his heels into a soldiers face. Landing lightly on his feet, Ikari flipped back, hoping to put some distance between himself and his dance partners. Matching his movements, they attacked in waves of two, pushing his ability to evade as he ducked, swayed, or twisted around their eager blades.

Ignoring the pain that shot through his leg as a sword grazed his thigh, Ikari hooked the arm of a soldier, locking it in place while he twisted and landed an elbow to the man's temple. Ikari then grabbed the man by the throat and flung him toward another soldier an instant before nailing them both with a spinning heel kick.

Shifting his attention to his left, Ikari jumped back to avoid getting sliced in two, and resumed his defensive dance as the soldier pressed his attack. Spotting a pattern in the soldiers attack, he ducked under a horizontal swing and stepped behind the soldier, scoring with a harsh kick. Reeling from his blow, the soldier failed to block a kick to his knee and dropped to a crouch a moment before Ikari yanked his head back by the hair and caved in his windpipe.

Spotting another of Gaou's men, Ikari darted forward, grateful that his armguard had done its job as he blocked a high strike, and landed a trio of blows. He started after the staggered soldier, hoping to finish him off, when he felt the cold steel from a sword slash across his back. Reeling from the sharp pain that jolted through his back, Ikari turned in time to see one of the soldiers boots crash into his jaw, sending him spiraling to the ground.

Landing hard on his aching back, he looked up and found a soldier diving toward him, ready to impale him. Ikari rolled to the side and twisted to his feet as the man landed, and threw a kick out of frantic desperation. Dashing toward the soldier that had cut him, Ikari blocked a downward slash and grabbed his wrist, unloading a harsh uppercut. Still holding the man's wrist, Ikari forced his arm into a locked position before slamming his palm into the man's elbow, breaking his arm. Twisting the mangled limb inwards, Ikari skewered the man with his own sword before letting him fall.

Ikari scanned the area and found the three remaining soldiers regrouping while Gaou cursed. Extending two fingers on each hand, Ikari took a deep breath, ignoring the pain throbbing from his wounds, and began to focus his energy into his fingers. Not waiting for the soldiers to surround him again, he bolted toward the man in the center and drove his knee into the man's nose. Spinning into a low sweep the instant his feet touched the ground, Ikari kicked the legs out from the soldier to his right. Allowing his momentum to spin him around completely, Ikari thrust his right arm into the falling man's torso, releasing the energy in his fingers with enough force to shatter the man's ribs.

Spinning back toward the man on the left, Ikari sidestepped an angry attack and stomped down on the soldier's sword as it hit the ground, prying it free from his grasp, and then kicked him in the throat. Still focusing his energy into his left fingers, Ikari turned toward the remaining soldier and rushed forward, blood pouring from his face. The soldier unleashed a torrent of attacks, forcing Ikari to dodge, but managed to land a solid kick to the stomach.

Ikari staggered back while the soldier lunged forward, attempting to skewer him, but Ikari rolled under the attack. Rising behind the soldier, Ikari twisted to his left, slamming his left hand into the man's exposed neck.

Taking a moment to force air back into his lungs as the last soldier fell, Ikari turned around in time to see Gaou's fist fly into his face. Reeling from both pain and surprise, Ikari felt Gaou's hand wrap around his throat, followed by another punch to the face.

"You look surprised. Didn't think I was this fast did ya?" Gaou punched Ikari again before pushing him back and unloading a kick to the chest. "Whatever Inara did to us is real good. The more time that passes the stronger I get."

"Swell." Ikari forced himself to his feet, wiping some of the blood from his face. Taking up an attack stance, Ikari glanced up the path, praying that Amy made it through the Gateway. "Let's see how strong you are."

* * *

Sprinting across a debris filled street with half a dozen useless nobles that had elected to dock at the eastern port, as he did, Genki was surprised to see the amount of damage Danothir's attack had caused in so short a time. Smoke poured from the buildings that remained intact after the explosions that shook the island. Evidence of Danothir's troops could be found easily enough as Genki stepped over another dead body.

"Sounds as if T'Chello has his hands full." Ryoma followed behind Genki as they moved down a narrow path that took them behind a row of two story buildings.

Genki nodded with a grunt, adjusting his grip on the axe he carried. "T'Chello's choice to join his troops was beneficial. He should keep Danothir distracted long enough for us to make our escape."

"Yes, much more preferable than actually helping," Ryoma replied.

"Disapprove of my methods as much as you like, but I've come to realize that you and I have much in common." Genki peered over his shoulder while turning down a wide alley that would lead back to the main road.

"I hadn't realized I was that self-centered."

"We're both well versed in the game of politics. And we both know the game Danothir started has to be played perfectly or we'll each lose everything. The only difference between us at the moment is that I'm aware of the other pieces on the board and you are not. However, you have good instincts, and you're at least smart enough to realize that there's more going on here than just Danothir's ambition. That is why you've only voiced concern about Danothir rather than actually moving against him. That's why you offered Ithor's support in aiding T'Chello, and that's why you keep trying to convince me to help you."

"And what exactly am I not seeing?" Ryoma inquired.

"Ritsuko Inara. You've been so focused on Danothir, and me, that you failed to notice her. Granted, she's been far more cautious than Danothir." Genki, and the group of nobles, reached the end of the alley and peered around the buildings corner. Empty, save for a few destroyed vendor stands and some abandoned carriages and wagons,

Genki's attention was drawn further up the road as he spotted Ritsuko exiting a large white building. "Speaking of whom."

Switching places with Genki, Ryoma looked up the road before turning back to Genki. "What is she doing leaving the library?"

"Let's ask her." Genki grinned, resting his axe on his shoulder.

"What about us?" the King of Fero asked.

"What about you?" Genki stared at the useless man for a moment.

Ryoma turned toward the nobles and gave them a reassuring smile. "Take the back streets the rest of the way and I'm sure you'll reach the port without incident."

Leaving the cowering nobles to fend for themselves, Genki headed toward the columned library, scanning the street for any signs of danger. Stopping a few yards away from Ritsuko, he noticed a large weathered book tucked under her arm. "I'd imagine the library is closed, given the current circumstances."

Ritsuko paused halfway down the wide stairs that led to the entrance and glanced to her left before glaring at the approaching men. "And here I was hoping that Danothir would at least succeed in riding the realm of one Sanada."

Ryoma took a step forward. "So you really are working with Danothir. Why?"

Ritsuko let a cold smile spread across her lips and continued down the stairs. "Oh, I've only been working with him since this morning. But, if I were you, I wouldn't worry about why right now. You have more pressing concerns."

"Those being?" Genki started to return her smile when he heard the sound of someone approaching from his right.

"Me." Turning in time to see a man with glowing blue scars punch him, Genki staggered back, clutching his jaw.

The man turned toward Ryoma and ducked under his blind attack, before driving his fist into the King's stomach. He then grabbed Ryoma by the back of his collar, pulled him back, and sent him tumbling backwards with a kick to the midsection. Genki darted forward, axe held ready to strike as the man's momentum spun him around, but a harsh kick to the sternum cut short his attack.

"Thade, if you would be so kind as to kill them." Ritsuko stepped past the brawny man and started down the road. "I'll be waiting on the ship. Don't take too long. We have errands to run."

"As you wish, my Lady." Thade bowed his head as Ritsuko strolled off before glaring at Genki and Ryoma. "Genki Sanada, I've been looking forward to testing my skills against the eldest of the Sanada family before I kill your siblings. I hope you're as skilled as they."

"Try me and find out." Genki held his weapon ready as Ryoma did the same.

"I intend to."

Switching to a left handed grip, Genki sprang forward, aiming his axe at Thade's neck as he swung it horizontally, but Thade swayed out of harm's way with ease. Genki reversed his swing, forcing Thade to jump back, and let the weight of the axe twist him around as he landed a side kick to the chest. Raising his weapon for an overhead strike, Genki pressed forward, planning to split the taller man in two, only to find his opponent had sidestepped his attack. Surprised by Thade's speed while his axe hit the ground, Genki's head flashed with pain as Thade's knee slammed into his face. Reeling from the first blow, Genki felt a large fist crash into his cheek, sending a second jolt of pain racing through his body.

Swinging his axe blindly as he spun away, Genki saw Ryoma rush passed him, and attack in a flurry of motion. Wearing an almost bored expression, Thade evaded each of Ryoma's well-aimed attacks. Missing with downward slash, Ryoma continued forward, changing the angle of his sword as he drove it up toward Thade's torso. Thade veered around the attack, and countered with a harsh kick to the ribs. Lunging after Ryoma, Thade pelted him with a trio of punches, before grabbing him by his tunic and hurling his next to Genki.

"How disappointing, I had hoped for a more spirited exchange." Thade stalked forward. "Or perhaps my strength has simply outgrown the Sanada."

Ryoma climbed to his feet, his bleeding face already showing signs of bruising. "I don't suppose you have any of your Sanyoshu lurking around."

"Not usually. Although, that's a practice I might start from now on." Genki shook his head, trying to force his vision to clear. Catching a nod from Ryoma, Genki shot forward, attacking from the left, while Ryoma attacked from the right.

Moving with a swiftness Genki wouldn't have thought possible for a human, Thade eluded every strike, every swing they threw at him. Using a barrage of attacks to push Thade toward a small shop, Genki lashed out with a vertical swing, hoping Thade would dodge and find himself impaled on Ryoma's sword. However, instead of dodging as he had expected, Thade caught the handle of his axe and nailed Ryoma with a harsh back fist, followed by a kick that sent him tumbling backwards. Thade then pulled forward on the axe, dragging Genki with it, and rammed his elbow into Genki's face.

Dropping his weapon, Genki heard himself gag as Thade wrapped his fingers around his throat. Gasping for air while his vision started to dim, Genki attempted a punch only to have it slapped away by Thade's free hand.

"I pray that before they die, your siblings give me more satisfaction." Thade tightened his grip, appearing to enjoy the sound Genki made as he struggled to free himself.

"Satisfaction, huh?" Genki managed to look up, while Thade turned toward the sound of the voice, and spotted Yuki flipping off the roof of the twenty foot high shop. Thrusting her heels into Thade's face, she sent him tumbling backwards into the street after rebounding off the surprised man and landed in a low crouch.

Freed from Thade's grasp, Genki fell to the ground, gasping for air, and watched Yuki sprint past him. Not wasting any time, Yuki pelted Thade with a string of punches, keeping him off balance. She landed another punch and went for a high kick, but Thade managed to catch her leg and throw her over his shoulder.

Darting out from between two buildings with their swords in hand, E'Lan and Saskai sped toward Thade, attacking in unison. Ducking from a high attack from Saskai, Thade was forced to jump over a low swing from E'Lan. Rolling to put some distance between himself and the pair of Sanyoshu, Thade spotted Yuki and leapt back to avoid a swift kick.

"What's with the disagreeable look?" Yuki took up an attack stance while Thade glanced from E'Lan and Saskai to her. "You asked for satisfaction, and I arrived with two of my friends. Don't tell me you've spent all your stamina on my brother."

Glancing to his side as Ryoma got back to his feet; Thade let a twisted smile adorn his face. "Not at all. I've simply kept Lady Ritsuko waiting for too long, but you and I will have our moment soon enough."

Not waiting for a reply, he sped toward Ryoma, punching him in the stomach, and ripped his sword free. Yuki started after him, but Thade turned and heaved the heavy weapon at her head before running off.

Sliding under the spiraling sword, Yuki popped back to her feet and extended her arm, stopping E'Lan and Saskai as they chased after Thade. "Don't bother. He's not an opponent the two of you can defeat. Besides, we've our own escape to make."

"Yes, Lady Yuki," E'Lan and Saskai replied in unison.

"What do you mean?" Genki stepped over to Yuki rubbing his aching throat while Saskai helped Ryoma up.

"Havent you heard? Danothir's little surprise attack has succeeded like the rising sun. T'Chello has ordered a full retreat." Yuki motioned toward the center of the island. "And as we speak, a mass of Borga's finest are headed this way. So unless you want to fight them all..."

"I get it. Let's go." Genki turned and started down the street, moving slower than he would have liked. "What about Ikari?"

"Believe it or not, but he's actually safer in Alextien than we are here." Pulling Genki's arm over her shoulder, Yuki helped him along, despite the annoyed look he gave her. "What about that one?"

"Ryoma can ride with us," Genki replied as they passed the injured King.

"Really?" Yuki smirked, clearly resisting the urge to say something more, and motioned for E'Lan and Saskai to help Ryoma. "That's twice I've saved you now, *your majesty.*"

"I'll have to find some way to repay you one of these days." Ryoma laughed, holding his side.

Trying to ignore the pain racking his body, Genki couldn't help but think about Thade and the damage he had done to Ryoma and himself. He had been trained to fight by the finest instructors in Austuria, and even though he wasn't in the same league as Yuki and Ikari, he had held his fighting prowess in high regard. All the same, Thade had managed to completely trounce him with what appeared to be little effort.

For the first time in his life, Genki felt a cold chill snake its way into his mind. Despite how battle crazed Yuki and Ikari became, he never really feared for their lives. He never worried because deep down he knew they'd always win. He knew no one could stand up to them. It was a comforting feeling he had taken for granted; and it was one that had just been taken from him.

Chapter Twenty-Five

Dirt, beautiful charred dirt. I forgot how kicking up the dust here stings the lungs.

Ikari tried not to think about the slight discomfort breathing in the dust caused him, focusing instead on blocking the barrage of punches being thrown at him and avoiding an even greater concern. More discomforting than the dirt, was the fact that he *needed* to focus on fighting Gaou. He had planned to simply incapacitate the pursuing soldiers and Gaou before following after Amy. Of course, at the time, he figured the soldiers would be pushovers and Gaou—as improved as he seemed at the warehouse—was still a lumbering brawler with no technique. Whatever Ritsuko had infected him with, it seemed to have enhanced his strength and speed to a level far beyond when they had last met. Even his technique, what little he displayed, seemed to have gotten better.

And I still have to find Amy.

Ikari knew that she would be safe enough with Gaius—even with the two soldiers that had gotten passed him chasing after them—assuming she made it to the Gateway and Gaius was at least as good as Hayate with a sword, and if Hayate was still alive. Getting poisoned by a member of the Assassins Guild was bad enough, but considering the poison had come from Alia, he had little hope of seeing the vexing knight alive.

Mind racing with concern for Amy, Ikari blocked a left hook only to feel Gaou's right fist slam into his ribs. Chastising himself for letting his mind wander, Ikari leapt forward, intending to deliver a knee to the head, however, Gaou blocked his attack and countered by grabbing him by the waist and slammed him onto the ground.

Ikari, resisting the urge to cry out as a fresh wave of pain rushed through his body, rolled backwards to avoid getting crushed by Gaou's large boot. Gaou pressed forward, landing a harsh punch that sent Ikari tumbling into a half dead tree and pounced instantly as he rebounded off the trunk, peppering him with a hail of strikes. Managing to duck under an attack, Ikari moved to get behind the larger man only to catch a fist to the head.

Falling forward, Ikari pushed off the ground, mule kicking Gaou as he tried to attack again. Pressing his advantage, he pelted Gaou with a punch of his own an instant before unleashing a torrent of kicks. Ikari poured all of his speed into his kicks, forcing his adversary to get defensive while pushing him back.

Ducking under a heel kick, Gaou threw an angry fist, but Ikari parried the strike, spun behind him, and hit him with an elbow between the shoulders. Ikari turned to follow up, but was surprised to find Gaou had already recovered and was caught off guard by a high kick. Spinning away, Ikari heard Gaou growling as he rushed forward and dropped back, hooking his arm, and threw him toward the wagon.

His body aching and eager to finish the fight, despite the excitement he felt, Ikari sprinted toward Gaou, when he saw him scoop something off the ground and hurl it at him. Realizing it was one of the soldiers swords, Ikari slid under the spiraling weapon, disconcerted by how close it had come to skewering his head, and closed the gap between them. Slamming his fist into Gaou's jaw, Ikari spun low, narrowly evading a second sword.

Using every ounce of speed he could muster to duck, dodge, or sway away from the frenzied assault, Ikari instinctively drew his own sword, blocking the increasing amount of attacks he couldn't evade. Ikari parried a wild slash and countered with a high kick, which Gaou managed to block and answered with kick to the chest. Pressing forward, Gaou released another flurry of high and mid attacks before going for a low sweep. Hopping over the sweep, Ikari spun to his right, blocking a high attack. Swords sparking as they clashed, Gaou swiveled around, aiming for Ikari's ankle.

Ikari flipped sideways, evading the low swing, and began somersaulting backwards, when he noticed another sword lying on the ground. Landing seven yards away from Gaou, Ikari took up a defensive stance while the brawler turned to sneer at him.

"What's wrong? Too scared to fight?" Gaou laughed, not nearly as winded as Ikari would have Hopped. "Can't say I blame ya, considering what I've become. With this strength, no one can beat me. Ya know it, don't ya? I can tell. I can tell you're scared 'cause you finally stopped making your lame jokes."

"You have no idea what she did to you, do you?" Ikari swallowed, fear chilling the pit of his stomach. "Do you even know what it is she has you fighting for?"

"All I need to know is that I'm about to be the man who killed Ikari Sanada."

"Really? Then by all means, give me everything you've got." Ikari forced a mocking grin to his face, wondering if Gaou could be more than just boasting. *Could you actually be the one to finally kill me?*

Fear, mixed with an almost euphoric sense of exhilaration rushed through Ikari as he rolled forward. Scooping up the sword he had spotted as he rolled to his feet, Ikari whipped the weapon at Gaou's head a spilt second before throwing his own sword. Batting the first sword away as he charged forward, Gaou lowered his blade in preparation to stab Ikari—who was rushing toward him—and failed notice the second sword until the blade found its mark. Gaou tried to raise his sword as he staggered back from the weapon sticking out of his torso but Ikari leapt forward, kicking his sword deeper into Gaou's chest, piercing his heart, before twisting in midair and scoring with a harsh kick to the jaw.

Landing on his feet with an exhausted thud, Ikari watched as Gaou tumbled back before coming to a motionless halt. Weary, Ikari stepped over to Gaou and glared down into the man's dimming eyes, desperate for air.

"Ordinarily, this is where I'd stop to make some witty remark before you died, but I'm tired and have places to be." Ikari reached down and ripped his sword out of the dead man's torso. "Who knew a bar brawler like you could give me a good fight."

Wiping off as much of the blood as he could, Ikari turned and started up the road, noticing an increasing amount of pain searing his body. Mustering all of his will to fight off collapsing, Ikari returned his weapon to its sheath and forced himself to run. As much as he would have liked to pass out, he knew he still had one task left to do. He had promised to get Amy back to Terra safely. And, to his surprise, that was one promise that he felt compelled to keep.

* * *

Chest pounding from terror and the adrenalin surging through her veins, Amy struggled to keep her balance while Hayate grew heavier, unable to keep his feet under him. Desperate to close the ten yards between them and the Gateway, she tried to ignore the cold sensation growing in the pit of her stomach and the overwhelming sense that she could feel Hayate fading from the warm spot in her mind that he had come to occupy. Behind her, the equally distressing sounds of swords banging together filled her ears as Gaius fought to buy her time. Stumbling as her foot hit a large rock, Amy fell to the ground, unable to balance herself and Hayate.

"Hayate." Amy rolled the knight to his back and moved to help him up when he feebly pushed her arm away.

"I... I'm not going to make it... through the Gateway," Hayate groaned, shivering as if he was submerged in ice water. "You have to go..."

Amy shook her head, powerless to stop the tears from flowing down her cheeks. "No I'm not leaving without you, so on your feet."

"Stay... and you die. You have to take the rose and go."

"To hell with the damn rose." Dropping the crimson jewel, Amy tried again to pull Hayate up, but stopped once she saw the pain twisting his face. Amy let herself drop to her knees, crying as she caressed his pale, cold cheek. "I don't want you to die."

A dusty breeze blew over the charred forest, carrying the gurgling cry of the last soldier as Gaius finished him off. Breathing heavily as he ran over to Amy, he peered around before kneeling next her. "We'd better get going. No telling how long we have till more soldiers show up."

"I'm not leaving Hayate and Ikari to die." Amy glared at Gaius for a moment before returning her attention to Hayate.

"Ikari's probably dead by now, and Hayate's..." Gaius let his voice trail off.

"Hayate's what?"

"I'm sorry. He's my friend as well, but whatever poison Tres used has done its job." Gaius placed a hand on her shoulder. "He'll never make it to Hapes or anyone who could save him. We came here on a mission. Ikari and Hayate died to see it through. We owe it to them to see it finished."

"He's right," Hayate stated between labored breaths and reached over to the rose. "Getting you home is all that matters."

"No it's not." Amy took the rose with her free hand, failing to keep her emotions in check. "What's the point of getting home if I can't take you with me to meet my dad, or show you off to my sister and friends?"

Hearing the sound of someone approaching, Amy glanced over her shoulder while Gaius turned and stepped forward with his sword at the ready when Ikari emerged out of a patch of dead trees.

"Ikari?" Gaius let out a surprised laugh and lowered his sword as he stepped over. "Still alive, huh? I'm glad to see Inara's soldiers are still not enough to do you in. Although, you've looked better."

"You should see the other guy." Ikari motioned toward Hayate. "How is he?"

"Not good. Poisons done its job well," Gaius replied.

Returning her attention to Hayate, Amy tried to return his smile as he caressed her cheek. "You promised to show me around Ithor, remember? As a knight, I'm holding you to that promise."

"I'm sorry I can't keep that promise, but I'm grateful that I got to meet you... I wish... I could have..." Hayate's hand fell from her face as his voice trailed off.

"Hayate?" Amy leaned in closer, holding his head, while tears poured down the sides of her face. Refusing to acknowledge that she no longer felt him in the back of her mind, Amy pressed her forehead against his, trying to will life back into him.

"Amy, he's... he's gone; Taken into the embrace of Ako'Reah," Gaius stated.

"Well she can't have him." Amy shoved Gaius back, tears pouring down her face as he tried to console her. Anguish twisting her features, she put her hands on Hayate's chest, wishing she had never asked him to bring her here. If she had just listened to him and stayed in Ithor, if she hadn't been so selfish and obsessed with finding a way back home, then Hayate would still be alive. He'd still be with her, and she would not have lost the one thing that still mattered to her.

"We have to go, before Tres catches up to us," Gaius stated from behind. Ignoring him, Amy laid her head on Hayate's chest, letting her emotions flood out of her.

"Amy?" Ikari whispered.

"I can't leave him."

"Amy," Ikari repeated, his voice carrying an odd inflection.

Amy spun toward Ikari, glaring through tear filled eyes while a surge of anger burned through her. "If you want to leave, then leave."

"Amy, Look!" Ikari pointed back to Hayate, radiating a sense of shock and confusion that she'd never felt from him before.

Amy turned back to Hayate, noticing a growing burning sensation traveling through her right arm and building within the crimson rose in her hand. Taken aback, Amy let the rose fall onto Hayate's chest as a pale, but comforting reddish light began to pulse out of it. Slowly, the warm light began to pour over the slain knight like thick syrup until it enveloped him completely.

Staring in awe despite feeling like her insides were fighting against gravity, Amy noticed a second bluish light and looked around to find its source before realizing that the light was radiating from her skin. Eyes wide, Amy reached out to Hayate, feeling drawn by the light surrounding him. Just as her fingers grazed the surface of the red light, the crimson shell shattered, disappearing in a blinding flash.

Unaffected by the burst of light, Amy watched as Hayate's eyes snapped open and he sucked air back into his lungs. "Hayate?" Overwhelmed with emotion, Amy fell on top of him, ecstatic that she could once again sense him occupying the loving portion in the back of her mind that she had gotten so used to feeling.

"Amy." Hayate smiled as he looked up and caressed her head.

"That's impossible," Ikari exclaimed in a soft voice.

"Gods, you really are a goddess aren't you?" Gaius stared down at Amy and Hayate for a long minute, clamping down on a sense of surprise. Taking a loud breath, Gaius twisted to his right, smashing the pommel of his sword onto Ikari's temple and sent him spinning to the ground. Gaius then grabbed a handful of Amy's hair and yanked her to her feet. "Quite a shame actually. I was really hoping you'd turn out to be just a pretty girl."

"What are you doing?" Hayate tried to push himself up, but his arms gave out a moment before Gaius pointed his sword at Hayate's neck.

"Following orders like a good knight. Lord Borga has paid me quite the King's ransom to deliver this little trinket to him." Gaius shoved Amy aside and picked up the rose before stepping over to the pedestal in front of the Gateway and opened the indigo portal. "Oh don't glare at me like that Hayate. I would have asked you to join me years ago, but I knew you were too mired in Ryoma's dogma to ever see the bigger picture."

"So you betrayed the King, your homeland, *me*, just to line your pockets with Borga's money?" Hayate climbed to his knees, glaring at the older knight. "Why?"

"Please, the man I serve has a vision for this realm the likes of which you can't imagine. Danothir's money is simply an added bonus." Gaius stepped in front of the portal, tucking the rose into an unseen pocket while keeping his sword at the ready. "Danothir wanted you dead and Amy brought back to him, but dragging her all the back to Nel'Oskow would be far too much of a hassle. And *because* we are friends, I've elected not to kill you."

"I'm not letting you leave with that rose." Hayate grabbed his sword and forced himself up, struggling to maintain his balance.

"As pleased as I am to see you alive and recovered, you can barely stand, let alone stop me. So rather than spend our last seconds together in so distasteful a manner, I'll take my leave. If we're fortunate, as saddening as the thought may be, we will never meet again.

Goodbye old friend." Waving, Gaius turned and disappeared into the shimmering portal.

"Gaius!" Hayate stared to follow, but stumbled as his legs almost gave out.

Mind swimming with concern, Amy hurried over to Hayate's side and helped him regain his balance. "Are you alright?"

"I'll be okay." Hayate stared into the portal for a long moment, burning with anger. Sheathing his sword, he wiped away a tear from her cheek. "Thanks to you."

"What just happened?" Ikari rolled to his back, holding his head. Sharing their smile for a moment longer, Hayate and Amy stepped over to Ikari and helped him to his feet. "I saw you die. You were dead, and now you're not. She was glowing, you were dead, and I got sucker punched by your pal. I'm still a little groggy, but no amount of magic or fancy armor can raise the dead. So will one of you, *any of you*, tell me what just happened?"

"I... I don't know," Amy stuttered, trying to think of an explanation besides the one she had wanted to avoid since falling out of that casket weeks ago.

"I'm a rational guy willing to believe in a lot, but..." Ikari trialed off as the sound of approaching horses caught everyone's attention.

"You can be surprised later." Hayate motioned toward the Gateway. "We need to go, now."

"Yeah," Ikari replied, regaining his composure. "I'm with you."

Taking Hayate's hand as Ikari limped through the portal, Amy followed behind him only to find herself feeling flabbergasted as they emerged on the other side. Expecting to see the pristine beauty of Hapes Romanesque structures, she was instead greeted by plumes of smoke. Hurrying onto the streets, they found buildings, charred by explosions, missing sections of walls while bodies lay strewn across the roads.

"What happened?" Amy glanced over the carnage, squeezing Hayate's hand.

"I'd guess Danothir made his move a little earlier than we expected." Ikari looked over the scene. "Which makes finding Gaius all the more harder."

"He could be anywhere. How're we supposed find him in all this?" Amy asked, picking up the sound of fighting a few blocks away.

"We're not," Hayate replied, anger narrowing his eyes.

"What about the rose?"

"No sense worrying about it now." Ikari turned back toward Amy and Hayate. "It's gone and we need to get off this island."

"Eastern docks?" Hayate motioned to his left.

"Unless either of you has learned to fly." Ikari nodded, starting down the debris filled street.

Chapter Twenty-Six

"So there's no way you can retake the island?" Ryoma stood on the opposite side of a well-polished circular table, rubbing the back of his neck.

Half listening to the conversation between Ryoma and T'Chello, Hayate stared down at a map of the realm laid out across the table and let his mind wander. The courtyards outside the castle were filled with the soldiers that had survived the retreat from Hapes. Not that he faulted them for retreating. He had seen for himself the strength of Danothir's forces while sneaking across the occupied island with Amy and Ikari and stealing the first boat they could sail out of port. After parting with Ikari, Hayate and Amy made their way back to Ithor without incident, save for the fact that they had barely spoken a word along the way.

Of course, he had no idea what he could say anyway. From the moment he had met her, he had believed Amy was the Protectorate Goddess. He *knew*, but he never had trouble talking to her before. It might have been because she was so certain that she wasn't. Maybe because, deep down, he didn't want to believe she was. But that was before he had died. He had died and she had brought him back, and he didn't know how to respond to that. After weeks of searching, they had found their proof, but he wasn't happy.

The trip to Ithor had been short, but Hayate could see the pain behind Amy's smile. He could see the weight this realization had brought on her, and it pained him to know that there was little he could do to help her. More vexing than that, was the realization that he was going to lose her. *How can she love me if she's a goddess? And what right do I have to even want it?*

"Not in the foreseeable future," T'Chello replied. "Borga positioned his forces well. He made sure the island was attacked on all sides. Trying to take it back now is a fool's errand."

"General, there was nothing more you could have done. Danothir's attack was too well planned, especially given the spies he placed in the island guards," Ryoma stated.

"Perhaps, but I should have been better prepared. I should have listened to you." T'Chello shook his head. "How goes the search for your own traitor?"

"I'll find him." Hayate looked over to the General, clenching his fist. "I promise you that."

Ryoma let out short sigh as he peered across the table. "Hayate…"

"Gaius Dualla is a traitor." Hayate slammed his fist on the table and turned away, stepping across the stone floor to lean against the window seal on the side wall. "I'm going to find him and see to it he's brought to justice; even if I have to hunt him across the realm to do it."

"I can appreciate how you're feeling right now, but I need your head clear if we're going to defeat Danothir." Ryoma leaned forward on the table before letting his voice soften. "How is Amy?"

"I… I don't know." Hayate shook his head. "She hasn't been the same simce Alextien."

"Understandable, given what happened."

Hayate let out a tired sigh and stepped back to the table. "I don't know what to say to her."

"I have no doubt that you'll work out what you need to say." Ryoma smiled.

"I heard about your resurrection in Alextien." T'Chello crossed his arms, sounding skeptical. "Rumors of your miracle have been floating through our camps since my men arrived in Ithor. Given that Ryoma was right about Danothir…"

"You don't believe that she's a goddess?" Hayate asked.

"I'm a practical man, a military man. I believe in what I can see or touch for myself, but your arguments, your own convictions seem to have swayed many of the men in my command," T'Chello replied. "But whether she is or not doesn't matter anymore. My men are willing to fight beside you, and by default, her, and so am I."

"We'd have a far easier fight if we weren't alone." Ryoma stared down at the map.

"What about the Sanada?" Hayate stifled a laugh, surprised that he had even thought of them.

"We'd sooner see a legless warg sail across the morning sky than receive help from the Sanada," Ryoma scoffed. "Genki made it clear that they weren't going to help."

"I'm not so sure." Hayate shook his head. "Amy thinks that they'll help, and… and I think she's right. Ikari nearly got himself killed trying to buy Amy time to drag me back to the Gateway. He could have left us the moment we reached the mainland, but he stayed and helped us get away. Amy says he'll help, and I've been wrong enough times to believe her."

"Well, for the moment we'll have to assume that we're on our own." T'Chello leaned forward and placed his finger on the map.

"Scouts say Borga is rallying his forces here, off the northeast corner of Hapes."

"Where is he heading?" Hayate glanced at the point of map, already knowing the answer.

"Ithor," T'Chello replied in a grim tone. "It looks as if he's planning to crush his opposition in one swipe, and he wants the girl."

"If your scout's numbers are accurate, then we can't allow Danothir's forces to reach Ithor." Ryoma turned toward T'Chello. "I won't let that madman butcher my people."

"I agree." T'Chello nodded, dragging his finger across the map. "That is why I suggest we ride out and meet him here, in the fields of Gelpher. It's far enough to keep any civilians out of the conflict, and with any luck, we'll be able to catch Borga off guard."

"I'm not thrilled with the idea of charging into battle, but it looks as if we have no other option." Ryoma shook his head.

"I'll make sure everyone is ready." Hayate nodded and started to turn away but stopped as Ryoma held up his hand.

"I'll have Holtz and Lynn spread the word." Ryoma stepped over to Hayate with a smile. "You, Hayate, need to go and talk with Amy."

Hayate let out a laugh, glancing out the open window and the afternoon sun. "Yeah, I know. Any idea on what I should say?"

"My friend, we're about to head out and fight for our lives in her name. I wouldn't know where to begin." Ryoma laughed, patting Hayate on the shoulder. "But I have faith that you'll figure out what to say, when the moments right."

* * *

Danothir marched down the hall of the lavish office he had requisitioned as his temporary camp site. Plush carpeting muffled the sound of his boots, allowing him to enjoy the clamor of his army through the open windows as they prepared to crush his enemies. Spotting his squire walking toward him, Danothir motioned for him to stop. "Lasaad, I'm expecting a guest. See to it she finds her way up here."

"Yes, Lord Borga." Lasaad nodded, stepping to the side. "Your other visitor is waiting in the office."

"Oh?" Danothir brushed passed the man and pushed open the door at the end of the hall. Stepping into the expensively decorated office, he noted the elegant woven tapestries hanging on the wooden walls. Sunlight filtered through tinted windows, reflecting off of a gaudy chandler that hung over a large mahogany desk. "You were supposed to be here days ago."

"Is that any way to greet a friend?" Sitting with his feet crossed on the polished desk, Gaius Dualla flashed an annoying smile while reaching into his tunic to pull out a leather pouch. "Especially one baring gifts."

Catching the pouch Gaius tossed to him, Danothir untied it and dumped the content into his open palm. "The last rose." Holding up the crimson jewel, Danothir let himself smile for a moment before a twinge of anger shot through him. "You were supposed to bring me the girl with it."

"Thank you is the customary response when someone does you a favor." Gaius glanced out the window as a group of soldiers marched passed.

"For as much as I'm paying you, you could have at least saved me the trouble of going to Ithor to take her."

"And spoil a motive for you to kill everyone in Ithor? That's hardly sporting. And I know how much you want Ryoma and T'Chello dead. You do know they're working together now, right?"

"Of course I do," Danothir spat, setting the rose down on the desk. "Which is why I want you to work with Svipdag. Together you can make a plan to counter any resistance Ryoma might conjure."

"Oh, gods no," Gaius laughed, dropping his feet to the wooden floor. "I'm not doing this because I care about your little uprising, and you're not paying me nearly enough to fight your battles for you. No, I've done everything I told you I would. Now, I expect to be well paid, not that I care much about your money."

"You'll have your money. Although I'm curious, if you're not willing to help me and you don't care about money, why get me the rose? Why betray your country?"

"Curiosity I suppose. I'm merely a purveyor of opportunities. And now that you have yours, I want to see what you make with it."

"Do you?" Danothir stared at the knight for a moment.

"Oh yes," Gaius replied. "For example, you wanted the roses and Amy in order to take control of the war god's army, despite the fact that you already control one of the largest armies in the realms. Why, or are you just that hungry for power?"

"To sow order out of chaos. I'm doing this not to gain power, but to bring peace. After I've wiped out T'Chello and Ryoma, I can unite the realm in a way no one has ever seen before."

Gaius smiled. "Under your militaristic dictatorship of course."

"Someone has to rule, and I am the one who's taken that right."

"So it's a holy war you've started?"

"I suppose it is. A war to avoid falling into chaos."

"Chaos, huh?" Gaius laughed. "How amusing."

Catching a shadow from behind, Danothir turned and saw Lasaad stepping through the doorway. "What is it?"

"Your other guests have arrived, my Lord."

"Bring them in." Danothir waved, noting that Lasaad had said guests.

"Well I can see you're busy, so I'll be on my way. After all, I do have a few errands to attend to before your little holy war reaches its conclusion." Gaius smirked as he rose to his feet and stepped around the desk. Pausing at the door as Lasaad led the two guests into the room, Gaius let out an amused laugh. "Ladies Inara."

Waiting until Lasaad and Gaius had left; Danothir forced the scowl from his face as he turned to greet Ritsuko and her daughter. "Welcome to Kalvor. What do you want?"

"You were right mother, he is rather boorish." Alia stepped passed Danothir and looked over the office.

"We came to see to our alliance." Ritsuko flashed a polite smiled while stepping past him to lean on the desk and picked up the crimson rose. "I see you managed to get this after all."

"I've been thinking over our last conversation, wondering why I should partner with you now that I have all three roses." Danothir stepped over to a tinted window and glanced over the soldiers gathered outside. "What is it that you have to offer?"

Ritsuko looked over her shoulder. "Besides the addition of my own augmented forces?"

"You mean the horde of assassins you brought with you."

"I thought we covered this," Ritsuko replied, letting the pleasantries drop from her voice. "I can give you the war god's army."

"You assume I can't get it myself. I did manage to get the rose despite your assurances that it was as good as yours."

"You can't," Alia stated from the back of the room. "Your schemes have worked well to get you this far, but no amount of scheming can conjure up an army. You need us more than you realize."

"Us?" Danothir shot the young woman an angry glare. "I don't remember inviting Ritsuko's spawn to participate."

"Yet here I am." Alia smirked.

"The fact of the matter is simple, Danothir," Ritsuko stated. "Together there isn't a force in the realm that can stop us. I will augment your soldiers, just as I did my own, and they will be more powerful than any army ever assembled. And after victory is at hand, I get the roses and use them to ascend, leaving you to rule the realm."

"And you're certain you can summon the armies of the slayer?" Danothir asked.

"So long as you bring me the girl, yes." Ritsuko nodded.

"When can you start augmenting my troops?"

"I've already taken the liberty." Alia stepped over to one of the tinted windows and pushed it open; playing with the jeweled pendant she wore around her neck. "You should see the results any moment now."

Ritsuko shot her daughter a surprised look while Danothir turned and opened the window behind him. "When did…"

"I had Thade dispense the potion as soon as we got here." Alia smiled and backed away from the window.

Gazing over the crowd of soldiers for a long minute, Danothir was about to turn around when he caught the sound of a man groaning. A moment later a chorus of multiple groans filled the air as waves of his soldiers doubled over in pain, dropping cups of purplish liquid or whatever else they might have been carrying. The pained cries began to fade, replaced by a sound he could only describe as stones rubbing together. Then, as suddenly as the sounds had started, they vanished, leaving the sea of soldiers completely motionless. Starring in disbelief at the army of stone statues frozen in front of him, Danothir spun toward Ritsuko only to find her mirroring the surprise he felt.

"You treacherous little witch." Danothir looked over to the smiling girl and yanked the knife he kept tucked in his belt free. Unable to keep his fury in check, he started forward when Ritsuko blocked his path.

"Alia, What have you done?" Ritsuko turned to glare at Alia, anger lining her voice.

"Did I forget to mention that I made a slight adjustment to your potion?" Alia laughed, enjoying the fury pouring off of them.

"Why?" Ritsuko demanded.

"Relax mother. It's completely reversible." Alia stepped back over to the window and held up the pendant by the chain, whispering to herself. Squeezing the pendant with her right hand, she closed her eyes a moment before a pale gray light began to slip through her fingers. Opening her hand in a burst light, Alia smirked as she opened her eyes. "See?"

Peering out of the window, Danothir felt an uneasy sense of relief as the stone skin encasing his soldiers crumbled away into dust. "I trust there was a point to this?"

"The point Lord Borga, was to get your attention. Both of you." Alia's eyes changed from an amused child's to an icy stare. "I just wanted you both to know what I could do if I don't get my way."

"What do you want?" Danothir returned her glare, surprised by the sudden shift in her demeanor.

"Ikari Sanada," Alia replied. "While the two of you are ascending or conquering, or whatever, I want you to see to it that Ikari is brought to me. Alive."

"And if I don't?" Danothir crossed his arms.

This time, it was Ritsuko who let out an amused laugh. "Isn't it obvious? If we don't, she turns your vast army back into garden decorations."

"You sound almost proud." Danothir shot a glare at Ritsuko, while the scent Alia's perfume filled his nostrils.

"Actually, I am." Ritsuko smiled, glancing at Alia.

"What makes you think the Sanada will even get involved?" Danothir asked, letting his anger subside as he grew more and more impressed with the younger Inara.

"I assure you they will," Ritsuko replied.

"Then they can burn with Ithor and T'Chello." Danothir felt Alia's glare digging into his side and turned to give her a reassuring nod. "Save for Ikari."

"Good." Alia nodded.

"Provided there are no more tricks," Danothir added, putting an edge to his voice. "You've managed to impress me little girl, I'd hate to have to cut into that pretty face of yours."

Alia flashed a coy smile. "So long as I get what I want, so can everyone else."

* * *

"You want to what?" Genki turned away from the large window in the central chamber of the Sanada estate to shoot his brother a confused glare.

Leaning against his sister's chair with his arms crossed, Ikari held his brother's gaze, unsurprised by his reaction. "I think we should help Ithor."

"Did you injure your head back in Alextien? Or have you forgotten that Danothir has Ryoma and T'Chello outnumbered two to one?"

"Three to one, actually," Yuki stated, stretching her legs across the other chairs. "Our scouts have reported that Lady Inara and her assassins have joined with Borga."

"All the more reason to follow the other Houses example and stay out of it." Genki waved his hand. "All of this was your idea, Ikari. We let everyone else kill each other, then finish of the rest."

"I know it was." Ikari let an angry note slip into his voice. "And it was a plan I intended to follow... but things changed."

"What's changed?" Genki inquired.

"Amy."

"Forget the girl." Genki rolled his eyes. "You can't actually believe she's the Protectorate Goddess?"

"Actually, I think I do," Ikari replied, surprised to hear himself admitting it. He had spent the last few days thinking over what he had witnessed at the foot of the Gateway, replaying every moment, every conversation he ever had with Amy, trying to figure out what happened. But, no matter how many times he ran through it, every scenario always brought him back to the same conclusion. "When she first came here, I thought she was just a girl, same as you. Since then, I've seen her do things, small things I ignored as coincidence, and she knows things. Things she shouldn't know, things she'd have no way of knowing."

"So she's intuitive." Genki shrugged. "I've seen you and Yuki do plenty of things I would not have thought possible."

"This goes beyond that. I watched Hayate die. He was as dead as dead gets, and she brought him back. No amount of magic, no technique, no mystical relic I know of can bring a man back from the dead." Ikari pushed off the chair and stepped toward Genki. "She *is* the Protectorate Goddess. I have no doubts about that."

"Even if she is, getting involved gains us nothing." Genki stepped passed Ikari, softening his voice as he walked over to a small rosewood cabinet near the side wall and pulled out a bottle of ale.

"We're already involved." Ikari spun to face Genki. "We started all of this when we sent Ithor reports about Danothir stealing their shipments. We made it worse by hiding proof of Danothir's treason. *We* made this scenario. We made it to gain power..."

"That's what we do." Genki's face flashed red. "That's what we've always done. We manipulate the situation to put us one step closer to taking our rightful place in ruling the realms."

Song of the Goddess

"Is that *all* we do? Manipulate people, spin things, twist the truth until it suites us?" Ikari turned away from Genki and started to pace around the three chairs. "I've spent my entire life following the will of the Sanada. I do whatever I have to do to keep us advancing down that path, but that can't be all there is for us. I refuse to believe that's all there is for us, for me. There has to be something more, something greater than our own ambitions for us to strive for. I'll walk the path of the Sanada, but I'm going to take my own way getting there. And right now, that path is telling me to help Amy."

"Ikari..."

"I'm with Ikari." Yuki hopped to her feet and strolled over to Genki, plucking the drink from his startled hand before stepping back to Ikari's side. "If Ikari believes she's a goddess then so do I."

"Yuki?" Ikari felt his eyebrows raise as he turned toward his sister—who smiled reassuringly at him after taking a sip of ale—astonished that she had taken his side.

"I don't believe this." Genki shook his head. "Of all the people in this room, I'd have thought you would be the one most against this."

"What can I say? Shying away from a good fight isn't in our nature." Yuki put her arm around Ikari's neck and shoved the bottle into his hands. "Besides, when have you ever heard Ikari sound so resolute about doing anything?"

Genki gazed at the twins for a long moment before letting out a defeated sigh. Walking over to Ikari, Genki took the bottle and tilted his head back, taking a long drink. "You two aren't going to let me win this are you, despite the fact that it gains us nothing."

"I wouldn't say it gains us nothing." Ikari smirked, following Genki as he sat in his chair, sensing that he was close to swaying his brother. "Think about it. If we help Amy, Ryoma, and T'Chello defeat Danothir, think about all the possibilities we gain by having a goddess owe us a favor. Not to mention what Ryoma and T'Chello will owe us, the latter of whom having significant influence on the selection of the next Chancellor."

Genki glanced up at Ikari. "And you think we can help, despite the numbers?"

"I really do." Ikari let a cocky grin slip through his serious demeanor. "This battle is going to decide the future of the entire realm. It's only fitting that the Sanada have a hand in deciding the outcome."

"I guess it is," Genki replied after taking another sip of ale and handing the bottle back to Yuki. "You've supported me all these years; it's only fair I do the same."

"So I guess you've finally found your higher purpose?" Yuki grinned at Ikari a moment before she took a swig from the bottle. "Here's to tomorrow, and a wild party."

Returning his sisters grin, Ikari grabbed the bottle and lifted it to his lips. "I'll drink to that."

* * *

Light from the two full moons gave the surrounding fields an eerie, beautiful glow while blades of grass swayed due to a cool, gentle breeze. Sitting alone on top of a high tower with her feet hanging over the edge, Amy stared out into the countryside, wondering what she was supposed to do. She knew what she *wanted* to do. She wanted to see her family again. She wanted to take Hayate with her to London and show him off to her friends. She wanted to stay with Hayate, to be someplace safe; someplace where she wasn't part of some legend. Someplace where no one was going to lead an army and slaughter innocent people just to get at her. Amy knew exactly what she wanted. Just as she knew she was never going to get any of it. Not now that she was coming to believe that Hayate had been right about her.

Maybe she was just destined to end up here. As a kid, her father had always told her that *fate smiles at us all. And when it does, all you can do is smile back and enjoy the ride.*

She had spent most of her teenage years trying to figure out what she wanted to do with her life, certain that she didn't want to follow in her dad's footsteps. Hoping to find what she wanted, she had run off to London to attend college only to find that circumstance after circumstance lead her back to what she had ran away from. Then she found herself getting pulled through a swirling portal and falling out of a casket. And more and more, fate seemed determined to drag her down the path of the Protectorate Goddess.

Sensing the approach of a familiar presence, Amy felt herself smile just as the oval door behind her opened. "Hayate."

Letting out a faint laugh, Hayate pushed the squeaky door closed and stepped over to her side. "It's both endearing and disturbing how you do that. Something Ikari taught you?"

"Kinda. Ikari picks out people as they get close." Amy shrugged; no longer surprised that she could feel him coming. "I sensed you coming from halfway across the castle."

"I see you found the tower of isolation," Hayate paused for a moment, catching a curious glance from Amy. "We call it that because, up here, it feels like you're the only one in the realm, and anyone who gets posted up here for sentry duty feels like he's being punished."

"I wanted to get some air and clear my head. Seemed like a good spot."

"If you want to be alone, I understand." Hayate started to turn away, but stopped as Amy reached over and grabbed his arm.

"Stay. Please."

"I'll stay as long you want." Nodding, Hayate climbed onto the wall and sat next to Amy. "I... I'm riding out with the King and General T'Chello in the morning. I wanted you to know... to know that I... I'm glad I met you."

"I know how you feel, and I feel the same way." Amy turned to face him, wishing the fear pulsing through her would stop. "But I don't want you to leave. Let someone else fight Danothir."

"I have to go. I have to stop him. He's not going to stop until he's murdered every man, woman, and child in Ithor, and taken you. I won't let him harm you."

"Then I'm coming with you."

"Absolutely not." Hayate looked at Amy, radiating fear. "I'm going out to stop him from finding you, to protect you. I'm not about to deliver you to him."

"I'm going. I'm not going stay here and wait to hear if you died. If I'm really supposed to be some kind of goddess then there has to be some way I can help. There has to be something I can do to protect *you*." Amy stared at Hayate, surprised to feel a sudden sense of determination rising up within her. "And it's not just you. Ryoma, and the other knights you've introduced me to, they're my friends too. What was the point to finding out who I am, the point of being the Protectorate Goddess, if I can't help the people I love?"

"Amy?" Hayate gazed at her for a long minute before letting a smile curve his lips. "And here I was wondering if you'd still want me around."

"I always will."

All fear melting away from him, Hayate kicked his feet back onto the tower floor and smiled as he reached out to Amy. "Come on."

"What?" Amy tilted her head, surprised by the shift she felt from the knight, but took his hand.

"When I was a kid, I sometimes snuck up here when the moons were full and stared up in the sky. I always found it relaxing." Hayate sat on the floor and pulled Amy down next to him before laying back and pointing at one of the moons. "See that red shadow on the moons edge? It means the mystic moon will be coming around in a day or so."

"And is that good or bad?" Amy smiled at Hayate, enjoying the innocent glow the moons light gave his eyes as she laid down next to him and stared up at the star filled sky.

"Many see it as a bad omen, but I always thought it brought good luck."

"Kinda like an albatross. Back home, an albatross was a kind of bird, one that brought good luck to sailing ships. It wasn't seen as bad until someone shot it."

"I'd stay out here all night sometimes and name the constellations."

"You got to name the constellations?" Amy arched an eyebrow.

"Oh yeah." Hayate looked over at her a moment before pointing to her left. "That one's called the Tiny Hog. That one, the Fearsome Borz, a borz is a small furry little lilac colored rodent kids keep as pets."

"Sounds cute," Amy laughed.

"That's what they want you to think." Hayate returned her smile, nudging her playfully. "They use their cuddle powers to lull you in. Their true purpose is sinister."

"Really?"

"True story." Hayate pointed to another cluster of stars. "I found this one a while ago but never picked out a name. How about the Albatross?"

"That one, right there?" Amy followed his finger.

"Yep."

"Bollocks. It doesn't even look like a bird."

"Sure it does. It's got the wings, and a beak, and... an extra leg, but definitely a bird. It's a little lopsided, maybe, but it'll fly true."

Pushing herself up to her elbow, Amy peered down into Hayate's eyes, wishing this moment could last forever. "Hayate, I don't want you to die. I don't want to lose you."

"You won't." Hayate sat up, staring her in the eyes.

"But how can you say that? How can you be so sure that nothing is going to happen?"

"Because I have faith in the people fighting alongside me. I have faith that you'll be watching over me," Hayate responded. "And I believe, when you're ready, you'll become the goddess I know you can be. Until then, no power in the realm will keep me from your side."

"Promise?"

"On my honor as a knight." Hayate held her gaze for moment longer before smiling and pointing to another patch of bright stars. "Oh, I almost forgot my favorite constellation, Captain Mittens."

Laughing as Hayate began to explain the reason for the name, Amy felt some of her apprehension peeling away. Amy put her hand on Hayate's cheek, cutting him off as she leaned forward and pressed her lips to his. Pulling back for a moment, a twinge of embarrassment shot through Amy, and she started to say something when she felt a surge of emotions rush through Hayate an instant before he kissed her back.

Smiling, Amy pulled back. "You know, I used to have a cat named mittens."

"Guess its fate that smiled on us and brought us together." Hayate beamed, wrapping his arms around her.

"Only thing we can do is smile back." Amy pressed her lips against his, letting his emotions pour into her as they fell to the floor.

Amy allowed herself to get lost within their passionate embrace, but even as she let her dreads wash away, a small, lingering fear refused to release its hold. She could feel it, an unshakable sense of terror pulling out her insides as it dragged her down a path she didn't want to follow. One stained with blood.

Chapter Twenty-Seven

The morning sun hung over the grassy plains of Gelpher. A strong, but warm breeze blew over the hills to the northeast while scores of men, clad in gray and black armor bearing the Borga family crest, marched across the blue-green field. Ritsuko's band of magically enhanced assassins and soldiers followed along behind them, wearing plain, nondescript black armor; not that Danothir cared whose crest Inara's men wore. So long as they lived up to Ritsuko's promise, he would be happy. He would be the realms unchallenged ruler. The man who grabbed the realm by the throat and ripped it from the trough's of chaos. The man who achieved his destiny and saved the realm.

Readjusting the eloquent tunic he wore over his custom made armor from atop his steed, Danothir glanced to his left and scowled. Riding in a large horse drawn palanquin, Ritsuko sat with her brat of a daughter, whispering behind a thin lavender veil. Marching along beside them, he spotted Thade and grimaced, wondering what depraved magic Ritsuko might have used to give him his glowing scars.

"Lord Borga."

Tearing his attention away from the stern looking general, Danothir looked up to find Svipdag riding toward him along with the assassin, Tres. "Something wrong?"

"Depends on your point of view, my Lord." Svipdag, dressed the same as the men he commanded, signaled for the army to stop. "Scouts just came back with some interesting news. Seems the good King and General T'Chello have come out to meet us. They're waiting just over the hill ahead."

"Then they can die that much sooner." Danothir smiled, enjoying the feeling of knowing that years of working in secret, of forcing himself to stomach the Consortiums endless squabbles, was about to come to fruition.

"Any preference on how we deal with them?" Svipdag inquired.

Danothir laughed, waving his hand. "So long as they die, I'll leave the details in your capable hands."

"So what's the plan," Tres asked.

"I'll take the cavalry in first and hit them hard, force out any tricks the bastards might be hiding." Svipdag turned toward Thade. "When you see your opening, bring in the infantry. Then we kill them all."

"Understood." Thade nodded.

Tres crossed his arms, glancing over each of them. "And what exactly I'm doing during all this?"

"You're an assassin, assassinate someone," Svipdag snorted. "You and your blue eyed freaks get to sneak around and flank them. Find the King and T'Chello and stick a knife in their throats."

"Well, that's a plan I can get behind." Tres laughed before turning to head toward his assassins.

"Let's find a better view point." Danothir waited until the two generals had left before riding to the right of his army. Finding a perfect vantage point, he gazed down at the field and smirked, watching as his enemies came into view.

"Don't forget our deal," Alia exclaimed as her palanquin pulled to a stop a few feet back. "Ikari is not to be harmed."

"Yes, yes. Assuming he actually shows, I've already instructed my men to give it their best effort." Danothir shifted his gaze to the younger Inara as she stepped out, followed by her mother.

"All their best effort will get you is a field full of statues." Alia narrowed her eyes, sending a spike of anger through Danothir as he caught a breath of her perfume.

"I'm a little tired of your threats. I make it a habit to kill mouthy little witches that cross me." Danothir glared at Alia, wondering for the first time why he hadn't slit her pretty little neck already. "If you don't want that dress of yours stained with blood, I suggest you focus on conjuring up the slayer's army."

"No need for idol threats, Danothir. Bring me Amy Price and I'll give you the army of a god." Ritsuko stepped over to his side and flashed one of her seductive smiles. "Also, that's the last time you get to threaten my daughter. She may be a bit... haughty at times, but do it again and I'll teach her how to make you choke on your own liquefied organs."

Growling in anger, Danothir started to reach for Ritsuko's throat, when he caught sight of Alia staring at him and decided against it. Turning back to the looming battle, he forced himself to take a breath. *I'm going to have to kill them sooner than I originally thought. But I can wait a little longer. Just a little longer, and the realm is mine.*

* * *

"Here they come," Ryoma stated, clad in a blue and gold variation of Ithorian armor.

Tightening his grip on his sheathed sword, Hayate watched as T'Chello and his troops rode toward the advancing enemies, trying to force any anxiety he felt out with each long breath. "There's more of them than I thought."

"It'll take make more than numbers to win this battle." Ryoma gave a reassuring smile to Hayate.

"But having them wouldn't hurt," Hayate whispered from atop his horse while T'Chello's forces crashed into Danothir's like waves hitting a beach.

"It really wouldn't," Ryoma laughed.

"I should be riding with the general." Hayate glanced over the ranks of knights and soldiers waiting behind them, then at Ryoma.

"You'll have your chance to fight. We all will." Ryoma patted his horse as it shook its head. "For now, we stick to T'Chello's plan. He wanted to go first, he needed to. T'Chello is a proud man, and he blames himself for what happened to the Chancellor. He had you wait because he's going to need someone with a clear head to back him up, someone to lead the second charge."

"He has you for that."

Ryoma smirked, shaking his head. "I have *you* for that. It's not me that the knights followed into battle. They have chosen their captain, and that's you my friend."

Swallowing, Hayate looked back toward the battle not knowing how to respond. Shouts of pain and anger filled the fields as swords struck metal and flesh. Hayate tried to locate T'Chello in the sea of swarming bodies, but failed to pick out the General. Surging forward, the Borga soldiers attacked with surprising furiousness, lashing out at any enemy like wild wolves. Watching with an uneasy anticipation, Hayate spotted Svipdag barking orders while hacking away at anyone near him.

Stifling a bolt of distress as he looked on, Hayate began to notice that T'Chello's forces were beginning to get pushed back, and turned toward Ryoma. "Majesty?"

"I know." Ryoma put on his helmet. "So much for waiting."

"It's strange," Hayate smiled, taking comfort in the warm breeze that blew over. "It almost feels like she's here, like Amy is watching over us."

"Maybe she is; despite you leaving her locked in your chamber when we left." Ryoma smirked. "But she doesn't seem the type to let that stop her. If we get through this, I don't much envy being the one to apologize to an angry goddess."

"I'll make it up to her." Hayate slid his helmet over his head and drew his sword.

"See that you do." Ryoma turned his horse toward the rest of his men and raised his sword over his head, electing a shout as the men snapped to attention. "Knights of Ithor, draw your swords. Our enemy's descend like rapid wolves gnawing at our doors, but they shall go no further. They would see our homes burned and our families butchered, but they will not succeed. For you are knights of Ithor, and you fear no evil." Ryoma paused as the knights heaved their swords into the air with an excited cry. "Ride forth and show our enemy that Ithor will never fall."

Adding his voice to the rallying shouts, Hayate sent his horse galloping alongside Ryoma's and plunged into the throng of enemy combatants, lashing out at any unfamiliar body. Blocking a strike from a soldier on foot, he planted his boot on the soldiers exposed face as he caught sight of Ryoma. Fighting off a man on horseback, Ryoma swayed under a high swing, stabbing the man in the belly before being forced to block the attack of another soldier.

Cutting down an axe wielding man, Hayate steered his steed toward Ryoma when his horse reared back. Hayate ducked to the side, trying to maintain his balance while evading a spear meant to impale him, and found a pair of spears being driven into the horse's neck. The two soldiers pressed forward, tipping the horse over and sent Hayate crashing to the ground.

Ripping their spears free, they each lunged at Hayate. Grabbing his sword as he rolled, Hayate kicked one of the spearmen and scrambled to his feet. He darted forward, not giving the second man a chance to ready his weapon, and impaled him with his sword. Pulling his weapon free, he felt a whisk of air shoot passed his ear and turned around in time to see an arrow plunge into a soldier's neck.

Tracing the arrow back to its source, Hayate spotted the familiar archer and nodded. "Lynn."

"You okay?" The young woman ran over to him.

"Fine." Hayate pointed to his left, directing her toward Ryoma. "Stay with the King."

Blocking an attack, Hayate pushed the enemy soldier back, retaliating with a string of slashes. Forty yards ahead, Hayate caught a flash of T'Chello furiously fighting his way through the center of Danothir's men. Elsewhere, allied forces struggled to hold their ground against wave after wave of soldiers. To his left, he found Ryoma fighting against a tall, portly man, with Lynn close to his side, arrows flying from her bow.

Catching the sound of marching boots, even over the endless clanging of swords and shields, Hayate finished off another foe and felt a wave of hopelessness wash over him. Moving in from their right flank, Hayate saw Thade closing in with a horde of soldiers dressed similar to the ones he had fought in Alextien.

"Not another wave," a knight gasped from Hayate's side. "We're barely holding as it is."

"We'll hold," Hayate shouted, knowing that they had no other choice. "Take a company and reinforce the King's position. Do not let them push you back."

"Understood." The knight hurried off to carry out his orders

"Reform the line! Archers to the front." Motioning for anyone not currently engaged in battle, Hayate began positioning whoever he could to hold off Thade's advance. Hayate raised his sword as he ordered the archers to take aim, trying to hide the growing fear bubbling inside of him. "Loose!"

* * *

Arrows soared across the clear sky, raining down upon the advancing forces of House Inara. Unabated by the volley, the soldiers picked up speed, closing in on Hayate's position radiating an eager aura. Taking in the chaos unfolding before him, Ikari strode down the northeastern hillside, allowing the sounds and smell of battle to push aside any lingering doubts he might have had about joining in.

"Looks like they started without us," Yuki sighed from his side. "Danothir and Ritsuko managed to put together a bigger army than I thought."

"Not too late for you and Genki to turn back." Ikari glanced over at Yuki. "I know he didn't want come along, and I know you..."

"...Would never miss out on such a spectacular fight," Yuki interrupted. "And for all his belly aching, Genki is still a Sanada. Fighting is in our blood."

"Fair enough." Ikari returned his attention to the battle and saw that Hayate and his knights were rushing toward Thade's soldiers. "I'll leave the mystical super soldiers to you and Genki. I'm going to go find Thade."

"Not alone you're not. I saw for myself how much stronger he got when I fought him on Hapes compared to when we first fought, and he's had even more time since then. Fighting Gaou almost got you killed. Plus, I have just as much of a score to settle with that man as you do, so we'll take him together. Let Genki, E'Lan, and Saskai handle the nameless flunkies."

"Alright then," Ikari replied. Letting a wave of excitement wash over him, he spotted Thade peering up at him as some of his men turned toward the Sanada. "Looks like they noticed us."

"Good."

Walking in unison and sharing the same enthusiastic smirk as Yuki, Ikari swung his arm to the right in a chopping motion while Yuki mirrored his signal with her left. An instant later, Saskai and E'Lan darted passed them with swords in hand, followed by all of the Sanyoshu under their command. At the opposite end of the field, Genki and his sect of Sanyoshu charged into view joining the embattled soldiers of Hapes. Channeling his energy, Ikari sprinted toward his target and leapt high into the air, sailing over the heads of his allies.

Thrusting his foot into the surprised face of one soldier, Ikari pivoted, using the soldiers face as footing while he fell and caught another combatant with a kick to the jaw. He leapt off the first soldier and used another's head to handspring over a bloody sword aiming for where he would have landed. Slamming his heels into an enemy chest plate and driving him to the ground, Ikari quickly caved in his windpipe before rolling to avoid getting beheaded. Instinct taking over as the Sanyoshu collided with the enemy, Ikari cut loose, striking at any target he could find when not evading opposing weapons. Attacking with a flurry of motion, two soldiers forced Ikari back, their eyes glowing an intense blue as the shock of his attack wore off.

Ikari ducked, avoiding losing the top of his skull, an instant before an upward swing forced him to sway back. Stepping back as he parried a mid-kick, he felt a large foot kick his legs out from under him and fell to the ground. Finding the man that had tripped him hoisting a sword to finish him off, Ikari scissored his legs, dragging the attacker to the ground. Rolling over the downed man's body and unwilling to allow himself to be impaled the horde around him, Ikari punched the closest foe in the stomach. Spinning around the doubled over soldier as he rose, Ikari hit another with a whip like kick before thrust kicking the doubled over man onto the rising sword of the tripped soldier. Catching a bestial cry, Ikari spun around, alarm pulsing through his body as another soldier swung his blade downward, only to find Yuki's foot crashing into the side of his face.

"Inara's men seem to be a bit tougher than I imagined." Yuki ducked under a vertical strike, thrusting her extended fingers into the man's throat as she rose.

"I noticed," Ikari replied, evading a string of attacks. "Ritsuko infected them with a watered down version of whatever she did to Thade."

"Speaking of whom." Yuki caught a man with an elbow then started toward the right. Dispatching the soldier in front of him, Ikari felt Thade's presence a moment before he saw him and followed Yuki. "It's bad form to keep a woman waiting."

"On the contrary, it's I who has been waiting for you, both of you." Thade stopped a few yards ahead of the twins, blood dripping from his hands while scars of luminescent blue light ran along his arms and half his face. Two fierce looking daggers with thick hand guards hung from the back of his belt, the metallic silver of their handles contrasting with his black and bloodied uniform. Watching Thade closely, Ikari noted that the horde of soldiers around them seemed to have given them a wide birth. Picking up on his curiosity, Thade smirked. "They all have been instructed to stay clear of our fight. I was ordered to ensure your survival, but that is one order I may not follow."

"Alia right?" Ikari smirked. "She really does like me, doesn't she?"

Thade flexed his arms, locking his gaze on the siblings. "The three of us will fight until this matter is settled. No more running, no more games, just us and glorious combat."

"I couldn't agree more," Yuki replied, taking up an attack stance. "So are you going to draw those daggers strapped to your hip, or are they just for show?"

"I will draw my weapons after you have drawn yours."

"Before that, I have to know." Ikari stared at Thade for a moment. "Why did you do this? Why did you let Ritsuko hook her venomous claws into you? You have to realize that whatever she did to you is going to kill you."

"Because I am a loyal servant of House Inara," Thade stated. "Because I, like you, have spent my life seeking worthy challenges. And just when I was near giving up hope of finding someone to test myself against, someone that could push me to my limit, I met you. I met you and Lady Inara calls for my aid to defeat you. How could I not answer? How could I not accept the opportunity to have my skills taken beyond anything I would have thought possible?"

Ikari gestured angrily. "Even if it means throwing away everything that made you human?"

"You and your sister are the same as I, inhuman beasts thriving in the chaos of battle and unfit to live in any other manner. People like us can only find contentment on the battlefield. It's what we were born for. It's how we will die." Thade flexed his shoulders, standing ready to attack. "That is why all that truly matters is the fight."

"You and I are a lot alike, that's probably why I actually respect you, but you're wrong. All the fighting in the realm doesn't matter if there's no higher propose to fight for. The Thade I met in Osaka Major knew that." Ikari narrowed his eyes, mirroring Yuki's stance. "I fight to find that purpose. You fight to get lost in it."

"We shall see." Thade shot forward, positioning himself between the twins.

Catching Ikari with a painful right hook, Thade pivoted and nailed Yuki with a harsh side kick that sent her stumbling back. Shaking off the blow to the jaw, Ikari blocked a string of swift strikes, startled by the speed and crispness of Thade's movements. Ikari focused his senses on Thade, letting the chaos surging around them fade from his thoughts as Thade's barrage continued. Blocking a punch, he grabbed Thade's wrist and threw a punch of his own, only to have it blocked. Thade flashed a twisted sneer as he gripped Ikari's wrist an instant before lashing out with unforgiving head-butt. Following up on his attack, Thade thrust a large boot onto Ikari's chest, knocking the air out of him as he tumbled backwards.

Sliding to a stop as he rolled to his feet, Ikari tried to ignore the pain ringing through his temple and looked up to see Yuki putting Thade on the defensive with a series of kicks. Missing with a high roundhouse, she continued her assault, but as well aimed as her attacks were, none managed to find their target. Moving with a grace usually found in dancers, Thade swayed around Yuki's attacks, parrying and blocking every blow she threw. Ikari dashed forward, watching as Yuki ducked under a counter from Thade and went for an uppercut. However, Thade caught her fist with one hand, twisting it as he pulled it down and locked her arm in place, before scoring with an elbow to her jaw.

Ikari leapt forward, catching Thade with a blocked kick and twisted in midair, forcing the General to duck under a crescent kick. Landing on his toes, Ikari stayed on the attack, determined to break through his opponent's defenses, and peppered him with a torrent of kicks. Eager to get back on the offensive, Thade parried a high punch and began his own assault, forcing Ikari to renew his evasive dance. Ikari drew on every ounce of speed he could muster, trying to stay ahead of his opponents fists, and smirked as a fist slipped through his guard and sent a jolt of pain shooting through him.

Letting the momentum from Thade's fist whip him around, Ikari spun low, extending a leg and sweeping the legs out from under Thade. Ikari rose, ready to press his advantage only to find that Yuki had beaten him to it. Flipping over her brother, Yuki kicked both feet out as she crashed in the ground, narrowly missing Thade's head as he rolled out of the way.

Not giving him a chance to recover, the twins attacked in unison, unleashing a storm of rapid punches and swift kicks. Azure scars flaring as Thade obstructed most of their strikes, Ikari spun to his left, aiming a high roundhouse kick at the back of Thade's head while Yuki twisted on her heels for a low sweep of his shins.

Diving into a forward roll to avoid their attack, Thade came to his feet and turned just in time to see them match his maneuver and drive their elbows into his face. Happy to see Thade could still feel pain, Ikari ducked under a wide punch along with Yuki and pressed forward. Rising back to back, the siblings each sent their foot crashing into Thade's jaw with a side kick.

Grinning, despite the taste of blood filling his mouth or the pain ringing throughout his body, Ikari watched as Thade managed to roll through his fall and wiped away some of the blood pouring out his busted lip. "Not bad old man. This is going to be more fun than I thought."

"Until the end then?" Thade returned his grin, standing ready to fight.

"Absolutely." Yuki flashed a twisted, excited smile before darting forward with Ikari, renewing their macabre ballet.

* * *

Blood from countless men and women stained the once green fields of Gelpher. Soldiers stained with blood danced across the field, weapons flashing under the morning sun, as they hacked away at eachother in a blur of motion. Generals barked orders, directing the flow of carnage while a King staved off an advancing enemy with his knights at his back. Further down the field, a young knight rallied his peers, leading the charge as they rushed toward another wave of opponents. Sanyoshu poured off the hillside, attacking soldiers with glowing blue eyes, leaving twin siblings free to combat a scared man who was just as eager to fight them.

Unable to shake the images rippling through her mind's eye, Amy felt as if she were staring through five feet of water, picking up broken bits of muffled sounds and momentary flashes of one fight or another.

Growing more and more frustrated, she started toward the large window, wondering for the eighth time if she could jump off the balcony and find a way to reach Hayate, when she stubbed her toe on one of the wooden bookcases along the stone wall.

"Bloody..." She hopped over to Hayate's bed and sat down, rubbing her sore foot. "I'm going to kill him."

Amy cursed, deciding to slip her boots on as she glanced around the knight's room hoping to discover some way out. She had woken up intending to accompany Hayate so she could keep him safe. Not that she knew how she was going accomplish that goal, but she was certain that she needed to be with him. Of course, that was before she had awakened to find he had snuck off and left her locked in his bedroom. Glaring at the oak door, Amy stood and marched over before pounding her fist against it.

"Hey. Open the sodding door." She kicked the door with a growl, hopping it would fly open as if she were in some over amped action movie. "I know you can bloody well hear me, so let me out!"

"I sorry miss," a woman's voice replied through the wooden door. "Sir Hayate told me not to let you out until he returns. Said he was protecting you."

"I'm supposed to protect him." Amy kicked the door again. "Prat!"

Amy turned away from the door, catching more flashes of violence and stepped back to the window, hopping the breeze would calm the pounding in her head. An uneasy tightness gripped her chest as she watched Hayate fight off a spear wielding soldier. Noticing something to his left, Hayate dived to the side just as a silver knife flew past his head. Scrambling to his feet, he deflected another spiraling knife, expanding Amy's view, as Tres lunged sword first toward the knight. Concern welling up inside of her, Amy could feel Tres's surprise to see Hayate alive, just as she could feel how excited he was to have another opportunity to hurt him.

Speaking too softly for Amy to hear, Tres lurched forward, attacking with a finesse that seemed contradictory to his brutal nature. Swords sparking as they collided with each other, Hayate and Tres fought in a flurry of motion, each keen on killing the other.

Hayate swayed, avoiding a stroke that would have cleaved his arm off at the shoulder and answered with an upward slash before reversing his strike. Sidestepping the second swing, Tres swung for his opponents head, planning to hit him with the pommel of his sword, however, Hayate blocked the attack and countered with a fist to the face.

Tres, reeling from the pain, lashed out blindly with a horizontal slash, forcing Hayate to jump back. Reversing his swing, Tres bound forward, aiming for his neck and followed up with a vertical strike. Hayate managed to block the strike, but Tres kicked his feet out from under him. Rolling to avoid getting impaled, Hayate scrambled back to his feet in time to catch a whip like kick to the side of his head.

"Hayate." Fear twisted Amy's voice as she watched, helpless as Hayate struggled to stay alive. "Why didn't you let me come with you?"

"And how precisely could you help him?" Surprise shooting through her, Amy turned around expecting to see the woman outside the door only to find a tall woman with elaborate, breaded hair staring at her with a raised eyebrow. The woman wore a long, lavish silver and white dress with expensive gold jewelry.

"Who… who are you? How did you get in here?" Amy took a step back.

"Stone walls can do little to one who travels as a voice in the wind." The woman smiled, holding her hands out to her sides as a torrent of wind blew through the window and began circling the room. Books and papers began to sail around them, followed by heavier objects as the gale increased. Hair wiping across her face, Amy watched in terror as the walls and floor were ripped away, colliding with broken bits of flying furniture and disappearing in bursts of light.

"Who are you?" Amy shouted over the roaring gale, noticing a familiar humming in the wind.

"I am the one responsible for your arrival in this realm. I am Araia, and it's time you and I talked."

* * *

Genki raised his battle axe over his head, hindering a sword meant to split his skull in two. Parrying the man's blade, Genki smacked him with the handle of his axe a moment before reversing and driving the end of his weapon into the soldier's temple. Pushing the soldier away with a kick to the chest, he turned to find another opponent and spotted T'Chello locked in combat with Svipdag.

Genki returned his attention to the chaos immediately surrounding him and leapt back to avoid an arching blade. Matching his movement, a man clad in the garb of the Assassin's Guild unleashed a hail of attacks. Genki blocked, grateful that his weapon's handle was made out of steal instead of wood, and hooked his opponent's sword with the curve of his axe. Yanking it downwards to pull the assassin off balance, Genki thrust the top of his axe into the man's gut and followed with a harsh punch.

Just as his fist found its target, Genki noticed the flash of another sword and swung his axe to block. Halting the enemy blade, he jumped backwards, trying to evade impalement at the hands of a second soldier, only to land right in the path of another. Recoiling from an unblocked kick, a wave of panic shoot through him as one of the soldiers lunged toward him sword first. He dove to the side, grunting as the blade slashed his midsection, sending a jolt of pain racing through him. Genki fell to the ground, growling through the pain as he forced himself to roll to his knees expecting to see the three soldiers pouncing on top of him, but was surprised to see a man in blue and white slamming shoulder first into the closest soldier. Recognizing the man as Ryoma, Genki rose to his feet while the Ithorian King slashed the first soldier across his back before exchanging blows with a second.

Shooting forward, Genki rammed the top of his weapon into the third soldiers exposed face, sending him staggering back an instant before driving his axe into the man's sternum. Genki yanked his axe free, unleashing a fresh wave of blood onto the trampled field, and took a moment to catch his breath.

"In a thousand years, I'd have never guessed that you would be here." Ryoma dispatched the soldier in front of him and scanned for any immediate danger.

"You can thank Ikari." Genki winced, standing straight as he stepped over to Ryoma. "He can be rather forceful when he wants to be. Dying out here with you wasn't part my plan."

"How's the wound?" Ryoma asked, wiping away some of the blood that poured from a gash on his forehead.

"I've had worse."

"I'm sure." Ryoma smirked, readying his sword as another pair of soldiers started toward them. "Hard to imagine the head of House Sanada getting slain by some regular in Danothir's army."

"There's nothing *regular* about them." Genki blocked a lateral strike from one of the soldiers while the other attacked Ryoma. Spotting a nod from Ryoma, Genki twisted on his heel, catching the man fighting the King off guard as his axe loped off his head, while Ryoma ducked underneath and plunged his sword into Genki's opponent.

"I noticed." Ryoma rose, wearing a grim look on his face as he pulled his sword free. "Lady Inara's handy work I presume. The question is what to do about it?"

"Nothing we can do now except fight and die." Genki glanced over the battlefield, knowing that even with the arrival of the Sanyoshu, Danothir still held the advantage. "You're the one that believes that girl is a goddess, pray."

"Despite my beliefs, I've always felt that acts of men are better than acts of gods."

Genki laughed, hefting his axe to attack. "And I've always felt that if you can't win, at least take as many of them with you as you can."

"So we have something in common after all." Ryoma smirked, charging into another group of enemy combatants.

"Damn. I guess we do," Genki whispered a moment before rushing after him.

Chapter Twenty-Eight

A jolt of pain shot through Ikari's arm, despite the armguards he wore, as he blocked another punch from Thade. To his left, Yuki attacked with a flurry of punches, trying to find an opening in Thade's defenses. Noticing a shift in stance as Thade moved to counter, Ikari threw a pair of swift strikes, forcing the older man to sway and duck to evade. Yuki—never one to miss an opportunity—nailed him with a harsh shot to the head.

Looking to stay on the attack, she stepped forward, punching with her right fist, however, Thade parried her attack with his left and grabbed her by the wrist, yanking her off balance. Putting his weight on his right leg, Thade caught Ikari with a kick to the chest and reached over to grab ahold of his arm. Thade's eyes flashed as he pulled the twins forward and off balance, twisting as he did, before throwing them both over his shoulder.

Landing hard on his back as he slid across the trampled grass, Ikari pushed off the ground, trying to gain control of his fall while Yuki did the same. Turning, just as his feet touched the ground, a sharp pain shot through his chest as Thade delivered a brutal kick to the sternum that sent him tumbling back further. Ikari struggled to get to his knees, groaning as a severe pain racked his torso, causing him to realize he had cracked a rib or two.

Up ahead, Yuki and Thade had resumed their dance, each moving in a blur of motion. Thade gained the advantage, scoring two hits to her one, and began to push her back. Landing a trio of rapid strikes, Thade pressed forward, throwing a fourth punch, but Yuki managed to block and countered with an uppercut. Thade recovered quickly, however, and parried her follow up attack with one hand while grabbing her by the throat with the other.

A cold panic surged through Ikari as he shot forward while Yuki struggled in vain to free herself. Close enough to hear his sister gasping for air; Ikari lunged at Thade, lashing out with a panicked punch. Relieved to see Thade release his hold on Yuki as he jumped back, Ikari twisted on his heel, missing with a high crescent kick. Ikari let the momentum from his kick spin him around while drawing his weapon with an upside down grip and caught Thade with a slash across the chest in one swift motion. Ikari then turned, moving into a right handed stance while making sure that he was in front of his sister.

"So…" Thade laughed, drawing his own weapons. "You're finally ready to use your sword."

"Guess so." Ikari shot forward, pouring all of his energy into his speed as he met Thade's advance.

Blades flashing as they reflected light from the afternoon sun, Ikari danced around Thade's attacks, trying to find an opening to counter. Ducking under a wide attack, Ikari went for an upward slash, but Thade side stepped, nailing him with a shot from the steal guard covering Thade's fingers. Recoiling from the force of the punch, Ikari felt the cold steel crash into his jaw as Thade uppercut him.

Not giving him a chance to recover, Thade shot forward, tackling Ikari while driving one dagger into his left shoulder and raising the other to finish him off. "Take solace knowing that we all must feel the embrace of the goddess someday."

"Not today." Yuki flipped over Thade, grabbing onto his shoulders while turning in mid descent, digging her heel into his back, and used her momentum to kick him over her.

Springing up to her feet, Yuki turned to face Thade—who had rolled through his fall—and pulled her sword from its sheath. Shooting forward with a feral snarl, she attacked, transitioning from one fluid move to another in a blur of motion. Yuki twirled her sword into a traditional grip, missing with a spinning kick, and unloaded a string of slashes intended to further scar the older man.

Ikari cried out in pain, removing the knife Thade had left in his shoulder while the sound of swords colliding filled his ears. Dashing toward Thade and Yuki's lethal dance, Ikari jumped, recognizing his sister's pattern of attack, and hit Thade with a solid kick to the chest just as Yuki ducked under him. Ikari surged after the staggered General and caught him with a heel to the chin.

Yuki fell into sync with Ikari, each using their swords to block Thade's dagger and attack with a variety of strikes. Missing with a roundhouse, Ikari followed with a vertical slash, but Thade managed to block and countered with a kick to his injured shoulder.

Ikari staggered back as a fresh wave of pain surged through him, while Yuki continued her assault, slicing Thade across the chest. Anger pouring off Thade as he spun away from her blade, he lashed out with his remaining dagger, forcing Yuki to roll to avoid getting her throat slit. Not allowing her to out maneuver him, Thade threw a series of quick stabs and slashes, all of which Yuki managed to deflect.

Watching Thade and Yuki exchange attacks for a moment, Ikari noticed Thade's movements were not as crisp as when they had first started and smirked. Thade had spent most of the fight separating him from Yuki to take them on one at a time. It was a good way to deal with multiple opponents, but it also took a lot of energy. As skilled as Thade was, he was a soldier, a General commanding armies and a warrior used to one on one bouts. Fighting two opponents as skilled as the Sanada twins was clearly taking its toll. Not that Ikari was fairing much better. At best, he figured he had a few minutes of fight left in him before Thade's dagger took up permanent residence in his skull. Yuki continued her exchange, but Ikari could tell that she too was nearing her limit.

Realizing that this might be his final few moments, Ikari smiled, dashing forward to join in on their dance, his mind free and content. Ikari evaded an arching kick, crouching down as he went for a low sweep. Hopping over the sweep, Thade blocked a pair of strikes from Yuki before rolling to avoid Ikari's raising kick. Cutting Yuki across the arm as he rose, Thade nailed her with a kick to the ribs and turned, catching Ikari with a boot to the sternum. Forcing himself to stay on his feet, Ikari ducked under Thade's follow up kick, slashing the underside of his leg as he did. Thade quickly reversed his kick, crying out in pain as he did, and smacked Ikari with his heel.

Turning to face them while Yuki staggered next to her brother, Thade landed a harsh fist to Ikari's jaw a second before connecting with a left hook. Refusing to succumb to the darkness edging his vision while Thade parried a strike from Yuki, Ikari rolled under his curving blade, trusting Yuki to evade his following roundhouse. Gald that Yuki had matched his maneuver as she rolled under Thade's kick and rose to his right, Ikari thrust his sword into the left side of Thade's midsection, while Yuki did the same on the right.

Ignoring Thade's pained roar, Ikari ripped his sword free, moving in unison with Yuki as they focused their remaining energy. Spinning in front of the wounded general while Yuki spun behind him, Ikari drove his sword into Thade's neck as Yuki sliced through from the opposite direction.

Lungs screaming for air, Ikari watched Thade's head fall from his shoulders, grimacing as the scars covering Thade's face faded, leaking an azure puss. "Fight well at the side of the slayer."

"And I... I wanted to stay away," Yuki laughed painfully between gasps for air.

"And miss all the fun?" Ikari let himself drop to his knees, desperate to remain conscious as he surveyed the field. "Of course, we're probably going to die out here."

"Not today." Yuki glanced around them before forcing a smile. "I promised someone I'd set them up on date with you."

"Gods, kill me now." Ikari returned her smile, stretching out his senses to get a feel for the battle, and swallowed a lump of fear. He had hoped to catch Danothir's and Ritsuko's forces off guard when he and the Sanyoshu arrived, but surprise, no matter how effective, wears off quickly. With it gone, Ritsuko's mystical enhancements gave the soldiers of House Borga more than enough edge to overrun the allied forces of Ithor, Hapes, and the Sanada, even if they weren't already out numbered. "I never thanked you for supporting me in all this."

"I'm your sister." Yuki stepped over and helped him up. "Of course, you realize you're going to pay me back for going through all of this just so you can help some funny talking twit."

"What can I say?" Ikari smirked, readying his sword as a group of assassins began to circle around them. "She was interesting."

* * *

Sparks flew as Hayate's sword collided with an arching attack from Tres. Pushing against the older man, Hayate parried his sword and hit Tres with a right hook. Tres recovered quickly however, retaliating with a fresh string of attacks. Mind numb to the anarchy flooding the fields, Hayate stepped back, relying on every skill and technique he could remember to avoid getting injured any further. Blots of fear coursed through him, giving his movements an unpolished, desperate feel as he parried another strike. Dying wasn't a thought that scared him. He was a knight; a knight in the middle of a battlefield fighting an army that outnumbered his three to one. Dying did not scare him.

Failing did.

Losing this fight meant losing Amy. It meant that he was too weak to help his friends fighting and dying at his side to protect their homes, and it meant that he would be unable to keep his promise to the woman he had fallen in love with. So he fought. He fought harder than he would have thought possible, refusing to submit to exhaustion or pain, and continued his dance of arching swords and angry counters.

Parrying a wide slash, Hayate thrust his sword forward, hoping to catch Tres unaware and end their duel. He pressed forward, attacking the assassin with a flurry of aggressive moves, switching from high to low attacks at random. Missing with a slash aimed at his opponents knees, Hayate brought his sword up, blocking a trio of counter attacks. Deflecting a fourth strike, he lashed out, grazing Tres across the stomach. Stifling a pained cry, Tres staggered back, turning away from Hayate as he grasped at his wound.

Eager to put an end to Tres, Hayate started forward but Tres turned back toward him, flinging a concealed knife with his free hand. Stopping with a surge of panic, he batted the spiraling dagger to the side and found Tres pouncing after him. Narrowly evading getting blinded as Tres's blade zipped passed his eyes, Hayate went back on the defensive.

Hayate repelled another attack, but Tres reversed his swing, sending a painful jolt through the young knight's arm as the cold steel grazed flesh. Recoiling, Hayate felt Tres's broad shoulder slam into his chest a moment before another fist collided with his jaw. Vision blurring for a moment, Hayate blocked a strike meant to split him in two, only to have his feet kicked out from under him.

Head bouncing harshly off the ground, Hayate looked up, trying to force the throbbing pain out of his mind, and felt an icy chill take its place. Terror drowning out the battle around him, Hayate spotted Tres diving toward him with his sword ready to turn the knight's torso into its new sheath.

* * *

"What is this?" Amy glanced around, trying to keep the panic out of her voice as she backed away. The howling squall whipping around them faded into a soft breeze, allowing the roar of battle to reach her ears. Glancing down, eyes wide with terror, Amy found herself floating over the blood soaked battlefield, standing on what felt like a thick, translucent glass floor.

"This is the culmination of events instigated by your arrival here," Araia stated, her voice taking on a smoky, regal tone.

"I started?" Images of individual battles began appearing around Amy, showing her scenes of violence and anguish only to disappear and be replaced with others.

"Yes. Your arrival drew the attention of Danothir Borga and Hayate Thane, who in turn pulled Ryoma, the Sanada, and the Inara's as well as their cohorts into play. Without you, none of them would be where they are today. The moment you fell out of my casket, you sent ripples through the sea of their lives that led them all to this moment."

"I never asked to be brought here." Amy turned toward the goddess, anger boiling in her voice. Ignoring the images that floated around her, a part of her couldn't help but wonder if what Araia was saying was true. "*You* tore me away from my family and dumbed me in this realm. I never wanted any of this to happen."

"It's not about what you want. It's about what *they* needed, and to an equal extent, what you needed." Araia motioned toward the battle as the swirling images disappeared. "The people of this realm have reached a crossroad. And it is at this point that it falls to you to choose their destiny."

"Why? Why me? Why any of this?"

"Ripples set in motion long before your arrival would have been the end of everyone below."

Amy stared at the field below them for a long moment, spotting familiar figures as they struggled to stay alive. Peering further up the field, she felt a cold chill blow over her and looked back toward Araia as recognition dawned on her. "This is the battle from my vision. The one I had when you first pulled me here."

"You have visions?" Araia raised an eyebrow for a moment before laughing to herself. "I chose you because you were lacking in any particular purpose or bias. You've spent your life searching for a purpose, a path to follow, so I gave you one. One you are far better suited to than any other option open to me. You were an impartial observer of this realm with no vested interest or preconceived notions. That makes you the ideal person to decide whether the people of Terra should face salvation or fall to damnation."

Amy shot the regal woman a furious glare. "I can't decide whether everyone in an entire realm lives or dies. I don't have that right. No one does."

"And if life were fair, you'd be right. You need to realize that your inaction would result in *everyone's* death, especially your friends. It is a heavy burden to bear, I know, but you are the one that must choose their destiny."

"And if I refuse, my friends die?"

"Ultimately, yes. However, you are free to choose whatever you want. I can return you to your homeland, to your father and sister if you desire, but believe me when I say that the fate that would befall Terra would be... unpleasant." Araia let the edge fall from her voice. "I know you are a loving, kind person. That is one reason I chose you. And in your travels, you have inspired those around you to greater heights than even I thought possible. That is why it has to be you. You have come to care for the people of this realm, a necessary quality for the Protectorate Goddess. Although in your case, you affection seems to be focused on a select few."

"I don't understand. It feels like you want them saved, but you're a goddess, why not just save them yourself? Why put us through all of this?"

Araia glanced to the left and held out a hand. Following her gaze, Amy felt a wave of fear flood over her as she saw Hayate struggling to stay alive while Tres kicked him in the ribs before moving to finish him off.

"Hayate?"

"Time is running out if you wish to save him…" Araia paused for a moment as an image of Ikari and Yuki slowly getting overrun formed to Amy's left. "…or them."

"Why are you doing this?" Amy reached for the image of Hayate, trying to pull him to safety while more images of Ryoma and Genki appeared around her.

"Because I want you to save them. More accurately, I want you to *want* to save them."

"I…"

"Before you respond—" Araia held up a slender finger. "—know that every action, no matter what you ultimately decide, will have its consequence."

"I don't care." Amy glared at Araia, tears filling her eyes as the crackle of lightning filled her ears. "I love Hayate. I'll do any bloody thing I have to if it means saving him and my friends, but I don't give a damn about you or the path you're pushing us to follow. I'm going to save the people I care about and, together, we'll live our lives following whatever path *we* choose."

"Spoken like a true protector." Araia smiled, waving away the images around them.

A new sensation radiating up from the embattled soldiers drew Amy's attention downward. Terror and astonishment filled her mind, drowning out everything else as she watched beings clad in intricate red and white armor pour out of multiple pools of shimmering crimson light. Faces covered with malevolent black masks, the crimson soldiers swarmed over the field, attacking with a frenzy and maliciousness far beyond the reaches of a human being.

"What…" Amy swallowed, shock mixing with horror, and began to search for Hayate.

"The immediate result of your decision. The crimson army of Sha'Kring; forever stained with the blood of their victims. A loan, from the god of war."

"What happens now?"

"For now, you go back to your knight. I assume you'll want to see him before coming with me. You and I still have much we need to discuss."

Amy looked up, eyebrows raised. "So that's it? I'm really a goddess?"

Araia smiled, stepping over to Amy's side, and peered down at the flowing horde of crimson soldiers. "You have come far in your journey Amy Price, but you are not a goddess yet."

* * *

Hayate.

Catching the sound of Amy's voice, Hayate felt a warm breeze blow over him, taking with it the panic that locked his body. Unsure of how he could have heard her or why he felt as if she were standing beside him, Hayate rolled, avoiding getting impaled by a snarling Tres. Trying to get to his feet, Tres kicked him in the ribs, sending a flood of pain racing through the knight. His left hand brushing against something metallic, Hayate cried out as Tres stomped on his weapon hand, pinning it to the ground.

"Don't know how you survived that poison, but I want you to know, I'm gonna kill that King you're so fond of real quick. Then I'm gonna take some time, get better acquainted with that leggy little lass you've been runnin' with. And when I'm done, I'm gonna make sure she dies nice and slow. You owe me a lot of time kid. Me and my knives are gonna have a ball takin' it out of her." Tres towered over Hayate with a twisted sneer, hoisting his sword to slay him. "Do have the common courtesy to stay dead this time."

Struggling to free himself, Hayate reached with his left hand, searching for anything he could use to get free, when he saw streaks of crimson lightning rain down from above. Splotches of red oozed across the once clear sky like puddles of water expanding on the ground, silencing the clatter of swords and cries of battle.

"What the…" Tres stood wide eyed, peering around as the sound of marching shook the ground.

Amy. Feeling her presence, Hayate grasped the object he had felt earlier, recognizing it as one of the knives Tres had thrown, and rolled to his right, stabbing the blade into the assassin's thigh.

Crying out in pain, Tres stumbled back, freeing Hayate, who shot to his feet. Tres let out a wild snarl, and lurched forward, lashing out with a high strike. Catching Tres's arm by the wrist, Hayate thrust his sword forward, stabbing Tres in the stomach. Exhaustion and relief washed over the knight as he wrenched his blade free and let Tres fall to ground.

Screams of agony and terror mixed with shouts of excitement filled the air as Hayate examined the field around him. Soldiers in crimson armor poured out of shimmering pools of red light, attacking the forces of House Borga. Sweeping over the field like rabid wolves, the crimson soldiers laid waste to anyone still fighting against them and slaughtered those that tried to flee. A cold, unpleasant shiver ran through Hayate as he watched, feeling both relieved that the battle was over, and terrified by the forces unleashed to save them.

"Quite the intimidating gift, huh?"

"Amy?" Hayate spun around to find Amy standing behind him and rushed over to her. Dropping his sword as he embraced her, he let his fear and distress fall with his weapon, taking comfort in seeing Amy. Pulling back after a long moment, he looked away from her. "Sorry. I didn't mean to... I'm getting blood on your clothes."

"Who cares?" Amy pulled him back to her and kissed him. Returning her kiss, Hayate felt a cool sensation wash over him, removing every ache or throbbing pain from his body as she pulled back. "Don't ever leave me locked up while you go off and almost die again."

"I promise." Hayate kissed her again before turning back to look over the field. "We went through so much to get to this moment, but now that it's here, I can't believe this is the end."

"I don't think it is," Amy replied.

"We should find the King, and Ikari, and everyone else. They might need our help." Hayate glanced at Amy, kicking himself for not thinking about them sooner, but relaxed as she smiled at him.

"They're all fine."

"What about Borga and Inara? This will all be for nothing if they escape."

Amy smiled again, nodding toward the hills to the north. "That won't be a problem."

"So what do we do now?"

"We find our friends." Amy's smile faded as she took his hand. "And then I say goodbye."

* * *

"Was this part of your destiny?" Alia mocked, while the last of Danothir's soldiers were slaughtered. "I wonder if Ikari had anything to do with this."

"Shut up." Danothir spun toward the young woman; spit flying from his mouth as his face burned with fury. "This isn't possible, even for the Sanada. I cannot be defeated. I won't be."

"And yet you are," Ritsuko replied, her voice cold. "And thanks to your ineptness, all of my plans have died with your pitiful little army."

"This is your fault." Danothir reached behind him and pulled a slender dagger from his belt an instant before grabbing Ritsuko by the throat. "You were supposed to make my army invincible."

Thrusting her ringed hand onto Danothir's chest, Ritsuko unleashed a pulse of light that sent him stumbling back. "My spells gave each of your men the strength of four. Don't blame me for the pathetic training of your people and their inability to wield what I gave them. And even with my spells, they were still men fighting an army forged by the slayer! *You* were supposed to bring the girl to me so that *I* would command that army."

"It's moot now." Alia stepped over to her mother's side. "All that can be done now is damage control."

"You're right, Alia," Ritsuko responded, taking a long, slow breath. "Did you bring what I asked you?"

"Of course, mother."

Turning away from the Inara's as they began whispering to each other, Danothir scowled at the field hoping to see some of his men still fighting. Fury and despair swelled inside of him while shouts of victory rose from the fields. Light from the afternoon sun began to filter through the fading red haze, returning the sky to its natural blue and blowing away the luminescent portals. Finished with their task, the crimson soldiers stood at attention, filling the air with the clank of armor a moment before getting carried off by the wind as specks of dust.

"This isn't how it was supposed to be." Danothir ran his hand through his hair, hardly noticing as he pulled some of it out. "I was supposed to rule. I was supposed to bring order. End chaos. This was supposed to be my destiny. The right to rule was supposed to be mine." Fury boiling over, Danothir hurled his dagger over the field, screaming until his lungs gave out.

Letting out another shout of rage, Danothir forced himself to breathe, trying to clear his vision and think. "We should leave, before they send someone looking for us." Danothir turned back around, realizing he no longer heard Ritsuko or Alia whispering, only to find himself standing alone. Swallowing a nervous lump, he glanced about, figuring that the two women might have entered their carriage, but found it empty. He began to back away from the carriage, electing to forget about the troublesome women, and stared toward his own horse when he spotted a familiar looking man stepping around the steed.

"Lord Borga, you will be coming with me." Recognizing the man as the Sanyoshu he had seen weeks earlier in the Consortium, Danothir stepped back, reaching for his dagger as Saskai stalked forward before remembering that he no longer had it.

"I won't be taken by some dog of the Sanada." Danothir turned to run, only to find a second Sanyoshu standing behind him. Trying to dart around her, he felt her elbow slam into his throat. Choking, Danothir clutched his throat while staggering back.

Drawing her sword with a cold smile, the woman kicked his legs out from under him an instant before driving the blade into his thigh. "Run and you'll die tired."

"E'Lan." Saskai stepped over to them, drawing his own weapon.

"He'll live."

"Now, Lord Borga, you have two options." Saskai stared down into Danothir's eyes while placing the tip of his sword against his neck. "You can surrender and come with us…"

"…or you can die screaming here and now," E'Lan finished for him, twisting her sword in Danothir's leg.

Chapter Twenty-Nine

"See to it that our wounded are treated." T'Chello stood a few yards away, dispatching men to various tasks as they scurried about. Knights carefully combed the stained field, gathering all the weapons they could find, while fallen enemy soldiers were stacked in piles to be buried. A few tents, being used as temporary medical stations, were set up about thirty yards away.

Standing next to Hayate as he conversed with Ryoma, Amy glanced over the fields, grateful that all of the fighting and danger was finally over. But as relieved as she was that her friends were safe, she knew the task awaiting her would be an uneasy one. It was an unavoidable task, one she knew she had to do, but it was one that would take her away from Hayate. And that tore at her more than she thought possible.

"Nothing's ever dull with you, is it?" Recognizing Ikari's voice, Amy turned, greeting him and his siblings with a smile.

"You really are the Protectorate Goddess aren't you?" Yuki gazed over the sea of bloodied grass and smiled. "I have to admit I had my doubts, but seeing the slayers army sweep over the field, slaughtering everything in their path, it's enough to make a girl weak in the knees."

"She's impressed," Ikari laughed. "That's rare."

Turning to face the Sanada, Ryoma shook his head, letting out a surprised laugh. "I'd never thought I'd see the day I was grateful to find the Sanyoshu amassed in Ithor."

Yuki stepped over to Ryoma with a playful smirk. "I'd have thought you'd be used to getting saved by a Sanada by now. Or have you simply tired of me already."

"Not as yet." Ryoma bowed at the waist. "So until then, I look forward to making it up to you."

"Don't worry, you will." Yuki smirked.

"Believe it or not, but Hayate never doubted that you would help," Ryoma stated.

"Really?" Ikari raised an eyebrow.

"I just figured you couldn't pass up a good fight." Hayate stepped closer to Amy. "Besides, Amy trusts you, so I might as well too."

Face sagging from exhaustion, T'Chello strode over to the group, greeting each of them with a nod before turning toward Amy. "So this is the woman responsible for our being here."

"Sorry 'bout that." Amy winced at the fierce tone in T'Chello's voice.

"I don't hold much credence in myths and legends..." T'Chello paused for moment, softening his voice. "...but everyone says I have you to thank for the crimson army that saved us. I don't know if you're a goddess or not, but you have my thanks."

"Seems you fared well enough throughout this ordeal, General," said Genki. "What do you intend to do next?"

"For now, I have my men searching for any survivors of Danothir's army. Assuming we find any, they'll be held for treason," T'Chello replied. "As will Danothir when we find him."

"Looks like you already have." Amy motioned to the right, focusing everyone's attention on a fuming Danothir as Saskai and E'Lan dragged him by the arms.

"I am a House Lord and you dogs have no authority over me. I demand that you release me. Now." Danothir's face burned red as he struggled to free himself from the pairs grasp. Sharing a brief glance, Saskai and E'Lan shoved him to the ground.

"We thought you might like a word with Lord Borga, General." Saskai moved to stand a few feet from the Sanada's side.

"What happened to his leg?" Ryoma asked, noting the blood pouring from a fresh wound.

E'Lan stepped over to join Saskai before glancing at the King. "He fell."

"Danothir Borga." T'Chello glared down at the fallen Lord, radiating waves of distain and anger. "You are charged with high treason against Terra and the Hapes Consortium, as well as the murder of Chancellor Malik Shen and everyone you slaughtered in your greed. You will be judged, sentenced, and executed. And I will take pleasure in carrying out that execution personally."

"Spare me your inane judgments." Glancing up from a patch of grass on the ground, Danothir shot T'Chello a seething, murderous look. "You, the most stalwart of insufferable blotches on the escutcheon of pointless chaos, have no right to judge me. Mine was the path of order. Mine was a righteous path that would have saved us all. But you, and your weak Ithorian fools, and the anarchy spreading Sanada, and her..." Danothir paused, shifting his gaze to Amy. "You cost me everything."

"I saw the result of your destiny." Amy swallowed, sensing his growing rage, while flashes of her vision ran through her mind. "You're daft if you think *that's* saving anyone."

"I won't be denied my destiny by some stupid little wench." Danothir jumped to his feet, scooping something off the ground with his right hand. Snarling as he lunged toward Amy, he hoisted a bloody knife over his head.

Fear seizing her body, Amy felt as if time had slowed around her. She could feel the surprise flowing through everyone. From the far right, she could see Saskai and E'Lan start to move to grab Danothir, but knew that they would reach him a second too late. She heard the distinct sound of Hayate's sword as he began to draw it, when a surge of energy caught her attention. Darting in front of her with a speed she'd never seen, Ikari drew his sword, slicing Danothir's throat in one swift motion.

Waiting until Danothir's body slumped to the ground, Ikari whipped his blade to the side, flinging off some of the blood before twirling his sword and returning it to its sheath. Turning back toward the group, Ikari froze, surprised to see everyone staring at him. "What?"

"You killed him." Genki glanced down at Danothir's body.

"And?"

"With your sword?" Yuki stared at her twin for a long moment. "You only use your sword when you have to, for something important."

"Ah." Ikari smirked, mulling over some thought that had surprised him. "Amy's grown on me."

"Thank you." Amy smiled at Ikari. "For everything."

"I'll see to it that Borga is burned with the rest of his men." T'Chello waved over two soldiers and instructed them to drag off Danothir's body before following after them.

"I suppose it's time we left as well," Genki stated, turning toward E'Lan and Saskai. "Gather the Sanyoshu."

"Yes, my Lord," E'Lan and Saskai responded in unison before heading off.

"You should come back in a few days." Ryoma stepped over to Genki and shook his hand. "It's customary in Ithor to celebrate our victories with a feast. And it seems we have cause to celebrate the birth of a new goddess among the heavens."

Yuki frowned, flashing Ryoma a hurt look. "Getting invited to your parties isn't nearly as fun as sneaking in."

"So what will you do now?" Ikari asked, glancing at Hayate and Amy.

"What else is there?" Hayate shrugged. "Amy ascends to the heavens as the Protectorate Goddess just as the legend ends."

"Well that's the thing..." Ikari flashed his customary grin. Taking Hayate's hand, Amy looked at the young knight, remembering what was waiting for her. "That's not how the story of the Protectorate Goddess really ends. There are always parts that get left out of these things."

"What do mean?" Amy looked back to Ikari.

"Well according to the legend, the goddess fell in love with a mortal. Together they rebelled against the other gods and ushered in an era of freedom and peace for the realm."

"So what happened to them?" Hayate asked.

"They were slaughtered horribly by the other gods," Yuki replied with a callus grin. "If you believe these things."

"Lovely story." Amy scowled, wishing there was a way she could stay with Hayate.

"The point is..." Ikari shot Yuki an annoyed glare. "...that you're both free to choose your own path. Don't let some ancient tales dictate what you do with your lives."

"I won't." Amy squeezed Hayate's hand, taking comfort in Ikari's words. Closing her eyes for a moment, she saw a flash of Ikari standing next to Hayate in an immense chamber, surrounded by a pillar of blinding light. "And promise me you'll keep searching for your own path, your own dreams. I'm sure you'll find it one day, and I'd like to see where it takes you."

Ikari smiled again, and brought Amy's free hand to his lips. "Until our paths cross again."

"Bye." Yuki waved as she and Genki followed after Ikari.

Watching for a moment as the Sanada headed off, Amy turned toward Hayate, trying to burn his smile into her mind. She gazed at him for a long moment, basking in the warmth of his hand and the emotions radiating off of him, when she noticed a faint but familiar voice rising on the cool breeze.

"What is that?" Confusion shot through Hayate, mixing with a hint of sadness, as he glanced around.

"You can hear her?" Surprised, Amy tucked some of her hair whipping around in the wind behind her ear, pleading for more time.

"You mean the oddly calming but eerie singing in the wind?" Ryoma asked. "Yes."

"I think its Araia's way of telling me it's time to go." Amy glanced over her shoulder and found the goddess standing with her back to sun. "But I really don't want to go."

"You said yourself that you have to." Hayate swallowed, forcing his emotions to the back of his mind and squeezed Amy's hand. "I would give anything to have you stay with me, but you have a duty to protect everyone in the realm. You can help people in a way I never could. You can be so much too so many, but not if you stay because of me. I love you. I want you to stay, but it's not about what we want. It's about what the realm needs."

"Hayate…" Amy looked away, trying to hide the tears rolling down her cheek. Not wanting to admit it, a part of her knew that he was right. Still, knowing about the needs of millions didn't make giving up her own any easier.

Hayate kissed her passionately before stepping back and releasing her hand. "Be well in the company of the gods."

"Bye love. Stay safe." Amy wiped some of the tears from her face and turned toward Araia. Staring at the regal woman as she walked, a twinge of anger shot through her as Araia held her pleasant smile. Twisting on her heel, Amy sprinted back to Hayate, wrapping her arms around his neck as she pressed her lips to his. Pulling back just far enough to talk, Amy smiled through her tears. "I don't care what Araia or any other god has planned. I promise I'm coming back to you. And when I do, no power in the heavens will keep us apart."

"And I'll be waiting. Now and forever, yours." Hayate held her tight, kissing her again.

Holding their embrace for a long minute, Amy backed away, keeping her eyes locked on Hayate's. Finally turning back to Araia, she marched over to the goddess, replacing all of her fear with a determination to find a way back to Hayate.

"Finally ready?" Araia glanced at Amy.

"Let's get this over with." Amy looked back to Hayate, silently promising to see him again. "I have someone waiting."

Araia titled her head. "Quite a bit of fire in you, isn't there? Good. You're going to need all of it."

Catching one last glance of Hayate, Amy smiled, burning his image into her mind. An instant later, he was gone.

* * *

Instruments ranging from violins and fiddles to flutes and horns filled the large Ithorian banquet hall with a blend of vivacious melodies.

Built a few miles from the castle, the hall had a simple, but elegant décor that had become quite common in Ithor. A few tapestries hung from the smooth stone walls. Intricate, wooden tables were set up in various sections allowing the occupants to sit and enjoy a wide variety of food and drinks. A round stage sat in the halls center, giving the minstrel's a place to play. Some of the guests were dancing near the stage, encouraging the band to play one song after another. Others seemed content with talking amongst themselves, commenting on the days since the battle in the fields or what they thought would happen next for the realm.

Making his way through the sea of people, Genki laughed, surprised to see Saskai playing a spirited violin alongside the band, undoubtedly at Ikari's behest. Scanning the area near the stage, he spotted his brother waving a flute in front of Yuki with a taunting smile.

"I havent had nearly enough to drink yet to make me play that thing." Yuki waved an indignant hand, chugging ale from the mug in her other hand.

"Didn't you say the flutiest had the musical talent of a roasting boar?" Ikari mocked.

Yuki shrugged, pushing Ikari back. "I also said I could play circles around him, but I'm not."

"It's a party dear sister, have a little fun."

"Yeah," someone—obviously not from Austuria since they were brave or foolish enough to shout at Yuki—encouraged from among the crowd. "Play."

Genki, not one for missing an opportunity to tease a sibling, paused, remembering days long forgotten when Yuki had spent most of her free time learning to play. A crucial skill for a warrior, or so the twins eccentric master had told them, was the mastery of some form of art. Lacking the patience to master the slow paced strategy games Ikari did, she had taken to the flute, finding it far more entertaining. Plus, she tended to enjoy using it as a weapon when the mood suited her. "Show us what you got."

"Fine." Yuki snatched the flute from Ikari's hand and started toward the stage when a mischievous smirk spread across her face. Veering over to E'Lan, Yuki whispered something in her ear, triggering a startled glance as her face reddened. Amused by E'Lan's response, Yuki stepped behind her before shoving her into Ikari. "But only if *you* dance with E'Lan."

Laughing as the two shared an awkward glance, Genki watched while Ikari took E'Lan's hand with a smirk, wondering which of the two Yuki was playing with.

"Try to keep up," Yuki ordered, climbing onto the stage next to Saskai. Bringing the flute to her lips as Ikari and E'Lan begun their dance, Yuki played along with the band, but soon increased the melodies tempo. To his credit, Saskai matched her pace with ease, playing as brilliantly as the luminescent stones lighting the hall.

Turning away from the cheering crowd and the show his siblings were putting on, Genki spotted Ryoma talking to T'Chello and made his way over to them. "Fine party, Ryoma. It's surprisingly lively."

"Glad you're enjoying yourself." Ryoma picked up a slender glass filled with sea green wine from the curved table behind him. The table was filled with assorted fruits and pastries as well as a wide variety of drinks. "Something to drink?"

"Please." Genki took a sip from the glass before looking toward T'Chello. "General, I never pegged you for the partying type."

"I'm not, as a rule, but they occasionally have uses," T'Chello replied. "Good for the men's moral."

"So how are things going on Hapes?" Genki asked.

"Slow, as expected." T'Chello drank from his glass. "It'll be some time before the damage done by Danothir's attack is repaired. My hope is to have enough done within the main chamber so we can begin choosing the new Chancellor."

Genki smiled, feigning disinterest while pondering how he could best take advantage of the situation. "Any ideas on who that might be?"

"None."

"I'm sure you'll have your hands full with that matter, General," Ryoma stated with a laugh. "I'm more concerned about Ritsuko Inara and her part in Danothir's plan."

"Thus far, I've seen no evidence to indicate that she was involved," T'Chello replied.

"Everyone in the Consortium suspected she was involved with the Assassins Guild." Ryoma glared at the General, a hint of anger lining his voice. "It's been days since the battle in the fields and no one has found a shred of evidence? Have you at least questioned her?"

"I understand your concern, Ryoma, but you must understand mine. My position has been left tenuous by Danothir's treachery. My priority is on securing Hapes and facilitating the transition of power to the next Chancellor. Despite my support or your beliefs, I cannot simply drag off the head of a House without due evidence. The other

Houses would never stand for it. At a time when the Hapes army is at its weakest, I can ill afford to risk a revolt of one of the major Houses." T'Chello turned to look over the hall, letting the edge fall from his voice. "Besides, I would gladly *ask* Lady Inara to come in for questioning, but no one has seen or heard from her in days."

"What?" Ryoma arched and eyebrow.

"You havent heard?" Genki finished his glass and stepped over to the table to pour himself some more. "Both Ritsuko and her daughter have vanished without a trace. Even I, despite my resources, haven't had any success in locating her. It's a situation I find curious, considering that there is nothing linking her to Danothir besides a dubious rumor."

"And what do you make of all this?" Ryoma turned an intrigued, yet cautious, eye on Genki.

"Ritsuko is as clever as she is beautiful. Whatever trappings are working through that head of hers is unlikely to bode well for the rest of us." Genki smirked and lifted his glass in salute. "Time and the gods will tell if we're up to weathering that storm when it comes."

* * *

Stepping around E'Lan as she twirled, Ikari felt his smile fade, noticing the scent of jasmine, despite the smell of ale and roasted meats permeating the air. Forcing the smile back to his face, he continued his dance, placing his hand on E'Lan's as they circled around each other. He began scanning the crowd, searching for the source of the perfume, already knowing who it was that had called his attention. Spotting a figure in a green hooded cloak stepping through the throng of partygoers, Ikari spun away from E'Lan.

Smiling as he turned to face her, Ikari bowed, keeping careful watch on the hooded figure. "Thank you for a lovely time, my Lady." Stepping passed the blushing Sanyoshu, Ikari ducked into the sea of guests, following after his target.

Pushing passed some pudgy Ithorian statesman as he tried to talk to him, Ikari glanced around again, finding the hooded figure heading toward the large columned archway that led to the halls entrance. A few yards from the archway, he spotted Hayate leaning against the wall and paused.

Considering whom he should follow, Ikari rolled his eyes with an annoyed groan and started over to the mopping knight. "You know, rumor has it there's a party somewhere around here. I even hear you're the guest of honor."

"Guess no one told the King *you* were coming." Hayate laughed mockingly. "What do you want Ikari?"

"Observing the situation." Ikari leaned against the wall next to Hayate, crossing his arms. "It's not often I get to observe the people of Ithor without sneaking around."

"Are you always so interested in the happenings of other people, or is it just me?"

"It's so funny… you think I care." Ikari returned his taunting smirk. "So what do you think Amy's up to?"

"Couldn't guess. Something beyond anything you and I are capable of doing. That much I know." Hayate leaned his head back, letting out a depressed sigh. "I can still feel her, not like before when she was here, it's more like a humming in the back of my head that I just got used to without realizing it. I'll be walking and swear that I can hear her voice."

"I've always believed that when people come together and really make a connection, they stay connected. No matter how much distance gets put between them."

"Doesn't make losing someone you love any easier though."

"Suppose it doesn't," Ikari replied after a moment. "Are you familiar with the origin of Protectorate Goddess?"

Hayate glanced at Ikari with a raised eyebrow. "Another part of the legend that's often forgotten?"

"Well, you know how these things go." Ikari laughed. "According to the tale, each person was originally born as two people in one. Hau Zo'Aroc eventually grew jealous of man and their potential, so he split them in two, forever dooming our spirits to search out their counterparts in another. Saddened by the god kings act, a goddess choose to spend her life acting as our protector from the other gods, and gave man the gift of love, so that he could find his other half and be at peace. If you believe such things."

"Huh, that actually makes me feel better." Hayate pushed off the wall, laughing as he shook his head. "This doesn't mean we're actually becoming friends does it?"

"No."

"Good." Hayate laughed again, stepping into the crowd. "See you around, Ikari."

"Enjoy your party." Ikari bounced off the wall, returning his attention to the archway. Still hanging in the air, Ikari followed the scent of jasmine through the wide hallway and pushed open the elegant mahogany doors. Stepping out into the grassy courtyard, he found his target standing near a curved tree, gazing up at the crimson moon lighting the night sky with its two siblings. Checking to be sure they were alone, he stepped over to the hooded woman. "Sorry to keep you waiting. I know how much you hate that, Alia."

"It's always worth waiting for you." Alia turned to face him, lowering her hood. "Although, I am disappointed that I wasn't the one dancing with you."

"There are a lot of people inside who'd be very interested in seeing you."

"And are you among them?" Alia raised an expectant eyebrow.

"Well, I'm certainly not, not interested," Ikari stated. "You're risking an awful lot by being here."

"I wanted to see you."

"And what does dear Ritsuko think about your sneaking out?"

"Mother is gone," Alia stated. "I haven't seen or heard from her in days. I had assumed she might have been taken by General T'Chello, but my sources on Hapes tell me he's just as lost as I am."

Interesting. So Ritsuko really is missing. Ikari held his gaze on Alia for a moment, searching her face for any signs of deception. "Any chance she simply ran off?"

"Why would she? We made sure there wasn't anything that could be traced back to us. Besides, we both know she's not the sort of woman to leave unfinished business, and she really wanted you dead."

"I have that effect on people. It's part of my charm."

"I noticed." Alia smiled seductively, running her hand across his chest. "I wanted to see you again before I left."

"Planning a vacation?"

"I'm going to look for mother. She may be a pain, but she is my mother, and I want to find the reason she disappeared."

"It is rather interesting." Ikari scanned the area again, wondering what or who could have made Ritsuko vanish and why.

"Is that all that has your interest?" Alia smiled again as she stepped in close to Ikari. "Can't you see that you and I are the same? You belong with me."

"I'll admit to finding you intriguing."

Ikari's eyes fell on Alia's. Amazed that he could see the stars reflected in her gaze, he mentally chastised himself, realizing that he held her gaze for a moment too long as she leaned in and kissed him. Resisting the impulse to push her away, he reached for her cheek, forgetting about the party inside and the breeze blowing around them.

Pushing her back into the tree, he continued their embrace, enjoying the warmth from her body as it pressed against his.

Ikari—finally pulling free—grinned, relishing the lingering taste of honeyed fruit on Alia's lips. "And you're certainly not the dull little brat I thought you were, but it would never work out between us. You're an Inara, I'm a Sanada, I'm pretty sure there's a law against it."

"I will make you mine, Ikari Sanada." Alia wrapped one arm around his neck while pulling him inches away from her face by the back of the head. "It's the will of Tai Re'l, and even you will be powerless to stop me from seeing it carried out. You and I are one, but I can wait, for a little while."

"And where is it you'll be going?"

"If you want to find out so badly, you're just going to have to find me." Pausing as she leaned in, Alia lightly licked the center of his lips before kissing him again. Running her fingers through his hair, she pulled back before slipping passed him. "Don't keep me waiting for too long."

"What makes think I'm going to come after you?" Ikari turned with a wide grin, watching her back toward the path that led out to the street.

"Because there were at least a dozen different ways you could have stopped me from kissing you, but you didn't. You're curious, and whatever you find interesting you pursue." Alia beamed, pulling her hood over her head. "Until the jubilant morrow when we meet again, and you are mine."

Watching as Alia disappeared into the night, Ikari turned away from the path and stared up into the star filled sky. Alia had left an impression on him, of that he had no doubt. Even better, Ritsuko was missing, Danothir was dead, Amy was in the havens, and she had given him a new puzzle to solve.

All is right in the realms. Noting the blood moon hanging over head, Ikari laughed, remembering the impassioned kiss he and Alia had just shared with a smirk. *So she wants me to come after her? Guess I have no choice.*

A renewed sense of excitement surged through him as he started back toward the party. Whatever future was awaiting him down his path, it was sure to be a puzzle, and he enjoyed solving puzzles.

"Could be fun."